The Literary Horse

The Literary Horse

GREAT MODERN STORIES ABOUT HORSES

Edited by Lilly Golden

THE ATLANTIC MONTHLY PRESS
NEW YORK

Published simultaneously in Canada
Printed in the United States of America

FIRST EDITION

Library of Congress Cataloging-in-Publication Data

The literary horse: great modern stories about horses / edited by Lilly Golden. — 1st ed.
ISBN 0-87113-595-7
1. Horses—Fiction. 2. Short stories. 3. Fiction—20th century. I. Golden, Lilly.
PN6120.95.H73L58 1995   808.83′10836—dc20   94-43628

Design by Laura Hammond Hough

The Atlantic Monthly Press
841 Broadway
New York, NY 10003

10 9 8 7 6 5 4 3 2 1

Contents

CONTENTS

CONTENTS

CONTENTS

The Literary Horse

LILLY GOLDEN

Introduction

For as long as I can remember, I have
been in love with horses. Something about horses appeals immensely to a
child's imagination. Is it their size, their silky noses, the wonderful way they
smell, or the warmth of their bodies on winter days? As a horse-crazed girl, I
found anything related to horses inherently more interesting than anything
else. And like anyone who has ever loved horses, I'm still smitten. Horses
are an abiding passion. I still look for them everywhere. And they still get
my full attention whenever I happen to see them. The same goes for horses
in film, in paintings, and especially in fiction, though my tastes have
matured since childhood, when all a story needed was a horse in it to be
good. Much more is required now.

The aim of this anthology is to bring together some of the best modern
horse stories from some of the best literary voices—stories that deserve to
be read because they are examples of great writing. Though most were written in the latter part of the twentieth century, a few stories from earlier in
the century (those by Rudyard Kipling, Saki, and Thorne Smith) are included, simply because they are too good to leave out. Some of the writers
here may surprise you. Many great names who aren't known for their writ-
ings about horses have a horse story or two in their literary cache. The
twenty-two stories within were selected because they impart with authentic-
ity the nature of riding and the relationship between people and horses.
Something in them is recognizable as the real thing.

The first group, "Horses as Heroes," includes stories in which the main

1

characters are horses, and in some we are even treated to the horse's point of view. The opening story, Kipling's "The Maltese Cat," was chosen not only because it is a venerable tale but because his horses help determine their own fate and the fate of the men riding them. In each of the stories in this section, horses save people's lives, literally or metaphorically. The horses in "The Maltese Cat," Patricia Highsmith's "Engine Horse," and Liam O'Flaherty's "The Old Hunter" are not youthful or lovely to look at, but they are soulful, wise, or ploddingly single-minded, and invincible despite their age and circumstances.

And then there are the "Rogues," horses that display unusually bad behavior. Included is Saki's "The Brogue," a story about a quirky animal whose dislikes have rendered him nearly unridable. Another is Thorne Smith's hilarious metamorphosed Mr. Lamb, whose roguish behavior lies in a more human realm; but because he is in a horse's body, he qualifies.

Then come the stories that are the truest portraits of both horse and human nature. Each story in "Horse and Child" features a child who dreams of nothing but having a horse—a child with whom all horse lovers can identify. But in John Steinbeck's "The Red Pony" and Wallace Stegner's "The Colt," when that dream is finally realized, something terrible happens. These stories are among the saddest ever written. All the sorrow of the world is conveyed in them—in the desperate hopes of a child, the brief and deceptive triumph, and then the tragic loss. They are stories about the loss of innocence and the dawn of a new, bitter knowledge that on the other side of happiness is the possibility of heartbreak. It is almost as if the combination of horse and child, both guileless and innocent, tempts fate.

But not all the horses in these stories suffer, and neither do all the children. There are also stories in which the child who dreams of having a horse is finally granted the wish. In these we wait for tragedy, bracing ourselves for the fall, and it seems nothing short of a miracle when it doesn't come.

In the stories in "Of Horses and Men" and "Women and Their Horses" the adults are often more frail than their hoofed counterparts. Recovering from war, as in Gretel Ehrlich's "Champ's Roan Colt," or struggling in poverty or despondence, as in "The Power of Horses" by Elizabeth Cook-Lynn, people turn to horses to help them heal or focus on them as objects of devotion and inspiration. There is a spiritual kinship between horse and rider, as if a remnant of an archetypal bond, a recognition.

In "Horses and Love" the main characters are men and women who are on the edge of revelation. In these stories they approach and round the corner, beyond which lies not happiness but an acknowledgment of a right to seek it. Two stories use the riding of horses as a stage on which seduction is played out: Pam Houston's "What Shock Heard" and Tess Slesinger's "Relax Is All." The final story, Rick Bass's "Wild Horses," is exquisite, encompassing everything already discussed: horses as heroes and rogues, human frailty, desire, heartbreak, and the search for happiness. Everything a short story, and a horse story, should be.

What emerges from the collection is a modern, complex look at the ageless relationship between horses and people. Readers will be pleased to discover that horses in fiction still embody notions of goodness, folly, strength, and vulnerability. And that horse stories are still vicariously thrilling. For all those who have grown from children who devoured horse stories into adults who demand good fiction: read on.

HORSES AS HEROES

RUDYARD KIPLING

The Maltese Cat

They had good reason to be proud, and better reason to be afraid, all twelve of them; for though they had fought their way, game by game, up the teams entered for the polo tournament, they were meeting the Archangels that afternoon in the final match; and the Archangels men were playing with half a dozen ponies apiece. As the game was divided into six quarters of eight minutes each, that meant a fresh pony after every halt. The Skidars' team, even supposing there were no accidents, could only supply one pony for every other change; and two to one is heavy odds. Again, as Shiraz, the grey Syrian, pointed out, they were meeting the pink and pick of the polo ponies of Upper India, ponies that had cost from a thousand rupees each, while they themselves were a cheap lot gathered, often from country carts, by their masters, who belonged to a poor but honest native infantry regiment.

"Money means pace and weight," said Shiraz, rubbing his black-silk nose dolefully along his neat-fitting boot, "and by the maxims of the game as I know it—"

"Ah, but we aren't playing the maxims," said the Maltese Cat. "We're playing the game; and we've the great advantage of knowing the game. Just think a stride, Shiraz! We've pulled up from bottom to second place in two weeks against all those fellows on the ground here. That's because we play with our heads as well as our feet."

"It makes me feel undersized and unhappy all the same," said Kittiwynk, a mouse-colored mare with a red brow band and the cleanest pair of legs that ever an aged pony owned. "They've twice our style, these others."

Kittiwynk looked at the gathering and sighed. The hard, dusty polo ground was lined with thousands of soldiers, black and white, not counting hundreds and hundreds of carriages and drags and dogcarts, and ladies with brilliant-colored parasols, and officers in uniform and out of it, and crowds of natives behind them; and orderlies on camels, who had halted to watch the game, instead of carrying letters up and down the station; and native horse dealers running about on thin-eared Baluchi mares, looking for a chance to sell a few first-class polo ponies. Then there were the ponies of thirty teams that had entered for the Upper India Free-for-All Cup—nearly every pony of worth and dignity, from Mhow to Peshawar, from Allahabad to Multan; prize ponies, Arabs, Syrian, Barb, country-bred, Deccanee, Waziri, and Kabul ponies of every color and shape and temper that you could imagine. Some of them were in mat-roofed stables, close to the polo ground, but most were under saddle, while their masters, who had been defeated in the earlier games, trotted in and out and told the world exactly how the game should be played.

It was a glorious sight, and the come and go of the little, quick hooves, and the incessant salutations of ponies that had met before on other polo grounds or racecourses were enough to drive a four-footed thing wild.

But the Skidars' team were careful not to know their neighbors, though half the ponies on the ground were anxious to scrape acquaintance with the little fellows that had come from the North, and, so far, had swept the board.

"Let's see," said a soft-gold-colored Arab, who had been playing very badly the day before, to the Maltese Cat; "didn't we meet in Abdul Rahman's stable in Bombay, four seasons ago? I won the Paikpattan Cup next season, you may remember?"

"Not me," said the Maltese Cat, politely. "I was at Malta then, pulling a vegetable cart. I don't race. I play the game."

"Oh!" said the Arab, cocking his tail and swaggering off.

"Keep yourselves to yourselves," said the Maltese Cat to his companions. "We don't want to rub noses with all those goose-rumped half-breeds of Upper India. When we've won this Cup they'll give their shoes to know *us.*"

"We shan't win the Cup," said Shiraz. "How do you feel?"

"Stale as last night's feed when a muskrat has run over it," said Polaris, a rather heavy-shouldered grey; and the rest of the team agreed with him.

"The sooner you forget that the better," said the Maltese Cat, cheerfully. "They've finished tiffin in the big tent. We shall be wanted now. If your saddles are not comfy, kick. If your bits aren't easy, rear, and let the *saises* know whether your boots are tight."

Each pony had his *sais*, his groom, who lived and ate and slept with the animal, and had betted a good deal more than he could afford on the result of the game. There was no chance of anything going wrong, but to make sure, each *sais* was shampooing the legs of his pony to the last minute. Behind the *saises* sat as many of the Skidars' regiment as had leave to attend the match—about half the native officers, and a hundred or two dark, black-bearded men with the regimental pipers nervously fingering the big, beribboned bagpipes. The Skidars were what they call a Pioneer regiment, and the bagpipes made the national music of half their men. The native officers held bundles of polo sticks, long cane-handled mallets, and as the grandstand filled after lunch they arranged themselves by ones and twos at different points round the ground, so that if a stick were broken the player would not have far to ride for a new one. An impatient British Cavalry Band struck up "If you want to know the time, ask a policeman!" and the two umpires in light dustcoats danced out on two little excited ponies. The four players of the Archangels' team followed, and the sight of their beautiful mounts made Shiraz groan again.

"Wait till we know," said the Maltese Cat. "Two of 'em are playing in blinkers, and that means they can't see to get out of the way of their own side, or they *may* shy at the umpires' ponies. They've *all* got white web reins that are sure to stretch or slip!"

"And," said Kittiwynk, dancing to take the stiffness out of her, "they carry their whips in their hands instead of on their wrists. Hah!"

"True enough. No man can manage his stick and his reins and his whip that way," said the Maltese Cat. "I've fallen over every square yard of the Malta ground, and I ought to know."

He quivered his little, flea-bitten withers just to show how satisfied he felt; but his heart was not so light. Ever since he had drifted into India on a troop ship, taken, with an old rifle, as part payment for a racing debt, the Maltese Cat had played and preached polo to the Skidars' team on the Skidars' stony polo ground. Now, a polo pony is like a poet. If he is born with a love for the game, he can be made. The Maltese Cat knew that bamboos grew solely in order that polo balls might be turned from their roots, that grain was given to ponies to keep them in hard condition, and that ponies were shod to prevent them slipping on a turn. But, besides all these things, he knew every trick and device of the finest game in the world, and for two seasons had been teaching the others all he knew or guessed.

"Remember," he said for the hundredth time, as the riders came up, "you *must* play together, and you *must* play with your heads. Whatever happens, follow the ball. Who goes out first?"

Kittiwynk, Shiraz, Polaris, and a short high little bay fellow with tremendous hocks and no withers worth speaking of (he was called Corks) were being girthed up, and the soldiers in the background stared with all their eyes.

"I want you men to keep quiet," said Lutyens, the captain of the team, "and especially not to blow your pipes."

"Not if we win, Captain Sahib?" asked the piper.

"If we win you can do what you please," said Lutyens with a smile, as he slipped the loop of his stick over his wrist and wheeled to canter to his place. The Archangels' ponies were a little bit above themselves on account of the many-colored crowd so close to the ground. Their riders were excellent players, but they were a team of crack players instead of a crack team; and that made all the difference in the world.

They honestly meant to play together, but it is very hard for four men, each the best of the team he is picked from, to remember that in polo no brilliancy in hitting or riding makes up for playing alone. Their captain shouted his orders to them by name, and it is a curious thing that if you call his name aloud in public after an Englishman you make him hot and fretty. Lutyens said nothing to his men, because it had all been said before. He pulled up Shiraz, for he was playing back, to guard the goal. Powell on Polaris was halfback, and Macnamara and Hughes on Corks and Kittiwynk were forwards. The tough bamboo ball was set in the middle of the ground, one hundred and fifty yards from the ends, and Hughes crossed sticks, heads up, with the captain of the Archangels, who saw fit to play forward; that is a place from which you cannot easily control your team. The little click as the cane shafts met was heard all over the ground, and then Hughes made some sort of quick wrist stroke that just dribbled the ball a few yards. Kittiwynk knew that stroke of old, and followed as a cat follows a mouse. While the Captain of the Archangels was wrenching his pony round, Hughes struck with all his strength, and next instant Kittiwynk was away, Corks following close behind her, their little feet pattering like raindrops on glass.

"Pull out to the left," said Kittiwynk between her teeth. "It's coming your way, Corks!"

The back and halfback of the Archangels were tearing down on her just as she was within reach of the ball. Hughes leaned forward with a loose rein, and cut it away to the left almost under Kittiwynk's foot, and it hopped and skipped off to Corks, who saw that if he was not quick it would run beyond the boundaries. That long bouncing drive gave the Archangels time to wheel and send three men across the ground to head off Corks. Kittiwynk stayed where she was; for she knew the game. Corks was on the ball half a fraction of a second before the others came up, and Macnamara, with a backhanded stroke, sent it back across the ground to Hughes, who saw the way clear to the Archangels' goal, and smacked the ball in before any one quite knew what had happened.

"That's luck," said Corks, as they changed ends. "A goal in three minutes for three hits, and no riding to speak of."

"Don't know," said Polaris. "We've made 'em angry too soon. Shouldn't wonder if they tried to rush us off our feet next time."

"Keep the ball hanging, then," said Shiraz. "That wears out every pony that is not used to it."

* * *

Next time there was no easy galloping across the ground. All the Arch-angels closed up as one man, but there they stayed, for Corks, Kittiwynk, and Polaris were somewhere on the top of the ball, marking time among the rattling sticks, while Shiraz circled about outside, waiting for a chance.

"We can do this all day," said Polaris, ramming his quarters into the side of another pony. "Where do you think you're shoving to?"

"I'll—I'll be driven in an *ekka* if I know," was the gasping reply, "and I'd give a week's feed to get my blinkers off. I can't see anything."

"The dust is rather bad. Whew! That was one for my off-hock. Where's the ball, Corks?"

"Under my tail. At least, the man's looking for it there! This is beauti-ful. They can't use their sticks, and it's driving 'em wild. Give old Blinkers a push and then he'll go over."

"Here, don't touch me! I can't see. I'll—I'll back out, I think," said the pony in blinkers, who knew that if you can't see all round your head, you cannot prop yourself against the shock.

Corks was watching the ball where it lay in the dust, close to his near foreleg, with Macnamara's shortened stick tap-tapping it from time to time. Kittiwynk was edging her way out of the scrimmage, whisking her stump of a tail with nervous excitement.

"Ho! They've got it," she snorted. "Let me out!" and she galloped like a rifle bullet just behind a tall lanky pony of the Archangels, whose rider was swinging up his stick for a stroke.

"Not today, thank you," said Hughes, as the blow slid off his raised stick, and Kittiwynk laid her shoulder to the tall pony's quarters, and shoved him aside just as Lutyens on Shiraz sent the ball where it had come from, and the tall pony went skating and slipping away to the left. Kit-tiwynk, seeing that Polaris had joined Corks in the chase for the ball up the ground, dropped into Polaris's place, and then "time" was called.

The Skidars' ponies wasted no time in kicking or fuming. They knew that each minute's rest meant so much gain, and trotted off to the rails, and their *saises* began to scrape and blanket and rub them at once.

12

"Whew!" said Corks, stiffening up to get all the tickle of the big vulcanite scraper. "If we were playing pony for pony, we would bend those Archangels double in half an hour. But they'll bring up fresh ones and fresh ones and fresh ones after that—you see."

"Who cares?" said Polaris. "We've drawn first blood. Is my hock swelling?"

"Looks puffy," said Corks. "You must have had rather a wipe. Don't let it stiffen. You'll be wanted again in half an hour."

"What's the game like?" said the Maltese Cat.

"Ground's like your shoe, except where they put too much water on it," said Kittiwynk. "Then it's slippery. Don't play in the center. There's a bog there. I don't know how their next four are going to behave, but we kept the ball hanging, and made 'em lather for nothing. Who goes out? Two Arabs and a couple of country-breds! That's bad. What a comfort it is to wash your mouth out!"

Kitty was talking with a neck of a lather-covered soda-water bottle between her teeth, and trying to look over her withers at the same time. This gave her a very coquettish air.

"What's bad?" said Grey Dawn, giving to the girth and admiring his well-set shoulders.

"You Arabs can't gallop fast enough to keep yourselves warm—that's what Kitty means," said Polaris, limping to show that his hock needed attention. "Are you playing back, Grey Dawn?"

"Looks like it," said Grey Dawn, as Lutyens swung himself up. Powell mounted the Rabbit, a plain bay country-bred much like Corks, but with mulish ears. Macnamara took Faiz-Ullah, a handy, short-backed little red Arab with a long tail, and Hughes mounted Benami, an old and sullen brown beast, who stood over in front more than a polo pony should.

"Benami looks like business," said Shiraz. "How's your temper, Ben?" The old campaigner hobbled off without answering, and the Maltese Cat looked at the new Archangel ponies prancing about on the ground. They were four beautiful blacks, and they saddled big enough and strong enough to eat the Skidars' team and gallop away with the meal inside them.

13

"Blinkers again," said the Maltese Cat. "Good enough!"

"They're chargers—cavalry chargers!" said Kittiwynk, indignantly. "*They'll* never see thirteen-three again."

"They've all been fairly measured, and they've all got their certificates," said the Maltese Cat, "or they wouldn't be here. We must take things as they come along, and keep your eyes on the ball."

The game began, but this time the Skidars were penned to their own end of the ground, and the watching ponies did not approve of that.

"Faiz-Ullah is shirking—as usual," said Polaris, with a scornful grunt.

"Faiz-Ullah is eating whip," said Corks. They could hear the leather-thonged polo quirt lacing the little fellow's well-rounded barrel. Then the Rabbit's shrill neigh came across the ground.

"I can't do all the work," he cried, desperately.

"Play the game—don't talk," the Maltese Cat whickered; and all the ponies wriggled with excitement, and the soldiers and the grooms gripped the railings and shouted. A black pony with blinkers had singled out old Benami, and was interfering with him in every possible way. They could see Benami shaking his head up and down, and flapping his underlip.

"There'll be a fall in a minute," said Polaris. "Benami is getting stuffy."

The game flickered up and down between goalpost and goalpost, and the black ponies were getting more confident as they felt they had the legs of the others. The ball was hit out of a little scrimmage, and Benami and the Rabbit followed it, Faiz-Ullah only too glad to be quiet for an instant.

The blinkered black pony came up like a hawk, with two of his own side behind him, and Benami's eye glittered as he raced. The question was which pony should make way for the other, for each rider was perfectly willing to risk a fall in a good cause. The black, who had been driven nearly crazy by his blinkers, trusted to his weight and his temper; but Benami knew how to apply his weight and how to keep his temper. They met, and there was a cloud of dust. The black was lying on his side, all the breath knocked out of his body. The Rabbit was a hundred yards up the ground with the ball, and Benami was sitting down. He had slid nearly ten yards on his tail, but he had had his revenge, and sat cracking his nostrils till the black pony rose.

"That's what you get for interfering. Do you want any more?" said Benami, and he plunged into the game. Nothing was done that quarter, because Faiz-Ullah would not gallop, though Macnamara beat him whenever he could spare a second. The fall of the black pony had impressed his companions tremendously, and so the Archangels could not profit by Faiz-Ullah's bad behavior.

But as the Maltese Cat said when time was called, and the four came back blowing and dripping, Faiz-Ullah ought to have been kicked all round Umballa. If he did not behave better next time the Maltese Cat promised to pull out his Arab tail by the roots and—eat it.

There was no time to talk, for the third four were ordered out.

The third quarter of a game is generally the hottest, for each side thinks that the others must be pumped; and most of the winning play in a game is made about that time.

Lutyens took over the Maltese Cat with a pat and a hug, for Lutyens valued him more than anything else in the world; Powell had Shikast, a little grey rat with no pedigree and no manners outside polo; Macnamara mounted Bamboo, the largest of the team; and Hughes Who's Who, alias the Animal. He was supposed to have Australian blood in his veins, but he looked like a clotheshorse, and you could whack his legs with an iron crowbar without hurting him.

They went out to meet the very flower of the Archangels' team; and when Who's Who saw their elegantly booted legs and their beautiful satin skins, he grinned a grin through his light, well-worn bridle.

"My word!" said Who's Who. "We must give 'em a little football. These gentlemen need a rubbing down."

"No biting," said the Maltese Cat, warningly; for once or twice in his career Who's Who had been known to forget himself in that way.

"Who said anything about biting? I'm not playing tiddlywinks. I'm playing the game."

The Archangels came down like a wolf on the fold, for they were tired of football, and they wanted polo. They got it more and more. Just after the game began, Lutyens hit a ball that was coming toward him rapidly, and it rolled in the air, as a ball sometimes will, with the whirl of a frightened partridge. Shikast heard, but could not see it for the minute, though he looked everywhere and up into the air as the Maltese Cat had taught him. When he saw it ahead and overhead he went forward with Powell as fast as he could put foot to ground. It was then that Powell, a quiet and levelheaded man as a rule, became inspired and played a stroke that sometimes comes off successfully after long practice. He took his stick in both hands, and, standing up in his stirrups, swiped at the ball in the air, Munipore fashion. There was one second of paralyzed astonishment, and then all four sides of the ground went up in a yell of applause and delight as the ball flew true (you could see the amazed Archangels ducking in their saddles to dodge the line of flight, and looking at it with open mouths), and the regimental pipes of the Skidars squealed from the railings as long as the pipers had breath.

Shikast heard the stroke; but he heard the head of the stick fly off at the same time. Nine hundred and ninety-nine ponies out of a thousand would have gone tearing on after the ball with a useless player pulling at their heads; but Powell knew him, and he knew Powell; and the instant he felt Powell's right leg shift a trifle on the saddle flap, he headed to the boundary, where a native officer was frantically waving a new stick. Before the shouts had ended, Powell was armed again.

Once before in his life the Maltese Cat had heard that very same stroke played off his own back, and had profited by the confusion it wrought. This time he acted on experience, and leaving Bamboo to guard the goal in case of accidents, came through the others like a flash, head and tail low—Lutyens standing up to ease him—swept on and on before the other side knew what was the matter, and nearly pitched on his head between the Archangels' goalpost as Lutyens kicked the ball in after a straight scurry of a hundred and fifty yards. If there was one thing more than another upon which the Maltese Cat prided himself, it was on this quick, streaking kind of run half across the ground. He did not believe in taking balls round the field unless you were clearly overmatched. After this they gave the Archangels five-minuted football; and an expensive fast pony hates football because it rumples his temper.

Who's Who showed himself even better than Polaris in this game. He did not permit any wriggling away, but bored joyfully into the scrimmage as if he had his nose in a feed box and was looking for something nice. Little Shikast jumped on the ball the minute it got clear, and every time an Archangel pony followed it, he found Shikast standing over it, asking what was the matter.

"If we can live through this quarter," said the Maltese Cat, "I shan't care. Don't take it out of yourselves. Let them do the lathering."

So the ponies, as their riders explained afterward, "shut up." The Archangels kept them tied fast in front of their goal, but it cost the Archangels' ponies all that was left of their tempers; and ponies began to kick, and men began to repeat compliments, and they chopped at the legs of Who's Who, and he set his teeth and stayed where he was, and the dust stood up like a tree over the scrimmage until that hot quarter ended.

They found the ponies very excited and confident when they went to their *saises*; and the Maltese Cat had to warn them that the worst of the game was coming.

"Now *we* are all going in for the second time," said he, "and *they* are trotting out fresh ponies. You think you can gallop, but you'll find you can't; and then you'll be sorry."

"But two goals to nothing is a halter-long lead," said Kittiwynk, prancing.

"How long does it take to get a goal?" the Maltese Cat answered. "For pity's sake, don't run away with a notion that the game is half won just because we happen to be in luck *now*. They'll ride you into the grandstand, if they can; you must not give 'em a chance. Follow the ball."

"Football, as usual?" said Polaris. "My hock's half as big as a nose bag."

"Don't let them have a look at the ball, if you can help it. Now leave me alone. I must get all the rest I can before the last quarter."

He hung down his head and let all his muscles go slack, Shikast, Bamboo, and Who's Who copying his example.

"Better not watch the game," he said. "We aren't playing, and we shall only take it out of ourselves if we grow anxious. Look at the ground and pretend it's fly time."

They did their best, but it was hard advice to follow. The hooves were drumming and the sticks were rattling all up and down the ground, and yells of applause from the English troops told that the Archangels were pressing the Skidars hard. The native soldiers behind the ponies groaned and grunted, and said things in undertones, and presently they heard a long-drawn shout and a clatter of hurrahs!

"One of the Archangels," said Shikast, without raising his head. "Time's nearly up. Oh, my sire—and *dam*."

"Faiz-Ullah," said the Maltese Cat, "if you don't play to the last nail in your shoes this time, I'll kick you on the ground before all the other ponies."

"I'll do my best when my time comes," said the little Arab, sturdily.

The *saises* looked at each other gravely as they rubbed their ponies' legs. This was the time when long purses began to tell, and everybody knew it. Kittiwynk and the others came back, the sweat dripping over their hooves and their tails telling sad stories.

"They're better than we are," said Shiraz. "I knew how it would be."

"Shut your big head," said the Maltese Cat. "We've one goal to the good yet."

"Yes, but it's two Arabs and two country-breds to play now," said Corks. "Faiz-Ullah, remember!" He spoke in a biting voice.

As Lutyens mounted Grey Dawn he looked at his men, and they did not look pretty. They were covered with dust and sweat in streaks. Their yellow boots were almost black, their wrists were red and lumpy, and their eyes seemed two inches deep in their heads; but the expression in the eyes was satisfactory.

"Did you take anything at tiffin?" said Lutyens; and the team shook their heads. They were too dry to talk.

"All right. The Archangels did. They are worse pumped than we are."

"They've got the better ponies," said Powell. "I shan't be sorry when this business is over."

That fifth quarter was a painful one in every way. Faiz-Ullah played like a little red demon, and the Rabbit seemed to be everywhere at once, and Benami rode straight at anything and everything that came in his way; while the umpires on their ponies wheeled like gulls outside the shifting game. But the Archangels had the better mounts—they had kept their racers till late in the game—and never allowed the Skidars to play football. They hit the ball up and down the width of the ground till Benami and the rest were outpaced. Then they went forward, and time and again Lutyens and Grey Dawn were just, and only just, able to send the ball away with a long, spitting backhander. Grey Dawn forgot that he was an Arab; and turned from grey to blue as he galloped. Indeed, he forgot too well, for he did not keep his eyes on the ground as an Arab should, but stuck out his nose and scuttled for the dear honor of the game. They had watered the ground once or twice between the quarters, and a careless waterman had emptied the last of his skinful all in one place near the Skidars' goal. It was close to the end of the play, and for the tenth time Grey Dawn was bolting after the ball, when his near hind foot slipped on the greasy mud, and he rolled over and over, pitching Lutyens just clear of the goalpost; and the triumphant Archangels made their goal. Then time was called—two goals all; but Lutyens had to be helped up, and Grey Dawn rose with his near hind leg strained somewhere.

"What's the damage?" said Powell, his arm around Lutyens.

"Collarbone, *of* course," said Lutyens, between his teeth. It was the third time he had broken it in two years, and it hurt him.

Powell and the others whistled.

"Game's up," said Hughes.

"Hold on. We've five good minutes yet, and it isn't my right hand. We'll stick it out."

19

"I say," said the captain of the Archangels, trotting up, "are you hurt, Lutyens? We'll wait if you care to put in a substitute. I wish—I mean—the fact is, you fellows deserve this game if any team does. Wish we could give you a man, or some of our ponies—or something."

"You're awfully good, but we'll play it to a finish, I think."

The captain of the Archangels stared for a little. "That's not half bad," he said, and went back to his own side, while Lutyens borrowed a scarf from one of his native officers and made a sling of it. Then an Archangel galloped up with a big bath sponge, and advised Lutyens to put it under his armpit to ease his shoulder, and between them they tied up his left arm scientifically; and one of the native officers leaped forward with four long glasses that fizzed and bubbled.

The team looked at Lutyens piteously, and he nodded. It was the last quarter, and nothing would matter after that. They drank out the dark golden drink, and wiped their mustaches, and things looked more hopeful.

The Maltese Cat had put his nose into the front of Lutyens' shirt and was trying to say how sorry he was.

"He knows," said Lutyens, proudly. "The beggar knows. I've played him without a bridle before now—for fun."

"It's no fun now," said Powell. "But we haven't a decent substitute."

"No," said Lutyens. "It's the last quarter, and we've got to make our goal and win. I'll trust the Cat."

"If you fall this time, you'll suffer a little," said Macnamara.

"I'll trust the Cat," said Lutyens.

"You hear that?" said the Maltese Cat proudly, to the others. "It's worthwhile playing polo for ten years to have that said of you. Now then, my sons, come along. We'll kick up a little bit, just to show the Archangels this team haven't suffered."

And, sure enough, as they went on to the ground, the Maltese Cat, after satisfying himself that Lutyens was home in the saddle, kicked out three or four times, and Lutyens laughed. The reins were caught up anyhow in the tips of his strapped left hand, and he never pretended to rely on them. He knew the Cat would answer to the least pressure of the leg, and by way of showing off—for his shoulder hurt him very much—he bent the little fellow in a close figure-of-eight in and out between the goalposts. There was a roar from the native officers and men, who dearly loved a piece of *dugabashi* (horse-trick work), as they called it, and the pipes very quietly and scornfully droned out the first bars of a common bazaar tune called "Freshly Fresh and Newly New," just as a warning to the other regiments that the Skidars were fit. All the natives laughed.

"And now," said the Maltese Cat, as they took their place, "remember that this is the last quarter, and follow the ball!"

"Don't need to be told," said Who's Who.

"Let me go on. All those people on all four sides will begin to crowd in—just as they did at Malta. You'll hear people calling out, and moving forward and being pushed back; and that is going to make the Archangel ponies very unhappy. But if a ball is struck to the boundary, you go after it, and let the people get out of your way. I went over the pole of a four-in-hand once, and picked a game out of the dust by it. Back me up when I run, and follow the ball."

There was a sort of an all-round sound of sympathy and wonder as the last quarter opened, and then there began exactly what the Maltese Cat had foreseen. People crowded in close to the boundaries, and the Archangels' ponies kept looking sideways at the narrowing space. If you know how a man feels to be cramped at tennis—not because he wants to run out of the court, but because he likes to know that he can at a pinch—you will guess how ponies must feel when they are playing in a box of human beings.

"I'll bend some of those men if I can get away," said Who's Who, as he rocketed behind the ball; and Bamboo nodded without speaking. They were playing the last ounce in them, and the Maltese Cat had left the goal undefended to join them. Lutyens gave him every order that he could to bring him back, but this was the first time in his career that the little wise grey had ever played polo on his own responsibility, and he was going to make the most of it.

"What are you doing here?" said Hughes, as the Cat crossed in front of him and rode off an Archangel.

"The Cat's in charge—mind the goal!" shouted Lutyens, and, bowing forward, hit the ball full, and followed on, forcing the Archangels toward their own goal.

"No football," said the Maltese Cat. "Keep the ball by the boundaries and cramp 'em. Play open order, and drive 'em to the boundaries."

Across and across the ground in big diagonals flew the ball, and whenever it came to a flying rush and a stroke close to the boundaries the Archangel ponies moved stiffly. They did not care to go headlong at a wall of men and carriages, though if the ground had been open they could have turned on a sixpence.

"Wriggle her up the sides," said the Cat. "Keep her close to the crowd. They hate the carriages. Shikast, keep her up this side."

Shikast and Powell lay left and right behind the uneasy scuffle of an open scrimmage, and every time the ball was hit away Shikast galloped on it at such an angle that Powell was forced to hit it toward the boundary; and when the crowd had been driven away from that side, Lutyens would send the ball over to the other, and Shikast would slide desperately after it till his friends came down to help. It was billiards, and no football, this time—billiards in a corner pocket; and the cues were not well chalked.

"If they get us out in the middle of the ground they'll walk away from us. Dribble her along the sides," cried the Maltese Cat.

So they dribbled all along the boundary, where a pony could not come on their right-hand side; and the Archangels were furious, and the umpires had to neglect the game to shout at the people to get back, and several blundering mounted policemen tried to restore order, all close to the scrimmage, and the nerves of the Archangels' ponies stretched and broke like cobwebs.

Five or six times an Archangel hit the ball up into the middle of the ground, and each time the watchful Shikast gave Powell his chance to send it back, and after each return, when the dust had settled, men could see that the Skidars had gained a few yards.

Every now and again there were shouts of "Side! Off side!" from the spectators; but the teams were too busy to care, and the umpires had all they could do to keep their maddened ponies clear of the scuffle.

At last Lutyens missed a short easy stroke, and the Skidars had to fly back helter-skelter to protect their own goal, Shikast leading. Powell stopped the ball with a backhander when it was not fifty yards from the goalposts, and Shikast spun round with a wrench that nearly hoisted Powell out of his saddle.

"Now's our last chance," said the Cat, wheeling like a cockchafer on a pin. "We've got to ride it out. Come along."

Lutyens felt the little chap take a deep breath, and, as it were, crouch under his rider. The ball was hopping toward the right-hand boundary, an Archangel riding for it with both spurs and a whip; but neither spur nor whip would make his pony stretch himself as he neared the crowd. The Maltese Cat glided under his very nose, picking up his hind legs sharp, for there was not a foot to spare between his quarters and the other pony's bit. It was as neat an exhibition as fancy figure skating. Lutyens hit with all the strength he had left, but the stick slipped a little in his hand, and the ball flew off to the left instead of keeping close to the boundary. Who's Who was far across the ground, thinking hard as he galloped. He repeated stride for stride the Cat's maneuvers with another Archangel pony, nipping the ball away from under his bridle, and clearing his opponent by half a fraction of an inch, for Who's Who was clumsy behind. Then he drove away toward the right as the Maltese Cat came up from the left; and Bamboo held a middle course exactly between them. The three were making a sort of Government-broad-arrow-shaped attack; and there was only the Archangels' back to guard the goal; but immediately behind them were three Archangels racing all they knew, and mixed up with them was Powell sending Shikast along on what he felt was their last hope. It takes a very good man to stand up to the rush of seven crazy ponies in the last quarters of a Cup game, when men are riding with their necks for sale, and the ponies are delirious. The Archangels' back missed his stroke and pulled aside just in time to let the rush go by. Bamboo and Who's Who shortened stride to give the Cat room, and Lutyens got the goal with a clean, smooth, smacking stroke that was heard all over the field.

But there was no stopping the ponies. They poured through the goalposts in one mixed mob, winners and losers together, for the pace had been terrific. The Maltese Cat knew by experience what would happen, and, to save Lutyens, turned to the right with one last effort, that strained a back-sinew beyond hope of repair. As he did so he heard the right-hand goalpost crack as a pony cannoned into it—crack, splinter, and fall like a mast. It had been sawed three parts through in case of accidents, but it upset the pony nevertheless, and he blundered into another, who blundered into the left-hand post, and then there was confusion and dust and wood. Bamboo was lying on the ground, seeing stars; an Archangel pony rolled beside him, breathless and angry; Shikast had sat down dog-fashion to avoid falling over the others and was sliding along on his little bobtail in a cloud of dust; and Powell was sitting on the ground, hammering with his stick and trying to cheer. All the others were shouting at the top of what was left of their voices, and the men who had been split were shouting too. As soon as the people saw no one was hurt, ten thousand native and English shouted and clapped and yelled, and before any one could stop them the pipers of the Skidars broke onto the ground, with all the native officers and men behind them, and marched up and down, playing a wild Northern tune called "Zakhme Bagan," and through the insolent blaring of the pipes and the high-pitched native yells you could hear the Archangels' band hammering, "For they are all jolly good fellows," and then reproachfully to the losing team, "Ooh, Kafoozalum! Kafoozalum! Kafoozalum!"

Besides all these things and many more, there was a commander in chief, and an inspector general of cavalry, and the principal veterinary officer of all India standing on the top of a regimental coach, yelling like schoolboys; and brigadiers and colonels and commissioners, and hundreds of pretty ladies joined the chorus. But the Maltese Cat stood with his head down, wondering how many legs were left to him; and Lutyens watched the men and ponies pick themselves out of the wreck of the two goalposts, and he patted the Maltese Cat very tenderly.

"I say," said the captain of the Archangels, spitting a pebble out of his mouth, "will you take three thousand for that pony—as he stands?"

"No thank you. I've an idea he's saved my life," said Lutyens, getting off and lying down at full length. Both teams were on the ground too, waving their boots in the air, and coughing and drawing deep breaths, as the *saises* ran up to take away the ponies, and an officious water carrier sprinkled the players with dirty water till they sat up.

"My aunt!" said Powell, rubbing his back, and looking at the stumps of the goalposts. "That was a game!"

They played it over again, every stroke of it, that night at the big dinner, when the Free-for-All Cup was filled and passed down the table, and emptied and filled again, and everybody made most eloquent speeches. About two in the morning, when there might have been some singing, a wise little, plain little, grey little head looked in through the open door.

"Hurrah! Bring him in," said the Archangels; and his *sais*, who was very happy indeed, patted the Maltese Cat on the flank, and he limped into the blaze of light and the glittering uniforms, looking for Lutyens. He was used to messes, and men's bedrooms, and places where ponies are not usually encouraged, and in his youth had jumped on and off a mess table for a bet. So he behaved himself very politely, and ate bread dipped in salt, and was petted all round the table, moving gingerly; and they drank his health, because he had done more to win the Cup than any man or horse on the ground.

That was glory and honor enough for the rest of his days, and the Maltese Cat did not complain much when the veterinary surgeon said that he would be no good for polo any more. When Lutyens married, his wife did not allow him to play, so he was forced to be an umpire; and his pony on these occasions was a flea-bitten grey with a neat polo tail, lame all round, but desperately quick on his feet, and, as everybody knew, Past Pluperfect Prestissimo Player of the Game.

LIAM O'FLAHERTY

The Old Hunter

Mr. Stephen Mullen, the horse dealer of Ballyhaggard, went to an auction one day. He was a tall, slim man with a red face and white eyebrows. Being a very popular man, on account of his dry wit and his good temper, he met many friends in the town where the auction was being held, and the result was that he spent the morning in the hotels drinking. Slightly intoxicated, he arrived at the auction when everything was sold except an old hunter called Morrissey.

Mr. Mullen went up to the auctioneer, a friend of his, and asked him had he anything left. The auctioneer pointed to the old hunter.

"That's the lot," he said.

"What's that?" said Mr. Mullen, shutting one eye and cocking his head sideways.

"Pooh!" said the auctioneer, "there's enough iron in that old rascal to keep a factory going for a month. Tell you what, these bank clerks and shopkeepers that are buying horses now with their ill-gotten gains don't know a . . ."

"Hech, hech," said Mr. Mullen, "let's have a look at him. I might give ye the price of a drink for him."

They walked over to the hunter. He was a finely built animal, but he looked like a man that had just left a nursing home after a serious nervous breakdown. His bones were sticking through his hide, and though he held his head proudly in the air, it was obvious that he did so out of respect for his ancestry and not because of any consciousness of his strength. He was of

26

a bay color and somebody had fired his left hind leg, so clumsily and in such a cruel manner that it appeared to have been done with a red-hot crowbar. The pelt was quite naked of hair and the flesh was singed in streaks.

"Look at that," said Mr. Mullen, pointing to the leg. "Did ye get him from a tinker, or what?"

"Lord have mercy on yer soul," said the auctioneer, "that fellah has a pedigree as long as yer arm. Come here, I'll show ye."

"Ye needn't bother," said Mr. Mullen. "What good is a pedigree to a dying man? The Master o' the Hounds might give a few bob for him for the pack."

Mr. Mullen wrinkled up his face in a smile and he looked at the auctioneer with his mouth open. He really wanted the horse because he liked the old fellow's head, but he wanted to get him for next to nothing. The auctioneer also wanted to get rid of him very badly, but still, he wanted to strike a good bargain.

"Now drop the coddin', Mr. Mullen," he said, "and buy the horse if ye want him. Sure I needn't tell you what a horse is, whether he is a horse or a mule. Man alive, sure a few square meals 'ud change that fellah so much ye wouldn't know him. Look at him . . ."

"Aye," said Mullen coldly, "let's have a look at them. I mean at his insides. I bet he's got a smoker's heart and a liver stitched together with the best silk thread. If I buy him, would ye get him carted home for me?"

"I can see it's out for coddin' me ye are," said the auctioneer, turning to go away.

"Very well," said Mr. Mullen, clearing his throat, "I'll make ye an offer for him."

"What's that?" said the auctioneer, halting abruptly and turning around to Mr. Mullen.

"I've got thirty bob on me," said Mullen, contracting his white eyebrows. "I'll give ye the lot, though it's good money wasted."

The auctioneer pursed up his lips and stared at Mr. Mullen for a few moments as if he were dumbfounded.

"D'ye really mean it?" he said.

Mr. Mullen nodded.

"Take him home, for God's sake," said the auctioneer, waving his hands.

Mr. Mullen paid for the horse and took him home. He led him along beside his own horse, and it was the devil of a job to keep him in hand. My boy, he had his head in the wind and champed along, rearing and trying to break loose.

"Good Lord," thought Mr. Mullen, "that fellah is a corker only for his age."

Mr. Mullen went to a party that night and there was heavy drinking. In his cups he began to boast about the old hunter he had bought for thirty shillings. Everybody made fun of him about it, so Mr. Mullen boasted that he would ride the old horse to the meet of the Ballyhaggard hounds next day.

"Wait till you see," he cried. "I'll leave you all so far behind that I'll have the fox's skin dressed before you arrive."

Next day Mr. Mullen's head was as big as a pot, and when he remembered his boast he was disgusted with himself. But he was a man of his word and he ordered the old hunter to be saddled for him. He drank a considerable amount of raw whisky and mounted him. Off he went to the meet.

Everybody in the district turns out with the hounds, from Lord Clonmore to Mr. Mulligan the butcher of Murren. All sorts of ungainly beasts appear. In fact, Mr. Murchison the new Protestant curate once joined, mounted on a cart horse, which a scoundrel called The Tiger Donnelly sold him as an Irish hunter. Since the war and the revolution all sorts of people have been thrown together in the district, so that, as Mr. Mullen says, "There's no class about anything nowadays." But when Mr. Mullen himself appeared that day on Morrissey, everybody agreed that such an extraordinary animal had never been seen before. It was like a mortally sick man appearing at a wedding, half drunk and insisting on being the most hilarious person present.

"Bravo, Mr. Mullen," said Lord Clonmore. "The dead have arisen. Eh?"

Everybody laughed and Mr. Mullen was mortally insulted, but when the Cavalcade set off, by Jove, Morrissey behaved himself marvelously. Like a good thoroughbred of the old school, he showed every ounce that was in him. He cleared the ditches and fences as lightly as those wonderful horses for which the Galway Blazers were famous, fellows that could live a week on a raw turnip and cross a bog without wetting their fetlocks. Mr. Mullen kept refreshing himself now and again with stimulants, and as a consequence rode even more daringly than was his custom; but the old hunter carried him all day without a single stumble, until at last, just before the finish, he arrived at the drain that flows from the workhouse, about a mile outside the town. There is no more filthy or evil-smelling drain in the world. There is no necessity to describe it.

But when Morrissey arrived at this drain at full speed, he stopped dead. Undoubtedly the animal was too well bred to face it. Mr. Mullen was pitched over the horse's head and he fell headlong into the stinking place. Several people pulled up, but Mr. Mullen crawled out, uninjured. Seeing him, everybody went into hysterics with laughter. He was indescribable, and in fact unrecognizable. Morrissey lowered his head, sniffed at Mr. Mullen and set off back at a mad canter.

"It must have turned his stomach," laughed a red-haired farmer.

"Yer a lot of scoundrels," shouted Mr. Mullen, struggling to his feet and holding out his dripping hands that were as black and sticky as if he had dipped them in tar.

Morrissey was found again and brought back to the stables. Mr. Mullen went home and had a bath, and by that time his anger had worn off and he himself was able to laugh at the joke. Next morning he went to look at Morrissey. The poor animal was quite stiff with his efforts of the previous day. But he still had his head in the air and he whinnied joyfully when he saw Mr. Mullen. That softened Mr. Mullen's heart towards him.

"Damn it," he said to the stable boy, "he's a great old horse. I'll take him down to the shore and give him a dip in the salt water to soften his legs."

He rode Morrissey down to the strand. It was a fine day, but there was a rather heavy ground swell and the waves broke on the sand with a thundering noise. This thundering noise and the menacing aspect of the dark green waves, rising suddenly within a few feet of the shore and falling with a thud, terrified the horse. It was impossible to get him to walk in the tide. At last Mr. Mullen managed to get him near the surf, when the tide had receded for a particularly long distance, as it does now and again, after a certain number of short waves have broken. Then as the horse was stamping about and snorting, trying to get away from the water, an enormous wave rose suddenly and almost enveloped him. Instead of trying to rush backward, he was so confused by the rush of water under his stomach that he plunged out to sea. Mr. Mullen tried to head him off, but it was no use. Presently another equally large wave arose, passed right over the horse and the rider, so that they both turned a somersault. Mr. Mullen was thrown from the saddle and he became entangled somehow in the horse's legs. When he came to the surface, after having saved himself, the horse was five yards away and Mr. Mullen was in deep water. He swam a few strokes, struck ground and then looked behind him. There was the horse, swimming mightily out towards the open sea.

"God Almighty!" cried Mr. Mullen. "With ten pounds worth of a saddle on him."

Mr. Mullen dashed up on to the strand and began to call some boatmen that were there. They ran over to him.

"Hey," he cried, "if he drowns, will he sink or float?"

"God save us," they cried, "who are ye talking about?"

"My horse, damn it," cried Mr. Mullen; "he's gone out to sea. Don't ye see him? Look."

"Aw, snakes alive," they said, when they saw the dark object, heaving along sideways, like an unwieldy porpoise.

"He'll float sure enough," said one man, "with the water he'll swallow."

"All right then," said Mr. Mullen, "get me a boat. I want to save the saddle. The horse isn't worth his keep, but the saddle is worth money. Get a boat for me."

They rushed down a boat and put to sea after the horse. When they had gone out almost half a mile, they met the horse swimming back towards them.

"There he is," cried one boatman.

"He's floating, sure enough," said Mr. Mullen. "Get alongside him and get the saddle."

"It's not floatin' he is but swimmin' like a warrior," said the boatman.

"God!" said Mr. Mullen.

They were all amazed and they lay on their oars, as Morrissey swept past them towards the beach, going at a terrific pace. They followed him, and when they reached the strand, Morrissey was standing there, shivering and exhausted. Mr. Mullen took off his hat and struck his forehead.

"Well, that horse beats all I ever saw," he said. "Here, I'll buy a bottle of whisky over this. Come on, men."

After that Mr. Mullen and the horse that went to sea became quite famous in the district. So that Mr. Mullen grew fond of the horse and he kept him all that winter in his stables with plenty of food. But he made no attempt to ride him, and although the fame of the horse spread afar, still nobody made an offer for him. Because even though he was famous for having swam a mile out to sea and then swam back again, he was also famous for having thrown Mr. Mullen into the workhouse drain.

Then in the following April another extraordinary thing happened to the horse. I must say that he had improved considerably during the winter. He had fattened a great deal and his hide was becoming almost glossy. The mark on his hind leg was not so outrageous, and to an ordinary person he seemed a perfectly sound horse. But to a horseman he was still an old crock. One of those game old things, whether they are old colonels who insist on wearing tight waists in their seventieth year, or old horses, or old battered fighting cocks that take a step ferociously and then glare, wagging their chaps aggressively as if they were in the prime of their lives—I say, he was one of those game old things that make a virtue of looking fit even when they might be excused drooping their heads and lying down to die. But all the buyers admired him and left him alone. Then Mr. Stanley Edwards came to the town.

Mr. Edwards might be called a crock as well as the old hunter. He spent a greater part of each year in a nursing home. The remainder of the year he spent in the pursuit of extravagant pleasures, not always very well considered. His money was tied up in this country, otherwise it is very probable that he would never spend a week in it. But when he had done a great bout in London, he always had to return to Ireland to get some more money. After one of those bouts and a month in the hospital, he engaged a villa in Ballyhaggard to take the sea air. A few days after his arrival in the town he came to Mr. Mullen. Mr. Mullen looked him up and down, rather surprised that such a weakling should come to him for anything.

"Well," he said, "what could I do for you?"

"Look here," said Mr. Edwards, "I have to live for a few months in this ghastly place. I'm sick and I have very little money. I have been here three days and I'm quite fed up with walking up and down the shore and talking to lunatics around here. I want a horse. Can you get me one?"

"Let me see," said Mr. Mullen, looking at him shrewdly, "you'd want a quiet horse, I suppose?"

"I want a horse," said Mr. Edwards pettishly. "It doesn't matter what he is. If he breaks my neck it might be a jolly good idea."

"I see," said Mr. Mullen. "I think I've got the very thing that'll suit you."

"Oh! Look here," said Mr. Edwards rather nervously. "I don't mean I want some . . . eh . . . crazy thing. You know . . . a . . . oh, well . . ."

"You leave it to me," said Mr. Mullen. "You can try him out before you buy him."

Morrissey was brought out and Mr. Edwards immediately mounted him and trotted off. Mr. Edwards looked a very poor figure on horseback. Some wit said that he was born to be a ragpicker, because his gaunt frame bent like a willow rod and his nose was so long that he could use it in the same way that an elephant uses the top of his trunk. But such a slight weight suited the old horse and he went off very gallantly indeed, with that twirl in his right hind leg, which is a sign of old age in a horse and which warns off the cunning buyer but which is very attractive; like the smart twirl of the spurred boot which tells the swagger cavalry officer.

Mr. Mullen looked after the horse, scratching his chin and thinking that he would be very glad to accept a five-pound note for him.

After an hour, Mr. Edwards returned, perspiring but looking very happy. A good hour's trotting on a well-bred horse on a fine spring morning would make a corpse almost come to life again.

"Go all right?" said Mr. Mullen, smiling his most engaging smile.

"Splendid," said Mr. Edwards, sitting the horse and wiping his forehead, as if he were loath to dismount. "How much do you want for him?"

"I'll take thirty pounds at a pinch," said Mr. Mullen, after a moment's apparent thought and looking at Mr. Edwards as if he were going to do him a favor, which, however, gave him a great deal of pain.

"Oh!" said Mr. Edwards, a little surprised.

Then he dismounted and looked curiously at Mr. Mullen.

"It's a lot," he said.

"Oh! Well," said Mr. Mullen, making a gesture with his hands, "a horse isn't a bicycle."

"Quite," said Mr. Edwards. "Now, let me see."

He walked around the horse and passed his hand over the horse's body in various places. Mr. Mullen was very glad to see that he touched the wrong places. Then Mr. Edwards stood at a distance from the horse and looked at him. He seemed very loath to leave him. Mr. Mullen began to feel very comfortable.

"Look here," said Mr. Edwards at length, "I'll come back tomorrow and have another ride. May I?"

"Why, certainly," said Mr. Mullen affably. "You can have a look at his pedigree now if you like."

"Oh, has he got a pedigree?" said Mr. Edwards.

"Lord, yes," said Mr. Mullen, "yards of it."

Here it must be stated that although Mr. Edwards was a wealthy country gentleman, he kept motorcars instead of horses and knew nothing about the animals except on race courses. So that a pedigree seemed to him as good a guarantee of perfection as the maker's name on a Rolls-Royce.

"Let's have a look at it," he said.

Mr. Mullen produced the pedigree and Mr. Edwards inspected it.

"In that case," he said, "I'll buy the horse right away."

"It's like taking milk from a child," thought Mr. Mullen, as Mr. Edwards wrote out the check.

Everybody expected Mr. Edwards to break his neck, and some people said that Mr. Mullen played rather a scurvy trick on the poor fellow, but during the whole of that summer the horse was seen on the roads almost every day, trotting along in the pink of condition. And what was more, Mr. Edwards became quite a new man. Whether it was the sea air or the riding that did it, he regained his health to an extraordinary extent. He did not become robust, but he was no longer an invalid and he led a decent healthy life. In fact, just before he went away, he came to Mr. Mullen and said: "Look here, Mr. Mullen, you've saved my life."

"Glad to hear it," said Mr. Mullen, without winking an eye.

In September Mr. Edwards left the district, but instead of going to England, as was his custom, he returned to his property in County Kilkenny. Nothing more was heard of him or of the horse for two years. And then two months ago I met Mr. Mullen in Dublin. We were having a drink together and talking about various things, when he suddenly gripped my arm and said:

"D'ye remember that horse, Morrissey, I had, the fellah that threw me into the drain?"

I nodded.

"Ye remember I sold him to a chap called Edwards from Kilkenny. Well, I've just been down there to a show. Met him there. He's still got the horse, going as strong as a three-year-old and . . . d'ye know what I'm going to tell ye? That horse saved his life, as he said himself. When I asked him

34

about the horse, he said: 'I wouldn't part with that horse for a thousand. I haven't left this district since I saw you last, and I can drink two bottles of port now after dinner without turning a hair.' "

So that, indeed, it seems that there is something in a pedigree.

PATRICIA HIGHSMITH

Engine Horse

When the big mare, Fanny, heard the rustle in the hay, she turned her head slowly, still chomping with unbroken rhythm, and her eyes, which were like large soft brown eggs, tried to look behind her and down. Fanny supposed it was one of the cats, though they seldom came close. There were two cats on the farm, one ginger, one black and white. Fanny's looking back had been casual. A cat often came into the stable in search of a quiet spot to nap in.

Still munching hay from her trough, Fanny looked for a second time and saw the little grey thing near her front foot. A tiny cat it was. Not one of the household, not one of the small cats belonging to either of the larger cats, because there weren't any just now.

It was sunset in the month of July. Gnats played around Fanny's eyes and nose, and made her snort. A small square window, closed in winter, was now open and the sun flooded directly into Fanny's eyes. She had not done much work that day, because the man called Sam, whom Fanny had known all her twelve years, had not come, either today or yesterday. Fanny had not done anything that she could remember except walk with the woman Bess to the water tank and back again. Fanny had a long period of munching in daylight, before she lay down with a grunt to sleep. Her vast haunch and rib cage, well covered with fat and muscle, hit the bed of hay like a carefully lowered barrel. It became cooler. The little grey kitten, which Fanny could now see more clearly, came and curled herself up in the reddish feathers behind Fanny's left hoof.

The little cat was not four months old, an ash-grey and black brindle, with a tail only the length of a king-sized cigarette, because someone had stepped in the middle of it when she was younger. She had wandered far that day, perhaps three or four miles, and turned in at the first shelter she had seen. She had left home, because her grandmother and great-grandmother had attacked her for an uncountable time, one time too many. Her mother had been killed by a car just a few days ago. The little cat had seen her mother's body on the road and sniffed it. So the little kitten, with an instinct for self-preservation, had decided that the great unknown was better than what she knew. She was already wiry of muscle, and full of pluck, but now she was tired. She had investigated the farmyard and found only some muddy bread and water to eat in the chickens' trough. And even at that hour in July the little cat was chilly. She had felt the warmth coming from the huge bulk of the red-brown mare, and when the horse lay down, the kitten found a nook, and collapsed.

The mare was somehow pleased. Such a dainty little creature! That size, that weight that was nothing at all!

The horse and the kitten slept.

And in the white, two-storey farmhouse, the people argued.

The house belonged to Bess Gibson, a widow for the last three years. Her grandson Harry had come with his bride Marylou a few days ago, for a visit, Bess had thought, and to introduce Marylou. But Harry had plans also. He wanted some money. His mother hadn't enough, or had refused him, Bess gathered. Bess's son Ed, Harry's father, was dead, and Harry's mother in California had remarried.

Now Harry sat in the kitchen, dressed in cowboy clothes, a toothpick alternating with a cigarette between his lips, and talked about the restaurant-drive-in-bar-and-café that he wanted to buy his way into.

"If you could only see, Gramma, that this farm isn't even paying its way, that the money's sitting here doing nothing! What've you got here?" He waved a hand. "You could get a hundred and twenty thousand for the house and land, and think for a minute what kind of apartment in town you could have for a fraction of that!"

"That's true, you know?" Marylou parroted. She was dawdling over her coffee, but she'd whipped out a nail file and was sawing away now.

Bess shifted her weight in the wooden chair, and the chair gave a creak. She wore a blue and white cotton dress and white sandals. She suffered from dropsy. Her hair had gone completely white in the last couple of years. She realized that Harry meant an apartment in town, and town was Danville, thirty miles away. Some poky little place with two flights of stairs to climb, probably belonging to someone else to whom she'd have to pay rent. Bess didn't want to think about an apartment, no matter how many modern conveniences it might have. "This place pays its way," Bess said finally. "It's not losing money. There's the chickens and ducks—people come to buy them or their eggs. There's the corn and the wheat. Sam manages it very well—I don't know about the immediate future, with Sam gone," she added with an edge in it, "but it's home to me and it's yours when I'm gone."

"But not even a tractor? Sam still uses a plough. It's ridiculous. That one horse. What century are you living in, Gramma?—Well, you could *borrow* on it," Harry said not for the first time, "if you really want to help me out."

"I'm not going to leave you or anybody a mortgaged house," Bess replied.

That meant she was not completely convinced of the safety of what he wanted to do. But since Harry had been over this ground, he was too bored to go over it again. He merely exchanged a glance with Marylou.

Bess felt her face grow warm. Sam, their handyman—hers and her husband Claude's for seventeen years, a real member of the family—had left two days ago. Sam had made a speech and said he just couldn't stand Harry, he was sorry. Sam was getting on in years, and Harry had tried to boss him around, as if he were a hired hand, Bess supposed. She wasn't sure, but she could imagine. Bess hoped Sam would write to her soon, let her know where he was, so she could ask him back when Harry left. When she remembered old Sam with his best jacket on and his suitcase beside him, hailing the bus on the main road, Bess almost hated her grandson.

"Gramma, it's as simple as this," Harry began in the slow, patient voice in which he always presented his case. "I need sixty thousand dollars to buy my half with Roscoe. I told you Roscoe's just a nickname for laughs. His name is Ross Levitt."

I don't care what his name is, Bess thought, but she said a polite "Um-hm."

"Well—with sixty thousand dollars each, it's a sure thing for both of us. It's part of a chain, you know, twelve other places already, and they're all coining money. But if I can't put up my part in a few days, Gramma—or can't give a promise of the money, my chances are gone. I'll pay you back, Gramma, naturally. But this is the chance of a lifetime!"

To use such words, Bess was thinking, and to be only twenty-two! Harry had a lot to learn.

"Ask your lawyer if you're in doubt, Gramma," Harry said. "Ask any banker. I'm not afraid of the facts."

Bess recrossed her thick ankles. Why didn't his mother advance the money, if it was so safe? His mother had married a well-to-do man. And here was her grandson, married, at twenty-two. Too early for Harry, Bess thought, and she didn't care for Marylou or her type. Marylou was pretty and silly. Might as well be a high-school crush, not a wife. Bess knew she had to keep her thoughts to herself, however, because there was nothing worse than meddling.

"Gramma, what fun is it here for you any more, all alone in the country? Both the Colmans dead in the last year, you told me. In town, you'd have a nice circle of friends who could . . ."

Harry's voice became a drone to Bess. She had three or four good friends, six or eight even in the district. She'd known them all a long time, and they rang up, they came to see her, or Sam drove her to see them in the pick-up. Harry was too young to appreciate what a home meant, Bess thought. Every high-ceilinged bedroom upstairs was handsome, everyone said, with curtains and quilts that Bess or her own mother had made. The local newspaper had even come to take photographs, and the article had been reprinted in the . . .

Bess was stirred out of her thoughts by Harry's getting up.

"Guess we'll be turning in, Gramma," he said.

Marylou got up with her coffee cup and took it to the sink. All the other dishes were washed. Marylou hadn't much to say, but Bess sensed a terrible storm in her, some terrible wish. And yet, Bess supposed, it probably wasn't any worse or any different from Harry's wish, which was simply to get his hands on a lot of money. They could live on the grounds behind the restaurant, Harry had said. A fine house with a swimming pool all their own. Bess could imagine Marylou looking forward to that.

The young people had gone up to the front bedroom. They'd taken the television set up there, because Bess had said she didn't often watch it. She did look at it nearly every night, but she'd wanted to be polite when Harry and Marylou first arrived. Now she wished she had the set, because she could have done with a little change of thoughts, a laugh maybe. Bess went to her own sleeping quarters, which in summer was a room off the back porch with screened windows against mosquitoes, though there weren't ever many in this region. She turned on her transistor radio, low.

Upstairs, Harry and Marylou talked softly, glancing now and then at the closed door, thinking Bess might knock with a tray of milk and cake, as she had done once since they'd been here.

"I don't think she'll be coming up tonight," Marylou said. "She's sort of mad at us."

"Well, that's too bad." Harry was undressing. He blew on the square toes of his cowboy boots and passed them once across the seat of his Levis to see if the shine came up. "Goddamn it, I've heard of these situations before, haven't you? Some old person who won't turn loose of the dough—which is really *coming* to me—just when the younger people damn well need it."

"Isn't there someone else you know who could persuade her?"

"Hell—around here?" They'd all be on his grandmother's side, Harry was thinking. Other people were the last thing they needed. "I'm for a small snort. How about you?" Harry pulled from a back corner of the closet a big half-empty bottle of bourbon.

"No, thanks. I'll have a sip of yours, if you're going to put water in it."

Harry splashed some water from the porcelain pitcher into his glass, handed the glass to Marylou for a sip, then added more bourbon for himself, and drank it almost off. "You know Roscoe wanted me to call him up yesterday or today? With an answer?" Harry wiped his mouth. He wasn't expecting a reply from Marylou and didn't get one. *I damn well wish she was dead now*, Harry thought, like a curse that he might have said aloud to get the resentment and anger out of his system. Then suddenly it came to him. An idea. Not a bad idea, not a horrible idea. Not too horrible. And safe. Well, ninety percent safe, if he did it wisely, carefully. It was even a simple idea.

"What're you thinking?" Marylou asked, propped up in bed now with the sheet pulled up to her waist. Her curly reddish hair glowed like a halo in the light of the reading lamp fixed to the bed.

"I'm thinking—if Gramma had something like a hip injury, you know—those things old people always get. She'd—" He came closer to the bed and spoke even more softly, knowing already that Marylou would be with him, even if his idea were more dangerous. "I mean, she'd have to stay in a town, wouldn't she—if she couldn't get around?"

Marylou's eyes swam in excited confusion, and she blinked. "What're you talking about?" she asked in a whisper. "Pushing her down the stairs?"

Harry shook his head quickly. "That's too obvious. I was thinking of— maybe going on a picnic, the way she says she does, you know? With the horse and wagon. A watermelon, sandwiches and all and—"

"And beer!" Marylou said, giggling nervously knowing the climax was coming.

"Then the wagon turns over somewhere," Harry said simply, shrugging. "You know, there's that ford by the stream. Well, *I* know it, anyway."

"Wagon turns over. What about us? If we're in it?"

"You don't have to be in it. You could've jumped off to lay the cloth, some damn thing. I'll do it."

A pause.

"You're serious?" Marylou asked.

Harry was thinking, with his eyes almost closed. Finally he nodded.

"Yes. If I can't think of anything else. Anything better. Time's getting short, even for promises to Roscoe. Sure. I'm serious." Then abruptly Harry went and switched on the television.

To the little grey cat, Fanny the horse had become a protectress, a fortress, a home. Not that Fanny did anything. Fanny merely existed, giving out warmth in the cold of the night before dawn. The grey kitten's only enemies were the two older cats, and fortunately these chose to be simply huffy, ready with a spit, a swipe of a paw full of claws. They made life unpleasant, but they were not out for the kill, or even to drive her off the premises, which was something.

The kitten spent not much time in the stable, however. She liked to play in the ducks' and the chickens' yard, to canter towards a chick as if with evil intent, then to dodge the lunge, the terrible beak of the mother hen. Then the kitten would leap to an upright of the wooden fence and sit, washing a paw, surveying alertly the area in front of her and the meadow behind her. She was half wild. She was not tempted to approach the back door of the house. She sensed that she wouldn't be welcome. She had never had anything but ill-treatment or indifference at best from the creatures that walked on two legs. With her grandmother and great-grandmother, she had eaten the remains of their kills, what was left of rats, birds, now and then a small rabbit, when her elders had eaten their fill. From the two-legged creatures came nothing reliable or abundant, maybe a pan of milk and bread, not every day, not to be counted on.

But the big red horse, so heavy, so slow, the grey kitten had come to recognize as a reliable friend. The kitten had seen horses before, but never any as huge as this. She had never come close to a horse, never touched one before. The kitten found it both amusing and dangerous. The kitten loved to feel amused, to feel as if she were playing tricks on other creatures (like the chickens) and on herself, because it eased the realities of existence, the fact that she could be killed—in a flash, as her mother had been—if the gigantic horse happened to step on her, for instance. Even the horse's big feet had metal bottoms: the kitten had noticed this one evening when the horse was lying down. Not soft, like the horse's long hair there, but hard, able to hurt.

Yet the kitten realized that the horse played with her too. The horse turned its great head and neck to look at her, and was careful not to step on her. Once when the horse was lying down, the kitten in a nervous rush of anxiety and mischief dashed up the horse's soft nose, up the bony front, and seized an ear and nipped it. Then at once the kitten had leapt down and crouched, fearing the worst in retaliation. But the horse had only tossed its head a little, showed its teeth, and snorted—disturbing some nearby wisps of hay—as if it were amused also. Therefore the grey kitten pranced without fear now on the horse's side and haunch, leapt to tackle the coarse hair of the horse's tail, and dodged the tail's slow flick with ease. The horse's eyes followed her. The kitten felt those eyes a kind of protection, like her mother's eyes which the kitten remembered. Now the kitten slept in the warm place under the horse's shoulder, next to the great body which radiated heat.

One day the fat woman caught sight of the little kitten. Usually the kitten hid at the first glimpse of a human figure coming from the house, but the kitten was caught unawares while investigating a well-pecked chicken bone outside the stable. The kitten crouched and stared at the woman, ready to run.

"Well, well! Where'd you come from!" said Bess, bending to see better. "And what's happened to your tail?—You're a tiny little thing!" When Bess moved closer, the kitten dashed into the raspberry bushes and disappeared.

Bess carried the bucket of oats into Fanny's stable—poor Fanny was standing and doing nothing now—set the oats on the corner of the trough, and led Fanny out for water. When Fanny had drunk, Bess opened a fence gate, and led Fanny into an enclosed meadow.

"You're having a fine holiday, aren't you, Fanny? But we're going on a picnic today. You'll pull the wagon. Down to the old brook where you can cool your feet." She patted the mare's side. The top of Fanny's back was on a level with Bess's eyes. A huge creature she was, but she didn't eat a lot, and she worked willingly. Bess remembered Harry at thirteen or so, sitting astride Fanny for his picture to be taken, legs all bowed out as if he were sitting on a barrel. Bess didn't like to recall those days. Harry had been a nicer boy then. Engine Horse, Harry had called Fanny, impressed by her strength, as who wouldn't be, seeing her pull a wagon-load of wheat sacks.

Bess went into the stable, poured the oats into Fanny's trough, then went back to the house, where she had a peach pie in the oven. She turned the oven off, and opened the oven door so it stayed ajar about four inches. Bess never measured or timed things, but her baking came out right. She ought to give the little kitten a roast beef rib to chew on, Bess thought. She knew the type this kitten was, half wild, full of beans, and she—or maybe it was a he—would make a splendid mouser, if it could hold its own against the pair of cats here till it grew up a little. Bess took the plate of leftover roast beef from the refrigerator and with a sharp knife cut off a rib about fourteen inches long. If she could manage to give it to the kitten without the other cats noticing and stealing it, it would do the kitten a power of good.

The ham and cheese sandwiches were already made, and it was only a quarter to twelve. Marylou had deviled half a dozen eggs this morning. Where was she now? They were both upstairs talking, Bess supposed. They did a lot of talking. Bess heard a floorboard squeak. Yes, they were upstairs, and she decided to go out now and see if she could find the kitten.

Bess approached the chicken yard in her waddling gait, calling, "Here kitty-kitty-kitty!" and holding the bone out. Her own two cats were away hunting now, probably, and just as well. Bess even looked in the stable for the little one, but didn't see her. Then when she glanced at Fanny in the meadow—Fanny with her head down, munching clover—Bess caught sight of the little kitten, gamboling and darting in the sunlight around Fanny's hooves, like a puff of smoke blown this way and that. The kitten's lightness and energy held Bess spellbound for a few moments. What a contrast, Bess was thinking, with her own awful weight, her slowness, her *age!* Bess smiled as she walked towards the gate. The kitten was going to be pleased with the bone.

"Puss-puss?" she called. "What'll we name you—if you stay?" Bess breathed harder, trying to walk and talk at the same time.

The kitten drew back and stared at Bess, her ears erect, yellow-green eyes wary, and she moved nearer the horse as if for protection.

"Brought you a bone," Bess said, and tossed it.

The kitten leapt backward, then caught the smell of meat and advanced, nose down, straight towards her objective. An involuntary, primal growl came from her small throat, a growl of warning, triumph, and voraciousness. With one tiny foot on the great bone, in case an intruder would snatch it, the kitten tore at the meat with baby teeth. Growling and eating at the same time, the kitten circled the bone, glancing all around her to see that no enemy or rival was approaching from any direction.

Bess chuckled with amusement and gratification. Certainly old Fanny wasn't going to bother the little cat with her bone!

Marylou was already loading the wagon with baskets and thermoses and the blankets to sit on. Bess pulled a fresh tablecloth out of the kitchen cabinet.

Harry went out to hitch up Fanny. He strode like a cowboy in his high-heeled boots, grabbed the curved brim of his Stetson and readjusted it to reassure himself, because he was not an expert at throwing a collar over a horse's head.

"*Whoa*, Fanny!" he yelled, when the mare drew back. He'd missed. Dammit, he wasn't going to call for Bess to help him, that'd be ridiculous. The mare circled Harry, facing him, but drawing back every time he tried to slip the heavy collar on. Harry jumped about like a bullfighter—except that the collar was getting damned heavy in his hands, not like something a bull-fighter had to carry. He might have to tie up the beast, he thought. He seized the bridle, which dangled from a halter. She hadn't even a bit in as yet. "Engine hoss! *Whoa*, girl!"

Fortified and exhilarated by her half-eaten banquet, the little grey kitten leapt about also, playing, pretending she had to guard her bone, though she knew the man hadn't even seen her.

"Whoa, I *said!*" Harry yelled, and lunged at Fanny and this time made it with the collar. Harry turned his ankle and fell to the ground. He got up, not at all hurt by the fall, and then he heard a cry, a rhythmic cry like something panting.

Harry saw the little grey animal, thought at first it was a rat, then realized it was a kitten with half its bowels out. He must have stepped on it, or the horse had. Or maybe he'd fallen on it. He'd have to kill it, that he saw right away. Annoyed and suddenly angry, Harry stepped hard on the kitten's head with the heel of his cowboy boot. Harry's teeth were bared. He was still getting his own breath back. His Gramma probably wouldn't miss the kitten, he thought. She usually had too many of them. But Harry picked the kitten up by its oddly short tail, swung it once, and hurled it as far as he could across the meadow, away from the house.

The mare followed the movement with her eyes, until the kitten—even before it landed on the ground—was lost to her vision. But she had seen the kitten smashed by the man falling on it. Fanny followed docilely as Harry led her towards the gate, towards the house. Fanny's awareness of what had happened came slowly and ponderously, even more slowly than she plodded across the meadow. Involuntarily, Fanny turned her head and tried to look behind her, almost came to a stop, and the man jerked her bridle.

"Come on, come on, Engine!"

The brook, sometimes called Latham's Brook, was about two miles from Bess's farm. Harry knew it from his childhood visits with his grandmother. It crossed his mind that the wooden bridge might be different—wider, maybe with a rail now—and was relieved to see that it was the same: a span of hardly twenty feet, and maybe eight or nine feet wide, not wide enough for two cars, but a car seldom came here, probably. The road was a single lane, unpaved, and there were lots of better roads around for cars.

"There's the old spot," said Bess, looking across the brook at the green grass, pleasantly sheltered by a few trees, where the family had come for years to picnic. "Hasn't changed, has it, Harry?" Bess was seated on a bench that let down from a side of the wagon, the right side.

Harry had the reins. "Nope. Sure hasn't."

This was where Marylou was to get down, and according to plan, she said, "Let me walk across, Harry! Is it shallow enough to wade?"

Harry tugged Fanny to a halt, sawing on her bit, and Fanny even backed a little, thinking that was what he wanted. "I dunno," said Harry in a frozen tone.

Marylou jumped down. She was in blue jeans, espadrilles, and a red-checked shirt. She trotted across the bridge, as if feeling happy and full of pep.

Harry clucked up Fanny again. He'd go over the right side of the bridge. He tugged Fanny to the right.

"Careful, Harry!" said Bess. "*Harry, you're—*"

The horse was on the bridge, the two right wheels of the wagon were not. There was a loud bump and scrape, a terrible jolt as the axles hit the edge of the bridge. Bess was thrown backward, balanced for a second with the wagon side in the small of her back, then she fell off into the water. Harry crouched, prepared to spring to safety, to jump towards the bank, but the falling wagon gave him nothing solid to leap from. Fanny, drawn backward and sideways by the weight of the wagon, was suddenly over the edge of the bridge, trapped in her shafts. She fell on Harry's shoulders, and Harry's face was suddenly smashed against stones, under water.

Fanny threshed about on her side, trying to regain her feet.

"*Har-ry!*" Marylou screamed. She had run on to the bridge. She saw a red stream coming from Harry's head, and she ran to the bank and waded into the water. "*Harry!*"

The crazy horse was somehow sideways in the wagon shafts, trampling all over Harry's legs now. Marylou raised her fists and shouted.

"*Back*, you idiot!"

Fanny, dazed with shock and fear, raised her front feet, not high, and when they came down, they struck Marylou's knees.

Marylou screamed, gave a panic-stricken, brandishing movement of her right fist to drive the horse off, then sank into the water up to her waist, gasping. Blood, terrifying blood, poured from her knees, through her torn blue jeans. And the stupid horse was now pitching and stomping, trying to get out of the shafts. Again the hooves came down on Harry, on his body.

It all happened so slowly. Marylou felt paralyzed. She couldn't even cry out. The horse looked like something in a slow-motion film, dragging now the broken wagon right across Harry. My God! And was it Bess yelling something now? Was it? Where? Marylou lost consciousness.

Bess was struggling to get to her feet. She'd been knocked out for a few minutes, she realized. What on earth had happened? Fanny was trying to climb the bank opposite, and the wagon was wedged between two trees. When Bess's eyes focused a bit better, she saw Harry almost covered by water, and then Marylou, who was nearer. Clumsily Bess waded into the deeper water of the brook, seized Marylou by one arm, and dragged her slowly, slowly over the stones, until her head was on the bank, clear of water.

But Harry was face down and under water! Bess had a horrible moment, had a desire to scream as loudly as she could for help. But all she did was wade towards Harry, hands outstretched, and when she reached him, she took as hard a grip as she could on his shirt, under his arm, and tugged with all her strength. She could not move him, but she turned him over, held his head in the air. His face was a pink and red blur, no longer a face. There was something wrong with his chest. It was crushed.

"*Help!*" Bess yelled. "Please!—*Help!*"

She waited a minute, and shouted again. She sat down finally on the grass of the bank. She was in shock, she realized. She shivered, then she began to tremble violently. A chill. She was soaking wet. Even her hair was wet. See about Marylou, she told herself, and she got up again and went to Marylou who was on her back, her legs twisted in an awful way, as if they were broken. But Marylou was breathing.

Bess made herself move. She unhitched Fanny. Bess had no purpose. She felt she was in some kind of nightmare, yet she knew she was awake, that it had all happened. She held on to a brass ring of Fanny's collar, and Fanny pulled her up the slope, onto the bridge. They walked slowly, the woman and the horse, back the way they had come. It was easily nearly a mile to any house, Bess thought. The Poindexter place, wasn't that the next?

When the Poindexter house was in sight, Bess saw a car approaching. She raised her arm, but found she hadn't strength to yell out loudly enough. Still, the car was coming, slowing down.

"Go to the bridge. The brook," Bess told the bewildered-looking man who was getting out of his car. "Two people—"

"You're hurt? You're bleeding," said the man, pointing to Bess's shoulder. "Get in the car. We'll go to the Poindexters' house. I know the Poindexters." He helped Bess into the car, then he took Fanny's dangling reins and pulled her into the long driveway of the Poindexters' property, so the horse would be off the road. He went back and drove the car into the driveway, past the horse, on to the house.

Bess knew the Poindexters too. They were not close friends, but good neighbors. Bess had enough of her wits about her to refuse to lie down on the sofa, as Eleanor Poindexter wished her to do, until they'd put newspapers down on it. Her clothes were still damp. Eleanor made her some tea. The man was already on the telephone. He came back and said he'd asked for an ambulance to go at once to the ford.

Eleanor, a gentle, rather pretty woman of fifty, saw to Bess's shoulder. It was a cut, not serious. "Whatever made your grandson go over the edge?" she said for the second time, as if in wonderment. "That bridge isn't all that narrow."

It was two or three days before Bess felt anything like her usual self. She hadn't needed to go into a hospital, but the doctor had advised her to rest a lot at home, which she had done. And Eleanor Poindexter had been an angel, and driven Bess twice to visit Marylou in the Danville hospital. Marylou's legs had been broken, and she'd need an operation on both knees. She might always walk with a limp, one doctor told Bess. And Marylou was strangely bitter about Harry—that shocked Bess the most, considering they were newlyweds, and Bess assumed much in love.

"Stupid—selfish—so-and-so," Marylou said. Her voice was bitter.

Bess felt Marylou might have said more, but didn't want to or didn't dare. Harry's body had been sent to California, to Harry's mother. After the brook, Bess had never seen Harry.

One day that same week, Bess took Fanny into the meadow for grazing. Bess was feeling a little happier. She'd had a letter from Sam, and he was willing to come back, providing Harry's visit was over (Sam didn't mince words), and Bess had just replied to him in a letter which the mailman would take away tomorrow morning.

Then Bess saw the dry and half-eaten body of the little grey cat, and a shock of pain went through her. She'd supposed the kitten had wandered on somewhere. What had happened to it? Crushed somehow. By what? A car or tractor never came into this meadow. Bess turned and looked at Fanny, whose thick neck was bent towards the ground. Fanny's lips and teeth moved in the grass. Fanny couldn't have stepped on the little thing, the kitten was much too quick, had been. Fanny had liked the kitten, Bess had seen that the morning she'd given the kitten the rib bone. And there, just a few feet away, was the long bone, stripped clean now by birds. Bess bent and picked it up. How the little kitten had loved this bone! Bess, after bracing herself, lifted the kitten's body up too. Hadn't Harry harnessed Fanny in the meadow that day? What had happened? What had happened to make Fanny so angry that day at the brook? It was Harry's hands that had driven the wagon over the edge. Bess had seen it. Fanny would never have gone so near the edge, if she hadn't been tugged that way.

In the afternoon, Bess buried the kitten in an old, clean dishtowel in a grave she dug in the far meadow, beyond the chickens' and the ducks' yard. It hadn't seemed right to dispose of the kitten in the garbage, even if she'd wrapped the body well. The kitten had been so full of life! Harry had somehow killed the kitten, Bess felt sure. And Fanny had seen it. Bess knew too that Harry had meant to kill her. It was horrid, too horrid to think about.

ROGUES

SAKI

The Brogue

The hunting season had come to an end, and the Mullets had not succeeded in selling the Brogue. There had been a kind of tradition in the family for the past three or four years, a sort of fatalistic hope, that the Brogue would find a purchaser before the hunting was over; but seasons came and went without anything happening to justify such ill-founded optimism. The animal had been named Berserker in the earlier stages of its career; it had been rechristened the Brogue later on, in recognition of the fact that, once acquired, it was extremely difficult to get rid of. The unkinder wits of the neighborhood had been known to suggest that the first letter of its name was superfluous. The Brogue had been variously described in sale catalogues as a lightweight hunter, a lady's hack, and, more simply, but still with a touch of imagination, as a useful brown gelding, standing 15.1. Toby Mullet had ridden him for four seasons with the West Wessex; you can ride almost any sort of horse with the West Wessex as long as it is an animal that knows the country. The Brogue knew the country intimately, having personally created most of the gaps that were to be met with in banks and hedges for many miles round. His manners and characteristics were not ideal in the hunting field, but he was probably rather safer to ride to hounds than he was as a hack on country roads. According to the Mullet family, he was not really road-shy, but there were one or two objects of dislike that brought on sudden attacks of what Toby called swerving sickness. Motors and cycles he treated with tolerant disregard, but pigs, wheelbarrows, piles of stones by the roadside, perambulators in a village street, gates painted too aggressively white, and sometimes, but not always, the newer kind of beehives, turned him aside from his tracks in vivid imitation of the zigzag course of forked lightning. If a pheasant rose noisily from the other side of a hedgerow the Brogue would spring into the air at the same moment, but this may have been due to a desire to be companionable. The Mullet family contradicted the widely prevalent report that the horse was a confirmed crib biter.

It was about the third week in May that Mrs. Mullet, relick of the late Sylvester Mullet, and mother of Toby and a bunch of daughters, assailed Clovis Sangrail on the outskirts of the village with a breathless catalogue of local happenings.

"You know our new neighbor, Mr. Penricarde?" she vociferated; "awfully rich, owns tin mines in Cornwall, middle-aged and rather quiet. He's taken the Red House on a long lease and spent a lot of money on alterations and improvements. Well, Toby's sold him the Brogue!"

Clovis spent a moment or two in assimilating the astonishing news; then he broke out into unstinted congratulation. If he had belonged to a more emotional race he would probably have kissed Mrs. Mullet.

"How wonderful lucky to have pulled it off at last! Now you can buy a decent animal. I've always said that Toby was clever. Ever so many congratulations."

"Don't congratulate me. It's the most unfortunate thing that could have happened!" said Mrs. Mullet dramatically. Clovis stared at her in amazement.

"Mr. Penricarde," said Mrs. Mullet, sinking her voice to what she imagined to be an impressive whisper, though it rather resembled a hoarse, excited squeak, "Mr. Penricarde has just begun to pay attentions to Jessie. Slight at first, but now unmistakable. I was a fool not to have seen it sooner. Yesterday, at the Rectory garden party, he asked her what her favorite flowers were, and she told him carnations, and today a whole stack of carnations has arrived, clove and malmaison and lovely dark red ones, regular exhibition blooms, and a box of chocolates that he must have got on purpose from London. And he's asked her to go round the links with him tomorrow. And now, just at this critical moment, Toby has sold him that animal. It's a calamity!"

"But you've been trying to get the horse off your hands for years," said Clovis.

"I've got a houseful of daughters," said Mrs. Mullet, "and I've been trying—well, not to get them off my hands, of course, but a husband or two wouldn't be amiss among the lot of them; there are six of them, you know."

"I don't know," said Clovis, "I've never counted, but I expect you're right as to the number; mothers generally know these things."

"And now," continued Mrs. Mullet, in her tragic whisper, "when there's a rich husband-in-prospect imminent on the horizon Toby goes and sells him that miserable animal. It will probably kill him if he tries to ride it; anyway it will kill any affection he might have felt towards any member of our family. What is to be done? We can't very well ask to have the horse back; you see, we praised it up like anything when we thought there was a chance of his buying it, and said it was just the animal to suit him."

"Couldn't you steal it out of his stable and send it to grass at some farm miles away?" suggested Clovis. "Write VOTE FOR WOMEN on the stable door, and the thing would pass for a Suffragette outrage. No one who knew the horse could possibly suspect you of wanting to get it back again."

"Every newspaper in the country would ring with the affair," said Mrs. Mullet; "can't you imagine the headline, 'Valuable Hunter Stolen by Suffragettes'? The police would scour the countryside till they found the animal."

"Well, Jessie must try and get it back from Penricarde on the plea that it's an old favorite. She can say it was only sold because the stable had to be pulled down under the terms of an old repairing lease, and that now it has been arranged that the stable is to stand for a couple of years longer."

"It sounds a queer proceeding to ask for a horse back when you've just sold him," said Mrs. Mullet, "but something must be done, and done at once. The man is not used to horses, and I believe I told him it was as quiet as a lamb. After all, lambs go kicking and twisting about as if they were demented, don't they?"

"The lamb has an entirely unmerited character for sedateness," agreed Clovis.

Jessie came back from the golf links next day in a state of mingled elation and concern.

"It's all right about the proposal," she announced, "he came out with it at the sixth hole. I said I must have time to think it over. I accepted him at the seventh."

"My dear," said her mother, "I think a little more maidenly reserve and hesitation would have been advisable, as you've known him so short a time. You might have waited till the ninth hole."

"The seventh is a very long hole," said Jessie; "besides, the tension was putting us both off our game. By the time we'd got to the ninth hole we'd settled lots of things. The honeymoon is to be spent in Corsica, with perhaps a flying visit to Naples if we feel like it, and a week in London to wind up with. Two of his nieces are to be asked to be bridesmaids, so with our lot there will be seven, which is rather a lucky number. You are to wear your pearl grey, with any amount of Honiton lace jabbed into it. By the way, he's coming over this evening to ask your consent to the whole affair. So far all's well, but about the Brogue it's a different matter. I told him the legend about the stable, and how keen we were about buying the horse back, but he seems equally keen on keeping it. He said he must have horse exercise now that he's living in the country, and he's going to start riding tomorrow. He's ridden a few times in the Row on an animal that was accustomed to carry octogenarians and people undergoing rest cures, and that's about all his experience in the saddle—oh, and he rode a pony once in Norfolk, when he was fifteen and the pony twenty-four; and tomorrow he's going to ride the Brogue! I shall be a widow before I'm married, and I do so want to see what Corsica's like; it looks so silly on the map."

Clovis was sent for in haste, and the developments of the situation put before him.

"Nobody can ride that animal with any safety," said Mrs. Mullet, "except Toby, and he knows by long experience what it is going to shy at, and manages to swerve at the same time."

"I did hint to Mr. Penricarde—to Vincent, I should say—that the Brogue didn't like white gates," said Jessie.

"White gates!" exclaimed Mrs. Mullet; "did you mention what effect a pig has on him? He'll have to go past Lockyer's farm to get to the high road, and there's sure to be a pig or two grunting about in the lane."

"He's taken rather a dislike to turkeys lately," said Toby.

"It's obvious that Penricarde mustn't be allowed to go out on that animal," said Clovis, "at least not till Jessie has married him, and tired of him. I tell you what: ask him to a picnic tomorrow, starting at an early hour; he's not the sort to go out for a ride before breakfast. The day after I'll get the rector to drive him over to Crowleigh before lunch, to see the new cottage hospital they're building there. The Brogue will be standing idle in the stable and Toby can offer to exercise it; then it can pick up a stone or something of the sort and go conveniently lame. If you hurry on the wedding a bit the lameness fiction can be kept up till the ceremony is safely over."

Mrs. Mullet belonged to an emotional race, and she kissed Clovis.

It was nobody's fault that the rain came down in torrents the next morning, making a picnic a fantastic impossibility. It was also nobody's fault, but sheer ill-luck, that the weather cleared up sufficiently in the afternoon to tempt Mr. Penricarde to make his first essay with the Brogue. They did not get as far as the pigs at Lockyer's farm; the rectory gate was painted a dull unobtrusive green, but it had been white a year or two ago, and the Brogue never forgot that he had been in the habit of making a violent curtsey, a backpedal and a swerve at this particular point of the road. Subsequently, there being apparently no further call on his services, he broke his way into the rectory orchard, where he found a hen turkey in a coop; later visitors to the orchard found the coop almost intact, but very little left of the turkey.

Mr. Penricarde, a little stunned and shaken, and suffering from a bruised knee and some minor damages, good-naturedly ascribed the accident to his own inexperience with horses and country roads, and allowed Jessie to nurse him back into complete recovery and golf-fitness within something less than a week.

In the list of wedding presents which the local newspaper published a fortnight or so later appeared the following item: "Brown saddle horse, 'The Brogue,' bridegroom's gift to bride."

"Which shows," said Toby Mullet, "that he knew nothing."

"Or else," said Clovis, "that he has a very pleasing wit."

THORNE SMITH

A Horse in Bed

There was an element of urgency sharpening the edges of Hebe's whisper that penetrated Sapho's vast unresponsiveness to mundane considerations. This woman of many parts and poses sat up in bed and looked upon her daughter as a glacier would regard a rose.

"Your humor, Hebe, is extremely malapropos," she brought forth.

"Sapho," replied Hebe, "I'm not trying to be funny. Things are funny enough. There's a horse or something very much like a horse in the major's bed."

Sapho still light-headed from a heavy sleep strove to adjust her brain to the reception of this extraordinary announcement. No good. The brain refused to accept it. "What do you mean, there's a horse in your father's bed?" she achieved after an effort.

"Exactly that," answered her daughter calmly. "Either father has turned into a horse or a horse has turned into father. It comes to the same thing. There's one other possibility. Some horse might have run father out of bed and taken his place or else gone to sleep on top of him."

"As if we didn't have enough on our hands with the Vacation Fund affair tonight," Mrs. Lamb complained as she sought for her robe and slippers. "If it isn't a horse, Hebe, I'll be very much vexed."

"And if it is?" Hebe inquired.

"God knows," sighed Mrs. Lamb, tiptoeing across the room.

Together they looked upon Mr. Lamb's bed and beheld a horse. As much of the covers as possible were over this horse, its head was upon the pillows, yet much remained exposed and dangling. Hoofs and legs were eloquently visible. It was obvious that only the most determined of horses would have been willing to sleep in such a cramped position merely for the sake of a bed.

"My God," breathed Mrs. Lamb. "What will the servants say?"

Under the scrutiny of the two women the horse stirred uneasily and opened one eye. It was enough. Mrs. Lamb indulged in a gasp. Hebe was merely interested. Not satisfied with this demonstration, the horse raised his head from the pillows and looked inquiringly at Hebe and Mrs. Lamb. Then his lips curled back in a sardonic grin displaying a powerful set of vicious-looking teeth. He rolled his eyes until only the whites remained and thrust one curved foreleg at Mrs. Lamb, a gesture eloquently suggestive of his intention to inflict some painful injury upon her body and person. Mrs. Lamb hastily withdrew to her bed where she took refuge beneath the covers.

"You do something about it, Hebe," came her muffled voice. "Get the creature out of the house without the servants knowing. It would never do to have them think your mother had a horse in the next room. You know what servants are."

The horse was listening intently, ears pitched forward, and at this last remark he winked slowly and deliberately at Hebe. The girl was amazed. It was her father all over. At that moment she accepted the fact that something strange had occurred.

Then after a few minutes of thoughtful consideration, looking this way and that as if to determine the best way of procedure, Mr. Lamb cautiously got himself out of bed, but not without considerable clattering and convolutions. Hebe watched him with amused interest. She knew it was her father.

"Hurry, Hebe," came her mother's voice. "We can't afford to miss church today—not with that affair on tonight."

Mr. Lamb thought of his best pajamas, and throwing back his head gave vent to a wild neigh. He was feeling rather wild and at the same time a trifle timid. He had often played horses as a child, but never actually been one. Now he tried to recall just how he had gone about it in those early days. He wondered how he looked, what sort of horse he was, and, remembering his full-length mirror, he stepped delicately across the room and, sitting down in a strangely unhorselike attitude, lowered his neck and gazed at his reflection. The effect was not pleasing. He saw a most despondent-looking creature regarding him from the glass. Hebe could not restrain a laugh, and Mr. Lamb turned his head and looked at her reproachfully, then continued his scrutiny.

"I'm not much of a horse in this position," he decided. "There must be some other way of being a horse. Perhaps—"

He rose from his strange position and backed away from the mirror, but was still unable to get the desired view. Bending an eloquent glance upon his daughter, he pointed with his hoof to the mirror. Obediently the girl went over to the mirror and after much shaking and nodding of her father's head, she adjusted it to his satisfaction.

"That's something like," thought Lamb, surveying his reflection with no little satisfaction.

He was a fine body of a horse—a sleek, strapping stallion. Black as night with a star on his forehead. He turned slowly, taking himself in from all angles.

"Rather indecent, though," he thought. "Wish I had a blanket, a long one. Oh, hell! I'm a horse, now. Horses don't mind. Still it doesn't seem quite—well, I just never did it before, that's all." He paused to reconsider his reflection, then continued his soliloquy, "Anyway, if that girl can go about in step-ins and such, I can go about in nothing at all."

He looked at his daughter proudly, and affectionately nuzzled her warm neck. She put up her arms and kissed him, then drew back and looked at him with a half smile. Lamb solemnly nodded his head, and Hebe understood. Then a pleasant idea occurred to him. He squeezed through the door into his wife's room and quietly approached the bed. Mrs. Lamb was still completely smothered by the covers. Slipping his nose through an aperture, he suddenly emitted a piercing scream sounding like a lost soul in hell. It was as if he had blown the good lady out of the bed. With amazing swiftness covers and all disappeared. Mrs. Lamb found herself on the floor on the other side of the bed, and she felt herself lucky to be there.

"Hebe, dear, for God's sake, what was that?" she wailed.

"The horse," answered Hebe shortly.

"Oh, what a horse!" quavered Mrs. Lamb. She was almost crying. "Can't you get him to go away? There's some Quaker Oats in the kitchen. Perhaps you can lure him out."

Thoroughly satisfied with the results of his first endeavor, Lamb's thoughts automatically turned to his brother-in-law. His spirit of enterprise was fired. He would stir farther afield. Still walking with highbred softness, he made his way to the quarters of Douglas Blumby. Hebe expectantly opened the door for him, and Lamb, with a courteous inclination of the head, passed through.

Brother Dug was at his shower. He was attacking it as only Brother Dug could. He was literally singing it into silence. Lamb stopped and considered, then gently parted the curtains and thrust in his head. Brother Dug, feeling a draft, reached blindly behind him to reclose the parted curtains. His hands encountered the wet nose of a horse. For a moment he fingered the nose thoughtfully. It was not a part of himself, he was sure of that. Then Lamb breathed heavily on his back, and Brother Dug gave up feeling and singing at the same moment. He turned uncertainly only to find a horse confronting him with every evil intent in its eyes.

Mr. Blumby's power lay in his throat, and this organ he now hastened to use with unprecedented vigor. It was a triumph of vocalization. He put his whole heart and soul into it, yet the horse remained. Realizing he could not shout the horse out of existence, Blumby crouched against the wall and held up two shaking hands as if to blot out the horrifying sight. For a moment he thought himself back in bed in the grip of some vividly terrifying nightmare. The horse still remained, water running grotesquely down either side of his nose. Mr. Lamb was killing two birds with one stone—refreshing himself and taking vengeance on his brother-in-law with whom he had never thought he would share a shower. He recalled the weeks, months, years of nausea this creature had caused him by his mere existence, and his anger rose. With one alarming foreleg he reached out and pressed down on the hot water lever. Cries of increased anguish from the occupant of the shower. Steam arose. Douglas attempted to escape, but Mr. Lamb implacably pushed him back. By this time Hebe had retired, having no desire to take part in a murder, no matter how justifiable.

Tiring at last of this sport, Mr. Lamb turned from the shower and devoted his talents to the room. This he proceeded to wreck, and, remarking Hebe's absence, gave other effective demonstrations of his scorn.

"Perhaps I shouldn't have done that," he said to himself as he left the room, "but after all I'm a horse; I'm not supposed to know any better."

Hebe met him at the door and suggested a breath of fresh air. Lamb gravely agreed. He was rather nervous and faltering in navigating the stairs, but with Hebe's moral encouragement he finally found himself in the lower hall. The girl opened the front doors and gave him an affectionate pat on the rump.

"That's rather a familiar thing to do even to one's father," Lamb decided.

He turned and subjected his daughter to a reproaching look, then with great dignity passed through the doors and descended the front steps. The Sunday papers had already been delivered. A headline caught his attention. He paused and endeavored to read, but found difficulty in focusing his eyes. Finally he hit upon the plan of using only one eye. This caused him to cock his head in rather an odd fashion for a horse. However, it served Lamb's purpose, and he became thoroughly interested. Having essentially a legal turn of mind, he had been following this murder trial in detail, and this report struck him as being unusually full and intelligent. With a deft hoof he flipped the paper over and continued reading, becoming more absorbed as he progressed.

Suddenly the maid, Helen, came out on the front veranda, hurried down the steps and snatched the paper from under his attentive nose. Lamb started after her up the steps, and the maid with a frightened cry darted into the house. Later she assured her mistress that she had been pursued across the lawn by a wild horse with blazing eyes. Mrs. Lamb was not hard to convince. That horse was capable of anything she thought.

Deprived of his newspaper, Lamb took stock of the world and his altered relations to it. It was a fair world and a brave day. Lamb felt better than he had in years. Nevertheless, he would very much like to finish that newspaper story. Perhaps the Walkers had not risen yet. Maybe their paper would still be out. With this hope at heart, he cantered down the drive and along High Hill Road until he had reached the Walkers' place. Here he turned in and bore down on the front porch as unobtrusively as he could, taking into consideration the fact that he was a stallion of striking appearance obviously on the loose.

Good. The paper was there. Lamb quickly found the exact place in the evidence he had been reading when interrupted and went on with the story. When it came to its continuation on page eighteen Lamb was nearly stumped, but by the happy expedient of applying a long red tongue to the paper, he was able to turn it to the desired page. Just as he had achieved this triumph some inner sense caused him to look up. Walker, clad in a bathrobe, was following his movements with every sign of amazement.

"Well, I'll be damned," said Walker softly. Then he called out: "Come here, May, if you want to see something funny—a horse reading the Sunday paper."

"Nonsense," said his wife, coming on to the porch and scanning the moist paper. "The poor fool's been trying to eat the paper, that's all. Such a beautiful horse, too. Wonder whose he is?"

"She called me a poor fool," said Lamb to himself, "and she's the biggest dunce in town. However, she has sense enough to see that I am beautiful. I am. Very."

He looked at her with arched brows, and Mrs. Walker was visibly impressed.

"He's an odd horse," she admitted. "Perhaps he was, in some strange way, interested in that paper."

Lamb made an approving noise.

Walker, having observed the horse's efforts, studied the page thoughtfully. There was only one continuation on it.

"I'll try him," he said, and he began reading the evidence aloud.

Lamb, forgetting he was a horse, promptly sat down and listened. From time to time, as a telling point was made, he nodded his head, and every time he did this Mr. Walker became so moved that he could hardly continue reading. Mrs. Walker drew up a wicker chair and sat down. She, too, became interested both in the horse and the evidence.

It was a strange Sunday morning scene: Mr. Walker comfortably seated on the top step reading diligently and a horse sitting in a weird position listening intently with ears cocked forward. Later when the Walkers attempted to tell the story at the Golf Club, they were jeered into rebellious silence.

Upon the completion of the story, Lamb arose and bowed courteously, so courteously, in fact, that Walker, in spite of himself, returned the bow with equal elaboration. Thereupon Mr. Lamb walked decently down the driveway and turned into High Hill Road.

"A good sort, Walker," thought Lamb. "I'll remember him if ever I get back to my former self. He believes in taking a chance."

Back on the Walker porch the man turned to his wife.

"Well, that's about the darndest horse I've ever seen," he said.

"An exceptionally interesting trial," mused Mr. Lamb as he ambled along High Hill Road. "If they can only get someone to corroborate that ragpicker's story the prosecution is going to have tough sledding."

Other considerations occupied his attention. He remembered with a pang that the morning had been lamentably free from any suggestion of bacon and eggs. Few things worse could happen to Mr. Lamb.

"Horses," he continued musing, "seem to get through the day pretty well on grass, but I won't eat grass. It would seem so desperate. What would Hebe think if I ever told her I had eaten grass?"

He looked contemplatively at a nearby tuft. They were about finishing breakfast at home now, well satisfied, gorged no doubt. Smelling agreeably of butter, they were preparing for church. Well, he would miss that in any event.

"That bit there doesn't look so bad," he thought, eyeing the tuft of grass with closer attention. "Suppose I try it just for fun?"

He glanced in either direction and approached the tuft.

"Well, here goes," he said to himself. "Might as well be a regular horse while I'm at it."

He nibbled the grass tentatively, throwing his head back the better to judge its taste.

"Not at all bad," he decided. "Not bad at all. Sort of like a rugged salad."

For the better part of an hour Mr. Lamb continued along the road fastidiously selecting choice patches of grass and experimenting with various combinations of weeds, clover, and wild flowers. Some he found palatable, others were hard to down. His appetite temporarily arranged for, Lamb bent his mind on other lines of activity. He was not like other horses, content to graze all day. Furthermore, he had come across a cow cropping grass, and this had rather damped his ardor. He had no intention at present of sharing breakfast with a cow. One had to draw the line somewhere. His thoughts involuntarily strayed to Sandra, and suddenly he remembered she had told him she was going riding today on Simonds's horse. She had also said some rather silly things about Simonds being a lovely man.

"I'll fix that horse," he muttered or attempted to mutter. "I'll make him rue this day."

With this edifying intention firmly fixed in his mind he cantered off in the direction of Simonds's home. He knew exactly where the horse passed most of its time—in a vacant lot directly back of Simonds's place. A high fence surrounded the lot, and behind this fence Simonds's horse was going about its own business. Mr. Lamb studied the innocent animal with growing animosity. He was the kind of horse Mr. Lamb most detested, a smug, plump horse, exactly like his master.

"He would have a fence to protect him," thought Lamb. "The coward. But I'll settle his hash. Wonder if I can make it?"

He backed off for some distance, gathered his powerful muscles together, and made a lunge at the fence, clearing it neatly. Once on the other side he suddenly changed his tactics. Instead of rushing at the horse and demolishing it as he had intended, he decided first to indulge in a little sport. He would be more subtle in his form of attack. He would confound this horse, terrify it within an inch of its life, put it out of commission for Sundays yet unborn.

Accordingly Mr. Lamb did things, things that no horse had ever done before or had ever thought of doing. He lowered his body close to the ground and curved his legs in a most unusual manner. Throwing his head to one side, he allowed his tongue to loll out of his mouth at one corner. With that careful attention to detail that marks the true artist, he flattened his ears and rolled his eyes more unpleasantly.

"Guess I look funny enough," thought Lamb. "Wish I could foam a bit. That would be the final touch."

He tried to work up a convincing-looking foam and succeeded partially. In this manner he approached his unwary enemy.

"Love to have a snapshot of myself," he reflected. "No one would ever believe it."

But several persons did believe it, among them being Simonds himself. He was standing at his bathroom window, and his eyes were starting out of their sockets. A few pedestrians also had stopped and now stood transfixed by the fence. This was more unusual than an appearance of Halley's comet, and years after they remembered the event far more vividly. Simonds, in a thin quivering voice, called to his wife, his son, and his daughter, and together in various stages of disarray, they witnessed the rout and almost total extinction of their horse.

When the horse first spied the strange-looking object creeping up on him he stopped what he was doing and gave his full attention to it. At first he felt no fear. The phenomenon was entirely outside his experience. But as Lamb drew nearer a certain anxiety took the place of curiosity and surprise.

And when the horse caught a glimpse of Mr. Lamb's lolling tongue and bloodshot eyes, he realized that here was something that would not improve upon closer acquaintance.

Slowly and deliberately Lamb circled round his enemy until he had reduced him to a state of abject terror. The horse's nerves were shot to pieces. He was trembling in every limb. Then Mr. Lamb, rolling his head drunkenly from side to side, his tongue sliding and slithering revoltingly between his bared teeth, began to close in on the aghast object of his enmity.

"A pretty picture I must make," thought Lamb, as he prepared for the final coup.

Within a few yards of the wretched horse, he paused and horrified the air with a series of heart-searing shrieks. The Simondses drew back from the window, the pedestrians hastily abandoned their points of vantage on the fence. The enemy almost swooned, but some half-numbed instinct warned him that to remain longer in the presence of that animal from hell was certain and painful death. Comparative safety lay only in flight, and flee the horse did. Thrice round the lot he sped, fear increasing his ambition to break all established speed records. Lamb, now at full height, followed just closely enough to keep the edge on the horse's terror.

On the third lap the horse decided that the enclosure was altogether too small to accommodate both of them. He made a dash at the fence. This time Lamb was not forced to jump, the enemy having gone clear through the fence and cleared the way. Out into the streets of the town the chase debouched. Fairfield Avenue swam past Mr. Lamb's vision like a dream. They came to a beautifully kept lawn and tore across it. The enemy rounded the corner of the house and came suddenly upon a breakfast party on the rear lawn. It was either his life, or the party's comfort, decided the horse. The party had to be sacrificed. Too late for turning now. Through the breakfast party the panting animal plowed, scattering table and dishes to the four winds. Lamb noticed as he passed through that one of the ladies had lost her kimono and was rushing about with the tablecloth over her head. He knew the people but had no time to apologize. His interest in the scene had caused him to lose slightly, and he now redoubled his efforts. The ground fairly thundered beneath his hooves as he dashed down the broad, quiet street at the end of which was situated the stately church he attended. This place of worship had broad doors on either side and a huge main entrance. They were all open to the breezes on this balmy July morning.

The fleeing horse, either mistaking the church for a stable or else deciding as a last resort to seek sanctuary, disappeared into the main entrance, paused in bewilderment, then as if realizing that this was no place for him, made a swift exit through one of the side doors.

Lamb in the heat of the pursuit followed without considering. He found the congregation in a state of wild confusion that was in no wise lessened by the sudden and tremendous appearance of a second and even more terrible horse. Protected by his pulpit the preacher looked boldly down upon his seething flock and for some odd reason began to sing "Nearer My God to Thee." Several women, believing he was summing up the situation altogether too mildly, fainted and lay in the aisles. All of the sleepers were wide awake and convinced that they would never sleep again.

It was at this moment that Lamb's better nature asserted itself. As he surveyed the scene of carnage he had been so instrumental in creating, his conscience smote him and he promptly sat down, hoping thereby to restore peace and harmony to the congregation.

Observing how quiet he was, one of the ushers timidly approached him and attempted to lead him out. Lamb resisted with dignity, and when the fellow persisted, he placed a hoof gently against his chest and gave him a slight push. The usher slid down the aisle as if it had been greased and brought up with a thump against a pew. No more attempts wee made to expel Mr. Lamb. He remained quietly seated in the rear of the church, paying strict attention to his own affairs. True, he was breathing hard, but so were many other members of the congregation including the preacher himself.

"This horse," announced the good man, peering at Mr. Lamb with puzzled eyes, "seems to be rather a different type of horse. I don't think he will disturb us and evidently he intends to stay. Who knows? Perhaps he is the first of equine converts."

Lamb's shoulders shook in encouraging mirth, and a polite noise is-sued from his throat. Several people turned and regarded him with timid reproval, and Lamb waved a placating hoof in their direction. Mistaking his meaning they immediately turned back and looked at him no more.

"Yes," continued the preacher as if in a dream, "a strangely odd horse. Never in my long experience—well, let's get on with the service."

Lamb followed the service closely, rising when the congregation rose and sitting when it sat. His kneeling was an artistic achievement and created such a stir that few people listened to the prayer in their efforts to observe his contortions. Even the preacher became distrait and found himself re-peating toward the end of the prayer, "God, what a horse! God all mighty what a horse!"

When the plate was passed for the offering, Mr. Lamb involuntarily reached for his change. The gesture was eloquent but futile. He averted his gaze, hoping no one had noticed his slip.

At the close of the service he was the first one to leave the church and, as was his custom, he waited outside for his family. He had gone this far, he thought to himself, he might as well see the thing through. He little reck-oned, however, on his reception by Mrs. Lamb. The docility of the horse throughout the service, his obvious reverence and piety, had somewhat re-assured this lady. She thought she knew how to deal with any person or creature who actually believed in God and took Him seriously. Conse-quently, as Lamb followed her and her daughter along the sidewalk, taking his proper place on the outside, she continually tried to "shoo" him, until Lamb in his exasperation gave vent to a piercing shriek.

That settled Mrs. Lamb. From then on Mr. Lamb was perforce ac-cepted as one of the party, much to Mrs. Lamb's humiliation. Time after time she passed acquaintances who in spite of their manners would not re-frain from asking her what she was doing with a horse. Mrs. Lamb dis-claimed any ownership of or responsibility for the animal. Lamb on his part invariably stepped courteously aside and gave the impression of following the conversation with polite attention. From time to time he nodded his head as if in agreement.

His wife particularly disliked this. It seemed to place her on a social level with a horse, and that was not to be tolerated. However, Lamb asserted his rights, and Mrs. Lamb no longer had the heart to challenge them. Hebe stuck to her father like a soldier, enjoying the situation with a maliciousness not at all compatible with her recent departure from a house of God. Toward the end of their progress the walk developed into a race, Mrs. Lamb endeavoring to leave the horse and Hebe behind, and the pair of them obstinately refusing to be left.

It was at this stage of the game that they encountered Sandra Rush. Mr. Lamb stopped in his tracks and fixed the girl with a triumphant eye. She met his gaze wonderingly for a moment, then turned to Hebe.

"Why, what a peculiar horse you have," she said. "For some reason he reminds me of your father. Something about the eyes. By the way, where is your father, the attenuated Lamb?"

Hebe was startled by her friend's instinctive recognition of the horse. Mrs. Lamb was returning reluctantly to join the conversation.

"I don't know exactly," she hastened to reply. "He's probably trailing about somewhere, or else just sitting. The major's an odd duck."

"A nice duck," said Sandra.

"What's this about ducks?" inquired Mrs. Lamb, as she joined the group in spite of the presence of the horse.

"I don't know," replied Sandra innocently. "I was just telling Hebe that I intended to go horseback riding this afternoon."

"On whose horse?" asked Hebe, and Mr. Lamb became immediately alert.

"That man Simonds's," said Sandra. "I ride on his horse each Sunday. Such a lovely horse."

"Well, he's far from a lovely horse now," replied Hebe sorrowfully. "From the glimpse I caught of him, that horse is a mental case. It will be many a long Sunday before he regains his reason, not to mention his health."

Sandra desired enlightenment, and Hebe told her all she had seen and heard of the chase. At the end of the stirring recital, Sandra turned and let her reproachful eyes dwell on Mr. Lamb. She found him looking noble and unrepentant, but under the pressure of her gaze, the great animal gradually wilted until finally his head hung low to the ground. Mrs. Lamb was outraged to see this demon stallion thus subjugated by this rather questionable friend of her daughter. As a matter of fact Mrs. Lamb resented Sandra's existence entirely. There were so many reasons—all of them good. Sandra was all that Mrs. Lamb would like to be and more than she had ever been.

"Why don't you ride this chap?" suggested Hebe. "It's all his fault."

"I shall," replied Sandra firmly. "I'll ride the devil to death. Simonds will lend me a saddle."

So, much to Mrs. Lamb's relief, the horse followed Sandra and was subsequently saddled and tethered in front of her house. When she came out from luncheon she found him leaning philosophically against a tree, his forelegs jauntily crossed.

"You'll have to cut this foolishness out," the girl said severely. "Only fake horses act like that. Don't make a spectacle of me."

Mr. Lamb turned an idle head and surveyed her long and approvingly. If she was as nice as that in riding togs, he considered, what wouldn't she be in underwear?

When Sandra had released the halter, he crouched close to the ground and peered round his shoulders at her. This proved a little too much for Sandra. The girl began to laugh, and Mr. Lamb shook himself impatiently. It was not the easiest position in the world to hold.

"I'll fix her," he said to himself.

When she finally decided to accept his grotesque invitation, Mr. Lamb crawled hastily forward, and the girl found herself sitting on his rump. She sat there only a moment before she slid slowly but inevitably to the street. Lamb rose to his full height and looked down at the young lady.

"That," she said from the gutter, "was a peculiarly snide trick. I don't know what sort of a horse you are, but if you were a human being I fancy you'd pull chairs from beneath people."

Mr. Lamb executed a neat little dance step and waited. This time Sandra mounted him in the accepted manner, and Mr. Lamb immediately set off backward, looking round from time to time to take his bearings.

"If you have any gentlemanly instincts at all," said Sandra at last, "you'll give up all this shilly-shallying and do your stuff like an honest-to-God horse."

Her mind was in a state of confusion. She had ridden all her life and met all types and conditions of horses, but she had never encountered one that had behaved so incredibly as this one. In its very resourcefulness there was something almost human.

At the girl's plea Mr. Lamb reversed his position and went forward majestically through the town. Sandra felt as if she were leading a circus parade. When they reached a dirt road he abandoned his little conceits and settled down to real business. He carried her swiftly, smoothly, and effortlessly over the ground. He was experiencing a sense of freedom and power—a total lack of responsibility save for the safety of the girl on his back. Sandra had never felt so exhilarated. Her mount was self-conducted. She had hardly to touch the reins. Presently they came to a fence that bordered a long rolling meadow. Lamb slowed down and looked back inquiringly at his passenger.

"It's all right with me, old boy," said Sandra. "Can you make it?"

Lamb showed her he could. He landed on the other side of the fence as if he were equipped with shock absorbers, then stretching his body he streamed away across the meadow. Sandra had a sensation of flying, and Lamb himself felt that his hooves were touching the ground only on rare occasions. After half an hour of swift running, Lamb came to a halt and sat down abruptly. The girl slid to the grass. When she attempted to rise, Lamb pushed her back with his nose and stood over her. For a moment she looked at the horse with startled eyes, then grinned.

"At it again," she said, pressing a cheek against his silky skin and giving him a small soft kiss.

Mr. Lamb stepped back a few paces and regarded the girl with heavy dignity. He was at a loss to know what to do about it. She had kissed him in broad daylight and made other affectionate advances. A stop should be put to this. Then something, some long restrained impulse seemed to snap in Mr. Lamb, and he began to prance joyously. He performed a dance of great vigor and elaboration after which he went racing round the meadow to give the girl some indication of what he could do when he set his mind to it. When he returned she was calmly reading a book she had fished from her pocket, *Green Mansions*, and as Lamb, now adept at reading horsewise, followed several pages over her shoulder, he became absorbed in the narrative and placed a restraining hoof against the margin of the page to prevent her from turning over before he had caught up with her.

In this manner some time slipped by, the horse reading over the girl's shoulder, until at last growing tired of the heavy breathing in her ear, she pushed his nose away and laid aside the book. Thereupon Lamb dropped to the grass beside her and placed his head in her lap, opening one large eye and looking up at her owlishly. Sandra picked up the book and continued to read. Lamb nudged her, and she gave him a sharp slap. He nudged her again and she commenced to read aloud. Lamb settled down to listen. The situation was much to his liking.

An hour later when it was time to return home, the girl had to pummel him to get him to wake up. Still half asleep, he struggled to his feet and automatically reached for a cigarette, then remembering he was a horse, frowned thoughtfully upon his companion. It was all too bewildering Lamb decided, but it had been an altogether satisfactory afternoon. Even while he had slept he had been deliciously aware of the closeness of the girl's body. Lamb was not insensitive to such things.

The stallion's appearance at the Vacation Fund affair that night was not an unqualified success. He first presented himself at the dining-room window where his wife and daughter and the leading actor, Mr. Leonard Gray, were indulging in a late, cold supper. Already the tables on the lawn were occupied. Other points of vantage were rapidly filling up. Cocktails were circulating freely. All those who dwelt on the right side of the tracks knew exactly the class of people for whom the Prohibition Act was intended.

They themselves were certainly not meant to be included. That went without saying.

Mr. Lamb announced his presence by thrusting his head through the window and unloosing a piercing scream. The dining room was filled with horror. . . . It took several minutes to find Mr. Gray, and several more to induce him to crawl from under the grand piano where he had apparently taken up permanent residence. Mrs. Lamb herself was none too well. When she and her leading man attempted to resume their dinner, their knives and forks clattered so violently against their plates, it sounded as if they were playing at beating the drum. The situation was saved by Hebe. That young lady of infinite composure, gathering up practically all the salad, made a quick exit through the window and led her father round behind some box bushes that encircled the field of activity. There was a convenient opening in the bushes at this spot through which, unobserved, Lamb could get an idea of what was going on.

Lamb thought the salad delicious. He had never tasted anything quite so wholeheartedly satisfying in his life. And when Hebe returned with a cocktail he felt that life was opening up indeed. A slight difficulty arose here, however. Lamb was unable to drink from so small a glass. He spilled most of its contents. His daughter with admirable resourcefulness thereupon fetched a bucket, a bottle of gin, some ice, and oranges. While Mr. Lamb looked on approvingly, she mixed this mighty cocktail and placed it before him. Lamb speedily inserted his nose, swallowed several cupfuls, and sank back with a sigh.

"All set now?" asked Hebe.

Lamb nodded enthusiastically.

"When it's empty, I'll fill it up," she assured him. "Sprawl here and get an eyeful. I'll send Mel around with a tray of sandwiches. This affair is going to be a riot."

At the time she little realized the remarkable accuracy of her prognostication.

When Melville Long appeared with the sandwiches he found Mr.

Lamb nose-down in the bucket, which from the sucking sounds that issued from it he judged to be empty. Mr. Lamb withdrew his head and received his visitor graciously. He literally beamed upon him, extending a hoof which Long seized and shook vigorously.

"A nice chap," thought Lamb. "One of the best. Wonder if he could mix me another cocktail? Everyone else is having a good time."

With the aid of an eloquent nose he drew the young man's attention to the dispiriting state of the bucket. The youth was not long in catching Mr. Lamb's meaning. With a curt "We'll fix that," he hastened away. When he returned he was carrying two bottles of gin and an armful of oranges.

"Hebe's bringing the ice," he explained as he poured the gin in the bucket and rapidly squeezed the oranges. "Didn't have room myself."

Together the young people arranged Mr. Lamb satisfactorily, then left him to his own devices, their presence being required elsewhere. Mr. Lamb was feeling remarkably well-disposed. He thrust his head through the aperture and eyed the lawn. At the unexpected appearance of the head an elderly lady jumped with the agility of a girl.

"God bless me!" she cried, spilling her cocktail down her dress. "Did you see that, Helen?"

Helen, her daughter, fortunately had not seen. She regarded the hole in the bushes nervously. It was empty. Turning back to her trembling mother, she endeavored to soothe her, but the old lady had been profoundly shocked. Mr. Lamb did not like this old lady nor was he exceedingly fond of her daughter. Arranging his face in its most demoniacal expression, he bided his time. When the two women were once more gazing nervously at the hole he suddenly popped his head through with instantaneous effect. Clinging to each other for support, mother and daughter cut a swath through the lawn party, uttering frightened little cries in their flight. Not until they were safely ensconced in their limousine and being driven rapidly home did they release their hold on each other. Then they sat up very erect and kept tapping their hands distractedly.

"I never saw such a face in my life. What was it?" asked the mother.

"Those eyes," intoned the daughter, and tightly closed her own.

Mr. Lamb's next opportunity to annoy someone came when a gentleman moved his chair close to the aperture and carelessly tossed his cigarette through it. The still lighted cigarette fell on Lamb's nose and burned it just a little. It was quite enough for Lamb. He promptly shot his head through the hole again and took a good look at the offender. Lamb did not like this man either. In his present state of liquor, Lamb hated the very sight of him. Therefore he withdrew his head and, thrusting a long leg through the hole, placed it against the chair and gave a tremendous shove. Man and chair parted company, but continued in the same general direction. The chair knocked the legs from under an innocent bystander, and its erstwhile occupant, passing completely through a group of ladies, came to rest on a rosebush. Extricating himself from this he hurried back to the hole and looked about for an enemy. None was to be found save an old gentleman quietly observing the colorful scene.

"Did you do that?" demanded the man in a hostile voice.

"Do what?" asked the old man amicably.

"Give me a clout just now," replied the other.

"Go away," said the old man deliberately. "You're drunk—drunker than you realize."

The assaulted man had reason to believe him, and quickly withdrew from the party. He did not feel quite drunk, but he imagined he must be. Those cocktails. They were strange concoctions. Just the same someone had given him a clout. There was no denying that. Drunk or sober, he knew when he had received a clouting.

This supine activity, in spite of its pleasing results, began to pall on Mr. Lamb. He yearned for larger fields. Taking another swig at his monolithic cocktail, he rose and, finding a gate in the box bushes, mingled with the party on the lawn. Although a trifle unsteady, he managed to maintain his dignity. He conducted himself as he conceived a gentle and unobtrusive horse should. The guests were rather surprised, some even alarmed, but after a short time they accepted him as a part of the evening's entertainment. Mrs. Lamb was so advanced.

From afar Mr. Lamb observed two particularly pretty girls in intimate conversation. Approaching the girls quietly he nipped one of them in an extremely ungentlemanly manner. The girl gave a startled exclamation and, heedless of the onlooker, tenderly rubbed the injured spot. Then she turned and saw the horse looking at her roguishly.

"My dear," she said to her companion, "you should know what that horse just did. Why, the creature's almost human."

When Lamb next tried this unmannerly trick the afflicted lady gave the gentleman she was conversing with a resounding slap in the face and followed it up with a piece of her mind. The poor man looked thoroughly mystified and wretched. The husband of the lady hurried to the spot and, upon learning what had occurred, drew back mightily and knocked the man down. He was literally dragged out. Today he is still wondering why.

Sapho had more than a suspicion that all was not going well with her party. The Vacation Fund affair was threatening to become a shambles. It was all the fault of that hell-born horse. Nothing could induce it to go away. She decided to put on the final act—the pièce de résistance of the night. Her act. In the meantime, having become bored with his surroundings, Mr. Lamb sat down and, leaning against a tree, fell into a light doze.

When he next opened his eyes the curtains had been parted on the flimsily constructed stage. His wife in his best pajamas was wallowing about in the arms of Leonard Gray, who was saying something about being "far from my own glade," in a high complaining voice. This bored Lamb beyond endurance. With a shriek of utter abandon he galloped toward the stage. Mr. Gray cast one horrified look at the speeding horse, then with amazing expedition got even farther from his own glade. Sapho also left at once, virtuously clutching the pants of Lamb's pajamas.

Springing to the stage, Lamb gave a drunken exhibition of a horse's idea of clog dancing. The audience was in confusion. In the midst of his hurricane efforts the stage collapsed, and Lamb disappeared beneath a small avalanche of scenery, planks, and trappings. Those who lingered to look back saw only a horse's head projecting from the ruins. The horse was either dead or asleep.

Later that night Lamb feebly dug himself out and sought his bucket.

Someone had thoughtfully replenished it. He drank avidly and made his way to the front of the house. He had some vague idea about sleeping in the hammock, but failed to retain it. Resting his head on the first step, he draped himself across the lawn and drifted off.

Mrs. Lamb was awakened the next morning by the maid announcing that a passerby had stopped to inform her that there was a dead horse on the lawn.

"I hope to God he is," said Mrs. Lamb, as she pulled the covers more securely over her head. Her only regret was that the animal was not buried and well out of sight.

After several other early commuters had informed the maid that a horse had passed out on the lawn Mrs. Lamb decided to look upon the gratifying sight herself. But when she reached the veranda the horse was no longer there, and the good lady was just as glad.

Lamb had awakened dizzily and made a tour of the ruins he had created. Vaguely only did he remember the events of the night. The little he did recall was sufficient to make him wish to forget.

"I'd better get the hell out of here," he said to himself. "There'll be no living within a mile of her for some time to come."

He cantered off to the station and hung about there for a while, getting in the way of hurrying commuters and keeping an eye out for Sandra. When that young lady undulated into view he trotted up to her and stopped. So did Sandy. She put her arms round his neck and gave him a good morning kiss. Lamb became a horse of stone. Dimly he heard an insistent honking of horns, but paid little attention to them. He had lost all traces of his headache. Sandy had kissed them away. He glanced about him and discovered he was blocking the way of two motors, the drivers of which were far from resigned. Stepping aside politely, he looked after the retreating figure of the girl.

"She shouldn't have done that," thought Lamb, "but I'm not altogether sorry she did."

At this point a state trooper tried to do things about the horse. Lamb reared back on his hind legs and pawed at the air. The trooper hurried else-where and returned with a long noose rope.

"Thinks he's Will Rogers," said Lamb to himself, as he watched the trooper out of the tail of his eye.

Craftily anticipating the man's fell purpose, he took immediate steps to outwit him. Carelessly Mr. Lamb maneuvered himself alongside one of the town's most revered citizens, Mr. Robert Bates, fat, fifty, and influential—a factor in local politics. As the noose came swishing through the air Lamb crouched close to the ground and observed the rope neatly pinion Mr. Rob-ert Bates's arms to his sides. Feeling the rope grow taut, the trooper tugged with a mighty effort and succeeded in pulling Mr. Bates completely over the back of the crouching horse. After that there were no impediments to bar the rapid progress of Mr. Robert Bates across the road.

The trooper wound the rope round a telegraph pole, secured it firmly, and turned to survey his prize. His prize lay struggling at his feet, emitting a long succession of unpleasant sounds terminating with "I'll break you for this, my man."

Naturally this little episode had neither gone unnoticed nor unappreci-ated. It was a pleasure to many to see Mr. Bates thus handled. It was no pleasure to the state trooper. The humor of the situation escaped him; but Mr. Bates did not escape. He would be with him always, the trooper feared. Mr. Lamb with a triumphant neigh left the poor fellow explaining to the sizzling first citizen that the unfortunate occurrence was entirely due to the horse, and thunderingly cleared the town. Thereafter all that remained of the horse was a not unblemished reputation.

Mr. Lamb was next discovered straining his neck to reach a particularly delectable blackberry on the edge of the woods. Several children, shep-herded by an elder sister, were regarding the enterprising horse. They had never seen a horse pick blackberries. The children decided that he was a "funny horse" and made a jubilant noise about it. Mr. Lamb, with a start of surprise, beheld his admiring audience and immediately fell to cropping grass in the conventionally accepted manner. The children then drew near the horse and patted him with small adventurous hands. The horse did tricks to amuse them, and they brought him a wild flower to smell. Amazingly the horse smelled it, rolling his eyes to show his appreciation. He was enjoying himself more than he had for years. Presently the horse took leave of the children and once more sought the road. The children returned home to hamper their mother's activities by telling about the funny horse.

After this pastoral interlude, Mr. Lamb continued cheerfully on his way. Many miles now separated him from Sapho. He regretted the absence of Hebe. A pity she, too, could not have turned into a horse. The little russet man was responsible for it all. Had Lamb only realized it at the time of their last conversation he would have arranged things differently—introduced an element of order. However, the little russet man had given him no chance. Now Lamb did not know how things stood, whether he was to be a horse permanently, or when he would stop being a horse. All such details should have been considered.

Mr. Lamb had taken to the more unfrequented roads and was now in a territory unknown to him. He was decidedly on the loose. He came to a meadow in which several sleek-looking mares were grazing. To Mr. Lamb they seemed quite girlish. Without further ado he leapt the fence and swaggered up to the mares. His unexpected arrival created quite a sensation. The mares were all atwitter. One began to tremble nervously from an excess of sex consciousness. The stouter of her girlfriends merely gazed at Mr. Lamb with an expressively submissive look. The third, however, was a mare of another color. She looked at Mr. Lamb for a long moment with a bold, appraising eye and seemingly found him to her liking. Then she trotted off to a secluded part of the meadow, occasionally glancing back at Mr. Lamb and tossing her head prettily.

This mare interested Mr. Lamb strangely. At the same time something urged him to proceed with caution. There was no good in that mare. Mr. Lamb followed her. There was something on his mind. He was trying to remember the image the mare evoked. Something about the eyes. Whose eyes were they?

When he reached the mare's side he peered into her eyes thoughtfully. The mare returned his gaze languorously and rubbed her nose against his.

Mr. Lamb started back offended. Then he remembered. This passionate creature had the eyes of Sapho when she was developing her art in the arms of Leonard Gray. Undeterred by the rebuff of her first effort, the mare circled round Mr. Lamb, gradually closing until she again stood at his side. Suddenly she turned and bit his neck, then sped away.

"Well, if she thinks I'm going to follow her," thought Mr. Lamb, "she has another think coming. They're all alike the world over. This mare is determined to get me into some compromising situation."

He spent the remainder of the afternoon alternately grazing and repulsing the mare's advances. Her two friends looked at him hopefully from time to time, but were ladylike enough to leave him to his own devices. Finally the mare, disgusted with this aloof, dignified, and apparently unemotional stallion, abandoned her attempts to seduce him and contented herself with gazing at him scornfully. She joined her companions, and the three of them put their heads close together. Occasionally they would lift them for a moment and look steadily at Mr. Lamb, then resume once more their intimate conversation. Lamb, growing uncomfortable under the continual scrutiny of the horses, sought another section of the meadow, but the mares, as if fascinated, followed him at a respectful distance and discussed his every move.

The situation was becoming intolerable, and Mr. Lamb was heartily thankful when at sunset the three mares trotted off to one end of the meadow and waited there expectantly. Lamb followed them at a casual amble, and when a sleepy-looking farmhand presently plodded up to the fence and opened a gate, Mr. Lamb slipped by unnoticed with the other horses and continued with them across the field to the stable.

"This is what might be termed crashing the gate," he said to himself, as he entered the stable and sought refuge in an empty stall.

He would have been perfectly satisfied with the oats the farmhand had provided had not the shameless mare kept thrusting her head over the partition in order the better to observe him crunch. Eating oats was a new experience to Lamb. He would have preferred to have practiced it alone, but every time he glanced up, the mare's large eyes were fixed upon him with such unabashed curiosity that Lamb immediately suspended action and pretended he had finished.

Apparently the acquisition of a strapping new stallion meant nothing in the life of the sleepy farmhand. He closed the stable doors and went his way, and Lamb, to escape the prying eyes of the abandoned animal in the next stall, lay down, placed his head on a bucket, and prepared to sleep. After the indulgence of the previous night, he was too tired to ponder over the radically altered circumstances of his existence. But before he took leave of consciousness Mr. Lamb once and for all washed his hands of the inquisitive mare, who was moving restlessly about in the next stall.

Mr. Burnham was not quite so unobservant as his handyman, the name being in this instance strictly a courtesy title. When he discovered the sleeping stallion the next morning his heart was filled with wonder and admiration.

"Why didn't you tell me of this, Sam?" he demanded of the farmhand.

"Didn't rightly notice it myself," replied that individual. "He acted so natural-like, seemed he must belong."

"And if a cavalry regiment had quartered here last night," observed Burnham, "I dare say it would have meant the same thing to you."

He looked at the three mares suspiciously and hummed under his breath.

"I wonder—" he continued as if to himself, then catching the look of disgust in the brazen mare's eyes, he shook his head and returned once more to the sleeping stallion.

"Funny way for a horse to sleep." Mr. Burnham drew his right arm's attention to the horse's head resting on the bucket. The right arm also had failed to notice this. He agreed, however. It was a funny way for a horse to sleep.

Mr. Burnham then applied a foot with insistent pressure to the stallion's rump, and Mr. Lamb looked up with sleepy indignation. Gazing for a moment at the two strange faces, he replaced his head on the bucket and closed his eyes.

"Get up, sir!" commanded Mr. Burnham, and this time the application of the foot was slightly more vigorous.

"If this sort of thing is going to continue," thought Lamb gloomily, "I might as well abandon all thoughts of sleep."

He rose, stretched his great body, and stepped out of his stall. The two men followed his movements in silence. Lamb walked out into the stable yard and, seeing a large trough full of water under the pump, plunged his head deep into it. Very busily he put in his front legs and twirled his hoofs around. Picking up an empty flour sack, he tossed it about his head until he was partially dry. After this Mr. Lamb felt considerably refreshed. He lifted his head proudly and looked down at the silently watching men. Even the farmhand had been able to detect something out of the ordinary in the actions of the horse.

"Well, Sam, what do you think of that?" asked Mr. Burnham, inhaling a deep breath.

Thinking was one of Sam's most vulnerable points. He was unable to put into words his confused mental reactions.

"It ain't right," was all he said.

"If nobody claims that stallion," declared Mr. Burnham, "I'm going to enter him in the show this Saturday. He's the finest body of a horse I've seen in years."

At this Mr. Lamb set himself and paced gallantly round the yard. He fully intended to earn his meal ticket. Sam eyed the horse with growing suspicion. His imagination was at last aroused.

"Feed him," said Mr. Burnham, "and keep him well groomed. I'm going to make inquiries. This seems like a gift from heaven. Those mares need entertainment."

Burnham made inquiries throughout the course of the week, but could find no claimant to the stallion. Those who had seen the horse, or who had even heard remotely about it, declared they would have nothing to do with it. They did not want that horse. As a result of his investigations, Mr. Burnham had no scruples in attaching the horse to himself. And Mr. Lamb was well pleased to be attached. He was living on the fat of the land, and Sam, in spite of his mental deficiencies, was proving himself to be an entirely satisfactory valet.

On Saturday Lamb was taken to the show. It was a semibucolic affair, a thing of barter and trade, but more than a thousand horse lovers were present and assembled about the field. Mr. Lamb was placed in a shack and carefully guarded by Sam. The stallion seemed greatly elated. Mr. Lamb was really anxious to win a prize—to establish a name for himself and Mr. Burnham.

It was a gala day for Sam. Lamb noticed that his valet was not too dumb to indulge copiously in corn whisky, a great bottle of which was reposing on a table in the shack. As time passed, Lamb began to grow nervous. He hated waiting. When Sam stepped outside to view the world, Mr. Lamb quickly elevated the bottle and drained its contents. His nervousness immediately left him. He knew he would win a prize. Nothing now could stop him. Sam returned and looked at the bottle with an injured expression.

"Someone's been in here," he muttered. "Like to catch 'em at it."

He departed again and presently returned with another bottle, which he uncorked and sampled appreciatively.

"Watch that bottle," he told the stallion when he next left to mingle with the throng. "And if anyone tries to get at it kick 'em through the shed."

Mr. Lamb made sure that no one would take liberties with the bottle. He introduced the fiery fluid into his system and felt even more convinced that he was certain to win practically all the prizes.

A few minutes later, when he was taken out to be judged, the whisky was taking full effect on him. Mr. Burnham was so keyed up himself, he failed to remark the staggering gait of the stallion. However, the judges and spectators noticed it as Mr. Lamb was led thrice past the stand. When he endeavored to prance bravely he got all tangled up in his legs.

"How many legs have I?" he wondered. "Seem to have grown an extra pair."

"That horse seems to think he's imitating a drunkard," observed a judge. "What on earth does he think he's doing?"

When he was brought up to be looked over at closer range Mr. Lamb almost fell over one of the judges. He succeeded in regaining his balance, only by stepping heavily on that shocked dignitary's foot. To make matters worse Lamb was seized with a violent attack of hiccoughs which he was unable to control. There was a strong smell of alcohol in the air. The judge regarded Mr. Burnham suspiciously.

"Got to do something to make up for all this," Mr. Lamb said to himself. "Wonder what I can do—some sort of a stunt—something a little different."

An idea grew and flourished in his dizzy brain.

"I'll be a hobbyhorse," he said to himself. "That's the very thing. I dare say nobody ever saw a live hobbyhorse before."

He thought for a moment, then stiffening his legs and placing his hooves close together, he began to rock forward and aft, gaining momentum with each swing. Every eye in the multitude was riveted on Mr. Lamb. The judge stepped back and regarded him indignantly. This animal was making a fool of them—taking their horse show altogether too lightly. Cheers of encouragement broke from the spectators. They went to Mr. Lamb's head. With gratified expression he redoubled his efforts. Mr. Burnham looked on helplessly, disgust written in every line of his face. He felt as if he had been betrayed. Mr. Lamb turned his head and winked at his owner as if to say, "We'll show these hicks something new in the line of a horse."

He did. Each rock was bringing him nearer to the ground. Finally, in an excess of zeal, Lamb made one supreme effort. He pitched recklessly forward, held his position for one breathless moment, then nose first continued to the ground where he remained with eyes tightly closed.

"I won't look," he said to himself. "This is the end. I'm disgraced."

"Will you please take that thing away?" asked one of the judges, turning to the humiliated Burnham. "We don't want it at this show."

Burnham tried to raise his crumpled horse—the heaven-sent—but Mr. Lamb refused to budge. One of the judges knelt down beside him and sniffed.

"How crude!" thought Lamb dreamily. "These judges!"

"Why, this horse has been drinking corn whisky," the judge announced, rising. "The animal is actually dead drunk. Disgraceful, Burnham, I say. Never heard of any such a thing in my life. Take him away."

Burnham, regarding the stallion, wondered exactly how the judge expected him to take his entry away. He certainly could not carry the besotted horse from the field in his arms. Nothing less than a derrick would be required to lift that body. The judges apparently were of this opinion, too, for they removed themselves to another section of the field and continued with the show. Lamb remained recumbent, gently snoring, in the center of the field. A circle of admiring spectators had gathered round him.

Before the day was done Mr. Burnham had sold the heaven-sent to a fancy truck farmer. The price given had reflected no credit on the value of Mr. Lamb. The truck farmer had turned in his own horse as part payment.

Darkness had fallen by the time Mr. Lamb had recovered sufficiently to be driven away. When he came to his senses he found himself harnessed to a light farm wagon. He was being driven along a country road.

"Sold down the river," he mused to himself. "Parted from family and friends."

Monotonously the fields and trees moved past. Lamb began to recognize the road. He remembered certain landmarks. They were going in the direction of his home. Presently his new master drew rein and, getting down from his seat, began to search in the back part of the wagon. Lamb fell into a light doze. When the farmer returned he found a man clad only in pajamas standing where just a moment ago his recently acquired horse had stood. The man seemed a bit dazed and was pulling at the shafts. At first the farmer was afraid to approach, then indignation got the better of his timidity. He strode up to the white-clad figure and looked at it wrathfully.

"What are you doing there?" he demanded.

Lamb started and looked down at himself.

"By God, I'm back," he said under his breath; then turning to the farmer, he replied, "Just fooling with these shafts."

"And what did you do with my horse?" continued the farmer.

Mr. Lamb dropped the shafts and seated himself by the roadside. The farmer followed his example.

"What could I have done with your horse?" asked Mr. Lamb. "Do you suppose that I tore him limb from limb and scattered his parts to the four winds?"

"No," said the man after a thoughtful pause. "You couldn't have done that."

He paused and considered Mr. Lamb with thoughtful eyes.

"Then you were the horse," he announced in positive tones. "You must have been the horse."

"What, me?" exclaimed Mr. Lamb. "You're crazy, sir. Do I faintly resemble a horse?"

"Not now, you don't," replied the man with conviction, "but a minute ago you did, and what's more, you acted like a horse—not a very good horse, but enough of a horse to get along with. Now you're no earthly good to me."

"Well, I'm relieved you recognize that fact," said Mr. Lamb. "What are we going to do about it?"

"Listen," said the man, as if endeavoring to explain the strange occurrence to himself. "This business isn't as simple as it seems to you. This evening at the show I bought you for a horse. You were dead drunk on the field in front of hundreds of people. In spite of that I bought you and gave you another chance. I was going to give you a nice home and keep you away from drink. I've been over the ropes myself. Don't object to a little fun within reason, but—"

"It's all right about that," put in Mr. Lamb. "Go on with this remarkable yarn."

"It does sound crazy when I hear myself telling it," admitted the man. "But it's true just the same, every word of it. I got you sort of sobered up and started off home with you. Everything was getting along nicely. At this spot I got down from my seat and turned my back on you for a minute. When I turned back—no horse. You were standing between the shafts pulling like the devil. Now answer me this," he continued in a reasonable voice, turning full on Mr. Lamb. "A minute ago there was a horse, or the dead image of a horse, standing between those shafts. If you weren't that horse, who was the horse or what was the horse? Answer me that."

Mr. Lamb did not want to answer him that. He realized that the man— any man—was mentally unequipped to be told the true state of affairs. He himself was reluctant to admit the terrible thing that had happened to him. It was too far removed from the kingdom of God as generally conceived. It was too mythological. Only a pagan would believe and understand. And back of it all, Lamb knew, was the little russet man.

"Well, I'll tell you," said Lamb slowly. "It was like this: when I was a very little boy I just loved to play horse. That's a fact. I played horse so much and so long that I was never able to break myself of the habit. To this day—would you believe it?—I still play horse. It's a weakness—a failing. It's like strong drink to other men."

Lamb halted to see what impression he was making on his erstwhile owner. The man seemed absorbed in the story. Lamb himself was beginning to believe it.

"Well tonight," he continued, "I gave a bit of a party, and I guess we all had a little too much. I remember after going to bed that it struck me as being rather a good idea to get up and play horse. I slipped from my bed, you understand, quiet as anything so as not to wake up my wife, who suffers from insomnia just like her mother, and whose brother has lumbago, poor chap. Without making any noise I crept downstairs, turned the key in the front door lock, and ran down the road. I ran and ran and ran. After a while I came to this wagon and crawled in between the shafts, and then you came along. That's how the whole thing happened."

The climax seemed rather smeared for a good story, but it was the best that Lamb could achieve at the moment. He looked at the man hopefully and regretted to see that the farmer's face had fallen considerably. Apparently he had lost interest in the story.

"It's all right," he said, "but it doesn't explain what became of my horse."

"There really wasn't ever any horse at all, was there?" asked Lamb, evasively.

"No," replied the farmer with elaborate sarcasm. "I was dragging this wagon along by myself just for exercise."

There followed an uncomfortable silence.

"Well, I'm sure," said Mr. Lamb at last, as he rose and stretched himself wearily, "I can't imagine what can have happened to your horse. You can see for yourself that I'm not anything like a horse."

"But I'm not so sure," the farmer replied, "that you weren't a horse a little while back. There's something queer about all this."

"All right, have it your way," said Lamb with a yawn. "I'm not your horse now. Have you any old bags in that wagon you don't need?"

The farmer tossed him a couple of sacks which Lamb draped about his long body.

"What am I going to do about the wagon?" demanded the farmer in a gloomy voice.

"Wait here for that horse," said Lamb. "He's sure to come back if he ever existed at all. I begin to fear he was not alone in his cups."

The farmer watched Mr. Lamb trudge off down the road, then seating himself once more on the moist leaves and grass, he thought over the strange events of the day until his head began to swim. Dawn found him still sitting there waiting for a horse that would never return.

"Why," Lamb asked himself, as he climbed quietly through one of the lower windows of his own house, "why, if that little russet chap took my silly outburst seriously, does he insist on making a practical joke of it?"

Like a thief he stole upstairs and crawled into bed.

CLARICE LISPECTOR

Dry Point of Horses

DESPOILMENT

The horse—naked.

FICTITIOUS DOMESTICATION

What is horse? It is freedom so indomitable that it becomes useless to imprison it to serve man: it lets itself be domesticated, but with a simple, rebellious toss of the head—shaking its mane like an abundance of free-flowing hair—it shows that its inner nature is always wild, translucent, and free.

FORM

The form of the horse exemplifies what is best in the human being. I have a horse within me who rarely reveals himself. But when I see another horse, then mine expresses himself. His form speaks.

GENTLENESS

What makes a horse be of glistening satin? It is the gentleness of one who has taken on life and its rainbow. This gentleness manifests itself in a smooth coat, suggesting elastic muscles, agile and controlled.

THE EYES OF THE HORSE

I once saw a blind horse: nature had erred. It was painful to feel him so restless, aware of the slightest sound caused by the breeze amongst the grasses, with his nerves ready to bristle in a shudder running throughout his alert body. What does a horse see so that not seeing his kind leaves him as if having lost his very self? It's just that when he looks, he sees outside himself what is inside himself. He is an animal who expresses himself through form. When he sees mountains, meadows, people, the sky—he takes dominion over men and over nature itself.

SENSITIVITY

All horses are wild and skittish when unsure hands touch them.

HE AND I

Trying to formulate my most hidden and subtle sensations—and disobeying an exigent need for truth—I would say: if I could have chosen, I would have wished to be born a horse. But—who knows—maybe the horse himself doesn't sense that great symbol of free life which we sense in him. Must I then conclude that the horse is there above all to be felt by me? Does the horse represent the beautiful and free animality of human beings? The best of the horse—does the human creature already have it? Then I abdicate being a horse and with glory pass on to my humanity. The horse tells me what I am.

THE ADOLESCENCE OF THE YOUNG GIRL-COLT

I already got along perfectly with horses. I remember myself as me-adolescent. Standing straight with the same haughtiness as the horse and passing my hand over his glistening hide. Through his aggressive, rugged mane. I felt as if something of me were seeing us from far away: "The Girl and the Horse."

DISPLAY

On the ranch, the white horse—the king of nature—hurled through the heights of the keen air his drawn-out whinny of splendor.

THE DANGEROUS HORSE

In the little country town—which would become a small metropolis one day—horses still reigned as the leading inhabitants. Due to the increasingly urgent need for transportation, droves of horses had invaded the hick town, and in the still-wild children there stirred the secret desire to gallop. A young bay gave a fatal kick to a boy who was mounting him. And the place where the daring child had died was regarded with censure by people who, in fact, didn't know at whom to direct it. With their shopping baskets on their arms, women would stop to stare. A newspaper took up the case, and, with a certain pride, you could read a brief notice under the title "The Horse's Crime." It was the Crime of one of the sons of that little town. The burg by then was mixing with its smell of stables an awareness of the strength bound within a horse.

ON THE SUN-BAKED STREET

But suddenly—in the silence of the two o'clock sun, with almost no one on the straggling streets—a pair of horses surged around a corner. For a moment they stood motionless, their hooves half raised. Gleaming at the mouth, as if unmuzzled. There, like statues. The few passersby daring to face the heat of the sun gazed at them, hard, isolated, without understanding in words what they saw. They just understood. The obfuscation of the apparition gone, the horses arched their necks, lowered their hooves, and continued on their way. The moment of recognition had passed. A moment fixed as if by a camera that has captured something which words will never say.

IN THE SETTING SUN

That day, as the sun was going down, gold spilled through the clouds and over the rocks. The faces of the townsfolk turned golden like armor and their flowing hair gleamed as well. Dust-covered factories gave forth prolonged whistles marking the end of the workday, a wagon wheel took on a gilded nimbus. In this gold, pallid from the breeze, there was a raising of an unsheathed sword. For that's how the equestrian statue of the square loomed in the softness of nightfall.

IN THE COLD DAWN

You could see the warm, moist breath—the radiant and peaceful breath that came from the tremulous, life-filled, flaring nostrils of stallions and mares in the cold of certain dawns.

IN THE MYSTERY OF NIGHT

But at night, horses released from their burdens and led to pasture would gallop lithe and free in the darkness. Colts, old nags, sorrels, long-legged mares, hardened hooves—suddenly a horse's head, cold and dark!—hooves pounding, frothy muzzles rising toward the air, enraged and murmuring. And sometimes a deep breath would chill the trembling blades of grass. Then the bay would come forward. He would walk sideways, head curved down to his chest, in a gentle cadence. The others attended without looking. Hearing the sound of the horses, I could imagine their dry hooves advancing, till coming to a halt at the highest point on the hill. And the head, dominating the little town, throwing out a long-drawn whinny. Fear gripped me in the shadows of my room, the fear of a king. I would have liked, gums bare, to give a whinny in response. In the envy of desire, my face took on the anxious nobility of a horse's head. Exhausted, jubilant, listening to the somnambulist trot. As soon as I left my room, my shape would start to fill out and purify, and by the time I reached the street, I would be galloping on sensitive feet, my hooves slipping at the bottom of the front steps. From the deserted pavement I would look around: one corner and the other. And I would see things as a horse sees them. That was what I wanted. From the house I would try, at least, to listen to the hillside pasture where, in the darkness, nameless horses were galloping, returned to a world of the hunt and of war.

The beasts did not abandon their secret life that goes on during the night. And if in the midst of the wild, milling herd a white colt appeared—it was wonderment in the dark. They all would stop in their tracks. The prodigious horse would *appear*, an apparition. It would show itself rearing for an instant. Immobile, the animals would wait, not looking at each other. But one of them would strike his hoof—and the sharp blow would break the vigil: whipped up, they would suddenly move with a new vigor, interweaving without any bumping, and among them the white horse would be lost.

Until a whinny of sudden rage alerted them—intent for a moment, they quickly fanned out once again, trotting in a new formation, their backs without horsemen, their necks so low their muzzles touched their chests. Their manes bristling. And they, cadenced, uncivilized.

Late night—while men were sleeping—would find them motionless in the dark. Solid and without weight. There they were, invisible, breathing. Waiting with their limited intelligence. Below, in the sleeping village, a cock fluttered up and settled on a windowsill. The hens looked at him. Beyond the railroad tracks a rat ready to flee. Then the dapple struck his hoof. He had no mouth to speak with, but he produced that small sign which surfaced now and then in the darkness. They looked about. Those animals with an eye for looking both ways at once—nothing had to be seen head-on by them, and that was the great night. The flanks of a mare rippled with rapid contractions. In the silence of the night, the mare gazed out as if surrounded by eternity. The most restless colt was still raising its mane in a muffled whinny. And then utter silence reigned.

Until the fragile luminosity of dawn revealed them. They were separate, standing on the hill. Exhausted, fresh. They had passed through the mystery of the nature of living beings, there in the darkness.

STUDY OF THE DIABOLIC HORSE

I will never rest easy again, for I have stolen the hunting horse of a King. Now I am worse than I myself! I will never rest easy again: I stole the King's hunting horse on the witching sabbath. If I fall asleep for a moment, the echo of a whinny awakens me. And it is useless to try not to go. In the dark of the night, a snorting makes me shiver. I pretend to be sleeping, but in the silence the jennet breathes. Every day it will be the same: already as the afternoon lengthens I begin to turn melancholy and pensive. I know that the first drum on the mountain of evil will make the night, I know that the third will have already enveloped me in its thunder. And at the fifth drum, I will be filled with desire for a ghost horse. Until at dawn, to the last and softest drumbeats, I will find myself, not knowing how, beside a fresh little stream, never knowing what I have done, next to the enormous tired head of a horse.

But tired from what? What did we do, I and the horse, we who trot in the hell of the vampire's joy? He, the King's steed, calls me. I have resisted in a bout of sweat and won't go. The last time I descended from his silver saddle, my human sadness at having been what shouldn't have been was so great that I swore—never again. The trot, however, continues inside me. I talk, straighten up the house, smile, but I know that the trot is inside me. I miss him like someone dying.

No, I cannot help but go.

And I know that at night, when he calls me, I will go. I want the horse to lead my thoughts one more time. It was with him that I learned. If this is thought, this hour between yelpings. I begin to grow sad because I know through my eyes—oh, without wanting to! it isn't my fault—with my eyes involuntarily resplendent now with evil glee—I know that I will go.

When at night he calls me to hell's allurements, I will go. I descend like a cat along the rooftops. No one knows, no one sees. Only dogs bark, sensing the supernatural.

And I present myself in the dark to the horse who awaits me, horse of royalty, I present myself in silence and in splendor. Obedient to the Beast.

Fifty-three flutes run after us. In front, a clarinet lights the way for us, shameless accomplices of the enigma. And nothing more is given me to know.

At dawn I will see us exhausted beside the little stream, without knowing what crimes we committed before reaching innocent dawn.

In my mouth and on his hooves the mark of great blood. What is it we have sacrificed?

At dawn I will be standing next to the jennet, now still, with the rest of the flutes still dripping from my hair. The first church bells from afar make us shiver and set us in flight, we dissolve before the cross.

The night is my life with the diabolic horse, I, witch of horror. The night is my life, it grows late, the sinfully happy night is the sad life that is my orgy—ah steal, steal from me the jennet, for from robbery to robbery even dawn I have stolen for myself and for my fantastical partner, and I have turned the dawn into a presentiment of the terror of demoniacal, unwholesome joy.

Free me, quickly steal the jennet while there is time, before it is too late, while there is still day without darkness, if indeed there still is time, for in stealing the jennet I had to kill the King, and killing him I stole the King's death. And the orgiastic joy of our murder consumes me in terrible pleasure. Quickly steal the King's perilous horse, steal him, steal me, before night falls and calls for me.

HORSE AND CHILD

JOHN STEINBECK

The Red Pony

At daybreak Billy Buck emerged from the bunkhouse and stood for a moment on the porch looking up at the sky. He was a broad, bandy-legged little man with a walrus mustache, with square hands, puffed and muscled on the palms. His eyes were a contemplative, watery grey and the hair which protruded from under his Stetson hat was spiky and weathered. Billy was still stuffing his shirt into his blue jeans as he stood on the porch. He unbuckled his belt and tightened it again. The belt showed, by the worn shiny places opposite each hole, the gradual increase of Billy's middle over a period of years. When he had seen to the weather, Billy cleared each nostril by holding its mate closed with his forefinger and blowing fiercely. Then he walked down to the barn, rubbing his hands together. He curried and brushed two saddle horses in the stalls, talking quietly to them all the time; and he had hardly finished when the iron triangle started ringing at the ranch house. Billy stuck the brush and currycomb together and laid them on the rail, and went up to breakfast. His action had been so deliberate and yet so wasteless of time that he came to the house while Mrs. Tiflin was still ringing the triangle. She nodded her grey head to him and withdrew into the kitchen. Billy Buck sat down on the steps, because he was a cowhand, and it wouldn't be fitting that he should go first into the dining room. He heard Mr. Tiflin in the house, stamping his feet into his boots.

The high jangling note of the triangle put the boy Jody in motion. He was only a little boy, ten years old, with hair like dusty yellow grass and with shy polite grey eyes, and with a mouth that worked when he thought. The triangle picked him up out of sleep. It didn't occur to him to disobey the harsh note. He never had: no one he knew ever had. He brushed the tangled hair out of his eyes and skinned his nightgown off. In a moment he was dressed—blue chambray shirt and overalls. It was late in the summer, so of course there were no shoes to bother with. In the kitchen he waited until his mother got from in front of the sink and went back to the stove. Then he washed himself and brushed back his wet hair with his fingers. His mother turned sharply on him as he left the sink. Jody looked shyly away.

"I've got to cut your hair before long," his mother said. "Breakfast's on the table. Go on in, so Billy can come."

Jody sat at the long table which was covered with white oilcloth washed through to the fabric in some places. The fried eggs lay in rows on their platter. Jody took three eggs on his plate and followed with three thick slices of crisp bacon. He carefully scraped a spot of blood from one of the egg yolks.

Billy Buck clumped in. "That won't hurt you," Billy explained. "That's only a sign the rooster leaves."

Jody's tall stern father came in then and Jody knew from the noise on the floor that he was wearing boots, but he looked under the table anyway, to make sure. His father turned off the oil lamp over the table, for plenty of morning light now came through the windows.

Jody did not ask where his father and Billy Buck were riding that day, but he wished he might go along. His father was a disciplinarian. Jody obeyed him in everything without questions of any kind. Now, Carl Tiflin sat down and reached for the egg platter.

"Got the cows ready to go, Billy?" he asked.

"In the lower corral," Billy said. "I could just as well take them in alone."

"Sure you could. But a man needs company. Besides your throat gets pretty dry." Carl Tiflin was jovial this morning.

Jody's mother put her head in the door. "What time do you think to be back, Carl?"

"I can't tell. I've got to see some men in Salinas. Might be gone till dark."

The eggs and coffee and big biscuits disappeared rapidly. Jody followed the two men out of the house. He watched them mount their horses and drive six old milk cows out of the corral and start over the hill toward Salinas. They were going to sell the old cows to the butcher.

When they had disappeared over the crown of the ridge Jody walked up the hill in back of the house. The dogs trotted around the house corner hunching their shoulders and grinning horribly with pleasure. Jody patted their heads—Doubletree Mutt with the big thick tail and yellow eyes, and Smasher, the shepherd, who had killed a coyote and lost an ear in doing it. Smasher's one good ear stood up higher than a collie's ear should. Billy Buck said that always happened. After the frenzied greeting the dogs lowered their noses to the ground in a businesslike way and went ahead, looking back now and then to make sure that the boy was coming. They walked up through the chicken yard and saw the quail eating with the chickens. Smasher chased the chickens a little to keep in practice in case there should ever be sheep to herd. Jody continued on through the large vegetable patch where the green corn was higher than his head. The cow pumpkins were green and small yet. He went on to the sagebrush line where the cold spring ran out of its pipe and fell into a round wooden tub. He leaned over and drank close to the green mossy wood where the water tasted best. Then he turned and looked back on the ranch, on the low, whitewashed house girded with red geraniums, and on the long bunkhouse by the cypress tree where Billy Buck lived alone. Jody could see the great black kettle under the cypress tree. That was where the pigs were scalded. The sun was coming over the ridge now, glaring on the whitewash of the houses and barns, making the wet grass blaze softly. Behind him, in the tall sagebrush, the birds were scampering on the ground, making a great noise among the dry leaves; the squirrels piped shrilly on the sidehills. Jody looked along at the farm buildings. He felt an uncertainty in the air, a feeling of change and of loss and of the gain of new and unfamiliar things. Over the hillside two big black buzzards sailed low to the ground and their shadows slipped smoothly and quickly ahead of them. Some animal had died in the vicinity. Jody knew it. It might be a cow or it might be the remains of a rabbit. The buzzards overlooked nothing. Jody hated them as all decent things hate them, but they could not be hurt because they made away with carrion.

After a while the boy sauntered downhill again. The dogs had long ago given him up and gone into the brush to do things in their own way. Back through the vegetable garden he went, and he paused for a moment to smash a green muskmelon with his heel, but he was not happy about it. It was a bad thing to do, he knew perfectly well. He kicked dirt over the ruined melon to conceal it.

Back at the house his mother bent over his rough hands, inspecting his fingers and nails. It did little good to start him clean to school for too many things could happen on the way. She sighed over the black cracks on his fingers, and then gave him his books and his lunch and started him on the mile walk to school. She noticed that his mouth was working a good deal this morning.

Jody started his journey. He filled his pockets with little pieces of white quartz that lay in the road, and every so often he took a shot at a bird or at some rabbit that had stayed sunning itself in the road too long. At the crossroads over the bridge he met two friends and the three of them walked to school together, making ridiculous strides and being rather silly. School had just opened two weeks before. There was still a spirit of revolt among the pupils.

It was four o'clock in the afternoon when Jody topped the hill and looked down on the ranch again. He looked for the saddle horses, but the corral was empty. His father was not back yet. He went slowly, then, toward the afternoon chores. At the ranch house, he found his mother sitting on the porch, mending socks.

"There's two doughnuts in the kitchen for you," she said. Jody slid to the kitchen, and returned with half of one of the doughnuts already eaten and his mouth full. His mother asked him what he had learned in school that day, but she didn't listen to his doughnut-muffled answer. She interrupted, "Jody, tonight see you fill the wood box clear full. Last night you crossed the sticks and it wasn't only about half full. Lay the sticks flat to-night. And Jody, some of the hens are hiding eggs, or else the dogs are eating them. Look about in the grass and see if you can find any nests."

Jody, still eating, went out and did his chores. He saw the quail come down to eat with the chickens when he threw out the grain. For some reason his father was proud to have them come. He never allowed any shooting near the house for fear the quail might go away.

When the wood box was full, Jody took his twenty-two rifle up to the cold spring at the brush line. He drank again and then aimed the gun at all manner of things, at rocks, at birds on the wing, at the big black pig kettle under the cypress tree, but he didn't shoot for he had no cartridges and wouldn't have until he was twelve. If his father had seen him aim the rifle in the direction of the house he would have put the cartridges off another year. Jody remembered this and did not point the rifle down the hill again. Two years was enough to wait for cartridges. Nearly all of his father's presents were given with reservations which hampered their value somewhat. It was good discipline.

The supper waited until dark for his father to return. When at last he came in with Billy Buck, Jody could smell the delicious brandy on their breaths. Inwardly he rejoiced, for his father sometimes talked to him when he smelled of brandy, sometimes even told things he had done in the wild days when he was a boy.

After supper, Jody sat by the fireplace and his shy polite eyes sought the room corners, and he waited for his father to tell what it was he contained, for Jody knew he had news of some sort. But he was disappointed. His father pointed a stern finger at him.

"You'd better go to bed, Jody. I'm going to need you in the morning."

That wasn't so bad. Jody liked to do the things he had to do as long as they weren't routine things. He looked at the floor and his mouth worked out a question before he spoke it. "What are we going to do in the morning, kill a pig?" he asked softly.

"Never you mind. You better get to bed."

When the door was closed behind him, Jody heard his father and Billy

Buck chuckling and he knew it was a joke of some kind. And later, when he lay in bed, trying to make words out of the murmurs in the other room, he heard his father protest, "But, Ruth, I didn't give much for him."

Jody heard the hoot owls hunting mice down by the barn, and he heard a fruit tree limb tap-tapping against the house. A cow was lowing when he went to sleep.

When the triangle sounded in the morning, Jody dressed more quickly even than usual. In the kitchen, while he washed his face and combed back his hair, his mother addressed him irritably. "Don't you go out until you get a good breakfast in you."

He went into the dining room and sat at the long white table. He took a steaming hotcake from the platter, arranged two fried eggs on it, covered them with another hotcake, and squashed the whole thing with his fork.

His father and Billy Buck came in. Jody knew from the sound on the floor that both of them were wearing flat-heeled shoes, but he peered under the table to make sure. His father turned off the oil lamp, for the day had arrived, and he looked stern and disciplinary, but Billy Buck didn't look at Jody at all. He avoided the shy questioning eyes of the boy and soaked a whole piece of toast in his coffee.

Carl Tiflin said crossly, "You come with us after breakfast!"

Jody had trouble with his food then, for he felt a kind of doom in the air. After Billy had tilted his saucer and drained the coffee which had slopped into it, and had wiped his hands on his jeans, the two men stood up from the table and went out into the morning light together, and Jody respectfully followed a little behind them. He tried to keep his mind from running ahead, tried to keep it absolutely motionless.

His mother called, "Carl! Don't you let it keep him from school."

They marched past the cypress, where a singletree hung from a limb to butcher the pigs on, and past the black iron kettle, so it was not a pig killing. The sun shone over the hill and threw long, dark shadows of the trees and buildings. They crossed a stubble field to shortcut to the barn. Jody's father unhooked the door and they went in. They had been walking toward the sun on the way down. The barn was black as night in contrast and warm from the hay and from the beasts. Jody's father moved over toward the one box stall. "Come here!" he ordered. Jody could begin to see things now. He looked into the box stall and then stepped back quickly.

A red pony colt was looking at him out of the stall. Its tense ears were forward and a light of disobedience was in its eyes. Its coat was rough and thick as an airedale's fur and its mane was long and tangled. Jody's throat collapsed in on itself and cut his breath short.

"He needs a good currying," his father said, "and if I ever hear of you not feeding him or leaving his stall dirty, I'll sell him off in a minute."

Jody couldn't bear to look at the pony's eyes any more. He gazed down at his hands for a moment, and he asked very shyly, "Mine?" No one answered him. He put his hand out toward the pony. Its grey nose came close, sniffing loudly, and then the lips drew back and the strong teeth closed on Jody's fingers. The pony shook its head up and down and seemed to laugh with amusement. Jody regarded his bruised fingers. "Well," he said with pride—"Well, I guess he can bite all right." The two men laughed, somewhat in relief. Carl Tiflin went out of the barn and walked up a sidehill to be by himself, for he was embarrassed, but Billy Buck stayed. It was easier to talk to Billy Buck. Jody asked again—"Mine?"

Billy became professional in tone. "Sure! That is, if you look out for him and break him right. I'll show you how. He's just a colt. You can't ride him for some time."

Jody put out his bruised hand again, and this time the red pony let his nose be rubbed. "I ought to have a carrot," Jody said. "Where'd we get him, Billy?"

"Bought him at a sheriff's auction," Billy explained. "A show went broke in Salinas and had debts. The sheriff was selling off their stuff."

The pony stretched out his nose and shook the forelock from his wild eyes. Jody stroked the nose a little. He said softly, "There isn't a—saddle?"

Billy Buck laughed. "I'd forgot. Come along."

In the harness room he lifted down a little saddle of red morocco leather. "It's just a show saddle," Billy Buck said disparagingly. "It isn't practical for the brush, but it was cheap at the sale."

Jody couldn't trust himself to look at the saddle either, and he couldn't speak at all. He brushed the shining red leather with his fingertips, and after a long time he said, "It'll look pretty on him though." He thought of the grandest and prettiest things he knew. "If he hasn't a name already, I think I'll call him Gabilan Mountains," he said.

Billy Buck knew how he felt. "It's a pretty long name. Why don't you just call him Gabilan? That means hawk. That would be a fine name for him." Billy felt glad. "If you will collect tail hair, I might be able to make a hair rope for you sometime. You could use it for a hackamore."

Jody wanted to go back to the box stall. "Could I lead him to school, do you think—to show the kids?"

But Billy shook his head. "He's not even halter-broke yet. We had a time getting him here. Had to almost drag him. You better be starting for school though."

"I'll bring the kids to see him here this afternoon," Jody said.

Six boys came over the hill half an hour early that afternoon, running hard, their heads down, their forearms working, their breath whistling. They swept by the house and cut across the stubble field to the barn. And then they stood self-consciously before the pony, and then they looked at Jody with eyes in which there was a new admiration and a new respect. Before today Jody had been a boy, dressed in overalls and a blue shirt—quieter than most, even suspected of being a little cowardly. And now he was different. Out of a thousand centuries they drew the ancient admiration of the footman for the horseman. They knew instinctively that a man on a horse is spiritually as well as physically bigger than a man on foot. They knew that Jody had been miraculously lifted out of equality with them, and had been placed over them. Gabilan put his head out of the stall and sniffed them.

"Why'n't you ride him?" the boys cried. "Why'n't you braid his tail with ribbons like in the fair?" "When you going to ride him?"

Jody's courage was up. He too felt the superiority of the horseman. "He's not old enough. Nobody can ride him for a long time. I'm going to train him on the long halter. Billy Buck is going to show me how."

"Well, can't we even lead him around a little?"

"He isn't even halter-broke," Jody said. He wanted to be completely alone when he took the pony out the first time. "Come and see the saddle."

They were speechless at the red morocco saddle, completely shocked out of comment. "It isn't much use in the brush," Jody explained. "It'll look pretty on him though. Maybe I'll ride bareback when I go into the brush."

"How you going to rope a cow without a saddle horn?"

"Maybe I'll get another saddle for every day. My father might want me to help him with the stock." He let them feel the red saddle, and showed them the brass chain throatlatch on the bridle and the big brass buttons at each temple where the headstall and brow band crossed. The whole thing was too wonderful. They had to go away after a little while, and each boy, in his mind, searched among his possessions for a bribe worthy of offering in return for a ride on the red pony when the time should come.

Jody was glad when they had gone. He took brush and currycomb from the wall, took down the barrier of the box stall, and stepped cautiously in. The pony's eyes glittered, and he edged around into kicking position. But Jody touched him on the shoulder and rubbed his high arched neck as he had always seen Billy Buck do, and he crooned, "So-o-o Boy," in a deep voice. The pony gradually relaxed his tenseness. Jody curried and brushed until a pile of dead hair lay in the stall and until the pony's coat had taken on a deep red shine. Each time he finished he thought it might have been done better. He braided the mane into a dozen little pigtails, and he braided the forelock, and then he undid them and brushed the hair out straight again.

Jody did not hear his mother enter the barn. She was angry when she came, but when she looked in at the pony and at Jody working on him, she felt a curious pride rise up in her. "Have you forgot the wood box?" she asked gently. "It's not far off from dark and there's not a stick of wood in the house, and the chickens aren't fed."

Jody quickly put up his tools. "I forgot, ma'am."

"Well, after this do your chores first. Then you won't forget. I expect you'll forget lots of things now if I don't keep an eye on you."

"Can I have carrots from the garden for him, ma'am?"

She had to think about that. "Oh—I guess so, if you only take the big tough ones."

"Carrots keep the coat good," he said, and again she felt the curious rush of pride.

Jody never waited for the triangle to get him out of bed after the coming of the pony. It became his habit to creep out of bed even before his mother was awake, to slip into his clothes and to go quietly down to the barn to see Gabilan. In the grey quiet mornings when the land and the brush and the houses and the trees were silver-grey and black like a photograph negative, he stole toward the barn, past the sleeping stones and the sleeping cypress tree. The turkeys, roosting in the tree out of coyotes' reach, clicked drowsily. The fields glowed with a grey frostlike light and in the dew the tracks of rabbits and of field mice stood out sharply. The good dogs came stiffly out of their little houses, hackles up and deep growls in their throats. Then they caught Jody's scent, and their stiff tails rose up and waved a greeting—Doubletree Mutt with the big thick tail, and Smasher, the incipient shepherd—then went lazily back to their warm beds.

It was a strange time and a mysterious journey, to Jody—an extension of a dream. When he first had the pony he liked to torture himself during the trip by thinking Gabilan would not be in his stall, and worse, would never have been there. And he had other delicious little self-induced pains. He thought how the rats had gnawed ragged holes in the red saddle, and how the mice had nibbled Gabilan's tail until it was stringy and thin. He usually ran the last little way to the barn. He unlatched the rusty hasp of the barn door and stepped in, and no matter how quietly he opened the door, Gabilan was always looking at him over the barrier of the box stall and Gabilan whinnied softly and stamped his front foot, and his eyes had big sparks of red fire in them like oakwood embers.

Sometimes, if the work horses were to be used that day, Jody found Billy Buck in the barn harnessing and currying. Billy stood with him and looked long at Gabilan and he told Jody a great many things about horses. He explained that they were terribly afraid for their feet, so that one must make a practice of lifting the legs and patting the hooves and ankles to re-move their terror. He told Jody how horses love conversation. He must talk to the pony all the time, and tell him the reasons for everything. Billy wasn't sure a horse could understand everything that was said to him, but it was impossible to say how much was understood. A horse never kicked up a fuss if someone he liked explained things to him. Billy could give examples, too. He had known, for instance, a horse nearly dead beat with fatigue to perk up when told it was only a little farther to his destination. And he had known a horse paralyzed with fright to come out of it when his rider told him what it was that was frightening him. While he talked in the mornings, Billy Buck cut twenty or thirty straws into neat three-inch lengths and stuck them into his hatband. Then during the whole day, if he wanted to pick his teeth or merely to chew on something, he had only to reach up for one of them.

Jody listened carefully, for he knew and the whole country knew that Billy Buck was a fine hand with horses. Billy's own horse was a stringy cayuse with a hammer head, but he nearly always won the first prizes at the stock trials. Billy could rope a steer, take a double half-hitch about the horn with his riata, and dismount, and his horse would play the steer as an angler plays a fish, keeping a tight rope until the steer was down or beaten.

Every morning, after Jody had curried and brushed the pony, he let down the barrier of the stall, and Gabilan thrust past him and raced down the barn and into the corral. Around and around he galloped, and some-times he jumped forward and landed on stiff legs. He stood quivering, stiff ears forward, eyes rolling so that the whites showed, pretending to be fright-ened. At last he walked snorting to the water trough and buried his nose in the water up to the nostrils. Jody was proud then, for he knew that was the way to judge a horse. Poor horses only touched their lips to the water, but a fine-spirited beast put his whole nose and mouth under, and only left room to breathe.

Then Jody stood and watched the pony, and he saw things he had never noticed about any other horse, the sleek, sliding flank muscles and the cords of the buttocks, which flexed like a closing fist, and the shine the sun put on the red coat. Having seen horses all his life, Jody had never looked at them very closely before. But now he noticed the moving ears which gave expression and even inflection of expression to the face. The pony talked with his ears. You could tell exactly how he felt about everything by the way his ears pointed. Sometimes they were stiff and upright and sometimes lax and sagging. They went back when he was angry or fearful, and forward when he was anxious and curious and pleased; and their exact position indicated which emotion he had.

Billy Buck kept his word. In the early fall the training began. First there was the halter-breaking, and that was the hardest because it was the first thing. Jody held a carrot and coaxed and promised and pulled on the rope. The pony set his feet like a burro when he felt the strain. But before long he learned. Jody walked all over the ranch leading him. Gradually he took to dropping the rope until the pony followed him unled wherever he went.

And then came the training on the long halter. That was slower work. Jody stood in the middle of a circle, holding the long halter. He clucked with his tongue and the pony started to walk in a big circle, held in by the long rope. He clucked again to make the pony trot, and again to make him gallop. Around and around Gabilan went thundering and enjoying it immensely. Then he called, "Whoa," and the pony stopped. It was not long until Gabilan was perfect at it. But in many ways he was a bad pony. He bit Jody in the pants and stomped on Jody's feet. Now and then his ears went back and he aimed a tremendous kick at the boy. Every time he did one of these bad things, Gabilan settled back and seemed to laugh to himself.

Billy Buck worked at the hair rope in the evenings before the fireplace. Jody collected tail hair in a bag, and he sat and watched Billy slowly constructing the rope, twisting a few hairs to make a string and rolling two strings together for a cord, and then braiding a number of cords to make the rope. Billy rolled the finished rope on the floor under his foot to make it round and hard.

The long halter work rapidly approached perfection. Jody's father, watching the pony stop and start and trot and gallop, was a little bothered by it.

"He's getting to be almost a trick pony," he complained. "I don't like trick horses. It takes all the—dignity out of a horse to make him do tricks. Why, a trick horse is kind of like an actor—no dignity, no character of his own." And his father said, "I guess you better be getting him used to the saddle pretty soon."

Jody rushed for the harness room. For some time he had been riding the saddle on a sawhorse. He changed the stirrup length over and over, and could never get it just right. Sometimes, mounted on the sawhorse in the harness room, with collars and hames and tugs hung all about him, Jody rode out beyond the room. He carried his rifle across the pommel. He saw the fields go flying by, and he heard the beat of the galloping hooves.

It was a ticklish job, saddling the pony the first time. Gabilan hunched and reared and threw the saddle off before the cinch could be tightened. It had to be replaced again and again until at last the pony let it stay. And the cinching was difficult, too. Day by day Jody tightened the girth a little more until at last the pony didn't mind the saddle at all.

Then there was the bridle. Billy explained how to use a stick of licorice for a bit until Gabilan was used to having something in his mouth. Billy explained, "Of course we could force-break him to everything, but he wouldn't be as good a horse if we did. He'd always be a little bit afraid, and he wouldn't mind because he wanted to."

The first time the pony wore the bridle he whipped his head about and worked his tongue against the bit until the blood oozed from the corners of his mouth. He tried to rub the headstall off on the manger. His ears pivoted about and his eyes turned red with fear and with general rambunctiousness.

Jody rejoiced, for he knew that only a mean-souled horse does not resent training.

And Jody trembled when he thought of the time when he would first sit in the saddle. The pony would probably throw him off. There was no disgrace in that. The disgrace would come if he did not get right up and mount again. Sometimes he dreamed that he lay in the dirt and cried and couldn't make himself mount again. The shame of the dream lasted until the middle of the day.

Gabilan was growing fast. Already he had lost the long-leggedness of the colt; his mane was getting longer and blacker. Under the constant currying and brushing his coat lay as smooth and gleaming as orange-red lacquer. Jody oiled the hooves and kept them carefully trimmed so they would not crack.

The hair rope was nearly finished. Jody's father gave him an old pair of spurs and bent in the side bars and cut down the strap and took up the chainlets until they fitted. And then one day Carl Tiflin said:

"The pony's growing faster than I thought. I guess you can ride him by Thanksgiving. Think you can stick on?"

"I don't know," Jody said shyly. Thanksgiving was only three weeks off. He hoped it wouldn't rain, for rain would spot the red saddle.

Gabilan knew and liked Jody by now. He nickered when Jody came across the stubble field, and in the pasture he came running when his master whistled for him. There was always a carrot for him every time.

Billy Buck gave him riding instructions over and over. "Now when you get up there, just grab tight with your knees and keep your hands away from the saddle, and if you get throwed, don't let that stop you. No matter how good a man is, there's always some horse can pitch him. You just climb up again before he gets to feeling smart about it. Pretty soon, he won't throw you no more, and pretty soon he *can't* throw you no more. That's the way to do it."

"I hope it don't rain before," Jody said.

"Why not? Don't want to get throwed in the mud?"

That was partly it, and also he was afraid that in the flurry of bucking

Gabilan might slip and fall on him and break his leg or his hip. He had seen that happen to men before, had seen how they writhed on the ground like squashed bugs, and he was afraid of it.

He practiced on the sawhorse how he would hold the reins in his left hand and a hat in his right hand. If he kept his hands thus busy, he couldn't grab the horn if he felt himself going off. He didn't like to think of what would happen if he did grab the horn. Perhaps his father and Billy Buck would never speak to him again, they would be so ashamed. The news would get about and his mother would be ashamed too. And in the school yard—it was too awful to contemplate.

He began putting his weight in a stirrup when Gabilan was saddled, but he didn't throw his leg over the pony's back. That was forbidden until Thanksgiving.

Every afternoon he put the red saddle on the pony and cinched it tight. The pony was learning already to fill his stomach out unnaturally large while the cinching was going on, and then to let it down when the straps were fixed. Sometimes Jody led him up to the brush line and let him drink from the round green tub, and sometimes he led him up through the stubble field to the hilltop from which it was possible to see the white town of Salinas and the geometric fields of the great valley, and the oak trees clipped by the sheep. Now and then they broke through the brush and came to little cleared circles so hedged in that the world was gone and only the sky and the circle of brush were left from the old life. Gabilan liked these trips and showed it by keeping his head very high and by quivering his nostrils with interest. When the two came back from an expedition they smelled of the sweet sage they had forced through.

Time dragged on toward Thanksgiving, but winter came fast. The clouds swept down and hung all day over the land and brushed the hilltops, and the winds blew shrilly at night. All day the dry oak leaves drifted down from the trees until they covered the ground, and yet the trees were unchanged.

Jody had wished it might not rain before Thanksgiving, but it did. The brown earth turned dark and the trees glistened. The cut ends of the stubble turned black with mildew; the haystacks greyed from exposure to the damp, and on the roofs the moss, which had been all summer as grey as lizards, turned a brilliant yellow-green. During the week of rain, Jody kept the pony in the box stall out of the dampness, except for a little time after school when he took him out for exercise and to drink at the water trough in the upper corral. Not once did Gabilan get wet.

The wet weather continued until little new grass appeared. Jody walked to school dressed in a slicker and short rubber boots. At length one morning the sun came out brightly. Jody, at his work in the box stall, said to Billy Buck, "Maybe I'll leave Gabilan in the corral when I go to school today."

"Be good for him to be out in the sun," Billy assured him. "No animal likes to be cooped up too long. Your father and me are going back on the hill to clean the leaves out of the spring." Billy nodded and picked his teeth with one of his little straws.

"If the rain comes, though—" Jody suggested.

"Not likely to rain today. She's rained herself out." Billy pulled up his sleeves and snapped his arm bands. "If it comes on to rain—why a little rain don't hurt a horse."

"Well, if it does come on to rain, you put him in, will you, Billy? I'm scared he might get cold so I couldn't ride him when the time comes."

"Oh sure! I'll watch out for him if we get back in time. But it won't rain today."

And so Jody, when he went to school, left Gabilan standing out in the corral.

Billy Buck wasn't wrong about many things. He couldn't be. But he was wrong about the weather that day, for a little after noon the clouds pushed over the hills and the rain began to pour down. Jody heard it start on the schoolhouse roof. He considered holding up one finger for permission to go to the outhouse and, once outside, running for home to put the pony in. Punishment would be prompt both at school and at home. He gave it up and took ease from Billy's assurance that rain couldn't hurt a horse. When school was finally out, he hurried home through the dark rain. The banks at the sides of the road spouted little jets of muddy water. The rain slanted and swirled under a cold and gusty wind. Jody dogtrotted home, slopping through the gravelly mud of the road.

From the top of the ridge he could see Gabilan standing miserably in the corral. The red coat was almost black, and streaked with water. He stood head down with his rump to the rain and wind. Jody arrived running and threw open the barn door and led the wet pony in by his forelock. Then he found a gunnysack and rubbed the soaked hair and rubbed the legs and ankles. Gabilan stood patiently, but he trembled in gusts like the wind.

When he had dried the pony as well as he could, Jody went to the house and brought hot water down to the barn and soaked the grain in it. Gabilan was not very hungry. He nibbled at the hot mash, but he was not very much interested in it, and he still shivered now and then. A little steam rose from his damp back.

It was almost dark when Billy Buck and Carl Tiflin came home. "When the rain started we put up at Ben Herche's place, and the rain never let up all afternoon," Carl Tiflin explained. Jody looked reproachfully at Billy Buck and Billy felt guilty.

"You said it wouldn't rain," Jody accused him.

Billy looked away. "It's hard to tell, this time of year," he said, but his excuse was lame. He had no right to be fallible, and he knew it.

"The pony got wet, got soaked through."

"Did you dry him off?"

"I rubbed him with a sack and I gave him hot grain."

Billy nodded in agreement.

"Do you think he'll take cold, Billy?"

"A little rain never hurt anything," Billy assured him.

Jody's father joined the conversation then and lectured the boy a little. "A horse," he said, "isn't any lapdog kind of thing." Carl Tiflin hated weakness and sickness, and he held a violent contempt for helplessness.

Jody's mother put a platter of steaks on the table and boiled potatoes and boiled squash, which clouded the room with their steam. They sat down to eat. Carl Tiflin still grumbled about weakness put into animals and men by too much coddling.

Billy Buck felt bad about his mistake. "Did you blanket him?" he asked.

"No. I couldn't find any blanket. I laid some sacks over his back."

"We'll go down and cover him up after we eat, then." Billy felt better about it then. When Jody's father had gone in to the fire and his mother was washing dishes, Billy found and lighted a lantern. He and Jody walked through the mud to the barn. The barn was dark and warm and sweet. The horses still munched their evening hay. "You hold the lantern!" Billy ordered. And he felt the pony's legs and tested the heat of the flanks. He put his cheek against the pony's grey muzzle and then he rolled up the eyelids to look at the eyeballs and he lifted the lips to see the gums, and he put his fingers inside the ears. "He don't seem so chipper," Billy said. "I'll give him a rubdown."

Then Billy found a sack and rubbed the pony's legs violently and he rubbed the chest and the withers. Gabilan was strangely spiritless. He submitted patiently to the rubbing. At last Billy brought an old cotton comforter from the saddle room, and threw it over the pony's back and tied it at neck and chest with string.

"Now he'll be all right in the morning," Billy said.

Jody's mother looked up when he got back to the house. "You're late up from bed," she said. She held his chin in her hard hand and brushed the tangled hair out of his eyes and she said, "Don't worry about the pony. He'll be all right. Billy's as good as any horse doctor in the country."

Jody hadn't known she could see his worry. He pulled gently away from her and knelt down in front of the fireplace until it burned his stomach. He scorched himself through and then went in to bed, but it was a hard thing to go to sleep. He awakened after what seemed a long time. The room was dark but there was a greyness in the window like that which precedes the dawn. He got up and found his overalls and searched for the legs, and then the clock in the other room struck two. He laid his clothes down and got back into bed. It was broad daylight when he awakened again. For the first time he had slept through the ringing of the triangle. He leaped up, flung on his clothes, and went out of the door still buttoning his shirt. His mother looked after him for a moment and then went quietly back to her work. Her eyes were brooding and kind. Now and then her mouth smiled a little but without changing her eyes at all.

Jody ran on toward the barn. Halfway there he heard the sound he dreaded, the hollow rasping cough of a horse. He broke into a sprint then. In the barn he found Billy Buck with the pony. Billy was rubbing its legs with his strong thick hands. He looked up and smiled gaily. "He just took a little cold," Billy said. "We'll have him out of it in a couple of days."

Jody looked at the pony's face. The eyes were half closed and the lids thick and dry. In the eye corners a crust of hard mucus stuck. Gabilan's ears hung loosely sideways and his head was low. Jody put out his hand, but the pony did not move close to it. He coughed again and his whole body constricted with the effort. A little stream of thin fluid ran from his nostrils.

Jody looked back at Billy Buck. "He's awful sick, Billy."

"Just a little cold, like I said," Billy insisted. "You go get some breakfast and then go back to school. I'll take care of him."

"But you might have to do something else. You might leave him."

"No, I won't. I won't leave him at all. Tomorrow's Saturday. Then you can stay with him all day." Billy had failed again, and he felt badly about it. He had to cure the pony now.

Jody walked up to the house and took his place listlessly at the table. The eggs and bacon were cold and greasy, but he didn't notice it. He ate his usual amount. He didn't even ask to stay home from school. His mother pushed his hair back when she took his plate. "Billy'll take care of the pony," she assured him.

He moped through the whole day at school. He couldn't answer any questions nor read any words. He couldn't even tell anyone the pony was sick, for that might make him sicker. And when school was finally out he started home in dread. He walked slowly and let the other boys leave him. He wished he might continue walking and never arrive at the ranch.

Billy was in the barn, as he had promised, and the pony was worse. His eyes were almost closed now, and his breath whistled shrilly past an obstruction in his nose. A film covered that part of the eyes that was visible at all. It was doubtful whether the pony could see any more. Now and then he snorted, to clear his nose, and by the action seemed to plug it tighter. Jody looked dispiritedly at the pony's coat. The hair lay rough and unkempt and seemed to have lost all of its old luster. Billy stood quietly beside the stall. Jody hated to ask, but he had to know.

"Billy, is he—is he going to get well?"

Billy put his fingers between the bars under the pony's jaw and felt about. "Feel here," he said and he guided Jody's fingers to a large lump under the jaw. "When that gets bigger, I'll open it up and then he'll get better."

Jody looked quickly away, for he had heard about that lump. "What is it the matter with him?"

Billy didn't want to answer, but he had to. He couldn't be wrong three times. "Strangles," he said shortly, "but don't you worry about that. I'll pull him out of it. I've seen them get well when they were worse than Gabilan is. I'm going to steam him now. You can help."

"Yes," Jody said miserably. He followed Billy into the grain room and watched him make the steaming bag ready. It was a long canvas nose bag with straps to go over a horse's ears. Billy filled it one-third full of bran and then he added a couple of handfuls of dried hops. On top of the dry substance he poured a little carbolic acid and a little turpentine. "I'll be mixing it all up while you run to the house for a kettle of boiling water," Billy said.

When Jody came back with the steaming kettle, Billy buckled the straps over Gabilan's head and fitted the bag tightly around his nose. Then through a little hole in the side of the bag he poured the boiling water on the mixture. The pony started away as a cloud of strong steam rose up, but then the soothing fumes crept through his nose and into his lungs, and the sharp steam began to clear out the nasal passages. He breathed loudly. His legs trembled in an ague, and his eyes closed against the biting cloud. Billy poured in more water and kept the steam rising for fifteen minutes. At last he set down the kettle and took the bag from Gabilan's nose. The pony looked better. He breathed freely, and his eyes were open wider than they had been.

"See how good it makes him feel," Billy said. "Now we'll wrap him up in the blanket again. Maybe he'll be nearly well by morning."

"I'll stay with him tonight," Jody suggested.

"No. Don't you do it. I'll bring my blankets down here and put them in the hay. You can stay tomorrow and steam him if he needs it."

The evening was falling when they went to the house for their supper. Jody didn't even realize that someone else had fed the chickens and filled the wood box. He walked up past the house to the dark brush line and took a drink of water from the tub. The spring water was so cold that it stung his mouth and drove a shiver through him. The sky above the hills was still light. He saw a hawk flying so high that it caught the sun on its breast and shone like a spark. Two blackbirds were driving him down the sky, glittering as they attacked their enemy. In the west, the clouds were moving in to rain again.

Jody's father didn't speak at all while the family ate supper, but after Billy Buck had taken his blankets and gone to sleep in the barn, Carl Tiflin built a high fire in the fireplace and told stories. He told about the wild man who ran naked through the country and had a tail and ears like a horse, and he told about the rabbit-cats of Moro Cojo that hopped into the trees for birds. He revived the famous Maxwell brothers who found a vein of gold and hid the traces of it so carefully that they could never find it again.

Jody sat with his chin in his hands; his mouth worked nervously and his father gradually became aware that he wasn't listening very carefully. "Isn't that funny?" he asked.

Jody laughed politely and said, "Yes, sir." His father was angry and hurt, then. He didn't tell any more stories. After a while, Jody took a lantern and went down to the barn. Billy Buck was asleep in the hay, and, except

that his breath rasped a little in his lungs, the pony seemed to be much better. Jody stayed a little while, running his fingers over the red rough coat,
and then he took up the lantern and went back to the house. When he was
in bed, his mother came into the room.

"Have you enough covers on? It's getting winter."

"Yes, ma'am."

"Well, get some rest tonight." She hesitated to go out, stood uncertainly. "The pony will be all right," she said.

Jody was tired. He went to sleep quickly and didn't awaken until dawn.
The triangle sounded, and Billy Buck came up from the barn before Jody
could get out of the house.

"How is he?" Jody demanded.

Billy always wolfed his breakfast. "Pretty good. I'm going to open that
lump this morning. Then he'll be better maybe."

After breakfast, Billy got out his best knife, one with a needle point. He
whetted the shining blade a long time on a little carborundum stone. He
tried the point and the blade again and again on his calloused thumb-ball,
and at last he tried it on his upper lip.

On the way to the barn, Jody noticed how the young grass was up and
how the stubble was melting day by day into the new green crop of volun-
teer. It was a cold sunny morning.

As soon as he saw the pony, Jody knew he was worse. His eyes were
closed and sealed shut with dried mucus. His head hung so low that his nose
almost touched the straw of his bed. There was a little groan in each breath,
a deep-seated, patient groan.

Billy lifted the weak head and made a quick slash with the knife. Jody
saw the yellow pus run out. He held up the head while Billy swabbed out the
wound with weak carbolic acid salve.

"Now he'll feel better," Billy assured him. "That yellow poison is what
makes him sick."

Jody looked unbelieving at Billy Buck. "He's awful sick."

Billy thought a long time what to say. He nearly tossed off a careless assurance, but he saved himself in time. "Yes, he's pretty sick," he said at last. "I've seen worse ones get well. If he doesn't get pneumonia, we'll pull him through. You stay with him. If he gets worse, you can come and get me."

For a long time after Billy went away, Jody stood beside the pony, stroking him behind the ears. The pony didn't flip his head the way he had done when he was well. The groaning in his breathing was becoming more hollow.

Doubletree Mutt looked into the barn, his big tail waving provocatively, and Jody was so incensed at his health that he found a hard black clod on the floor and deliberately threw it. Doubletree Mutt went yelping away to nurse a bruised paw.

In the middle of the morning, Billy Buck came back and made another steam bag. Jody watched to see whether the pony improved this time as he had before. His breathing eased a little, but he did not raise his head.

The Saturday dragged on. Late in the afternoon Jody went to the house and brought his bedding down and made up a place to sleep in the hay. He didn't ask permission. He knew from the way his mother looked at him that she would let him do almost anything. That night he left a lantern burning on a wire over the box stall. Billy had told him to rub the pony's legs every little while.

At nine o'clock the wind sprang up and howled around the barn. And in spite of his worry, Jody grew sleepy. He got into his blankets and went to sleep, but the breathy groans of the pony sounded in his dreams. And in his sleep he heard a crashing noise which went on and on until it awakened him. The wind was rushing through the barn. He sprang up and looked down the lane of stalls. The barn door had blown open, and the pony was gone.

He caught the lantern and ran outside into the gate, and he saw Gabilan weakly shambling away into the darkness, head down, legs working slowly and mechanically. When Jody ran up and caught him by the forelock, he allowed himself to be led back and put into his stall. His groans were louder, and a fierce whistling came from his nose. Jody didn't sleep any more then. The hissing of the pony's breath grew louder and sharper.

He was glad when Billy Buck came in at dawn. Billy looked for a time at the pony as though he had never seen him before. He felt the ears and flanks. "Jody," he said, "I've got to do something you won't want to see. You run up to the house for a while."

Jody grabbed him fiercely by the forearm. "You're not going to shoot him?"

Billy patted his hand. "No. I'm going to open a little hole in his windpipe so he can breathe. His nose is filled up. When he gets well, we'll put a little brass button in the hole for him to breath through."

Jody couldn't have gone away if he had wanted to. It was awful to see the red hide cut, but infinitely more terrible to know it was being cut and not to see it. "I'll stay right here," he said bitterly. "You sure you got to?"

"Yes. I'm sure. If you stay, you can hold his head. If it doesn't make you sick, that is."

The fine knife came out again and was whetted again just as carefully as it had been the first time. Jody held the pony's head up and the throat taut, while Billy felt up and down for the right place. Jody sobbed once as the bright knife point disappeared into the throat. The pony plunged weakly away and then stood still, trembling violently. The blood ran thickly out and up the knife and across Billy's hand and into his shirtsleeve. The sure square hand sawed out a round hole in the flesh, and the breath came bursting out of the hole, throwing a fine spray of blood. With the rush of oxygen, the pony took a sudden strength. He lashed out with his hind feet and tried to rear, but Jody held his head down while Billy mopped the new wound with carbolic salve. It was a good job. The blood stopped flowing and the air puffed out the hole and sucked it in regularly with a little bubbling noise.

The rain brought in by the night wind began to fall on the barn roof. Then the triangle rang for breakfast. "You go up and eat while I wait," Billy said. "We've got to keep this hole from plugging up."

Jody walked slowly out of the barn. He was too dispirited to tell Billy how the barn door had blown open and let the pony out. He emerged into the wet grey morning and sloshed up to the house, taking a perverse pleasure in splashing through all the puddles. His mother fed him and put dry

clothes on. She didn't question him. She seemed to know he couldn't answer questions. But when he was ready to go back to the barn she brought
him a pan of steaming meal. "Give him this," she said.

But Jody did not take the pan. He said, "He won't eat anything," and
ran out of the house. At the barn, Billy showed him how to fix a ball of
cotton on a stick, with which to swab out the breathing hole when it became
clogged with mucus.

Jody's father walked into the barn and stood with them in front of the
stall. At length he turned to the boy. "Hadn't you better come with me? I'm
going to drive over the hill." Jody shook his head. "You better come on, out
of this," his father insisted.

Billy turned on him angrily. "Let him alone. It's his pony, isn't it?"

Carl Tiflin walked away without saying another word. His feelings were
badly hurt.

All morning Jody kept the wound open and the air passing in and out
freely. At noon the pony lay wearily down on his side and stretched his nose
out.

Billy came back. "If you're going to stay with him tonight, you better
take a little nap," he said. Jody went absently out of the barn. The sky had
cleared to a hard thin blue. Everywhere the birds were busy with worms that
had come to the damp surface of the ground.

Jody walked to the brush line and sat on the edge of the mossy tub. He
looked down at the house and at the old bunkhouse and at the dark cypress
tree. The place was familiar, but curiously changed. It wasn't itself any
more, but a frame for things that were happening. A cold wind blew out of
the east now, signifying that the rain was over for a little while. At his feet
Jody could see the little arms of new weeds spreading out over the ground.
In the mud about the spring were thousands of quail tracks.

Doubletree Mutt came sideways and embarrassed up through the vegetable patch, and Jody, remembering how he had thrown the clod, put his
arm about the dog's neck and kissed him on his wide black nose. Doubletree Mutt sat still, as though he knew some solemn thing was happening. His
big tail slapped the ground gravely. Jody pulled a swollen tick out of Mutt's

neck and popped it dead between his thumbnails. It was a nasty thing. He washed his hands in the cold spring water.

Except for the steady swish of the wind, the farm was very quiet. Jody knew his mother wouldn't mind if he didn't go in to eat his lunch. After a little while he went slowly back to the barn. Mutt crept into his own little house and whined softly to himself for a long time.

Billy Buck stood up from the box and surrendered the cotton swab. The pony still lay on his side and the wound in his throat bellowsed in and out. When Jody saw how dry and dead the hair looked, he knew at last that there was no hope for the pony. He had seen the dead hair before on dogs and on cows, and it was a sure sign. He sat heavily on the box and let down the barrier of the box stall. For a long time he kept his eyes on the moving wound, and at last he dozed, and the afternoon passed quickly. Just before dark his mother brought a deep dish of stew and left it for him and went away. Jody ate a little of it, and, when it was dark, he set the lantern on the floor by the pony's head so he could watch the wound and keep it open. And he dozed again until the night chill awakened him. The wind was blowing fiercely, bringing the north cold with it. Jody brought a blanket from his bed in the hay and wrapped himself in it. Gabilan's breathing was quiet at last; the hole in his throat moved gently. The owls flew through the hayloft, shrieking and looking for mice. Jody put his hands down on his head and slept. In his sleep he was aware that the wind had increased. He heard it slamming about the barn.

It was daylight when he awakened. The barn door had swung open. The pony was gone. He sprang up and ran out into the morning light.

The pony's tracks were plain enough, dragging through the frostlike dew on the young grass, tired tracks with little lines between them where the hoofs had dragged. They headed for the brush line halfway up the ridge. Jody broke into a run and followed them. The sun shone on the sharp white quartz that stuck through the ground here and there. As he followed the plain trail, a shadow cut across in front of him. He looked up and saw a high circle of black buzzards, and the slowly revolving circle dropped lower and lower. The solemn birds soon disappeared over the ridge. Jody ran faster then, forced on by panic and rage. The trail entered the brush at last and followed a winding route among the tall sage bushes.

At the top of the ridge Jody was winded. He paused, puffing noisily. The blood pounded in his ears. Then he saw what he was looking for. Below, in one of the little clearings in the brush, lay the red pony. In the distance, Jody could see the legs moving slowly and convulsively. And in a circle around him stood the buzzards, waiting for the moment of death they know so well.

Jody leaped forward and plunged down the hill. The wet ground muffled his steps and the brush hid him. When he arrived, it was all over. The first buzzard sat on the pony's head and its beak had just risen dripping with dark eye fluid. Jody plunged into the circle like a cat. The black brotherhood arose in a cloud, but the big one on the pony's head was too late. As it hopped along to take off, Jody caught its wing tip and pulled it down. It was nearly as big as he was. The free wing crashed into his face with the force of a club, but he hung on. The claws fastened on his leg and the wing elbows battered his head on either side. Jody groped blindly with his free hand. His fingers found the neck of the struggling bird. The red eyes looked into his face, calm and fearless and fierce; the naked head turned from side to side. Then the beak opened and vomited a stream of putrefied fluid. Jody brought up his knee and fell on the great bird. He held the neck to the ground with one hand while his other found a piece of sharp white quartz. The first blow broke the beak sideways and black blood spurted from the twisted, leathery mouth corners. He struck again and missed. The red fearless eyes still looked at him, impersonal and unafraid and detached. He struck again and again, until the buzzard lay dead, until its head was a red pulp. He was still beating the dead bird when Billy Buck pulled him off and held him tightly to calm his shaking.

Carl Tiflin wiped the blood from the boy's face with a red bandana. Jody was limp and quiet now. His father moved the buzzard with his toe. "Jody," he explained, "the buzzard didn't kill the pony. Don't you know that?"

"I know it," Jody said wearily.

It was Billy Buck who was angry. He had lifted Jody in his arms, and had turned to carry him home. But he turned back on Carl Tiflin. "'Course he knows it," Billy said furiously, "Jesus Christ! man, can't you see how he'd feel about it?"

WILLIAM SAROYAN

The Summer of the Beautiful White Horse

One day back there in the good old days when I was nine and the world was full of every imaginable kind of magnificence, and life was still a delightful and mysterious dream, my cousin Mourad, who was considered crazy by everybody who knew him except me, came to my house at four in the morning and woke me up by tapping on the window of my room.

Aram, he said.

I jumped out of bed and looked out the window.

I couldn't believe what I saw.

It wasn't morning yet, but it was summer and with daybreak not many minutes around the corner of the world it was light enough for me to know I wasn't dreaming.

My cousin Mourad was sitting on a beautiful white horse.

I stuck my head out of the window and rubbed my eyes.

Yes, he said in Armenian. It's a horse. You're not dreaming. Make it quick if you want a ride.

I knew my cousin Mourad enjoyed being alive more than anybody else who had ever fallen into the world by mistake, but this was more than even I could believe.

In the first place, my earliest memories had been memories of horses and my first longings had been longings to ride.

This was the wonderful part.

In the second place, we were poor.

This was the part that wouldn't permit me to believe what I saw.

We were poor. We had no money. Our whole tribe was poverty-stricken. Every branch of the Garoghlanian family was living in the most amazing and comical poverty in the world. Nobody could understand where we ever got money enough to keep us with food in our bellies, not even the old men of the family. Most important of all, though, we were famous for our honesty. We had been famous for our honesty for something like eleven centuries, even when we had been the wealthiest family in what we liked to think was the world. We were proud first, honest next, and after that we believed in right and wrong. None of us would take advantage of anybody in the world, let alone steal.

Consequently, even though I could see the horse, so magnificent; even though I could *smell* it, so lovely; even though I could *hear* it breathing, so exciting; I couldn't *believe* the horse had anything to do with my cousin Mourad or with me or with any of the other members of our family, asleep or awake, because I *knew* my cousin Mourad couldn't have *brought* the horse, and if he couldn't have bought it he must have *stolen* it, and I refused to believe he had stolen it.

No member of the Garoghlanian family could be a thief.

I stared first at my cousin and then at the horse. There was a pious stillness and humor in each of them which on the one hand delighted me and on the other frightened me.

Mourad, I said, where did you steal this horse?

Leap out of the window, he said, if you want a ride.

It was true, then. He *had* stolen the horse. There was no question about it. He had come to invite me to ride or not, as I chose.

Well, it seemed to me stealing a horse for a ride was not the same thing as stealing something else, such as money. For all I knew, maybe it wasn't stealing at all. If you were crazy about horses the way my cousin Mourad and I were, it wasn't stealing. It wouldn't become stealing until we offered to sell the horse, which of course I knew we would never do.

Let me put on some clothes, I said.

All right, he said, but hurry.

130

I leaped into my clothes.

I jumped down to the yard from the window and leaped up onto the horse behind my cousin Mourad.

That year we lived at the edge of town, on Walnut Avenue. Behind our house was the country: vineyards, orchards, irrigation ditches, and country roads. In less than three minutes we were on Olive Avenue, and then the horse began to trot. The air was new and lovely to breathe. The feel of the horse running was wonderful. My cousin Mourad who was considered one of the craziest members of our family began to sing. I mean, he began to roar.

Every family has a crazy streak in it somewhere, and my cousin Mourad was considered the natural descendant of the crazy streak in our tribe. Before him was our uncle Khosrove, an enormous man with a powerful head of black hair and the largest mustache in the San Joaquin Valley, a man so furious in temper, so irritable, so impatient that he stopped anyone from talking by roaring, *It is no harm; pay no attention to it.*

That was all, no matter what anybody happened to be talking about. Once it was his own son Arak running eight blocks to the barber shop where his father was having his mustache trimmed to tell him their house was on fire. The man Khosrove sat up in the chair and roared, It is no harm; pay no attention to it. The barber said, But the boy says your house is on fire. So Khosrove roared, Enough, it is no harm, I say.

My cousin Mourad was considered the natural descendant of this man, although Mourad's father was Zorab, who was practical and nothing else. That's how it was in our tribe. A man could be the father of his son's flesh, but that did not mean that he was also the father of his spirit. The distribution of the various kinds of spirit of our tribe had been from the beginning capricious and vagrant.

We rode and my cousin Mourad sang. For all anybody knew we were still in the old country where, at least according to our neighbors, we belonged. We let the horse run as long as it felt like running.

At last my cousin Mourad said, Get down. I want to ride alone.

Will you let me ride alone? I said.

That is up to the horse, my cousin said. Get down.

The *horse* will let me ride, I said.

We shall see, he said. Don't forget that I have a way with a horse.

Well, I said, any way you have with a horse, I have also.

For the sake of your safety, he said, let us hope so. Get down.

All right, I said, but remember you've got to let me try to ride alone.

I got down and my cousin Mourad kicked his heels into the horse and shouted, *Vazire,* run. The horse stood on its hind legs, snorted, and burst into a fury of speed that was the loveliest thing I had ever seen. My cousin Mourad raced the horse across a field of dry grass to an irrigation ditch, crossed the ditch on the horse, and five minutes later returned, dripping wet.

The sun was coming up.

Now it's my turn to ride, I said.

My cousin Mourad got off the horse.

Ride, he said.

I leaped to the back of the horse and for a moment knew the awfulest fear imaginable. The horse did not move.

Kick into his muscles, my cousin Mourad said. What are you waiting for? We've got to take him back before everybody in the world is up and about.

I kicked into the muscles of the horse. Once again it reared and snorted. Then it began to run. I didn't know what to do. Instead of running across the field to the irrigation ditch the horse ran down the road to the vineyard of Dikran Halabian where it began to leap over vines. The horse leaped over seven vines before I fell. Then it continued running.

My cousin Mourad came running down the road.

I'm not worried about you, he shouted. We've got to get that horse. You go this way and I'll go this way. If you come upon him, be kindly. I'll be near.

I continued down the road and my cousin Mourad went across the field toward the irrigation ditch.

It took him half an hour to find the horse and bring him back.

132

All right, he said, jump on. The whole world is awake now.

What will we do? I said.

Well, he said, we'll either take him back or hide him until tomorrow morning.

He didn't sound worried and I knew he'd hide him and not take him back. Not for a while, at any rate.

Where will you hide him? I said.

I know a place, he said.

How long ago did you steal this horse? I said.

It suddenly dawned on me that he had been taking these early morning rides for some time and had come for me this morning only because he knew how much I longed to ride.

Who said anything about stealing a horse? he said.

Anyhow, I said, how long ago did you begin riding every morning?

Not until this morning, he said.

Are you telling the truth? I said.

Of course not, he said, but if we are found out, that's what you're to say. I don't want both of us to be liars. All you know is that we started riding this morning.

All right, I said.

He walked the horse quietly to the barn of a deserted vineyard which at one time had been the pride of a farmer named Fetvajian. There were some oats and dry alfalfa in the barn.

We began walking home.

It wasn't easy, he said, to get the horse to behave so nicely. At first it wanted to run wild, but as I've told you, I have a way with a horse. I can get it to want to do anything *I* want it to do. Horses understand me.

How do you do it? I said.

I have an understanding with a horse, he said.

Yes, but what sort of an understanding? I said.

A simple and honest one, he said.

Well, I said, I wish I knew how to reach an understanding like that with a horse.

You're still a small boy, he said. When you get to be thirteen you'll know how to do it.

I went home and ate a hearty breakfast.

That afternoon my uncle Khosrove came to our house for coffee and cigarettes. He sat in the parlor, sipping and smoking and remembering the old country. Then another visitor arrived, a farmer named John Byro, an Assyrian who, out of loneliness, had learned to speak Armenian. My mother brought the lonely visitor coffee and tobacco and he rolled a cigarette and sipped and smoked, and then at last, sighing sadly, he said, My white horse which was stolen last month is still gone. I cannot understand it.

My uncle Khosrove became very irritated and shouted, It's no harm. What is the loss of a horse? Haven't we all lost the homeland? What is this crying over a horse?

That may be all right for you, a city dweller, to say, John Byro said, but what of my surrey? What good is a surrey without a horse?

Pay no attention to it, my uncle Khosrove roared.

I walked ten miles to get here, John Byro said.

You have legs, my uncle Khosrove shouted.

My left leg pains me, the farmer said.

Pay no attention to it, my uncle Khosrove roared.

That horse cost me sixty dollars, the farmer said.

I spit on money, my uncle Khosrove said.

He got up and stalked out of the house, slamming the screen door.

My mother explained.

He has a gentle heart, she said. It is simply that he is homesick and such a large man.

The farmer went away and I ran over to my cousin Mourad's house.

He was sitting under a peach tree, trying to repair the hurt wing of a young robin which could not fly. He was talking to the bird.

What is it? he said.

The farmer, John Byro, I said. He visited our house. He wants his horse. You've had it a month. I want you to promise not to take it back until I learn to ride.

It will take you a *year* to learn to ride, my cousin Mourad said.

We could keep the horse a year, I said.

My cousin Mourad leaped to his feet.

What? he roared. Are you inviting a member of the Garoghlanian family to steal? The horse must go back to its true owner.

When? I said.

In six months at the latest, he said.

He threw the bird into the air. The bird tried hard, almost fell twice, but at last flew away, high and straight.

Early every morning for two weeks my cousin Mourad and I took the horse out of the barn of the deserted vineyard where we were hiding it and rode it, and every morning the horse, when it was my turn to ride alone, leaped over grapevines and small trees and threw me and ran away. Nevertheless, I hoped in time to learn to ride the way my cousin Mourad rode.

One morning on the way to Fetvajian's deserted vineyard we ran into the farmer John Byro who was on his way to town.

Let me do the talking, my cousin Mourad said. I have a way with farmers.

Good morning, John Byro, my cousin Mourad said to the farmer.

The farmer studied the horse eagerly.

Good morning, sons of my friends, he said. What is the name of your horse?

My Heart, my cousin Mourad said in Armenian.

A lovely name, John Byro said, for a lovely horse. I could swear it is the horse that was stolen from me many weeks ago. May I look into its mouth?

Of course, Mourad said.

The farmer looked into the mouth of the horse.

Tooth for tooth, he said. I would swear it *is* my horse if I didn't know your parents. The fame of your family for honesty is well known to me. Yet the horse is the twin of my horse. A suspicious man would believe his eyes instead of his heart. Good day, my young friends.

Good day, John Byro, my cousin Mourad said.

Early the following morning we took the horse to John Byro's vineyard and put it in the barn. The dogs followed us around without making a sound.

The dogs, I whispered to my cousin Mourad. I thought they would bark.

They would at somebody else, he said. I have a way with dogs.

My cousin Mourad put his arms around the horse, pressed his nose into the horse's nose, patted it, and then we went away.

That afternoon John Byro came to our house in his surrey and showed my mother the horse that had been stolen and returned.

I do not know what to think, he said. The horse is stronger than ever. Better-tempered, too. I thank God.

My uncle Khosrove, who was in the parlor, became irritated and shouted, Quiet, man, quiet. Your horse has been returned. Pay no attention to it.

CATHERINE PETROSKI

Beautiful My Mane in the Wind

I am a horse, perhaps the last mustang. This is my yard, this is my pasture. And I told her I hate her. My dam-mother. She does not understand horses. She doesn't even try. There are many things she doesn't notice about me.

Horses move their feet like this.

Horses throw their heads like this, when they are impatient, about to dash away to some shady tree. See how beautiful my mane in the wind.

Horses snort.

Horses whinny.

Horses hate her.

I am a girl horse. I am building a house under the loquat tree. It is taking me a long time.

My house is made of logs, logs that Daddy doesn't want. That is because our fireplace goes nowhere. It is just a little cave in the wall because this is Texas and it is mostly hot here. Our fireplace has a permanent fake log. I am six.

I will be six next month.

Anyway that is why I got the real logs when our weeping willow died and Mama pushed it over one Sunday afternoon. The bottom of the trunk was rotten and the tree just fell over and Mama laughed and the baby laughed and I didn't laugh. I hate her.

I hate also the baby who is a Botherboy.

Daddy cut the willow tree into pieces I could carry and gave them to me and now I am building a horsehouse under the loquat and waiting for a man-horse to come along, which is the way it is supposed to happen.

I saw a picture of one and its name was Centaur.

Of a Sunday afternoon, in her stable

My room I also hate. Bother loves it best and squeals when he gets to its door, because he thinks it's nicer than his own room, nicer than the big room, nicer than any place at all. He likes best all the blocks and the toy people. I build temples and bridges sometimes but then he comes along. He throws blocks when he plays because he's just a baby. And a boy. And not a horse.

What I hate most about this room is picking up pieces of the lotto game when he throws it all over, picking up pieces of jigsaw puzzles that he has thrown all over. Picking up the spilled water, the blocks, the people. I hate his messes. I know that horses are not this messy. Mama says it is our fate to be left with the mess, but I don't think she likes it any more than I do.

She pays very little attention to me actually. She thinks I just read and I'm pretty sure she doesn't realize about the change. To a horse. She acts as though I'm still a girl. She doesn't observe closely.

Administering herself first aid

The fact is there is a fossil in my hoof.

At school we have a hill that is called Fossilhill because there are a lot of fossils to be found there. Actually the fossils are very easy to find. You just pick up a handful of dirt and you come up with fossils. The trick is to find big fossils. I can always find the biggest fossils of anybody, snails and funny sea snakes and shells of all kinds.

The boys run up and down Fossilhill and don't look where they're going. It's no wonder they don't find many fossils. They come and pull Horse's mane. They scuff through where Horse is digging with her hoof. They sometimes try to capture Horse, since she is perhaps the last mustang and of great value. But mostly they are silly, these boys. They don't make much sense, just a mess.

Today I was trotting on the side of the hill and found the biggest fossil I have ever found in my life, which in horse is I think twelve or maybe twenty-four years old. Then I found more and more fossils and other children came to the hill, even the girlygirls who never look for fossils because they always play games I don't know how to play. House and Shopping and Bad Baby. But they tried to find fossils today and asked me if this was a fossil or that, and they found many, many fossils. And we all had a good time. And when we had found all the fossils we had time to find, our teacher said, Put them in your pockets, children, and if you don't have pockets put them in your socks. And we did, and that's why there is a fossil in my hoof.

Girlygirls vs. Boyannoys vs. Horse

In my kindergarten there is a girl whose name is Larch. It is a funny name for a girl. It might not be such a funny name for a horse, but Larch isn't a horse because she is in fact the girl leader because she decides what games are going to be played and will let the boys tie her up. And the other girls too. When they tie people up they don't use real rope because our teacher wouldn't allow that. If they tie me up with their pretend rope it doesn't work. They think I just don't want to play, but the truth is I'm a horse and stronger than a girl and can break their girlygirl rope.

It's more fun being a horse. More fun than being a girl too, because they just play Housekeeping Area and none of them really knows yet how to read even though they pretend to. I can tell because they can't get the hard words. So they don't let me play with them. My mother says it's all right because they wish they could enjoy stories themselves and next year they will all read and everything will be all right.

The reading is the real problem between the horse and the girls, I guess. But sometimes they do let me play with them, if they need a victim or a hostage or an offering.

Herself among the others

Horses are I think lucky. They do not seem to have friends, such as people, you know, for they do not seem to need friends. They have enemies—the snakes, the potholes, the cougars, the fancy-booted cowboys who don't know the difference between a canter and a hand gallop. What friends they have are on a very practical basis. Other horses with the same problems.

The wind.

A talk with herself

If I tell her what I am she will not believe me.

If I tell the others what I am they may rope me and tell me to pull their wagon.

If I tell a boy what I am he will invade my loquat house, and maybe it will be good and maybe it will be bad.

If I tell Daddy what I am he will act interested for a minute and then drink some beer and start reading again.

And if I tell Bother he will not understand even the words but will grab my mane and pull it until he has pulled some of it out.

What does it matter? What does it all matter? I will whinny and run away.

Who could blame me? Horses should not be abused, ignored, or made fun of.

Discussing the weather or nothing at all

Just a little while ago, when I needed to go out to race a bit and throw my head in the wind, she stopped me, my dam-mother, and asked me who I thought I was. A girl? A horse? My name? I know what she's thinking. The others at school ask me the same question.

So I said, A girl, because I know that's what I'm supposed to think. One thing I know, not a girlygirl, which would be stupid playing games talking teasing being tied to the jungle gym. I won't. Sometimes it's hard not telling her what I really think, what I know. That sometimes I'm a girl, sometimes I'm a horse. When there are girl-things to do, like read, which a horse never does, or go in the car to the stock show or for ice cream or any of those things, I have to be a girl, but when there are hillsides of grass and forests with low-hanging boughs and secret stables in loquat trees, I am a horse.

Maybe someday there will be no changing back and forth and I will be stuck a horse. Which will be all right with me. Because horses think good easy things, smooth green and windy things, without large people or Bothers or other kids or school, and they have enough grass to trot in forever and wind to throw their manes high to the sky and cool sweet stream water to drink, and clover.

WALLACE STEGNER

The Colt

It was the swift coming of spring that let things happen. It was spring, and the opening of the roads, that took his father out of town. It was spring that clogged the river with floodwater and ice pans, sent the dogs racing in wild aimless packs, ripped the railroad bridge out and scattered it down the river for exuberant townspeople to fish out piecemeal. It was spring that drove the whole town to the riverbank with pikepoles and coffeepots and boxes of sandwiches for an impromptu picnic, lifting their sober responsibilities out of them and making them whoop blessings on the Canadian Pacific Railway for a winter's firewood. Nothing might have gone wrong except for the coming of spring. Some of the neighbors might have noticed and let them know; Bruce might not have forgotten; his mother might have remembered and sent him out again after dark.

But the spring came, and the ice went out, and that night Bruce went to bed drunk and exhausted with excitement. In the restless sleep just before waking he dreamed of wolves and wild hunts, but when he awoke finally he realized that he had not been dreaming the noise. The window, wide open for the first time in months, let in a shivery draught of fresh, damp air, and he heard the faint yelping far down in the bend of the river.

He dressed and went downstairs, crowding his bottom into the warm oven, not because he was cold but because it had been a ritual for so long that not even the sight of the sun outside could convince him it wasn't necessary. The dogs were still yapping; he heard them through the open door.

142

"What's the matter with all the pooches?" he said. "Where's Spot?"

"He's out with them," his mother said. "They've probably got a porcupine treed. Dogs go crazy in the spring."

"It's dog days they go crazy."

"They go crazy in the spring, too." She hummed a little as she set the table. "You'd better go feed the horses. Breakfast won't be for ten minutes. And see if Daisy is all right."

Bruce stood perfectly still in the middle of the kitchen. "Oh my gosh!" he said. "I left Daisy picketed out all night!"

His mother's head jerked around. "Where?"

"Down in the bend."

"Where those dogs are?"

"Yes," he said, sick and afraid. "Maybe she's had her colt."

"She shouldn't for two or three days," his mother said. But just looking at her, he knew that it might be bad, that there was something to be afraid of. In another moment they were out the door, running.

But it couldn't be Daisy they were barking at, he thought as he raced around Chance's barn. He'd picketed her higher up, not clear down in the U where the dogs were. His eyes swept the brown, wet, close-cropped meadow, the edge of the brush where the river ran close under the north bench. The mare wasn't there! He opened his mouth and half turned, running, to shout at his mother coming behind him, and then sprinted for the deep curve of the bend.

As soon as he rounded the little clump of brush that fringed the cutbank behind Chance's he saw them. The mare stood planted, a bay spot against the gray brush, and in front of her, on the ground, was another smaller spot. Six or eight dogs were leaping around, barking, sitting. Even at that distance he recognized Spot and the Chapmans' Airedale.

He shouted and pumped on. At a gravelly patch he stooped and clawed and straightened, still running, with a handful of pebbles. In one pausing, straddling, aiming motion he let fly a rock at the distant pack. It fell far short, but they turned their heads, sat on their haunches, and let out defiant short barks. Their tongues lolled as if they had run far.

143

Bruce yelled and threw again, one eye on the dogs and the other on the chestnut colt in front of the mare's feet. The mare's ears were back, and as he ran Bruce saw the colt's head bob up and down. It was all right then. The colt was alive. He slowed and came up quietly. Never move fast or speak loud around an animal, Pa said.

The colt struggled again, raised its head with white eyeballs rolling, spraddled its white-stockinged legs and tried to stand. "Easy, boy," Bruce said. "Take it easy, old fella." His mother arrived, getting her breath, her hair half down, and he turned to her gleefully. "It's all right, Ma. They didn't hurt anything. Isn't he a beauty, Ma?"

He stroked Daisy's nose. She was heaving, her ears pricking forward and back; her flanks were lathered, and she trembled. Patting her gently, he watched the colt, sitting now like a dog on its haunches, and his happiness that nothing had really been hurt bubbled out of him. "Lookit, Ma," he said. "He's got four white socks. Can I call him Socks, Ma? He sure is a nice colt, isn't he? Aren't you, Socks, old boy?" He reached down to touch the chestnut's forelock, and the colt struggled, pulling away.

Then Bruce saw his mother's face. It was quiet, too quiet. She hadn't answered a word to all his jabber. Instead she knelt down, about ten feet from the squatting colt, and stared at it. The boy's eyes followed hers. There was something funny about . . .

"Ma!" he said. "What's the matter with its front feet?"

He left Daisy's head and came around, staring. The colt's pasterns looked bent—*were* bent, so that they flattened clear to the ground under its weight. Frightened by Bruce's movement, the chestnut flopped and floundered to its feet, pressing close to its mother. And it walked, Bruce saw, flat on its fetlocks, its hooves sticking out in front like a movie comedian's too-large shoes.

Bruce's mother pressed her lips together, shaking her head. She moved so gently that she got her hand on the colt's poll, and he bobbed against the pleasant scratching. "You poor broken-legged thing," she said with tears in her eyes. "You poor little friendly ruined thing!"

Still quietly, she turned toward the dogs, and for the first time in his life

Bruce heard her curse. Quietly, almost in a whisper, she cursed them as they sat with hanging tongues just out of reach. "God damn you," she said. "God damn your wild hearts, chasing a mother and a poor little colt."

To Bruce, standing with trembling lip, she said, "Go get Jim Enich. Tell him to bring a wagon. And don't cry. It's not your fault."

His mouth tightened, a sob jerked in his chest. He bit his lip and drew his face down tight to keep from crying, but his eyes filled and ran over.

"It is too my fault!" he said, and turned and ran.

Later, as they came in the wagon up along the cut-bank, the colt tied down in the wagon box with his head sometimes lifting, sometimes bumping on the boards, the mare trotting after with chuckling vibrations of solicitude in her throat, Bruce leaned far over and tried to touch the colt's haunch. "Gee whiz!" he said. "Poor old Socks."

His mother's arm was around him, keeping him from leaning over too far. He didn't watch where they were until he heard his mother say in surprise and relief, "Why, there's Pa!"

Instantly he was terrified. He had forgotten and left Daisy staked out all night. It was his fault, the whole thing. He slid back into the seat and crouched between Enich and his mother, watching from that narrow space like a gopher from its hole. He saw the Ford against the barn and his father's big body leaning into it, pulling out gunnysacks and straw. There was mud all over the car, mud on his father's pants. He crouched deeper into his crevice and watched his father's face while his mother was telling what had happened.

Then Pa and Jim Enich lifted and slid the colt down to the ground, and Pa stooped to feel its fetlocks. His face was still, red from windburn, and his big square hands were muddy. After a long examination he straightened up.

"Would've been a nice colt," he said. "Damn a pack of mangy mongrels, anyway." He brushed his pants and looked at Bruce's mother. "How come Daisy was out?"

"I told Bruce to take her out. The barn seems so cramped for her, and I thought it would do her good to stretch her legs. And then the ice went out, and the bridge with it, and there was a lot of excitement. . . . " She spoke very fast, and in her voice Bruce heard the echo of his own fear and guilt. She was trying to protect him, but in his mind he knew he was to blame.

"I didn't mean to leave her out, Pa," he said. His voice squeaked, and he swallowed. "I was going to bring her in before supper, only when the bridge . . . "

His father's somber eyes rested on him, and he stopped. But his father didn't fly into a rage. He just seemed tired. He looked at the colt and then at Enich. "Total loss?" he said.

Enich had a leathery, withered face, with two deep creases from beside his nose to the corner of his mouth. A brown mole hid in the left one, and it emerged and disappeared as he chewed a dry grass stem. "Hide," he said.

Bruce closed his dry mouth, swallowed. "Pa!" he said. "It won't have to be shot, will it?"

"What else can you do with it?" his father said. "A crippled horse is no good. It's just plain mercy to shoot it."

"Give it to me, Pa. I'll keep it lying down and heal it up."

"Yeah," his father said, without sarcasm and without mirth. "You could keep it lying down about one hour."

Bruce's mother came up next to him, as if the two of them were standing against the others. "Jim," she said quickly, "isn't there some kind of brace you could put on it? I remember my dad had a horse once that broke a leg below the knee, and he saved it that way."

"Not much chance," Enich said. "Both legs, like that." He plucked a weed and stripped the dry branches from the stalk. "You can't make a horse understand he has to keep still."

"But wouldn't it be worth trying?" she said. "Children's bones heal so fast, I should think a colt's would too."

"I don't know. There's an outside chance, maybe."

"Bo," she said to her husband, "why don't we try it? It seems such a shame, a lovely colt like that."

"I know it's a shame!" he said. "I don't like shooting colts any better than you do. But I never saw a broken-legged colt get well. It'd just be a lot of worry and trouble, and then you'd have to shoot it finally anyway."

"Please," she said. She nodded at him slightly, and then the eyes of both were on Bruce. He felt the tears coming up again, and turned to grope for the colt's ears. It tried to struggle to its feet, and Enich put his foot on its neck. The mare chuckled anxiously.

"How much this hobble brace kind of thing cost?" the father said finally. Bruce turned again, his mouth open with hope.

"Two–three dollars, is all," Enich said.

"You think it's got a chance?"

"One in a thousand, maybe."

"All right. Let's go see MacDonald."

"Oh, good!" Bruce's mother said, and put her arm around him tight.

"I don't know whether it's good or not," the father said. "We might wish we never did it." To Bruce he said, "It's your responsibility. You got to take complete care of it."

"I will!" Bruce said. He took his hand out of his pocket and rubbed below his eye with his knuckles. "I'll take care of it every day."

Big with contrition and shame and gratitude and the sudden sense of immense responsibility, he watched his father and Enich start for the house to get a tape measure. When they were thirty feet away he said loudly, "Thanks, Pa. Thanks an awful lot."

His father half turned, said something to Enich. Bruce stopped to stroke the colt, looked at his mother, started to laugh, and felt it turn horribly into a sob. When he turned away so that his mother wouldn't notice he saw his dog Spot looking inquiringly around the corner of the barn. Spot took three or four tentative steps and paused, wagging his tail. Very slowly (never speak loud or move fast around an animal) the boy bent and found a good-sized stone. He straightened casually, brought his arm back, and threw with all his might. The rock caught Spot squarely in the ribs. He yiped, tucked his tail, and scuttled around the barn, and Bruce chased him, throwing clods and stones and gravel, yelling, "Get out! Go on, get out of here or I'll kick you apart. Get out! Go on!"

So all that spring, while the world dried in the sun and the willows emerged from the floodwater and the mud left by the freshet hardened and caked among their roots, and the grass of the meadow greened and the river brush grew misty with tiny leaves and the dandelions spread yellow among the flats, Bruce tended his colt. While the other boys roamed the bench hills with .22's looking for gophers or rabbits or sage hens, he anxiously superintended the colt's nursing and watched it learn to nibble the grass. While his gang built a darkly secret hideout in the deep brush beyond Hazard's, he was currying and brushing and trimming the chestnut mane. When packs of boys ran hare and hounds through the town and around the river's slow bends, he perched on the front porch with his slingshot and a can full of small round stones, waiting for stray dogs to appear. He waged a holy war on the dogs until they learned to detour widely around his house, and he never did completely forgive his own dog, Spot. His whole life was wrapped up in the hobbled, leg-ironed chestnut colt with the slow-motion lunging walk and the affectionate nibbling lips.

Every week or so Enich, who was now working out of town at the Half Diamond Bar, rode in and stopped. Always, with that expressionless quiet that was terrible to the boy, he stood and looked the colt over, bent to feel pastern and fetlock, stood back to watch the plunging walk when the boy held out a handful of grass. His expression said nothing; whatever he thought was hidden back of his leathery face as the dark mole was hidden in the crease beside his mouth. Bruce found himself watching that mole sometimes, as if revelation might lie there. But when he pressed Enich to tell him, when he said, "He's getting better, isn't he? He walks better, doesn't he, Mr. Enich? His ankles don't bend so much, do they?" the wrangler gave him little encouragement.

"Let him be awhile. He's growin', sure enough. Maybe give him another month."

May passed. The river was slow and clear again, and some of the boys were already swimming. School was almost over. And still Bruce paid attention to nothing but Socks. He willed so strongly that the colt should get well that he grew furious even at Daisy when she sometimes wouldn't let the colt suck as much as he wanted. He took a butcher knife and cut the long tender grass in the fence corners, where Socks could not reach, and fed it to his pet by the handful. He trained him to nuzzle for sugar lumps in his pockets. And back in his mind was a fear: in the middle of June they would be going out to the homestead again, and if Socks weren't well by that time he might not be able to go.

"Pa," he said, a week before they planned to leave. "How much of a load are we going to have, going out to the homestead?"

"I don't know, wagonful, I suppose. Why?"

"I just wondered." He ran his fingers in a walking motion along the round edge of the dining table, and strayed into the other room. If they had a wagon-load, then there was no way Socks could be loaded in and taken along. And he couldn't walk fifty miles. He'd get left behind before they got up on the bench, hobbling along like the little crippled boy in the Pied Piper, and they'd look back and see him trying to run, trying to keep up.

That picture was so painful that he cried over it in bed that night. But in the morning he dared to ask his father if they couldn't take Socks along to the farm. His father turned on him eyes as sober as Jim Enich's, and when he spoke it was with a kind of tired impatience. "How can he go? He couldn't walk it."

"But I want him to go, Pa!"

"Brucie," his mother said, "don't get your hopes up. You know we'd do it if we could, if it was possible."

"But, Ma . . ."

His father said, "What you want us to do, haul a broken-legged colt fifty miles?"

"He'd be well by the end of the summer, and he could walk back."

"Look," his father said. "Why can't you make up your mind to it? He isn't getting well. He isn't going to get well."

"He is too getting well!" Bruce shouted. He half stood up at the table, and his father looked at his mother and shrugged.

"Please, Bo," she said.

"Well, he's got to make up his mind to it sometime," he said.

Jim Enich's wagon pulled up on Saturday morning, and Bruce was out the door before his father could rise from his chair. "Hi, Mr. Enich," he said.

"Hello, Bub. How's your pony?"

"He's fine," Bruce said. "I think he's got a lot better since you saw him last."

"Uh-huh." Enich wrapped the lines around the whipstock and climbed down. "Tell me you're leaving next week."

"Yes," Bruce said. "Socks is in the back."

When they got into the backyard Bruce's father was there with his hands behind his back, studying the colt as it hobbled around. He looked at Enich. "What do you think?" he said. "The kid here thinks his colt can walk out to the homestead."

"Uh-huh," Enich said. "Well, I wouldn't say that." He inspected the chestnut, scratched between his ears. Socks bobbed, and snuffled at his pockets. "Kid's made quite a pet of him."

Bruce's father grunted. "That's just the damned trouble."

"I didn't think he could walk out," Bruce said. "I thought we could take him in the wagon, and then he'd be well enough to walk back in the fall."

"Uh," Enich said. "Let's take his braces off for a minute."

He unbuckled the triple straps on each leg, pulled the braces off, and stood back. The colt stood almost as flat on his fetlocks as he had the morning he was born. Even Bruce, watching with his whole mind tight and apprehensive, could see that. Enich shook his head.

"You see, Bruce?" his father said. "It's too bad, but he isn't getting better. You'll have to make up your mind—"

"He will get better, though!" Bruce said. "It just takes a long time, is all." He looked at his father's face, at Enich's, and neither one had any hope in it. But when Bruce opened his mouth to say something else his father's

150

eyebrows drew down in sudden, unaccountable anger, and his hand made an impatient sawing motion in the air.

"We shouldn't have tried this in the first place," he said. "It just tangles everything up." He patted his coat pockets, felt in his vest. "Run in and get me a couple cigars."

Bruce hesitated, his eyes on Enich. "Run!" his father said harshly.

Reluctantly he released the colt's halter rope and started for the house. At the door he looked back, and his father and Enich were talking together, so low that their words didn't carry to where he stood. He saw his father shake his head, and Enich bend to pluck a grass stem. They were both against him, they both were sure Socks would never get well. Well, he would! There was some way.

He found the cigars, came out, watched them both light up. Disappointment was a sickness in him, and mixed with the disappointment was a question. When he could stand their silence no more he burst out with it. "But what are we going to *do*? He's got to have some place to stay."

"Look, kiddo." His father sat down on a sawhorse and took him by the arm. His face was serious and his voice gentle. "We can't take him out there. He isn't well enough to walk, and we can't haul him. So Jim here has offered to buy him. He'll give you three dollars for him, and when you come back, if you want, you might be able to buy him back. That is, if he's well. It'll be better to leave him with Jim."

"Well . . ." Bruce studied the mole on Enich's cheek. "Can you get him better by fall, Mr. Enich?"

"I wouldn't expect it," Enich said. "He ain't got much of a show."

"If anybody can get him better, Jim can," his father said. "How's that deal sound to you?"

"Maybe when I come back he'll be all off his braces and running around like a house afire," Bruce said. "Maybe next time I see him I can ride him." The mole disappeared as Enich tongued his cigar.

"Well, all right then," Bruce said, bothered by their stony-eyed silence. "But I sure hate to leave you behind, Socks, old boy."

151

"It's the best way all around," his father said. He talked fast, as if he were in a hurry. "Can you take him along now?"

"Oh, gee!" Bruce said. "Today?"

"Come on," his father said. "Let's get it over with."

Bruce stood by while they trussed the colt and hoisted him into the wagon box, and when Jim climbed in he cried out, "Hey, we forgot to put his hobbles back on." Jim and his father looked at each other.

His father shrugged. "All right," he said, and started putting the braces back on the trussed front legs.

"He might hurt himself if they weren't on," Bruce said. He leaned over the endgate stroking the white blazed face, and as the wagon pulled away he stood with tears in his eyes and the three dollars in his hand, watching the terrified straining of the colt's neck, the bony head raised above the endgate and one white eye rolling.

Five days later, in the sun-slanting, dew-wet spring morning, they stood for the last time that summer on the front porch, the loaded wagon against the front fence. The father tossed the key in his hand and kicked the door-jamb. "Well, good-bye, Old Paint," he said. "See you in the fall."

As they went to the wagon Bruce sang loudly,

> Good-bye, Old Paint, I'm leavin' Cheyenne,
> I'm leavin' Cheyenne, I'm goin' to Montana,
> Good-bye, Old Paint, I'm leavin' Cheyenne.

"Turn it off," his father said. "You want to wake up the whole town?" He boosted Bruce into the back end, where he squirmed and wiggled his way neck-deep into the luggage. His mother, turning to see how he was settled, laughed at him. "You look like a baby owl in a nest," she said.

His father turned and winked at him. "Open your mouth and I'll drop in a mouse."

It was good to be leaving; the thought of the homestead was exciting. If he could have taken Socks along it would have been perfect, but he had to admit, looking around at the jammed wagon box, that there sure wasn't any room for him. He continued to sing softly as they rocked out into the road and turned east toward MacKenna's house, where they were leaving the keys.

At the low, sloughlike spot that had become the town's dumpground the road split, leaving the dump like an island in the middle. The boy sniffed at the old familiar smells of rust and tar paper and ashes and refuse. He had collected a lot of old iron and tea lead and bottles and broken machinery and clocks, and once a perfectly good amber-headed cane, in that old dumpground. His father turned up the right fork, and as they passed the central part of the dump the wind, coming in from the northeast, brought a rotten, unbearable stench across them.

"Pee-you!" his mother said, and held her nose.

Bruce echoed her. "Pee-you! Pee-you-willy!" He clamped his nose shut and pretended to fall dead.

"Guess I better get to windward of that coming back," said his father.

They woke MacKenna up and left the key and started back. The things they passed were very sharp and clear to the boy. He was seeing them for the last time all summer. He noticed things he had never noticed so clearly before: how the hills came down into the river from the north like three folds in a blanket, how the stovepipe on the Chinaman's shack east of town had a little conical hat on it. He chanted at the things he saw. "Good-bye, old Chinaman. Good-bye, old Frenchman River. Good-bye, old Dumpground, good-bye."

"Hold your noses," his father said. He eased the wagon into the other fork around the dump. "Somebody sure dumped something rotten."

He stared ahead, bending a little, and Bruce heard him swear. He slapped the reins on the team till they trotted. "What?" the mother said. Bruce, half rising to see what caused the speed, saw her lips go flat over her teeth, and a look on her face like the woman he had seen in the traveling dentist's chair, when the dentist dug a living nerve out of her tooth and then got down on his knees to hunt for it, and she sat there half raised in her seat, her face lifted.

"For gosh sakes," he said. And then he saw.

He screamed at them. "Ma, it's Socks! Stop, Pa! It's Socks!"

His father drove grimly ahead, not turning, not speaking, and his mother shook her head without looking around. He screamed again, but neither of them turned. And when he dug down into the load, burrowing in and shaking with long smothered sobs, they still said nothing.

So they left town, and as they wound up the dugway to the south bench there was not a word among them except his father's low, "For Christ sakes, I thought he was going to take it out of town." None of them looked back at the view they had always admired, the flat river bottom green with spring, its village snuggled in the loops of river. Bruce's eyes, pressed against the coats and blankets under him until his sight was a red haze, could still see through it the bloated, skinned body of the colt, the chestnut hair left a little way above the hooves, the iron braces still on the broken front legs.

MANUEL BUAKEN

The Horse of the Sword

"Boy, get rid of that horse," said one of the wise old men from Abra where the racing horses thrive on the good Bermuda grass of Luzon uplands. "That's a bandit's horse. See that Sign of Evil on him. Something tragic will happen to you if you keep him."

But another one of the old horse traders who had gathered at that auction declared, "That's a good omen. The Sword he bears on his shoulder means leadership and power. He's a true mount for a chieftain. He's a free man's fighting horse."

As for me, I knew this gray colt was a wonder horse the moment I saw him. These other people were blind. They only saw that this gray, shaggy horse bore the marks of many whips, that his ribs almost stuck through his mangy hide, that his great eyes rolled in defiance and fear as the auctioneer approached him. They couldn't see the meaning of that Sword he bore—a marking not in the color, which was a uniform gray, but in the way that the hair had arranged itself permanently: it was parted to form an outline of a sword that was broad on his neck and tapered to a fine point on his shoulder.

Father, too, was blind against this horse. He argued with me and scolded, "Maning, when I promised you a pony as a reward for good work in high school English, I thought you'd use good judgment in choosing. It is true, this horse has good blood, for he came from the Santiago stables— they have raised many fine racers, but this colt has always been worthless. He is bad-tempered, would never allow himself to be bathed and curried,

155

and no one has ever been able to ride him. Now, that black over there is well trained—"

"Father, you promised I could choose for myself," I insisted. "I choose this horse. None of them can tame him, but I can. He's wild because his mouth is very tender—see how it is bled. That's his terrible secret."

My father always kept his promises, so he paid the few pesos they asked for this outlaw colt and made arrangements to have the animal driven, herded, up to our summer home in the hills.

"I used to play, but now I have work to do," I told Father. "I'll show you and everybody else what a mistake you made about my horse."

Father agreed with me solemnly, and smiled over my head at Mother, but she wasn't agreeing at all. "Don't you go near that bad horse your father foolishly let you buy. You know he has kicked so many people."

It hurt me to disobey Mother, and I consoled myself with the thought she'd change her mind when I had tamed my Horse of the Sword.

But could I win where all others, smart grown men, had failed? I could, if I was right. So early in the morning I slipped off to the meadow. The Horse of the Sword was cropping the grass industriously, but defiantly, alert for any whips. He snorted a warning at me, and backed away skittishly as I approached. "What a body you have," I said, talking to accustom him to my voice and to assure him of my peaceful intentions. "Wide between the shoulders—that's for strength and endurance. Long legs for speed, and a proud arched neck, that's some Arabian aristocracy you have in you, Sword Horse."

I kept walking slowly toward him and talking softly, until he stopped backing away. He neighed defiance at me, and his eyes rolled angrily, those big eyes that were so human in their dare and their appeal. He didn't move now as I inched closer, but I could see his muscles twitch. Very softly and gently I put my hand on his shoulder. He jumped away. I spoke softly and again put my hand on the Sword of his shoulder. This time he stood. I kept my hand on his shaggy shoulder. Then slowly I slipped it up to his head, then down again to his shoulder, down his legs to his fetlocks. It was a major victory.

That very day I began grooming him, currying his coat, getting out the collection of insects that had burrowed into his skin. He sometimes jumped away, but he never kicked at me. And next day I was able to lead my gray horse across the meadow to the spring, with my hand on his mane as his only guide—this "untamable outlaw" responded to my light touch. It was the simple truth—his mouth was too tender for a jerking bridle bit. The pain just drove him wild; that's all that had made him an outlaw. Gentle handling, no loud shouts, no jerks on his tender mouth, good food and a cleaned skin—these spelled health and contentment. Kindness had conquered. In a few days the gaunt hollows filled out with firm flesh to give the gray horse beauty. Reckless spirit he always had.

Every morning I slipped off to the meadow—Mother was anxious to have the house quiet so Father could write his pamphlet on the language and Christianization of the Tinggians, so I had a free hand. It didn't take more than a month to change my find from a raging outlaw to a miracle of glossy horseflesh. But was his taming complete? Could I ride him? Was he an outlaw at heart?

In the cool of a late afternoon, I mounted to his back. If he threw me I should be alone in my defeat and my fall would be cushioned by the grass. He trembled a little as I leaped to his back. But he stood quiet. He turned his head, his big eyes questioning me. Then, obedient to my "Kiph"—"Go"— he trotted slowly away.

I knew a thrill then, the thrill of mastery and of fleet motion on the back of this steed whose stride was so smooth, so much like flying. He ran about the meadow eagerly, and I turned him into the mountain lane. "I know how a butterfly feels as he skims along," I crowed delightedly. Down the lane where the trees made dappled shade around our high-roofed bungalow we flew along. Mother stood beside her cherished flame tree, watching sister Dominga as she pounded the rice.

The Horse of the Sword pranced into the yard. Mother gasped in amazement. "Mother, I disobeyed you," I blurted out quickly. "I'm sorry, but I had to show you, and you were wrong, everybody was wrong about this horse."

Mother tried to be severe with me, but soon her smile warmed me, and she said, "Yes, I was wrong, Maning. What have you named your new horse?"

"A new name for a new horse, that's a good idea. Mother, you must name him."

Mother's imagination was always alive. It gave her the name at once. "Glory, that's his name. *MoroGlorioso*. Gray Glory." So MoroGlory it was.

Too soon, vacation was over and I had to go back to school. But Moro-Glory went with me. "You take better care of that horse than you do of yourself," Father complained. "If you don't stop neglecting your lessons, I'll have the horse taken up to the mountain pasture again."

"Oh, no, Father, you can't do that," I exclaimed. "MoroGlory must be here for his lessons too. Every day I teach him and give him practice so that next spring, at the Feria, he is going to show his heels to all those fine horses they boast about so much."

Father knew what I meant. Those boasts had been mosquito bites in his mind too; for our barrio was known to be horse-crazy.

For instance, it was almost a scandal the way the Priest, Father Anastacio, petted his horse Tango. Tango ate food that was better than the priest's, they said. He was a beauty, nobody denied that, but the good Father's boasts were a little hard to take, especially for the Presidente.

The Presidente had said in public, "My Bandirado Boyo is a horse whose blood lines are known back to an Arabian stallion imported by the Conquistadores—these others are mere plow animals."

But the horse that really set the tongues wagging in Santa Lucia and in Candon was Allahsan, a gleaming sorrel who belonged to Bishop Aglipay and was said to share the Bishop's magic power. There were magic wings on his hooves, it was said, that let him carry the Bishop from Manila to Candon in one flying night.

Another boaster was the Municipal Treasurer—the Tesero, who had recently acquired a silver-white horse, Purao, the horse with the speed and power of the foam-capped waves.

The Chief of Police hung his head in shame now. His Castano had once been the pride of Santa Lucia, had beaten Katarman—the black satin horse from the nearby barrio of Katarman who had so often humbled Santa Lucia's pride. Much as the horses of Santa Lucia set their owners to boasting against one another, all united against Katarman. Katarman, so the tale went, was so enraged if another horse challenged him that he ran until the muscles of his broad withers parted and blood spattered from him upon his rider, but he never faltered till his race was won.

These were the boasts and boasters I had set out to dust with defeat.

Winter was soon gone, the rice harvested and the sugar cane milled. Graduation from high school approached. At last came the Feria day, and people gathered, the ladies in sheer flowing gowns of many colors, the men in loose flowing shirts over cool white trousers. Excitement was a wild thing in the wind at the Feria, for the news of the challenge of the wonder horse MoroGlory had spread. I could hear many people shouting "*Caballo a Bintuangin*—The Horse of the Sword." These people were glad to see the once-despised outlaw colt turn by magic change into the barrio's pride. They were cheering for my horse, but the riders of the other horses weren't cheering. I was a boy, riding an untried and yet feared horse. They didn't want me there, so they raised the entrance fee. But Father had fighting blood also, and he borrowed the money for the extra fee.

As we paraded past the laughing, shouting crowds in the Plaza, the peddlers who shouted "Sinuman—Delicious Cascarones" stopped selling these coconut sweets and began to shout the praises of their favorite. I heard them calling: "Allahsan for me. Allahsan has magic hooves." The people of Katarman's village were very loud. They cried out: "Katarman will win. Katarman has the muscles of the carabao. Katarman has the speed of the deer."

The race was to be a long-distance trial of speed and endurance—run on the Provincial Road for a racetrack. A mile down to the river, then back to the Judge's stand in the Plaza.

MoroGlory looked them over, all the big-name horses. I think he measured his speed against them and knew they didn't have enough. I looked them over too. I was so excited, yet I knew I must be on guard as the man who walks where the big snakes hide. These riders were experienced; so were their horses. MoroGlory had my teaching only. I had run him this same course many times. MoroGlory must not spend his strength on the first mile; he must save his speed for a sprint. In the high school, I had made the track team. An American coach had taught me, and I held this teaching in my head now.

The starter gave his signal and the race began. Allahsan led out at a furious pace; the other horses set themselves to overtake him. It hurt my pride to eat the dust of all the others—all the way out the first mile. I knew it must be done. "Oomh, easy," I commanded, and MoroGlory obeyed me as always. We were last, but MoroGlory ran that mile featherlight on his feet.

At the river's bank all the horses turned quickly to begin the fateful last mile. The Flagman said, "Too late, Boy," but I knew MoroGlory.

I loosened the grip I held and he spurted ahead in flying leaps. In a few space-eating strides he overtook the tiring Allahsan. The pacesetter was breathing in great gasps. "Where are your magic wings?" I jeered as we passed.

"*Kiph*," I urged MoroGlory. I had no whip. I spoke to my horse and knew he would do his best. I saw the other riders lashing their mounts. Only MoroGlory ran as he willed.

Oh, it was a thrill, the way MoroGlory sped along, flew along, his hooves hardly seeming to touch the ground. The wind whipped at my face and I yelled just for pleasure. MoroGlory thought I was commanding more speed and he gave it. He flattened himself closer to the ground as his long legs reached forward for more and more. Up, and up. Past the strong horses from Abra, past the bright Tango. Bandirado Boyo was next in line. "How the Presidente's daughter will cry to see her Bandirado Boyo come trailing home, his banner tail in the dust," I said to myself as MoroGlory surged past him. The Tesero's Purao yielded his place without a struggle.

Now there was only Katarman, the black thunder horse ahead, but several lengths ahead. Could MoroGlory make up this handicap in this short distance, for we were at the Big Mango tree—this was the final quarter.

"Here it is, MoroGlory. This is the big test." I shouted. "Show Katarman how your Sword conquers him."

Oh, yes, MoroGlory could do it. And he did. He ran shoulder to shoulder with Katarman.

I saw that Katarman's rider was swinging his whip wide. I saw it came near to MoroGlory's head. I shouted to the man and the wind brought his answering curse at me. I must decide now—decide between MoroGlory's danger and the winning of the race. That whip might blind him. I knew no winning was worth that. I pulled against him, giving up the race.

MoroGlory had always obeyed me. He always responded to my lightest touch. But this time my sharp pull at his bridle brought no response. He had the bit between his teeth. Whip or no whip, he would not break his stride. And so he pulled ahead of Katarman.

"MoroGlory—The Horse of the Sword," the crowd cheered as the gray horse swept past the judges, a winner by two lengths.

I leaped from his back and caught his head. Blood streamed down the side of his head, but his eyes were unharmed. The Sword on his shoulder was touched with a few drops of his own blood.

Men also leaped at Katarman, dragged his rider off and punished him before the Judges could interfere. The winner's wreath and bright ribbon went to MoroGlory, and we paraded in great glory. I was so proud. The Horse of the Sword had run free, without a whip, without spurs. He had proved his leadership and power. He had proved himself a "true mount for a chieftain, a free man's fighting horse," as the old Wise Man had said.

Golden days followed for MoroGlorioso. Again and again we raced—in Vigan, in Abra, and always MoroGlory won.

Then came the day when my Father said, "The time has come for you, my son, to prove your Sword, as MoroGlory proved his. You must learn to be a leader," Father said.

And so I sailed away to America, to let the world know my will. As MoroGlory had proved himself, so must I.

OF HORSES AND MEN

JOYCE CARY

Bush River

A black pony, tied by one leg to the stump of a tree, was eating corn from a wooden bowl. A little brown soldier groomed it furiously, prancing round it in poses of dramatic violence, and twisting his face, like his body, every moment into some unexpected form. Sweat poured down his cheeks and bare chest, on which an identity disc and a leather amulet, on separate cords, performed a kind of African minuet. After every few strokes, he fell back a yard, passing his quivering hand, as small and nervous as a child's, upwards over his whole face and cried loudly in Hausa, "Oh—beautiful—oh, the lovely one. Oh, God bless him. See how he shines."

A young officer with an eyeglass in his right eye walked slowly round pony and groom. Now and then he glanced severely upon both. Everything about him, his clipped hair which left him almost bald, his clipped moustache, even his eyeglass increased this air of severity, of an austere and critical aloofness.

"Now then, Mamadu," he said impatiently, "get on with it. What about the tail?"

"Oh, what a tail. Did you ever see such a tail?"

"I never saw such a dirty one."

The little soldier pulled his face into a long, dolorous oval and sent his eyebrows to the top of his skull. But the officer did not notice this performance. He had walked down to the riverbank.

The river was an African river never yet banked up, tamed, dredged, canalized; a river still wild. It poured along in tan-colored flood, carrying with it whole trees, and every part of its surface showed a different agitation. Here it was all in foaming breakers, suddenly cut off by a spear-shaped eddy like pulled brown silk; beyond the eddy was a dark sea, with crisp waves jumping, like a wind flaw; and over on the far side, long manila ropes of water which seemed to turn upon themselves as they were dragged under the banks. This savage river not only moved with agile power; it worked. One saw it at work, digging out its own bed, eating at its banks. Every moment some bluff crumbled; stones, bushes fell and vanished.

The young officer, like most people, found a certain attraction in all rivers and moving waters. But African rivers fascinated him. Looking at them he understood that old phrase "the devouring element." He asked himself how Africa survived against such destruction. At the same time, he thought, how magnificent was the gesture with which Africa abandoned herself to be torn, like a lioness who stretches herself in the sun while her cubs bite at her.

A thin old sergeant, with extremely bandy legs, marched up, gave a sketchy wartime salute, and said in a grumbling voice, "Captain Corner, sir."

"Yes, sergeant?"

"Germans, sir. They come."

Young Corner withdrew his eyes slowly from the fascinating river and looked once more at the pony, which had taken its nose from the bowl to nibble at the orderly's legs. He said severely, "Don't forget the tail, Mamadu."

And once more he walked slowly round, frowning through his eyeglass at the pony.

It was a Barbary stallion, jet black except beneath the belly, which showed a tinge of bronze. It had legs which looked too fine for its body, a crest like the Parthenon chargers and a forelock swinging to its nose. The little head, with full round eyes and tilted nostrils, was like a stag's. The ears were small and pointed, curled like the husks of an almond.

Corner had never before owned a pony of such quality and he was obsessed with the creature. Indeed he had already committed a great folly for its sake. A week before he had received a command regarded by himself and most of his brother officers as a special distinction, a step to promotion. He was to take charge of a sticky and dangerous operation, the planning of a route through the heart of enemy country, by which a heavy gun could be dragged, in secret, to Mora mountain, a German stronghold that had held out against two assaults. It was thought that the fire of this gun, taking the Germans by surprise, would not only smash their defenses on the mountaintop but break the morale of their local troops, who could have no experience of high explosive.

This was the year 1915, before the days of bombing by planes. The Cameroons campaign of 1914–16, against the German army of occupation, was a war of raids, ambushes, sieges, enormous marches, and especially surprises. There was no reconnaissance by air, no radio, and intelligence could only be got by scouts and spies. Whole columns would disappear for weeks together, to burst out, a thousand miles away, upon a panic-stricken capital. Two patrols would stumble upon each other by accident in high jungle and stare with amazement for a few seconds before grabbing their rifles.

The strategy of such a war was that of the old bush fighters who knew the jungle, who did not expect a field of fire in order to secure a position, who understood how to place a listening sentry in a tree, who could distinguish between the cough of a leopard and a husky, bored Negro *hauptmann* wandering from his post to look for a chicken, who could take a thousand men in line through thick scrub without losing touch and change front without their shooting each other.

Corner's instructions were to avoid anything like a road or even a used track. They were likely to be watched. He was not even to cross a road by daylight. He was to plot his line as far as possible through untouched bush, to avoid any indication that might put the enemy patrols on the alert, and to hide by night.

Officers in that campaign were allowed their horses, but only in the main column—never on scout, point, or patrol duty. For one thing, Nigerian horses in use are all stallions; they will scream at the most distant scent of a mare. For another, a man on a horse can be seen above the top of all but the tallest grass. Corner's assignment was actually that of a man on scout duty all the way. But he had not been able to persuade himself to leave his darling pony behind in some horse lines to be neglected by strangers, starved by thieving camp orderlies, or borrowed by some subaltern for a forced march, or be left dying in a swamp. Few men who parted from their horses in that war ever saw them again. Corner knew his duty, but he said to himself that most of his course lay through high bush where a horse would be as easily hidden as a man. "And as for mares, there won't be any about— the villages are empty." But already twice Satan had imagined mares and sent out a trumpet as good as a bugle call for every German within a mile.

Each of these tremendous neighs had scattered the men, diving for cover, and startled the young man out of himself. Each time, in the awful silence which followed, he had sat waiting for a shot, and thinking with amazement, "My God, what a goddamn bloody fool I was to bring this bloody pony. What a hell-fired ass I am." And the amazement was even stronger than the anger. It was as though he discovered for the first time his own folly, his own mysterious power to forget, simply to abolish common sense and walk gravely, with the most reasonable, dignified air, into impossible situations.

The men creeping back from the scrub would look sulkily at the barb still walking on his toes with ears cocked and nostrils flared. They hated Satan for these alarums. And that was why the young man now said to the sergeant, "After all the row you've been making down there." He was defending his darling. He was saying, "You complain of my pony, but what about your chatter?" And even while he said it, he was ashamed of himself, he was amazed at his own small-mindedness. "Not like that, Mamadu— don't tear at it." He took the comb out of the man's hands.

"Captain, sir. Captain Corner, sir." The sergeant made another wartime salute, and cried in a voice unexpectedly shrill, "We see 'em, sir."

Corner, understanding these words at last, looked with surprise at the sergeant and said, "Who see who, Sargy?"

"Germans, sir. We see 'em, over the river. And the river too big. He too big."

"That's the style," Corner murmured to the orderly. He took the excuse of stroking the pony's croup, as if to test the grooming. He did not like to show too openly his passion before Mamadu in case of provoking the latter's admiring outcries, which, for some reason, got on his nerves. His severe air was in fact a defense against this noise and exaggerated praise. "Gently does it," he said, and Mamadu cried, "Oh, what hair—what a tail. God save us, it touches the ground."

Corner carefully unraveled the tail; Satan, having ground up every bit of corn in the bowl, turned his delicate nose and began to eat the tree stump. His tail switched in the young man's hand, and he glanced sideways at his master. The large black eyes, more brilliant under the thick short lashes than any woman's, expressed something which always gave Corner acute pleasure, though he could scarcely have described it, except by the words, "The little bastard don't give a damn for me or anybody else."

He frowned and said, "Eating still—this horse would eat anything."

The sergeant turned and walked off, humping his right shoulder in a peculiar manner.

"Oh, a lovely eater—it's a marvel how he eats. Why, he'll eat a desert round himself wherever he is."

The orderly quite understood that Corner's critical look was simply the outward manner of his obsession; a lover's constraint. Like a lady's maid, he easily penetrated his master's mind. And Corner, like a lady, slightly resented it. He said illogically, "Then why don't you groom him properly? Look at that mane—look at the dust in the roots."

"But, sir, it's too thick—just see how thick. Holy God, a wonder for thickness."

The sergeant reappeared under the huge trees which surrounded the little mud flat. His shoulder was now almost at his ear and he had also begun to limp. He said flatly, "We no cross here, sir—he too bad place."

"But we have to cross here; it's the only good place for the gun."

The duty of the party was to discover if it were practicable to drag a French 75 a hundred miles through the unmapped bush to a certain rendezvous. The idea was to surprise the Germans with this gun, which ranked, in Africa, as heavy artillery.

"The men, they say they no fit to cross."

"Why?" Corner was startled. He looked thoughtfully at the sergeant. "There's nobody there, you're not afraid of demons, are you?" he asked.

Sergeant Umaru had, in fact, a great terror of demons, especially in strange bush, and his fear sometimes infected his men. But the men were already frightened of the river, the Germans, or demons. Corner found them huddled in a group on the bank, staring through the scrub across the roaring stream. Their faces had the look of panic, a loosened appearance of the flesh had turned soft and sagged a little from the bone. Mouths were hanging slack; one young soldier was showing his lower teeth.

"What's the trouble?" Corner was saying. "There's no Germans within miles. And this river is too fast for crocodiles or water spirits."

He was fond of his men and knew them well—brave and cool in action, but subject to unexpected and mysterious panics.

"It's a bad place," a lance corporal muttered, rolling his eyes about like a child in a cellar.

"Nonsense, it's a very good place. Mamadu, saddle up. Where are the swimmers for the loads?"

On the evening before, there had been eight volunteers eager to take charge of the loads—rifles, ammunition, and rations floated on gourds—but now there were none. Corner looked round him with an air of surprise, which was purely formal. His mind was scarcely interested in this crisis. He was preoccupied with the river. "A very good place," he murmured. "Where's the guide for the ford?"

"No guide, sir—he no come."

"No guide." He was startled. And then at once he felt a peculiar sense of anticipation. Not of pleasure, scarcely of excitement. It was as if an opportunity had opened itself before the young man, a gate in the wall of his routine, through which his mind already began to flow. Or rather the force

170

which poured eagerly through this gap was not his at all but that peculiar energy which had possessed him for days; the energy of his passion for Satan, for the wild bush, especially for the wild river. The different streams rushed together at the same gap, and their joined forces where overwhelming. They swept away the whole bank, the whole wall. Young Corner looked severely upon his men and said in a voice of resignation, "I suppose you want me to give you a lead. Bring Satan, Mamadu."

Satan was brought. He stretched out his shining neck and nibbled the tassel on the sergeant's fez. But no one laughed. The men were quite dissolved in panic. While Corner mounted, they gazed at him with round eyes which seemed to be liquefying with fear.

The little sergeant alone had his surly veteran's composure. He hitched up his whole right arm and muttered, "Very bad river, sir. Them crocodiles live, sir. Them Germans live other side, I see 'em."

But Corner did not even listen to him. He had been carried far away from any notion of Germans, of crocodiles. He had no mind for anything but the river and Satan beneath him, who, by means of the magnificent river, was going to achieve a triumph. He held out each leg in turn to Mamadu to pull off his boots. Bare-legged, he hooked his big toe through the sides of the stirrup irons, gave his eyeglass an additional screw, and jammed on his hat, a disreputable terai. Then, for the first time, he examined the river, not as a fascinating object, but as an obstacle. He measured the weight of the current and the direction of the eddies.

He had swum horses before, but only for a few yards—once on a road after a storm, once in a river pool—never in flood water.

It was not a thing one set out to do. On an ordinary journey, the groom took horses across unbridged rivers from a boat, holding them short by head ropes to keep their noses up. A man who chose to swim his own horse when a boat or a ford was available would have seemed quite mad; and if he managed to drown himself or his horse, he would also seem irresponsible.

Corner, at twenty-six, was an extremely conventional young officer, a little bit of a dandy, a good deal of a coxcomb. He had a strong prejudice against the unusual. It seemed to him affected and he hated affectation. And what gave him a calm personal delight in this opportunity seized upon so eagerly by the forces which possessed him was the knowledge that he *had* to swim this river. He had a first-class excuse for doing what he had often wanted to do. He told himself that he was not his own master, not in any sense of the word.

Satan stepped into the water, moving as usual with the precise muscular liveliness of a dancer, and obeying signals that his rider had not consciously given, the shade of a leg pressure, the very beginning of a wrist turn.

A corporal called out suddenly, "Don't go there, sir—we find them ford, sir."

Satan's breast was already under water. He lifted his head; he was swimming within five yards of the bank.

Corner, up to the neck as Satan's hindquarters sank beneath him, took his feet out of the stirrups, hooked his right hand into the pommel of the saddle and floated over it. He found at once that he had no control over the pony. He could only talk to him in Hausa, "Keep at it, friend—straight ahead."

And when he spoke, he felt an affection for the little horse, an exultant pride in his courage, so different in quality from anything he had known before that it could not be described. It was more than sympathy, more than the bantering love of a friend; it was a feeling so strong that it seemed to have its own life, full of delight and worship; laughing at Satan and rejoicing in all devotion and courage; the mysterious greatness of the spirit. He wanted to laugh, to call out, like Mamadu. But again, as if constrained by decorum or a sense of what was proper to his responsibilities, he merely looked severe and repeated, this time in English, "Keep it up, old boy—that's the stuff."

They were now in mid-current. At this level, the river seemed a mile wide and the waves a little ocean storm. The far bank was a mere line on the horizon. A tree trunk, turning its branches like an enormous screw, went swinging past, three yards from Satan's nose. Satan turned an ear back as if expecting some remark, but his nose never deviated an inch from the course. It pointed like a compass at the opposite bank, now passing at a speed which seemed like a train's.

Once only he showed some emotion, when a wave splashed into his nose. He then gave a snort, not the short loud snort of indignation or surprise, but the longer exhalation which means enquiry and suspended judgment. The bank was now close and it proved to be extremely high and steep—what's more, the eddy under the bank was like a millstream. Satan seemed to be deeper in the water. Another wave struck him in the nose and he snorted loud and sharp. Corner thought, "If he turns back, we're done."

But Satan obviously had no notion of turning back. Possibly he was too stupid to think of it; or perhaps wise enough to know its danger. Perhaps it was not in the habit of his mind and breeding to turn back. He struck with his forefeet at the clay, now flying past at the rate of four miles an hour. But it was as hard as brick above water level, and his unshod hooves brought down only small shoots of dust. Corner murmured, "That's it, old boy, go at it." But he did not see exactly what was to be gone at. They whirled along the bank and Satan continued to stab at it furiously; he sank suddenly over his nose and, coming up again with a terrific snort, again stabbed and again sank.

They were carried round a point and struck a snag, itself caught against a stump. The cliff behind was breached by some recent avalanche which was heaped among the roots of the stump. Corner threw himself on the snag and backed up the slope, hauling on the reins. Satan made a powerful effort and heaved himself out of the river. In a moment both were on the level ground ten feet above, among short bushes.

Corner felt as if he too had swum a river. He was tired as only a swimmer can be. He chose a patch of young grass and lay flat on his back, holding Satan by the loose rein.

Suddenly he heard a click and turned his head towards it. Over a bush, not ten yards away, he saw the outline of a head in a German soldier's cap and a rifle barrel.

"The Germans," he thought, or rather the realization exploded inside his brain like a bomb on a time fuse, illuminating a whole landscape of the mind. He was stupefied again by the spectacle of his own enormous folly, but also by something incomprehensible behind it and about it. And it was with a kind of despair that he said to himself, "You've done it at last, you fool. You asked for it. But why, why—"

He hadn't even a revolver, so he lay quite still, fatalistic, but not resigned. For he was resentful. He detested this monster of his own stupidity.

At the same time, he was in great terror, the calm helpless terror of the condemned. He was holding his breath for the shot. He had a queer sensation so vivid that he still remembered it twenty years after, of floating lightly off the ground.

Nothing happened. There was a deep silence. And then suddenly a cold touch on his bare calf made him shiver. But he perceived at once that it was Satan's nose. The pony wanted a tuft of grass that was just under his leg.

The young man jumped up and looked angrily at the bushes. But no German fired.

"Captain." The sergeant's voice behind was full of exultation. Dripping, he saluted almost well enough for a recruit on parade.

"Oh, you've got over at last." Corner turned upon the man.

"All present, sir." And he saluted again. "We find them ford—dem guide come."

"I suppose he was there all the time. We stop here. We'll have to ramp this bank. Put out two pickets at once. And tell the men to keep on the alert."

The men, shouting and laughing in triumph as they climbed the bank, were annoyed to be put on picket. They were quite sure that there were no Germans within miles. As the sergeant said in Hausa, "If the Germans were here, they would have fired before this."

Corner, with a brisk efficient air, marched up and down, inspected the pickets, pegged out a section of bank to be cut away. He could hear the orderly's voice raised in a song of praise loud enough to reach his ear, and intended to do so.

"Oh, the marvelous swimmer. Oh, the brave horse. Oh, princely horse—the worthy son of kings among horses. Look at him, my brothers. How nobly he moves his lovely ears. Oh, wise horse, he's as wise as a clerk.

God bless him in his bravery—in his beauty. Oh, God bless him in his eating."

Corner frowned and walked further away, as if from contagion. Why had that German not fired—orders to give no alarms?—panic at the sudden appearance of his own men coming up the bank in force? But what was the good of wondering at chance, at luck, here in Africa? Next time it would be different.

He turned his thought from the event, from Satan—he would not even look at the river. But all the more, they were present to his feeling, the feeling of one appointed to a special fate, to gratitude.

We'll Have Fun

It was often said of Tony Costello that there was nothing he did not know about horses. No matter whom he happened to be working for—as coachman, as hostler, as blacksmith—he would stop whatever he was doing and have a look at an ailing horse and give advice to the owner who had brought the horse to Tony. His various employers did not object; they had probably sometime in the past gotten Tony's advice when he was working for someone else, and they would do so again sometime in the future. A year was a long time for Tony to stay at a job; he would quit or he would get the sack, find something else to do, and stay at that job until it was time to move on. He had worked for some employers three or four times. They would rehire him in spite of their experience with his habits, and if they did not happen to have a job open for him, they would at least let him bed down in their haylofts. He did not always ask their permission for this privilege, but since he knew his way around just about every stable in town—private and livery—he never had any trouble finding a place to sleep. He smoked a pipe, but everybody knew he was careful about matches and emptying the pipe and the kerosene heaters that were in most stables. And even when he was not actually in the service of the owner of a stable, he more than earned his sleeping privilege. An owner would go out to the stable in the morning and find that the chores had been done. "Oh, hello, Tony," the owner would say. "Since when have you been back?"

"I come in last night."

"I don't have a job for you," the owner would say.

"That's all right. Just a roof over me head temporarily. You're giving that animal too much oats again. Don't give him no oats at night, I told you."

"Oh, all right. Go in the kitchen and the missus will give you some breakfast. That is, if you want any breakfast. You smell like a saloon."

"Yes, this was a bad one, a real bad one. All I want's a cup of coffee, if that's all right?"

"One of these nights you'll walk in front of a yard engine."

"If I do I hope I'll have the common sense to get out of the way. And if I don't it'll be over pretty quick."

"Uh-huh. Well, do whatever needs to be done and I'll pay you two dollars when I get back this evening."

The owner could be sure that by the end of the day Tony would have done a good cleaning job throughout the stable, and would be waiting in patient agony for the money that would buy the whiskey that cured the rams. "I got the rams so bad I come near taking a swig of the kerosene," he would say. He would take the two dollars and half walk, half run to the nearest saloon, but he would be back in time to feed and bed down the owner's horse.

It would take a couple of days for him to get back to good enough shape to go looking for a steady job. If he had the right kind of luck, the best of luck, he would hear about a job as coachman. The work was not hard, and the pay was all his, not to be spent on room and board. The hardest work, though good pay, was in a blacksmith's shop. He was not young any more, and it took longer for his muscles to get reaccustomed to the work. Worst of all, as the newest blacksmith he was always given the job of shoeing mules, which were as treacherous as a rattlesnake and as frightening. He hated to shoe a mule or a Shetland pony. There were two shops in town where a mule could be tied up in the stocks, the apparatus that held the animal so securely that it could not kick; but a newly shod mule, released from the stocks, was likely to go crazy and kill a man. If he was going to die that way, Tony wanted his executioner to be a horse, not a goddamn mule.

And if he was going to lose a finger or a chunk of his backside, let it be a horse that bit him and not a nasty little bastard ten hands high. Blacksmithing paid the best and was the job he cared the least for, and on his fiftieth birthday Tony renounced it forever. "Not for fifty dollars a week will I take another job in a blacksmith's," he swore.

"You're getting pretty choosy, if you ask me," said his friend Murphy. "Soon there won't be no jobs for you of any kind, shape, or form. The ottomobile is putting an end to the horse. Did you ever hear tell of the Squadron A in New York City?"

"For the love of Jesus, did I ever hear tell of it? Is that what you're asking me? Well, if I was in New York City I could lead you to it blindfolded, Ninety-something-or-other and Madison Avenue, it is, on the right-hand side going up. And before I come to this miserable town the man I worked for's son belonged to it. Did I ever hear tell of the Squadron A!"

"All right. What is it now?" said Murphy.

"It's the same as it always was—a massive brick building on the right-hand side—"

"The organ-i-zation, I'm speaking of," said Murphy.

"Well, the last I seen in the papers, yesterday or the day before, this country was ingaged in mortal combat with Kaiser Wilhelm the Second. I therefore hazard the guess that the organ-i-zation is fighting on our side against the man with the withered arm."

"Fighting how?"

"Bravely, I'm sure."

"With what for weapons?"

"For weapons? Well, being a cavalry regiment I hazard the guess that they're equipped with sabre and pistol."

"There, you see? You're not keeping up to date with current happenings. Your Squadron A that you know so much about don't have a horse to their name. They're a machine-gun outfit."

"Well, that of course is a God damn lie, Murphy."

"A lie, is it? Well how much would you care to bet me—in cash?"

"Let me take a look and see how much I have on me?" said Tony. He placed his money on the bar. "Eighteen dollars and ninety-four cents. Is this even money, or do I have to give you odds?"

Murphy placed nineteen dollars on the bar. "Even money'll be good enough for me, bein's it's like taking the money off a blind man."

"And how are we to settle who's right?" said Tony.

"We'll call up the newspaper on the telephone."

"What newspaper? There's no newspaper here open after six P.M."

"We'll call the New York *World*," said Murphy.

"By long distance, you mean? Who's to pay for the call?"

"The winner of the bet," said Murphy.

"The winner of the bet? Oh, all right. I'll be magnanimous. How do you go about it? You can't put that many nickels in the slot."

"We'll go over to the hotel and get the operator at the switchboard, Mary McFadden. She's used to these long-distance calls."

"Will she be on duty at this hour?"

"Are you trying to back out? It's only a little after eight," said Murphy.

"Me back out? I wished I could get the loan of a hundred dollars and I'd show you who's backing out," said Tony.

In silence they marched to the hotel, and explained their purpose to Mary McFadden. Within fifteen minutes they were connected with the office of *The World*, then to the newspaper library. "Good evening, sir," said Murphy. "This is a long-distance call from Gibbsville, Pennsylvania. I wish to request the information as to whether the Squadron A is in the cavalry or a machine-gun organ-i-zation." He repeated the question and waited. "He says to hold the line a minute."

"Costing us a fortune," said Tony.

"Hello? Yes, I'm still here. Yes? Uh-huh. Would you kindly repeat that information?" Murphy quickly handed the receiver to Tony Costello, who listened, nodded, said "Thank you," and hung up.

"How much do we owe you for the call, Mary?" said Murphy.

"Just a minute," said the operator. "That'll be nine dollars and fifty-five cents."

"Jesus," said Tony. "Well, one consolation. It's out of your profit, Murphy."

"But the profit is out of your pocket," said Murphy. "Come on, we'll go back and I'll treat you. Generous in victory, that's me. Like Ulysses S. Grant. He give all them Confederates their horses back, did you ever know that, Costello?"

"I did not, and what's more I don't believe it."

"Well, maybe you'd care to bet on that, too? Not this evening, however, bein's you're out of cash. But now will you believe that the ottomobile is putting an end to the horse?"

"Where does the ottomobile come into it? The machine gun is no ottomobile."

"No, and I didn't say it was, but if they have no use for the cavalry in a war, they'll soon have no use for them anywhere."

"If you weren't such a pinch of snuff I'd give you a puck in the mouth. But don't try my patience too far, Mr. Murphy. I'll take just so much of your impudence and no more. With me one hand tied behind me I could put you in hospital."

"You're kind of a hard loser, Tony. You oughtn't to be that way. There's more ottomobiles in town now than horses. The fire companies are all motorizing. The breweries. And the rich, you don't see them buying a new pair of cobs no more. It's the Pierce-Arrow now. Flannagan the undertaker is getting rid of his blacks, he told me so himself. Ordered a Cunningham 8."

"We'll see where Flannagan and his Cunningham 8 ends up next winter, the first time he has to bring a dead one down from the top of Fairview Street. Or go up it, for that matter. There's hills in this town no Cunningham 8 will negotiate, but Flannagan's team of blacks never had the least trouble. Flannagan'll be out of business the first winter, and it'll serve him right."

"And here I thought he was a friend of yours. Many's the time you used his stable for a boudoir, not to mention the funerals you drove for him. Two or three dollars for a half a day's work."

"There never was no friendship between him and I. You never saw me stand up to a bar and have a drink with him. You never saw me set foot inside his house, nor even his kitchen for a cup of coffee. The rare occasions that I slept in his barn, he was never the loser, let me tell you. Those blacks that he's getting rid of, I mind the time I saved the off one's life from the colic. Too tight-fisted to send for Doc McNary, the vet, and he'd have lost the animal for sure if I wasn't there. Do you know what he give me for saving the horse? Guess what he give me."

"Search me," said Murphy.

"A pair of gloves. A pair of gauntlets so old that the lining was all wore away. Supposed to be fleece-lined, but the fleece was long since gone. 'Here, you take these, Tony,' said Mr. Generous Flannagan. I wanted to say 'Take them and do what with them?' But I was so dead tired from being up all night with the black, all I wanted to do was go up in his hayloft and lie down exhausted. Which I did for a couple of hours, and when I come down again there was the black, standing on his four feet and give me a whinny. A horse don't have much brains, but they could teach Flannagan gratitude."

After the war the abandonment of horses became so general that even Tony Costello was compelled to give in to it. The small merchants of the town, who had kept a single horse and delivery wagon (and a carriage for Sunday), were won over to Ford and Dodge trucks. The three-horse hitches of the breweries disappeared and in their place were big Macks and Garfords. The fire companies bought American LaFrances and Whites. The physicians bought Franklins and Fords, Buicks and Dodges. (The Franklin was air-cooled; the Buick was supposed to be a great hill climber.) And private citizens who had never felt they could afford a horse and buggy, now went into debt to purchase flivvers. Of the three leading harness shops in the town, two became luggage shops and one went out of business entirely. Only two of the seven blacksmith shops remained. Gone were the Fleischmann's Yeast and Grand Union Tea Company wagons, the sorrels and greys of the big express companies. The smooth-surface paving caused a high mortality rate among horses, who slipped and broke legs and had to be shot and carried away to the fertilizer plant. The horse was retained only by the rich and the poor; saddle horses for the rich, and swaybacked old nags for the junk men and fruit peddlers. For Tony Costello it was not so easy as it once had been to find a place to sleep. The last livery stable closed in 1922, was converted into a public garage, and neither the rats nor Tony Costello had a home to go to, he said. "No decent, self-respecting rat will live in a garridge," he said. "It's an inhuman smell, them gazzoline fumes. And the rats don't have any more to eat there than I do meself."

The odd jobs that he lived on made no demands on his skill with horses, but all his life he had known how to take proper care of the varnish and the brightwork of a Brewster brougham, the leather and the bits and buckles of all kinds of tack. He therefore made himself useful at washing cars and polishing shoes. Nobody wanted to give him a steady job, but it was more sensible to pay Tony a few dollars than to waste a good mechanic on a car wash. He had a flexible arrangement with the cooks at two Greek restaurants who, on their own and without consulting the owners, would give him a meal in exchange for his washing dishes. "There ain't a man in the town has hands any cleaner than mine. Me hands are in soapy water morning, noon, and night," he said.

"It's too bad the rest of you don't get in with your hands," said Murphy. "How long since you had a real bath, Tony?"

"Oh, I don't know."

"As the fellow says, you take a bath once a year whether you need it or not," said Murphy. "And yet I never seen you need a shave, barring the times you were on a three-day toot."

"Even then I don't often let her grow more'n a couple days. As long as I can hold me hand steady enough so's I don't cut me throat. That's a temptation, too, I'll tell you. There's days I just as soon take the razor in me hand and let nature take its course."

"What stops you?" said Murphy.

"That I wonder. Mind you, I don't wonder too much or the logical conclusion would be you-know-what. My mother wasn't sure who my father was. She didn't keep count. She put me out on the streets when I was eight or nine years of age. 'You can read and write,' she said, which was more than she could do. With my fine education I was able to tell one paper from another, so I sold them."

"You mean she put you out with no place to sleep?"

"Oh, no. She let me sleep there, providing she didn't have a customer. If I come home and she had a customer I had to wait outside."

"I remember you telling me one time your father worked for a man that had a son belonged to the Squadron A. That time we had the bet."

"That was a prevarication. A harmless prevarication that I thought up on the spur of the moment. I ought to know better by this time. Every time I prevaricate I get punished for it. That time I lost the bet. I should have said I knew about the Squadron A and let it go at that, but I had to embellish it. I always knew about the Squadron A. From selling newspapers in the Tenderloin I got a job walking hots at the race track, and I was a jock till I got too big. I couldn't make the weight any more, my bones were too heavy regardless of how much I starved myself and dried out. That done something to me, those times I tried to make a hundred and fifteen pounds and my bones weighed more than that. As soon as I quit trying to be a jock my weight jumped up to a hundred and fifty, and that's about what I am now."

"What do you mean it done something to you?" said Murphy.

"Be hard for you to understand, Murphy. It's a medical fact."

"Oh, go ahead, Doctor Costello."

"Well, if you don't get enough to eat, the blood thins out and the brain don't get fed properly. That changes your whole outlook on life, and if the brain goes too long without nourishment, you get so's you don't care any more."

"Where did you get that piece of information?"

"I trained for a doctor that owned a couple trotters over near Lancaster. Him and I had many's the conversation on the subject."

"I never know whether to believe you or call you a liar. Did you get so's you didn't care any more?"

"That's what I'm trying to get through your thick skull, Murphy. That's why I never amounted to anything. That's why poor people stay poor. The brain don't get enough nourishment from the blood. Fortunately

I know that, you see. I don't waste my strength trying to be something I ain't."

"Do you know what I think, Tony? I think you were just looking for an excuse to be a bum."

"Naturally! I wasn't looking for an excuse, but I was looking for some reason why a fellow as smart as I am never amounted to anything. If I cared more what happened to me, I'd have cut my throat years ago. Jesus! The most I ever had in my life was eight hundred dollars one time a long shot came in, but I don't care. You know, I'm fifty-five or -six years of age, one or the other. I had my first woman when I was fifteen, and I guess a couple hundred since then. But I never saw one yet that I'd lose any sleep over. Not a single one, out of maybe a couple hundred. One is just like the other, to me. Get what you want out of them, and so long. So long till you want another. And I used to be a pretty handsome fellow when I was young. Not all whores, either. Once when I was wintering down in Latonia—well, what the hell. It don't bother me as much as it used to do. I couldn't go a week without it, but these days I just as soon spend the money on the grog. I'll be just as content when I can do without them altogether."

One day Tony was washing a brand-new Chrysler, which was itself a recent make of car. He was standing off, hose in hand, contemplating the design and colors of the car, when a young woman got out of a plain black Ford coupe. She was wearing black and white saddle shoes, bruised and spotted, and not liable to be seriously damaged by the puddles of dirty water on the garage floor, but Tony cautioned her. "Mind where you're walking, young lady," he said.

"Oh, it won't hurt these shoes," she said. "I'm looking for Tony Costello. I was told he worked here."

"Feast your eyes, Miss. You're looking right at him," he said.

"You're Tony Costello? I somehow pictured an older man," she said.

"Well, maybe I'm older than I look. What is there I can do for you?"

She was a sturdily built young woman, past the middle twenties, handsome if she had been a man, but it was no man inside the grey pullover. "I was told that you were the best man in town to take care of a sick horse," she said.

"You were told right," said Tony Costello. "And I take it you have a sick horse? What's the matter with him, if it's a him, or her if it's a her?"

"It's a mare named Daisy. By the way, my name is Esther Wayman."

"Wayman? You're new here in town," said Tony.

"Just this year. My father is the manager of the bus company."

"I see. And your mare Daisy, how old?"

"Five, I think, or maybe six," said Esther Wayman.

"And sick in what way? What are the symptoms?"

"She's all swollen up around the mouth. I thought I had the curb chain on too tight, but that wasn't it. I kept her in the stable for several days, with a halter on, and instead of going away the swelling got worse."

"Mm. The swelling, is it accompanied by, uh, a great deal of saliva?"

"Yes, it is."

"You say the animal is six years old. How long did you own her, Miss Wayman?"

"Only about a month. I bought her from a place in Philadelphia."

"Mm-hmm. Out Market Street, one of them horse bazaars?"

"Yes."

"Is this your first horse? In other words, you're not familiar with horses?"

"No, we've always lived in the city—Philadelphia, Cleveland, Ohio, Denver, Colorado. I learned to ride in college, but I never owned a horse before we came here."

"You wouldn't know a case of glanders if you saw it, would you?"

"No. Is that a disease?" she said.

"Unless I'm very much mistaken, it's the disease that ails your mare Daisy. I'll be done washing this car in two shakes, and then you can take me out to see your mare. Where do you stable her?"

"We have our own stable. My father bought the Henderson house."

"Oh, to be sure, and I know it well. Slept in that stable many's the night."

"I don't want to take you away from your work," she said.

"Young woman, you're taking me *to* work. You're not taking me away from anything."

He finished with the Chrysler, got out of his gum boots, and put on his shoes. He called to the garage foreman, "Back sometime in the morning," and did not wait for an answer. None came.

On the way out to the Wayman-Henderson house he let the young woman do all the talking. She had the flat accent of the Middle West and she spoke from deep inside her mouth. She told him how she had got interested in riding at cawlidge, and was so pleased to find that the house her father bought included a garage that was not really a garage but a real stable. Her father permitted her to have a horse on condition that she took complete care of it herself. She had seen the ad in a Philadelphia paper, gone to one of the weekly sales, and paid $300 for Daisy. She had not even looked at any other horse. The bidding for Daisy had started at $100; Esther raised it to $150; someone else went to $200; Esther jumped it to $300 and the mare was hers.

"Uh-huh," said Tony. "Well, maybe you got a bargain, and maybe not."

"You seem doubtful," she said.

"We learn by experience, and you got the animal you wanted. You'll be buying other horses as you get older. This is only your first one."

They left the car at the stable door. "I guess she's lying down," said Esther.

Tony opened the door of the box stall. "She is that, and I'm sorry to tell you, she's never getting up."

"She's dead? How could she be? I only saw her a few hours ago."

"Let me go in and have a look at her. You stay where you are," he said. He had taken command and she obeyed him. In a few minutes, three or four, he came out of the stall and closed the door behind him.

"Glanders, it was. Glanders and old age. Daisy was more like eleven than five or six."

"But how could it happen so quickly?"

"It didn't, exactly. I'm not saying the animal had glanders when you bought her. I do say they falsified her age, which they all do. Maybe they'll give you your money back, maybe they won't. In any case, Miss Wayman, you're not to go in there. Glanders is contagious to man and animal. If you want me to, I'll see to the removal of the animal. A telephone call to the fertilizer plant, and they know me there. Then I'll burn the bedding for you and fumigate the stable. You might as well leave the halter on. It wouldn't be fair to put it on a well horse."

The young woman took out a pack of cigarettes and offered him one. He took it, lit hers and his. "I'm glad to see you take it so calmly. I seen women go into hysterics under these circumstances," he said.

"I don't get hysterics," she said. "But that's not to say I'm not in a turmoil. If I'd had her a little while longer I *might* have gotten hysterical."

"Then be thankful that you didn't have her that much longer. To tell you the truth, you didn't get a bargain. There was other things wrong with her that we needn't go into. I wouldn't be surprised if she was blind, but that's not what I was thinking of. No, you didn't get a bargain this time, but keep trying. Only, next time take somebody with you that had some experience with horses and horse dealers."

"I'll take you, if you'll come," she said. "Meanwhile, will you do those other things you said you would?"

"I will indeed."

"And how much do I owe you?" she said.

He smiled. "I don't have a regular fee for telling people that a dead horse is dead," he said. "A couple dollars for my time."

"How about ten dollars?"

"Whatever you feel is right, I'll take," he said. "The state of my finances is on the wrong side of affluence."

"Is the garage where I can always reach you?" she said.

"I don't work there steady."

"At home, then? Can you give me your telephone number?" she said.

187

"I move around from place to place."

"Oh. Well, would you like to have a steady job? I could introduce you to my father."

"I couldn't drive a bus, if that's what you had in mind. I don't have a license, for one thing, and even if I did they have to maintain a schedule. That I've never done, not that strict kind of a schedule. But thanks for the offer."

"He might have a job for you washing buses. I don't know how well it would pay, but I think they wash and clean those buses every night, so it would be steady work. Unless you're not interested in steady work. Is that it?"

"Steady pay without the steady work, that's about the size of it," he said.

She shook her head. "Then I don't think you and my father would get along. He lives by the clock."

"Well, I guess he'd have to, running a bus line," said Tony. He looked about him. "The Hendersons used to hang their cutters up there. They had two cutters and a bob. They were great ones for sleighing parties. Two–three times a winter they'd load up the bob and the two cutters and take their friends down to their farm for a chicken-and-waffle supper. They had four horses then. A pair of sorrels, Prince and Duke. Trixie, a bay mare, broke to saddle. And a black gelding named Satan, Mr. Henderson drove himself to work in. They were pretty near the last to give up horses, Mr. and Mrs. Henderson."

"Did you work for them?"

"Twice I worked for them. Sacked both times. But he knew I used to come here and sleep. They had four big buffalo robes, two for the bob and one each for the cutters. That was the lap of luxury for me. Sleep on two and cover up with one. Then he died and she moved away, and the son Jasper only had cars. There wasn't a horse stabled in here since Mrs. moved away, and Jasper wouldn't let me sleep here. He put in that gazzoline pump and he said it wasn't safe to let me stop here for the night. It wasn't me he was worried about. It was them ottomobiles. Well, this isn't getting to the telephone."

During the night he fumigated the stable. The truck from the fertilizer plant arrived at nine o'clock and he helped the two men load the dead mare, after which he lit the fumigating tablets in the stalls and closed the doors and windows. Esther Wayman came up from the house at ten o'clock or so, just as he was closing the doors of the carriage house. "They took her away?" she said.

"About an hour ago. Then I lit candles for her," he said.

"You what?"

"That's my little joke, not in the best of taste perhaps. I don't know that this fumigating does any good, but on the other hand it can't do much harm. It's a precaution you take, glanders being contagious and all that. You have to think of the next animal that'll be occupying that stall, so you take every precaution—as much for your own peace of mind as anything else, I guess."

"Where did you get the fumigating stuff?"

"I went down to the drugstore, Schlicter's Pharmacy, Sixteenth and Market. I told them to charge it to your father. They know me there."

"They know you everywhere in this town, don't they?"

"Yes, I guess they do, now that I stop to think of it."

"Can I take you home in my car?"

"Oh, I guess I can walk it."

"Why should you when I have my car? Where do you live?"

"I got a room on Canal Street. That's not much of a neighborhood for you to be driving around in after dark."

"I'm sure I've been in worse, or just as bad," she said.

"That would surprise me," he said.

"I'm not a sheltered hothouse plant," she said. "I can take care of myself. Let's go. I'd like to see that part of town."

When they got to Canal Street she said, "It isn't eleven o'clock yet. Is there a place where we can go for a drink?"

"Oh, there's places aplenty. But I doubt if your Dad would approve of them for you."

"Nobody will know me," she said. "I hardly know anybody in this town. I don't get to know people very easily. Where shall we go?"

"Well, there's a pretty decent place that goes by the name of the Bucket of Blood. Don't let the name frighten you. It's just a common ordinary saloon. I'm not saying you'll encounter the Ladies Aid Society there, but if it didn't have that name attached to it—well, you'll see the kind of place it is."

It was a quiet night in the saloon. They sat at a table in the back room. A man and woman were at another table, drinking whiskey by the shot and washing it down with beer chasers. They were a solemn couple, both about fifty, with no need to converse and seemingly no concern beyond the immediate appreciation of the alcohol. Presently the man stood up and headed for the street door, followed by the woman. As she went out she slapped Tony Costello lightly on the shoulder. "Goodnight, Tony," she said.

"Goodnight, Marie," said Tony Costello.

When they were gone Esther Wayman said, "She knew you, but all she said was goodnight. She never said hello."

"Him and I don't speak to one another," said Tony. "We had some kind of a dispute there a long while back."

"Are they husband and wife?"

"No, but they been going together ever since I can remember."

"She's a prostitute, isn't she?"

"That's correct," said Tony.

"And what does he do? Live off her?"

"Oh, no. No, he's a trackwalker for the Pennsy. One of the few around that ain't an I-talian. But she's an I-talian."

"Are you an Italian? You're not, are you?"

"Good Lord, no. I'm as Irish as they come."

"You have an Italian name, though."

"It may sound I-talian to you, but my mother was straight from County Cork. My father could be anybody, but most likely he was an Irishman, the neighborhood I come from. I'm pretty certain he wasn't John Jacob Astor or J. Pierpont Morgan. My old lady was engaged in the same occupation as Marie that just went out."

"Doesn't your church—I mean, in France and Italy I suppose the prostitutes must be Catholic, but I never thought of Irish prostitutes."

"There's prostitutes wherever a woman needs a dollar and doesn't have to care too much how she gets it. It don't even have to be a dollar. If they're young enough they'll do it for a stick of candy, and the dollar comes later. This is an elevating conversation for a young woman like yourself."

"You don't know anything about myself, Mr. Costello," she said.

"I do, and I don't," he said. "But what I don't know I'm learning. I'll make a guess that you were disappointed in love."

She laughed. "Very."

"What happened? The young man give you the go-by?"

"There was no young man," she said. "I have never been interested in young men or they in me."

"I see," he said.

"Do you?"

"Well, to be honest with you, no. I don't. I'd of thought you'd have yourself a husband by this time. You're not at all bad looking, you know, and you always knew where your next meal was coming from."

"This conversation *is* beginning to embarrass me a little," she said. "Sometime I may tell you all about myself. In fact, I have a feeling I will. But not now, not tonight."

"Anytime you say," said Tony. "And one of these days we'll go looking for a horse for you."

"We'll have fun," she said.

BERYL MARKHAM

The Splendid Outcast

The stallion was named after a star, and when he fell from his particular heaven, it was easy enough for people to say that he had been named too well. People like to see stars fall, but in the case of Rigel, it was of greater importance to me. To me and to one other—to a little man with shabby cuffs and a wilted cap that rested over eyes made mild by something more than time.

It was at Newmarket, in England, where, since Charles I instituted the first cup race, a kind of court has been held for the royalty of the turf. Men of all classes come to Newmarket for the races and for the December sales. They come from everywhere—some to bet, some to buy or sell, and some merely to offer homage to the resplendent peers of the Stud Book, for the sport of kings may, after all, be the pleasure of every man.

December can be bitterly cold in England, and this December was. There was frozen sleet on buildings and on trees, and I remember that the huge Newmarket track lay on the downs below the village like a noose of diamonds on a tarnished mat. There was a festive spirit everywhere, but it was somehow lost on me. I had come to buy new blood for my stable in Kenya, and since my stable was my living, I came as serious buyers do, with figures in my mind and caution in my heart. Horses are hard to judge at best, and the thought of putting your hoarded pounds behind that judgment makes it harder still.

I sat close on the edge of the auction ring and held my breath from time to time as the bidding soared. I held it because the casual mention of ten thousand guineas in payment for a horse or for anything else seemed to me wildly beyond the realm of probable things. For myself, I had five hundred pounds to spend and, as I waited for Rigel to be shown, I remember that I felt uncommonly maternal about each pound. I waited for Rigel because I had come six thousand miles to buy him, nor was I apprehensive lest anyone should take him from me; he was an outcast.

Rigel had a pedigree that looked backward and beyond the pedigrees of many Englishmen—and Rigel had a brilliant record. By all odds, he should have brought ten thousand guineas at the sale, but I knew he wouldn't, for he had killed a man.

He had killed a man—not fallen upon him, nor thrown him in a playful moment from the saddle, but killed him dead with his hooves and with his teeth in a stable. And that was not all, though it was the greatest thing. Rigel had crippled other men and, so the story went, would cripple or kill still more, so long as he lived. He was savage, people said, and while he could not be hanged for his crimes, like a man, he could be shunned as criminals are. He could be offered for sale. And yet, under the implacable rules of racing, he had been warned off the turf for life—so who would buy?

Well, I for one—and I had supposed there would not be two. I would buy if the price were low enough, because I had youth then, and a corresponding contempt for failure. It seemed probable that in time and with luck and with skill, the stallion might be made manageable again, if only for breeding—especially for breeding. He could be gentled, I thought. But I found it hard to believe what I saw that day. I had not known that the mere touch of a hand could, in an instant, extinguish the long-burning anger of an angry heart.

I first noticed the little man when the sale was already well on its way, and he caught my attention at once, because he was incongruous there. He sat a few benches from me and held his lean, interwoven fingers upon his knees. He stared down upon the arena as each horse was led into it, and he listened to the dignified encomiums of the auctioneer with the humble attention of a parishioner at mass. He never moved. He was surrounded by men and women who, by their impeccable clothes and by their somewhat bored familiarity with pounds and guineas, made him conspicuous. He was like a stone of granite in a jeweler's window, motionless and grey against the glitter.

You could see in his face that he loved horses—just as you could see, in some of the faces of those around him, that they loved the idea of horses. They were the cultists, he the votary, and there were, in fact, about his grey eyes and his slender lips, the deep, tense lines so often etched in the faces of zealots and of lonely men. It was the cast of his shoulders, I think, the devotion of his manner that told me he had once been a jockey.

A yearling came into the ring and was bought, and then another, while the pages of catalogues were quietly turned. The auctioneer's voice, clear but scarcely lifted, intoned the virtues of his magnificent merchandise as other voices, responding to this magic, spoke reservedly of figures: "A thousand guineas . . . two thousand . . . three . . . four! . . ."

The scene at the auction comes to me clearly now, as if once again it were happening before my eyes.

"Five, perhaps?" The auctioneer scans the audience expectantly as a groom parades a dancing colt around the arena. There is a moment of near silence, a burly voice calls, "Five!" and the colt is sold while a murmur of polite approval swells and dies.

And so they go, one after another, until the list is small; the audience thins, and my finger traces the name, Rigel, on the last page of the catalogue. I straighten on my bench and hold my breath a little, forgetting the crowd, the little man, and a part of myself. I know this horse. I know he is by Hurry On out of Bounty—the sire unbeaten, the dam a great steeplechaser—and there is no better blood than that. Killer or not, Rigel has won races, and won them clean. If God and Barclays Bank stay with me, he will return to Africa when I do.

And there, at last, he stands. In the broad entrance to the ring, two powerful men appear with the stallion between them. The men are not grooms of ordinary size; they have been picked for strength, and in the clenched fist of each is the end of a chain. Between the chain and the bit there is on the near side a short rod of steel, close to the stallion's mouth—a rod of steel, easy to grasp, easy to use. Clenched around the great girth of the horse, and fitted with metal rings, there is a strap of thick leather that brings to mind the restraining harness of a madman.

Together, the two men edge the stallion forward. Tall as they are, they move like midgets beside his massive shoulders. He is the biggest thorough-bred I have ever seen. He is the most beautiful. His coat is chestnut, flecked with white, and his mane and tail are close to gold. There is a blaze on his face—wide and straight and forthright, as if by this marking he proclaims that he is none other than Rigel, for all his sins, for all the hush that falls over the crowd.

He is Rigel and he looks upon the men who hold his chains as a cap-tured king may look upon his captors. He is not tamed. Nothing about him promises that he will be tamed. Stiffly, on reluctant hooves, he enters the ring and flares his crimson nostrils at the crowd, and the crowd is still. The crowd whose pleasure is the docile beast of pretty paddocks, the gainly horse of cherished prints that hang upon the finest walls, the willing winner of the race—upon the rebel this crowd stares, and the rebel stares back.

His eyes are lit with anger or with hate. His head is held disdainfully and high, his neck an arc of arrogance. He prances now—impatience in the thudding of his hooves upon the tanbark, defiance in his manner—and the chains jerk tight. The long stallion reins are tightly held—apprehensively held—and the men who hold them glance at the auctioneer, an urgent ques-tion in their eyes.

The auctioneer raises his arm for silence, but there is silence. No one speaks. The story of Rigel is known—his breeding, his brilliant victories, and finally his insurgence and his crimes. Who will buy the outcast? The auctioneer shakes his head as if to say that this is a trick beyond his magic. But he will try. He is an imposing man, an experienced man, and now he clears his throat and confronts the crowd, a kind of pleading in his face.

"This splendid animal—" he begins—and does not finish. He cannot finish.

Rigel has scanned the silent audience and smelled the unmoving air, and he—a creature of the wind—knows the indignity of this skyless temple.

He seems aware at last of the chains that hold him, of the men who cling forlornly to the heavy reins. He rears from the tanbark, higher and higher still, until his golden mane is lifted like a flag unfurled and defiant. He beats the air. He trembles in his rising anger, and the crowd leans forward.

A groom clings like a monkey to the tightened chain. He is swept from his feet while his partner, a less tenacious man, sprawls ignobly below, and men—a dozen men—rush to the ring, some shouting, some waving their arms. They run and swear in lowered voices; they grasp reins, chains, rings, and swarm upon their towering Gulliver. And he subsides.

With something like contempt for this hysteria, Rigel touches his fore-hooves to the tanbark once more. He has killed no one, hurt no one, but they are jabbing at his mouth now, they are surrounding him, adding fuel to his fiery reputation, and the auctioneer is a wilted man.

He sighs, and you can almost hear it. He raises both arms and forgoes his speech. "What," he asks with weariness, "am I offered?" And there is a ripple of laughter from the crowd. Smug in its wisdom, it offers nothing.

But I do, and my voice is like an echo in a cave. Still there is triumph in it. I will have what I have come so far to get—I will have Rigel.

"A hundred guineas!" I stand as I call my price, and the auctioneer is plainly shocked—not by the meagerness of the offer, but by the offer itself. He stares upward from the ring, incredulity in his eyes.

He lifts a hand and slowly repeats the price. "I am offered," he says, "one hundred guineas."

There is a hush, and I feel the eyes of the crowd and watch the hand of the auctioneer. When it goes down, the stallion will be mine.

But it does not go down. It is still poised in midair, white, expectant, compelling, when the soft voice, the gently challenging voice is lifted. "Two hundred!" the voice says, and I do not have to turn to know that the little jockey has bid against me. But I do turn.

He has not risen from the bench, and he does not look at me. In his hand he holds a sheaf of bank notes. I can tell by their color that they are of small denomination, by their rumpled condition that they have been hoarded long. People near him are staring—horrified, I think—at the vulgar spectacle of cash at a Newmarket auction.

I am not horrified, nor sympathetic. Suddenly I am aware that I have a competitor, and I am cautious. I am here for a purpose that has little to do with sentiment, and I will not be beaten. I think of my stable in Kenya, of the feed bills to come, of the syces to be paid, of the races that are yet to be won if I am to survive in this unpredictable business. No, I cannot now yield an inch. I have little money, but so has he. No more, I think, but perhaps as much.

I hesitate a moment and glance at the little man, and he returns my glance. We are like two gamblers bidding each against the other's unseen cards. Our eyes meet for a sharp instant—a cold instant.

I straighten and my catalogue is crumpled in my hand. I moisten my lips and call, ''Three hundred!'' I call it firmly, steadily, hoping to undo my opponent at a stroke. It is a wishful thought.

He looks directly at me now, but does not smile. He looks at me as a man might look at one who bears false witness against him, then soundlessly he counts his money and bids again, ''Three fifty!''

The interest of the crowd is suddenly aroused. All these people are at once conscious of being witnesses, not only before an auction, but before a contest, a rivalry of wills. They shift in their seats and stare as they might stare at a pair of duelists, rapiers in hand.

But money is the weapon, Rigel the prize. And prize enough, I think, as does my adversary.

I ponder and think hard, then decide to bid a hundred more. Not twenty, not fifty, but a hundred. Perhaps by that I can take him in my stride. He need not know there is little more to follow. He may assume that I am one of the casual ones, impatient of small figures. He may hesitate, he may withdraw. He may be cowed.

Still standing, I utter, as indifferently as I can, the words, ''Four fifty!'' and the auctioneer, at ease in his element of contention, brightens visibly.

I am aware that the gathered people are now fascinated by this battle of pounds and shillings over a stallion that not one of them would care to own. I only hope that in the heat of it some third person does not begin to bid. But I need not worry; Rigel takes care of that.

The little jockey has listened to my last offer, and I can see that he is already beaten—or almost, at least. He has counted his money a dozen times, but now he counts it again, swiftly, with agile fingers, as if hoping his previous counts had been wrong.

I feel a momentary surge of sympathy, then smother it. Horse training is not my hobby. It is my living. I wait for what I am sure will be his last bid, and it comes. For the first time, he rises from his bench. He is small and alone in spirit, for the glances of the well-dressed people about him lend him nothing. He does not care. His eyes are on the stallion and I can see that there is a kind of passion in them. I have seen that expression before—in the eyes of sailors appraising a comely ship, in the eyes of pilots sweeping the clean, sweet contours of a plane. There is reverence in it, desire—and even hope.

The little man turns slightly to face the expectant auctioneer, then clears his throat and makes his bid. "Four eighty!" he calls, and the slight note of desperation in his voice is unmistakable, but I force myself to ignore it. Now, at last, I tell myself, the prize is mine.

The auctioneer receives the bid and looks at me, as do a hundred people. Some of them, no doubt, think I am quite mad or wholly inexperienced, but they watch while the words "Five hundred" form upon my lips. They are never uttered.

Throughout the bidding for Rigel, Rigel has been ignored. He has stood quietly enough after his first brief effort at freedom; he has scarcely moved. But now, at the climax of the sale, his impatience overflows, his spirit flares like fire, his anger bursts through the circle of men who guard him. Suddenly, there are cries, shouts of warning, the ringing of chains and the cracking of leather, and the crowd leaps to its feet. Rigel is loose. Rigel has hurled his captors from him and he stands alone.

It is a beautiful thing to see, but there is terror in it. A thoroughbred stallion with anger in his eye is not a sight to entrance anyone but a novice. If you are aware of the power and the speed and the intelligence in that towering symmetrical body, you will hold your breath as you watch it. You will know that the teeth of a horse can crush a bone, that hooves can crush a man. And Rigel's hooves have crushed a man.

He stands alone, his neck curved, his golden tail a battle plume, and he turns, slowly, deliberately, and faces the men he has flung away. They are not without courage, but they are without resource. Horses are not tamed by whips or by blows. The strength of ten men is not so strong as a single stroke of a hoof; the experience of ten men is not enough, for this is the unexpected, the unpredictable. No one is prepared. No one is ready.

The words "Five hundred" die upon my lips as I watch, as I listen. For the stallion is not voiceless now. His challenging scream is shrill as the cry of winter wind. It is bleak and heartless. His forehooves stir the tanbark. The auction is forgotten.

A man stands before him—a man braver than most. He holds nothing in his hands save an exercise bat; it looks a feeble thing, and is. It is a thin stick bound with leather—enough only to enrage Rigel, for he has seen such things in men's hands before. He knows their meaning. Such a thing as this bat, slight as it is, enrages him because it is a symbol that stands for other things. It stands, perhaps, for the confining walls of a darkened stable, for the bit of steel, foreign, but almost everpresent in his mouth, for the tightened girth, the command to gallop, to walk, to stop, to parade before the swelling crowd of gathered people, to accept the measured food gleaned from forbidden fields. It stands for life no closer to the earth than the sterile smell of satin on a jockey's back or the dead wreath hung upon a winner. It stands for servitude. And Rigel has broken with his overlords.

He lunges quickly, and the man with a bat is not so quick. He lifts the pathetic stick and waves it in desperation. He cries out, and the voice of the crowd drowns his cry. Rigel's neck is outstretched and straight as a sabre. There is dust and the shouting of men and the screaming of women, for the stallion's teeth have closed on the shoulder of his forlorn enemy.

The man struggles and drops his bat, and his eyes are sharp with terror, perhaps with pain. Blood leaves the flesh of his face, and it is a face grey and pleading, as must be the faces of those to whom retribution is unexpected and swift. He beats against the golden head while the excitement of the crowd mounts against the fury of Rigel. Then reason vanishes. Clubs, whips, and chains appear like magic in the ring, and a regiment of men advance upon the stallion. They are angry men, brave in their anger, righteous and justified in it. They advance, and the stallion drops the man he has attacked, and the man runs for cover, clutching his shoulder.

I am standing, as is everyone. It is a strange and unreal thing to see this trapped and frustrated creature, magnificent and alone, away from his kind, remote from the things he understands, face the punishment of his minuscule masters. He is, of course, terrified, and the terror is a mounting madness. If he could run, he would leave this place, abandoning his fear and his hatred to do it. But he cannot run. The walls of the arena are high. The doors are shut, and the trap makes him blind with anger. He will fight, and the blows will fall with heaviness upon his spirit, for his body is a rock before these petty weapons.

The men edge closer, ropes and chains and whips in determined hands. The whips are lifted, the chains are ready; the battle line is formed, and Rigel does not retreat. He comes forward, the whites of his eyes exposed and rimmed with carnelian fire, his nostrils crimson.

There is a breathless silence, and the little jockey slips like a ghost into the ring. His eyes are fixed on the embattled stallion. He begins to run across the tanbark and breaks through the circle of advancing men and does not stop. Someone clutches at his coat, but he breaks loose without turning, then slows to an almost casual walk and approaches Rigel alone. The men do not follow him. He waves them back. He goes forward, steadily, easily and happily, without caution, without fear, and Rigel whirls angrily to face him.

Rigel stands close to the wall of the arena. He cannot retreat. He does not propose to. Now he can focus his fury on this insignificant David who has come to meet him, and he does. He lunges at once as only a stallion can—swiftly, invincibly, as if escape and freedom can be found only in the destruction of all that is human, all that smells human, and all that humans have made.

He lunges and the jockey stops. He does not turn or lift a hand or otherwise move. He stops, he stands, and there is silence everywhere. No one speaks; no one seems to breathe. Only Rigel is motion. No special hypnotic power emanates from the jockey's eyes; he has no magic. The stallion's teeth are bared and close, his hooves are a swelling sound when the jockey turns. Like a matador of nerveless skill and studied insolence, the jockey turns his back on Rigel and does not walk away, and the stallion pauses.

Rigel rears high at the back of the little man, screaming his defiant scream, but he does not strike. His hooves are close to the jockey's head, but do not touch him. His teeth are sheathed. He hesitates, trembles, roars wind from his massive lungs. He shakes his head, his golden mane, and beats the ground. It is frustration—but of a new kind. It is a thing he does not know—a man who neither cringes in fear nor threatens with whips or chains. It is a thing beyond his memory perhaps—as far beyond it as the understanding of the mare that bore him.

Rigel is suddenly motionless, rigid, suspicious. He waits, and the grey-eyed jockey turns to face him. The little man is calm and smiling. We hear him speak, but cannot understand his words. They are low and they are lost to us—an incantation. But the stallion seems to understand at least the spirit if not the sense of them. He snorts, but does not move. And now the jockey's hand goes forward to the golden mane—neither hurriedly nor with hesitance, but unconcernedly, as if it had rested there a thousand times. And there it stays.

There is a murmur from the crowd, then silence. People look at one another and stir in their seats—a strange self-consciousness in their stirring, for people are uneasy before the proved worth of their inferiors, unbelieving of the virtue of simplicity. They watch with open mouths as the giant Rigel, the killer Rigel, with no harness save a head collar, follows his Lilliputian master, his new friend, across the ring.

All has happened in so little time—in moments. The audience begins to stand, to leave. But they pause at the lift of the auctioneer's hand. He waves it and they pause. It is all very well, his gestures say, but business is, after all, business, and Rigel has not been sold. He looks up at me, knowing that I have a bid to make—the last bid. And I look down into the ring at the stallion I have come so far to buy. His head is low and close to the shoulder of the man who would take him from me. He is not prancing now, not moving. For this hour, at least, he is changed.

I straighten, and then shake my head. I need only say, "Five hundred," but the words won't come. I can't get them out. I am angry with myself—a sentimental fool—and I am disappointed. But I cannot bid. It is too easy—twenty pounds too little, and yet too great an advantage.

No. I shake my head again, the auctioneer shrugs and turns to seal his bargain with the jockey.

On the way out, an old friend jostles me. "You didn't really want him then," he says.

"Want him? No. No, I didn't really want him."

"It was wise," he says. "What good is a horse that's warned off every course in the Empire? You wouldn't want a horse like that."

"That's right. I wouldn't want a horse like that."

We move to the exit, and when we are out in the bright cold air of Newmarket, I turn to my friend and mention the little jockey. "But he wanted Rigel," I say.

And my old friend laughs. "He would," he says. "That man has himself been barred from racing for fifteen years. Why, I can't remember. But it's two of a kind, you see—Rigel and Sparrow. Outlaws, both. He loves and knows horses as no man does, but that's what we call him around the tracks—the Fallen Sparrow."

GRETEL EHRLICH

Champ's Roan Colt

I told my roan colt one afternoon how I was gut shot, wounded in the leg, went goofy for a while, then sent back into action, but I didn't get any sympathy. Works on the girls, what's wrong with this damned horse? McKay can walk right out into the pasture and catch him, but me—you'd think the Loch Ness monster had just arrived. Maybe it's the cane. The goddamned wooden third leg. Can't walk. Can't stand right, can't get on a horse right, gimp, gimp, gimp. Is that what scares him? Well it scares me too.

Okay, so I'm warped beyond recognition, but I always was and the horses used to like that because they knew I didn't give a damn. That's the thing, that's the difference. Now I do care, because I've got to rope and ride with the best of them or else, what the hell will I do?

All I've ever wanted to do is ranch—ranch and get laid—but things sure do get deep around here with McKay feeling sorry for himself and Ted quietly going off his rocker, and Bobby fussing around like an old maid. Where the hell does that leave me? Maybe I ought to hire on elsewhere, but that's nothing new. Everyone keeps saying things have changed since the war, but hell, I think they're the same, except now all the dark corners show a little brighter. Bobby says McKay is like Prince Genji, whoever the hell that is— some romantic girl-chasing bastard from a thousand years ago. No telling what he calls me. We always did grate on each other's nerves. In fact I think I cause quite a bit of unhappiness around here. I go into town a lot. Now they're having regular dances again. So what if I limp, at least I've got two legs and something that hangs between them.

Today I got the colt in the round corral and stood in the middle leaning on my cane while he whirled around like something on the end of a rubber band. "Too much of this could make a man dizzy," I told him, trying to sound nonchalant. But I lied. I was madder than hell. Why didn't he just settle down? Then I thought I'd try something I'd seen Pinkey do—sit down in the middle of the corral and close my eyes like I was sleeping. Get real relaxed, then the colt would lose his fear. He trotted around, then finally I heard him stop. I peered through the slits of my eyes and saw him with his rump toward me, looking over his shoulder to see if I was cheating. And I was. He threw his head over the top rail, whinnied, then started trotting again.

I guess I lost my patience. I didn't have all day. Got up off my ass and kicked dirt at him. The colt jumped and tried to get away. "Jump again, damnit," I said, going toward him. You could scare a horse into standing still and that's what I was trying to do. As I got closer, he did stand, nervous and twitching, with his ears laid back listening to my footsteps. The muscle in his shoulder was shaking. When I got almost close enough to touch him, I watched to see if he would cock a back leg and fire at me. "Fire away. I'm used to it," I said. "I've been fired on by worse than you." But what good does bragging do with a horse? He dug in, spun, and ran spraying me with clods of dirt. I spit and wiped my face, thinking of the beach where I had been under fire, watching ammunition hit the sand, blasting it into the air, then when I was hit, it felt like sand had been driven all through me, my veins and bones, like human slurry, the stinging mixed up with the deep cold of pain.

The colt had been trotting but finally stopped. He was blowing pretty hard and sweat spread up his neck from his shoulder. "What in the hell buggered you, anyway?" It was an honest question. He laid his ears back in response. Was he laughing at me or was he just pissed? I leaned back on my cane because my leg hurt—there were snow clouds coming in—and breathed deeply. After, the horse sighed, then worked his mouth a little. He was relaxing. "That's good, Blue," I said. When I thought about it, I could feel how tense I'd been. "A horse knows even before you come out to catch him," Pinkey always said. But hell, you can't be perfect all the time, can you?

The thing is I'd had about enough. My little brother, Prince Charming McKay, gives me grief about my taste in women, about my pool game, about my roping, about, for god's sake, my morals, and Bobby is after me about getting married, and now this horse. What is it about me that he didn't like? From a horse it's different, it really gets to me because I thought we were pals, I thought all horses liked me.

Funny how something like this can get you down—a horse that won't be caught. . . . Once I got close enough to touch his shoulder, but when I slid my hand up his neck holding the halter rope he pulled away. "You sonofabitch," I yelled as he flew by. The second time around I stuck my cane out, and he fired at me with a back leg, almost got me in the face. He jerked to a stop on his front feet, and I threw my cane, end over end. It hit him square on the hocks and broke in two. He lunged at the gate, breaking the top rail and the middle one. Then he jumped through and ran, across the irrigation ditch, out into the horse pasture. In the distance I could see McKay on a horse watching me. "Go screw yourself," I yelled to him, though he probably couldn't hear me. He rode away. Some present he'd given me. He must have trained this horse to run from me so everyone could laugh.

From my bedroom window the next morning I saw McKay run my colt back into the round corral and leave him there. "Shithead," I said, then slept some more. But what I saw when I went out there broke my heart: the colt's front legs were wirecut and swollen.

This time he stood. He worked his ears as I approached but didn't move a muscle. The game was over, but I had lost. I knelt, running my hand down one mangled leg. "Jesus, Blue, what the hell did you get so scared for?" But it was me who had been scared, not of the horse, but of my own incompetence, scared of this everlasting limp.

Went to the house for medicine and when I came back he had something in his mouth. I'll be goddamned if it wasn't a piece of my cane he was packing around like a puppy. When I went close to doctor his legs he touched his muzzle to my hand, and as I crouched down beside him, talking softly, he dropped the piece of cane on top of my bad knee as if to say, "That's what it's for, dummy, not for me."

After doctoring him for a month, I never did have trouble catching him again.

WOMEN AND THEIR HORSES

JAMES SALTER

Twenty Minutes

This happened near Carbondale to a woman named Jane Vare. I met her once at a party. She was sitting on a couch with her arms stretched out on either side and a drink in one hand. We talked about dogs.

She had an old greyhound. She'd bought him to save his life, she said. At the tracks they put them down rather than feed them when they stopped winning, sometimes three or four together, threw them in the back of a truck and drove to the dump. This dog was named Phil. He was stiff and nearly blind, but she admired his dignity. He sometimes lifted his leg against the wall, almost as high as the door handle, but he had a fine face.

Tack on the kitchen table, mud on the wide-board floor. In she strode like a young groom in a worn jacket and boots. She had what they called a good seat and ribbons layered like feathers on the wall. Her father had lived in Ireland where they rode into the dining room on Sunday morning and the host died fallen on the bed in full attire. Her own life had become like that. Money and dents in the side of her nearly new Swedish car. Her husband had been gone for a year.

Around Carbondale the river drops down and widens. There's a spidery trestle bridge, many times repainted, and they used to mine coal.

It was late in the afternoon and a shower had passed. The light was silvery and strange. Cars emerging from the rain drove with their headlights on and the windshield wipers going. The yellow road machinery parked along the shoulder seemed unnaturally bright.

It was the hour after work when irrigation water glistens high in the air, the hills have begun to darken, and the meadows are like ponds.

She was riding alone up along the ridge. She was on a horse named Fiume, big, well formed, but not very smart. He didn't hear things and sometimes stumbled when he walked. They had gone as far as the reservoir and then come back, riding to the west where the sun was going down. He could run, this horse. His hooves were pounding. The back of her shirt was filled with wind, the saddle was creaking, his huge neck was dark with sweat. They came along the ditch and toward a gate—they jumped it all the time.

At the last moment something happened. It took just an instant. He may have crossed his legs or hit a hole but he suddenly gave way. She went over his head and as if in slow motion he came after. He was upside down— she lay there watching him float toward her. He landed on her open lap.

It was as if she'd been hit by a car. She was stunned but felt unhurt. For a minute she imagined she might stand up and brush herself off.

The horse had gotten up. His legs were dirty and there was dirt on his back. In the silence she could hear the clink of the bridle and even the water flowing in the ditch. All around her were meadows and stillness. She felt sick to her stomach. It was all broken down there—she knew it although she could feel nothing. She knew she had some time. Twenty minutes, they always said.

The horse was pulling at some grass. She rose to her elbows and was immediately dizzy. "God damn you!" she called. She was nearly crying. "Git! Go home!" Someone might see the empty saddle. She closed her eyes and tried to think. Somehow she could not believe it—nothing that had happened was true.

It was that way the morning they came and told her Privet had been hurt. The foreman was waiting in the pasture. "Her leg's broken," he said.

"How did it happen?"

He didn't know. "It looks like she got kicked," he guessed.

The horse was lying under a tree. She knelt and stroked its boardlike nose. The large eyes seemed to be looking elsewhere. The vet would be driving up from Catherine Store trailing a plume of dust, but it turned out to be a long time before he came. He parked a little way off and walked over. Afterward he said what she had known he would say, they were going to have to put her down.

She lay remembering that. The day had ended. Lights were appearing in parts of distant houses. The six o'clock news was on. Far below she could see the hayfield of Piñones and much closer, a hundred yards off, a truck. It belonged to someone trying to build a house down there. It was up on blocks, it didn't run. There were other houses within a mile or so. On the other side of the ridge the metal roof, hidden in trees, of old man Vaughn who had once owned all of this and now could hardly walk. Further west the beautiful tan adobe Bill Millinger built before he went broke or whatever it was. He had wonderful taste. The house had the peeled log ceilings of the Southwest, Navajo rugs, and fireplaces in every room. Wide views of the mountains through windows of tinted glass. Anyone who knew enough to build a house like that knew everything.

She had given the famous dinner for him, unforgettable night. The clouds had been blowing off the top of Sopris all day, then came the snow. They talked in front of the fire. There were wine bottles crowded on the mantel and everyone in good clothes. Outside the snow poured down. She was wearing silk pants and her hair was loose. In the end she stood with him near the doorway to her kitchen. She was filled with warmth and a little drunk, was he?

He was watching her finger on the edge of his jacket lapel. Her heart thudded. "You're not going to make me spend the night alone?" she asked.

He had blond hair and small ears close to his head. "Oh . . ." he began. "What?"

"Don't you know? I'm the other way."

Which way, she insisted. It was such a waste. The roads were almost closed, the house lost in snow. She began to plead—she couldn't help it—and then became angry. The silk pants, the furniture, she hated it all.

In the morning his car was outside. She found him in the kitchen making breakfast. He'd slept on the couch, combed his longish hair with his fingers. On his cheeks was a blond stubble. "Sleep well, darling?" he asked.

Sometimes it was the other way around—in Saratoga in the bar where the idol was the tall Englishman who had made so much money at the sales. Did she live there? he asked. When you were close his eyes looked watery but in that English voice which was so pure, "It's marvelous to come to a place and see someone like you," he said.

She hadn't really decided whether to stay or leave and she had a drink with him. He smoked a cigarette.

"You haven't heard about those?" she said.

"No, what about them?"

"They'll give thee cancer."

"Thee?"

"It's what the Quakers say."

"Are you really a Quaker?"

"Oh, back a ways."

He had her by the elbow. "Do you know what I'd like? I'd like to fuck thee," he said.

She bent her arm to remove it.

"I mean it," he said. "Tonight."

"Some other time," she told him.

"I don't have another time. My wife's coming tomorrow, I only have tonight."

"That's too bad. I have every night."

She hadn't forgotten him, though she'd forgotten his name. His shirt had elegant blue stripes. "Oh, damn you," she suddenly cried. It was the horse. He hadn't gone. He was over by the fence. She began to call him, "Here, boy. Come here," she begged. He wouldn't move.

She didn't know what to do. Five minutes had passed, perhaps longer. Oh, God, she said, oh, Lord, oh God our Father. She could see the long stretch of road that came up from the highway, the unpaved surface very pale. Someone would come up that road and not turn off. The disastrous road. She had been driving it that day with her husband. There was something he had been meaning to tell her, Henry said, his head tilted back at a funny angle. He was making a change in his life. Her heart took a skip. He was breaking off with Mara, he said.

There was a silence.

Finally she said, "With who?"

He realized his mistake. "The girl who . . . in the architect's office. She's the draftsman."

"What do you mean, breaking it off?" It was hard for her to speak. She was looking at him as one would look at a fugitive.

"You knew about that, didn't you? I was sure you knew. Anyway it's over. I wanted to tell you. I wanted to put it all behind us."

"Stop the car," she said. "Don't say any more, stop here."

He drove alongside her trying to explain but she was picking up the biggest stones she could find and throwing them at the car. Then she cut unsteadily across the fields, the sage bushes scratching her legs.

When she heard him drive up after midnight she jumped from bed and shouted from the window, "No, no! Go away!"

"What I never understood is why no one told me," she used to say. "They were supposed to be my friends."

Some failed, some divorced, some got shot in trailers like Doug Portis who had the excavation business and was seeing the policeman's wife. Some like her husband moved to Santa Barbara and became the extra man at dinner parties.

It was growing dark. Help me, someone, help me, she kept repeating. Someone would come, they had to. She tried not to be afraid. She thought of her father who could explain life in one sentence, "They knock you down and you get up. That's what it's all about." He recognized only one virtue. He would hear what had happened, that she merely lay there. She had to try to get home, even if she went only a little way, even a few yards.

Pushing with her palms she managed to drag herself, calling the horse as she did. Perhaps she could grab a stirrup if he came. She tried to find him. In the last of the light she saw the fading cottonwoods but the rest had disappeared. The fence posts were gone. The meadows had drifted away.

She tried to play a game, she wasn't lying near the ditch, she was in another place, in all the places, on Eleventh Street in that first apartment above the big skylight of the restaurant, the morning in Sausalito with the maid knocking on the door and Henry trying to call in Spanish, not now, not now! And postcards on the marble of the dresser and things they'd bought. Outside the hotel in Haiti the cabdrivers were leaning on their cars and calling out in soft voices, Hey, *blanc*, you like to go to a nice beach? Ibo beach? They wanted thirty dollars for the day, they said, which meant the price was probably about five. Go ahead, give it to him, she said. She could be there so easily, or in her own bed reading on a stormy day with the rain gusting against the window and the dogs near her feet. On the desk were photographs: horses, and her jumping, and one of her father at lunch outside when he was thirty, at Burning Tree. She had called him one day—she was getting married, she said. Married, he said, to whom? A man named Henry Vare, she said, who is wearing a beautiful suit, she wanted to add, and has wonderful wide hands. Tomorrow, she said.

"Tomorrow?" He sounded farther away. "Are you sure you're doing the right thing?"

"Absolutely."

"God bless you," he said.

That summer was the one they came here—it was where Henry had been living—and bought the place past the Macraes'. All year they fixed up the house and Henry started his landscaping business. They had their own world. Up through the fields in nothing but shorts, the earth warm under their feet, skin flecked with dirt from swimming in the ditch where the water was chilly and deep, like two sun-bleached children but far better, the screen door slamming, things on the kitchen table, catalogues, knives, new everything. Autumn with its brilliant blue skies and the first storms coming up from the west.

It was dark now, everywhere except up by the ridge. There were all the

214

things she had meant to do, to go East again, to visit certain friends, to live a year by the sea. She could not believe it was over, that she was going to be left here on the ground.

Suddenly she started to call for help, wildly, the cords standing out in her neck. In the darkness the horse raised his head. She kept shouting. She already knew it was a thing she would pay for, she was loosing the demonic. At last she stopped. She could hear the pounding of her heart and beyond that something else. Oh, God, she began to beg. Lying there she heard the first solemn drumbeats, terrible and slow.

Whatever it was, however bad, I'm going to do it as my father would, she thought. Hurriedly she tried to imagine him and as she was doing it a length of something went through her, something iron. In one unbelievable instant she realized the power of it, where it would take her, what it meant.

Her face was wet and she was shivering. Now it was here. Now you must do it, she realized. She knew there was a God, she hoped it. She shut her eyes. When she opened them it had begun, so utterly unforeseen and with such speed. She saw something dark moving along the fence line. It was her pony, the one her father had given her long ago, her black pony going home, across the broad fields, across the grassland. Wait, wait for me!

She began to scream.

Lights were jerking up and down along the ditch. It was a pickup coming over the uneven ground, the man who was sometimes building the lone house and a high school girl named Fern who worked at the golf course. They had the windows up and, turning, their lights swept close to the horse but they didn't see him. They saw him later, coming back in silence, the big handsome face in the darkness looking at them dumbly.

"He's saddled," Fern said in surprise.

He was standing calmly. That was how they found her. They put her in the back—she was limp, there was dirt in her ears—and drove into Glenwood at eighty miles an hour, not even stopping to call ahead.

That wasn't the right thing, as someone said later. It would have been better if they had gone the other way, about three miles up the road to Bob

Lamb's. He was the vet but he might have done something. Whatever you said, he was the best doctor around.

They would have pulled in with the headlights blooming on the white farmhouse as happened so many nights. Everyone knew Bob Lamb. There were a hundred dogs, his own among them, buried in back of the barn.

KAY BOYLE

Episode in the Life of an Ancestor

What a gold mine it was to come into the stable on an early morning that sparkled with rain and to start the horses tossing their manes on their shoulders, stamping and lashing with fury because she passed by them. Even more active was the one she would slap under the belly and throw the saddle over. She would stand close to him, whichever one he was, tapping him on the ribs with her knuckles until he blasted what breath he had in him straight out and drew his waist in tapering and fine. At the moment she passed his head with the single bit in her hand he would stand quiet, venturing to crane out his head and nibble with his soft loose lips at her shoulder.

The smallest horse was the favorite, and when he saw her he lifted his trim hind legs and shot them at the sides of the stall. His delicate hooves ran like a regiment over the blackened timber. He kicked in a frenzy, but his eyes were precisely on every move she was making, and his teeth, small and sweet and unlike a horse's teeth, were ready to smile. Even with his ears flat as a rabbit's as he kicked, there was a flicker of knowledge in the tips of them that waited patiently for her decision of whether she would fling the saddle over him or whether she would go on to another stall, leaving him ready to cry with impatience.

Her father was proud of the feminine ways there were in her, and especially of the choir voice she used in church. It was no pride to him to hear it turned hard and thin in her mouth to quiet a horse's ears when some fright had set them to fluttering on the beak of its head. But at a time when the

Indian fires made a wall that blossomed and faded at night on three sides of the sky, this grandmother was known as one of the best horsewomen in Kansas.

They were used to seeing her riding with a sunbonnet on her head—not in pants, but with wide skirts hullabalooing out behind her in the wind. At this time of the century nobody was very particular about the great length of the distances covered, and a day's ride from one town to another was like nothing at all. Kansas was like any other place on the map to them, and there was nothing strange about it to their minds. The horses that grew up there were simple enough not to shy away from skirts that slapped at their sides, and reserved their skittishness for lightning or for the occasion of the moon rising suddenly at night out of the dust of the highway. Trains were no trouble to them, for they could see them only in the distance on an edge they never approached, but for cows, that they knew capable of ripping open their sides, they had no antics, only ungarnished cowardice. Smoke, like the railway, was another thing too remote to be taken into account. They were used to seeing it along the edge of the prairie, twisting up from the Indian encampments and becoming a part of the wind woven of many odors that blew through the long tunnels of their noses but never interfered.

To her father it was a real sorrow that a needle and thread were rarely seen in her fingers. His wife was dead and it seemed to him that he must set flowing in his daughter the streams of gentleness and love that cooled the blood of true women. The idea was that she be sweetened by the honey of the ambitions he had for her. There was this irritation in him that could not be quieted: her indifference to the things that were his, his house, or the color and strength of his beard, and her interest in the sumac trees at the time they were ripe, or the sky with the crows flying across it in search of the shortest distance between two points (and finding it with a dignity and patience that was a shame to mankind).

Her father would listen for her to come down the hill from the stable, for she would often be singing aloud as she came around the side of it. It was he who had first taught her to ride, and even in the first months before year after year in the saddle had rubbed any tenderness out of her flesh, he had seen her way with horses. What she had no pity for, but a kind of arrogance instead, was for the melting eyes, the rich false chocolate drops of despair in a horse's head. But a horse's eye rolled in the socket back at her in fear over his foaming shoulder, tied fast with its own bloody veins, was a treasure. Rather than see this fact in her, her father preferred to lower his gaze and contemplate the patent tips of his boots.

One day as she was coming down from the stable he heard this miracle: she was singing and her voice struck some hollow in the opposite hill and curved and warbled there like the voice of a second singer. For a full minute he stood listening while the two voices sang together, her own voice deep and voluptuous and full like that of an older woman, and the other voice fresh and thin, singing always a note or two behind the other. Once she rounded the side of the barn there was nothing more to it, and she came down singing, and not suspecting that the other hill had taken the notes out of her mouth and piped them back at her father.

To please him maybe, but he was never sure enough if it were for that, she'd do the things that were to be done in the kitchen. She could stuff a cod very nicely, stitch up its belly, and see that it baked. From the French side she had learned to put fresh mackerel in kegs with white wine and lemon peel and a bouquet of spice. But on these occasions her beautiful red hair would be pulled back from her face, tight into a net at the back of her head, as naturally as if it had of itself recoiled in distaste from the monotony of the tasks performed before it.

There was a special flavor to the snuffle that a mount splattered out of his nose on the wind and back onto the face and mouth. What a feast of splatters when she would come out from a long time in the kitchen and walk in upon the beasts who were stamping and sick with impatience for her in the barn! She would find them in fury at every hole in the stallboards, and at the hay fleas jumping through the fodder in the manger, and at the soft balls of manure packed solid in their hoofs. An ovation of splatters would shower out before her. It was early fall and black as a pocket when she came out from a whole day in the house and saddled the smallest horse and rode him out the door.

Her father saw her riding off alone this way and he sat home thinking of the things that might become of his daughter. He sat away from the window, thinking that the sight of the darkness outside was no help to him and that with his paper down on his knees and his eyes closed he was better off. Outside she was riding away, any way, hammering off through the dark with nobody knowing what was going on inside her or what she was filled with, the hooves of the horse hammering tack tracks in the blackness that was maybe the road, or the dust, or the prairie, that blew richly from side to side. Her father was thinking that someday she might go off and be married, and he was willing for her to marry a gentleman someday, but these were not the feminine ways he thought of stirring in her. He was more concerned with the cooking and the sewing ways that would be a comfort to him and keep him to his own satisfaction.

The thought of her marrying made him think of the schoolmaster who was the only gentleman in the countryside. Her father sat with the points of the fingers of his two hands together and with his elbows resting on the arms of his rocking chair. He sat rocking gently back and forth with his thoughts, and then it came to him that early in the evening he had seen the young schoolmaster walking out as well onto the prairie. He had sat by the window, watching the small strong figure of the schoolmaster making his way up the road over the prairie, and he began wondering how it would be to have the schoolmaster in the family, married to his daughter and living with them there every day in the house. This was a quiet enough thought to him and it kept him rocking gently back and forth for a while.

But with his daughter off in the night this way he became restless, and presently he started up and found himself at the window, looking out for her. He was surprised to find that in the little time he had been sitting in his chair the moon had come up and was lighting up all the country around. He could see very clearly the softly flowering goldenrod, white as flax under the moon, and the deep valleys and gulfs of the whole blossoming prairie. All along the edge of it were the Indian fires burning as hard and bright as peonies.

He asked himself what in the world his daughter could be doing out at this time of the night. It was such a strange thing that he crossed the room and went up the stairs that had a narrow ribbon of carpet running down the middle of them like a spine. He opened the door of her room and looked in, but it was empty. Only with the lamp in his hand he saw something that caught his eye. It was the corner of a volume sticking out from under her folded quilt. Maybe she had intended to hide it away in her quilt, but the old man took it out by the end and turned its face up to the light. Poetry it was, he saw, with pictures engraved through it of a kind that brought the blood flying to his face. His fingers trembled on the flyleaf and there he saw the name of the schoolmaster inscribed in the young man's long leaning hand, while the book itself had been left open at the picture entitled *The Creation of Eve*. Under it he read the words the poet had written:

> . . . *To the Nuptial Bowre*
> *I led her blushing like the Morn: all Heav'n*
> *And happie Constellations on that houre*
> *Shed thir selectest influence; the Earth*
> *Gave sign of gratulation, and each Hill;*
> *Joyous the Birds; fresh Gales and gentle Aires*
> *Whisper'd it to the Woods, and from thir wings*
> *Flung Rose, flung Odours from the spicie Shrub,*
> *Disporting, till the amorous Bird of Night*
> *Sung Spousal, and bid haste the Evening Starr*
> *On his Hill top, to light the bridal Lamp.*

You fine example to the young, screamed the father's mind. You creeping out into the night to do what harm you can, creeping out and doing God knows what harm, God knows. He went quivering down the stairs, his mind in a fury. The low educated fellow forgetting his precious learning and out after the poor girl after dark on the prairie, he was thinking. Very clearly in his rage he could see the meeting of the eyebrows over the schoolmaster's nose, so hateful had he become to him, seeing them in detail, the black sprinkling of hairs that grew down between the schoolmaster's eyes. In his mind he thought of every part of the young man's face, and especially of the pores in the wings of his nose, and he began to walk back and forth in a fury in the house.

The horse on which the grandmother was riding had come to some kind of incline in the ground, and there he slowed his pace and began feeling his way with great delicacy through the bushes that flowed back over his thin knees. The grandmother's hands let the rein ride loose on his neck, and he flicked his ears forward and back in the dark for some sound from her. He kept chewing with his teeth at the bit in his mouth and tossing the rings of the mouthpiece so that they rang aloud. There was no movement even in her legs that hung down around his belly, and with the interest of selecting his own way absorbing him, without any display of fear he watched the moon coming up, straining his ears almost out of his head as he followed it edging up ahead of him through the prairie grass.

It was at this moment that he was startled by a faint stir in the bushes, and to quiet his heart's beating he drew several long cool blasts into his lungs the better to listen for what was to come. No help was given him by the grandmother who had never before abandoned him to his own wits, and trying to keep his head clear and away from fright he was left to discover all by himself that the wind had risen with the moon.

After the first moment it went out of his head to make a scene about the wind and he went on, pointing his ears to the sound of it in the grass and clicking his heels sharply on every stone he passed over. The wind was lifting off the bunches of white feather from the milkweed pods that had burst dry and floury in the September night. It was taking the ripe milkweed seeds with the cotton crowning them and blowing them over the crust of the prairie. First it was this, a simple rising and falling of the breath as the tufted seeds went, and then as fold of the wind opened on fold, out they came in a tide, leaving the empty husks rattling and hissing like snakes behind them.

Presently the milkweed blow had strengthened so that it was sweeping across the whole upper reaches of the prairie. To the eye it seemed knee-deep and ravenous, but it came only to the crests of the little horse's hooves and there washed delicately about them. He gave many humorous leaps and cavorts in the blowing tide, spraying it with splutter from his nose and si- dling prettily up to the moon. Only when he ventured a sharp glance out over any distance did the terror of the enormous shifting plain, seething as it was with the milkweed blow, disturb him.

This was tame idle sport, suited to ladies, this romping in the milkweed cotton across the miles of piecrust. Suddenly he felt this anger in the grand- mother's knees and it caught and swung him about in the wind. Without any regard for him at all, so that he was in a quiver of admiration and love for her, she jerked him up and back, rearing his wild head high, his front hooves left clawing at the space that yapped under them. To such a frenzy of kicking she urged him that he was ready to faint with delight. Even had she wished to now she could never have calmed him, and she started putting him over bushes and barriers, setting his head to them and stretching him thin as a string to save the smooth nut of his belly from scraping, reeling him so close to the few pine trunks that streamed up like torrents that he leaped sideways to save his fair coat from ripping open on their spikes. It was a long way to travel back, but he never stopped until his hooves thundered into the barn that had shrunk too small for him. There he stood in the darkness, wet and throbbing like a heart cut out of the body.

The leap of the grandmother down off his back startled him afresh into such terror that he sprang off as light as a frog across the boards of the floor. The leather of the saddle was steaming with his sweat, and after she had stripped him she brushed him down quickly and slapped him into his stall.

In the parlor of the house the father was sitting quite still at the table. He was asking himself in great self-pity how he was to know what had become of her during the night. A great many things that had nothing to do with it went through his mind, and one thing was that it was sad to have no one of his own time to talk to. When she came into the room she was there in front of him in the same way that the roses on the floor were woven straight across the rug. Where have you been to, he wanted to say to her, but he could not bring himself to speak. With someone of his own years, maybe, speech would already have been running nimble between them. He was ready to say right out that he had seen the schoolmaster walking out early in the evening up on the road that led nowhere except out onto the prairie. Well, now, what have you been up to with the schoolmaster, he was ready to say.

But the grandmother in anger had seen her book and picked it up from the table, and put it close to her under her arm. In his sorrow for himself the father turned his head away from the sight of her. With this woman in the room with him he was beginning to see the poor little schoolmaster, the poor squat little periwinkle with his long nose always thrust away in a book. He began to remember that the horse his daughter had been out riding all night had once backed up on just such a little whippersnapper as was the schoolmaster and kicked his skull into a cocked hat. He began to worry for the sake of the schoolmaster who was such a timid little fellow and not used to Kansas, who might get into harm's way.

The father kept turning his head away from the sight of this woman. She stood by the table with her eyes staring like a hawk's eyes straight into the oil lamp's blaze. The farm and the prairie, he thought in anger, and the sky with the moon in it would only be remembered because this woman would carry them off in her own hard heart. They would not be remembered for anything else at all.

"What have you done to the schoolmaster?" he wanted to say to her. The words were right there in his mouth but he couldn't get them out.

ELIZABETH SPENCER

The Girl Who Loved Horses

I

She had drawn back from throwing a pan of bird scraps out the door because she heard what was coming, the two-part pounding of a full gallop,
not the graceful triple notes of a canter. They were mounting the drive now,
turning into the stretch along the side of the house; once before someone
appearing at the screen door had made the horse shy, so that, barely held
beneath the rider, barely restrained, he had plunged off into the flower beds.
So she stepped back from the door and saw the two of them shoot past,
rounding a final corner, heading for the straight run of drive into the cattle
gate and the barn lot back of it.

She flung out the scraps, then walked to the other side of the kitchen
and peered through the window, raised for spring, toward the barn lot. The
horse had slowed, out of habit, knowing what came next. And the white
shirt that had passed hugged so low as to seem some strange part of the
animal's trappings, or as though he had run under a low line of drying laun-
dry and caught something to an otherwise empty saddle and bare withers,
now rose up, angling to an upright posture. A gloved hand extended to pat
the lathered neck.

"Lord have mercy," the woman said. The young woman riding the
horse was her daughter, but she was speaking also for her son-in-law who
went in for even more reckless behavior in the jumping ring the two of them
had set up. What she meant by it was that they were going to kill themselves

225

before they ever had any children, or if they did have children safely they'd bring up the children to be just as foolish about horses and careless of life and limb as they were themselves.

The young woman's booted heel struck the back steps. The screen door banged.

"You ought not to bring him in hot like that," the mother said. "I do know that much."

"Cottrell is out there," she said.

"It's still March, even if it has got warm."

"Cottrell knows what to do."

She ran water at the sink, and cupping her hand drank primitive fashion out of it, bending to the tap, then wet her hands in the running water and thrust her fingers into the dusty, sweat-damp roots of her sand-colored hair. It had been a good ride.

"I hope he doesn't take up too much time," the mother said. "My beds need working."

She spoke mildly but it was always part of the same quarrel they were in like a stream that was now a trickle, now a still pool, but sometimes after a freshet could turn into a torrent. Such as: "Y'all are just crazy. Y'all are wasting everything on those things. And what are they? I know they're pretty and all that, but they're not a thing in the world but animals. Cows are animals. You can make a lot more money in cattle, than carting those things around over two states and three counties."

She could work herself up too much to eat, leaving the two of them at the table, but would see them just the same in her mind's eye, just as if she'd stayed. There were the sandy-haired young woman, already thirty—married four years and still apparently with no intention of producing a family (she was an only child and the estate, though small, was a fine piece of land)— and across from her the dark spare still young man she had married.

She knew how they would sit there alone and not even look at one another or discuss what she'd said or talk against her; they would just sit there and maybe pass each other some food or one of them would get up for the coffeepot. The fanatics of a strange cult would do the same, she often thought, loosening her long hair upstairs, brushing the gray and brown together to a colorless patina, putting on one of her long cotton gowns with the ruched neck, crawling in between white cotton sheets. She was a widow and if she didn't want to sit up and try to talk to the family after a hard day, she didn't have to. Reading was a joy, lifelong. She found her place in *Middlemarch*, one of her favorites.

But during the day not even reading (if she'd had the time) could shut out the sounds from back of the privet hedge, plainly to be heard from the house. The trudging of the trot, the pause, the low directive, the thud of hooves, the heave and shout, and sometimes the ring of struck wood as a bar came down. And every jump a risk of life and limb. One dislocated shoulder—Clyde's, thank heaven, not Deedee's—a taping, a sling, a contraption of boards, and pain "like a hot knife," he had said. A hot knife. Wouldn't that hurt anybody enough to make him quit risking life and limb with those two blood horses, quit at least talking about getting still another one while swallowing down painkiller he said he hated to be sissy enough to take?

"Uh-huh," the mother said. "But it'll be Deborah next. You thought about that?"

"Aw, now, Miss Emma," he'd lean back to say, charming her through his warrior's haze of pain. "Deedee and me—that's what we're hooked on. Think of us without it, Mama. You really want to kill us. We couldn't live."

He was speaking to his mother-in-law but smiling at his wife. And she, Deborah, was smiling back.

Her name was Deborah Dale, but they'd always, of course, being from LaGrange, Tennessee, right over the Mississippi border, that is to say, real South, had a hundred nicknames for her. Deedee, her father had named her, and "Deeds" her funny cousins said—"Hey, Deeds, how ya' doin'?" Being on this property in a town of pretty properties, though theirs was a little way out, a little bit larger than most, she was always out romping, swimming in forbidden creeks, climbing forbidden fences, going barefoot too soon in the spring, the last one in at recess, the first one to turn in an exam paper. ("Are you quite sure that you have finished, Deborah?" "Yes, ma'am.")

When she graduated from ponies to that sturdy calico her uncle gave her, bringing it in from his farm because he had an eye for a good match, there was almost no finding her. "I always know she's somewhere on the place," her mother said. "We just can't see it all at once," said her father. He was ailing even back then but he undertook walks. Once when the leaves had all but gone from the trees, on a warm November afternoon, from a slight rise, he saw her down in a little-used pasture with a straight open stretch among some oaks. The ground was spongy and clotted with damp and a child ought not to have tried to run there. But there went the calico with Deedee clinging low, going like the wind, and knowing furthermore out of what couldn't be anything but long practice, where to turn, where to veer, where to stop.

"One fine afternoon," he said to himself, suspecting even then (they hadn't told him yet) what his illness was, "and Emma's going to be left with nobody." He remarked on this privately, not without anguish and not without humor.

They stopped her riding, at least like that, by sending her off to boarding school, where a watchful ringmaster took "those girls interested in equitation" out on leafy trails, "at the walk, at the trot, and at the canter." They also, with that depth of consideration which must flourish even among those Southerners unlucky enough to wind up in the lower reaches of hell, kept her young spirit out of the worst of the dying. She just got a call from the housemother one night. Her father had "passed away."

After college she forgot it, she gave it up. It was too expensive, it took a lot of time and devotion, she was interested in boys. Some boys were interested in her. She worked in Memphis, drove home to her mother every night. In winter she had to eat breakfast in the dark. On some evenings the phone rang; on some it was silent. Her mother treated both kinds of evenings just the same.

* * *

To Emma Tyler it always seemed that Clyde Mecklin materialized out of nowhere. She ran straight into him when opening the front door one evening to get the paper off the porch, he being just about to turn the bell or knock. There he stood, dark and straight in the late light that comes after first dark and is so clear. He was clear as anything in it, clear as the first stamp of a young man ever cast.

"Is Deb'rah here?" At least no Yankee. But not Miss Tyler or Miss Deborah Tyler, or Miss Deborah. No, he was city all right.

She did not answer at first.

"What's the matter, scare you? I was just about to knock."

She still said nothing.

"Maybe this is the wrong place," he said.

"No, it's the right place," Emma Tyler finally said. She stepped back and held the door wider. "Come on in."

"Scared the life out of me," she told Deborah when she finally came down to breakfast the next day, Clyde's car having been heard to depart by Emma Tyler in her upstairs bedroom at an hour she did not care to verify. "Why didn't you tell me you were expecting him? I just opened the door and there he was."

"I liked him so much," said Deborah with grave honesty. "I guess I was scared he wouldn't come. That would have hurt."

"Do you still like him?" her mother ventured, after this confidence.

"He's all for outdoors," said Deborah, as dreamy over coffee as any mother had ever beheld. "Everybody is so indoors. He likes hunting, going fishing, farms."

"Has he got one?"

"He'd like to have. All he's got's this job. He's coming back next weekend. You can talk to him. He's interested in horses."

"But does he know we don't keep horses anymore?"

"That was just my thumbnail sketch," said Deborah. "We don't have to run out and buy any."

"No, I don't imagine so," said her mother, but Deborah hardly remarked the peculiar turn of tone, the dryness. She was letting coast through her head the scene: her mother (whom she now loved better than she ever had in her life) opening the door just before Clyde knocked, so seeing unexpectedly for the first time, that face, that head, that being. . . . When he had kissed her her ears drummed, and it came back to her once more, not thought of in years, the drumming hooves of the calico, and the ghosting father, behind, invisible, observant, off on the bare distant November rise.

It was after she married that Deborah got beautiful. All LaGrange noticed it. "I declare," they said to her mother or sometimes right out to her face, "I always said she was nice looking but I never thought anything like that."

II

Emma first saw the boy in the parking lot. He was new.

In former days she'd parked in front of nearly any place she wanted to go—hardware, or drugstore, or courthouse: change for the meter was her biggest problem. But so many streets were one-way now and what with the increased numbers of cars, the growth of the town, those days were gone; she used a parking lot back of a cafe, near the newspaper office. The entrance to the lot was a bottleneck of a narrow drive between the two brick buildings; once in, it was hard sometimes to park.

That day the boy offered to help. He was an expert driver, she noted, whereas Emma was inclined to perspire, crane, and fret, fearful of scraping a fender or grazing a door. He spun the wheel with one hand; a glance told him all he had to know; he as good as sat the car in place, as skillful (she reluctantly thought) as her children on their horses. When she returned an hour later, the cars were denser still; he helped her again. She wondered whether to tip him. This happened twice more.

"You've been so nice to me," she said, the last time. "They're lucky to have you."

"It's not much of a job," he said. "Just all I can get for the moment. Being new and all."

"I might need some help," she said. "You can call up at the Tyler place if you want to work. It's in the book. Right now I'm in a hurry."

On the warm June day, Deborah sat the horse comfortably in the side yard and watched her mother and the young man (whose name was Willett? Williams?), who, having worked the beds and straightened a fence post, was now replacing warped fence boards with new ones.

"Who is he?" she asked her mother, not quite low enough, and meaning what a Southern woman invariably means by that question, not what is his name but where did he come from, is he anybody we know? What excuse, in other words, does he have for even being born?

"One thing, he's a good worker," her mother said, preening a little. Did they think she couldn't manage if she had to? "Now don't you make him feel bad."

"Feel bad!" But once again, if only to spite her mother, who was in a way criticizing her and Clyde by hiring anybody at all to do work that Clyde or the Negro help would have been able to do if only it weren't for those horses—once again Deborah had spoken too loudly.

If she ever had freely to admit things, even to herself, Deborah would have to say she knew she not only looked good that June day, she looked sexy as hell. Her light hair, tousled from a ride in the fields, had grown longer in the last year; it had slipped its pins on one side and lay in a sensuous lock along her cheek. A breeze stirred it, then passed by. Her soft poplin shirt was loose at the throat, the two top buttons open, the cuffs turned back to her elbows. The new horse, the third, was gentle, too much so (this worried them); she sat it easily, one leg up, crossed lazily over the flat English pommel, while the horse, head stretched down, cropped at the tender grass. In the silence between their voices, the tearing of the grass was the only sound except for a shrill jay's cry.

"Make him feel bad!" she repeated.

231

The boy looked up. The horse, seeking grass, had moved forward; she was closer than before, eyes looking down on him above the rise of her breasts and throat; she saw the closeness go through him, saw her presence register as strongly as if the earth's accidental shifting had slammed them physically together. For a minute there was nothing but the two of them. The jay was silent; even the horse, sensing something, had raised his head.

Stepping back, the boy stumbled over the pile of lumber, then fell in it. Deborah laughed. Nothing, that day, could have stopped her laughter. She was beautifully, languidly, atop a fine horse on the year's choice day at the peak of her life.

"You know what?" Deborah said at supper, when they were discussing her mother's helper. "I thought who he looks like. He looks like Clyde."

"The poor guy," Clyde said. "Was that the best you could do?"

Emma sat still. Now that she thought of it, he did look like Clyde. She stopped eating, to think it over. What difference did it make if he did? She returned to her plate.

Deborah ate lustily, her table manners unrestrained. She swobbed bread into the empty salad bowl, drenched it with dressing, bit it in hunks.

"The poor woman's Clyde, that's what you hired," she said. She looked up.

The screen door had just softly closed in the kitchen behind them. Emma's hired man had come in for his money.

It was the next day that the boy, whose name was Willett or Williams, broke the riding mower by running it full speed into a rock pile overgrown with weeds but clearly visible, and left without asking for pay but evidently taking with him in his car a number of selected items from barn, garage, and tack room, along with a transistor radio that Clyde kept in the kitchen for getting news with his early coffee.

Emma Tyler, vexed for a number of reasons she did not care to sort out (prime among them was the very peaceful and good time she had been having with the boy the day before in the yard before Deborah had chosen to ride over and join them), telephoned the police and reported the whole mat-

232

ter. But boy, car, and stolen articles vanished into the nowhere. That was all, for what they took to be forever.

III

Three years later, aged thirty-three, Deborah Mecklin was carrying her fine head higher than ever uptown in LaGrange. She drove herself on errands back and forth in car or station wagon, not looking to left or right, not speaking so much as before. She was trying not to hear from the outside what they were now saying about Clyde, how well he'd done with the horses, that place was as good as a stud farm now that he kept ten or a dozen, advertised and traded, as well as showed. And the money was coming in hard and fast. But, they would add, he moved with a fast set, and there was also the occasional gossip item, too often, in Clyde's case, with someone ready to report firsthand; look how quick, now you thought of it, he'd taken up with Deborah, and how she'd snapped him up too soon to hear what his reputation was, even back then. It would be a cold day in August before any one woman would be enough for him. And his father before him? And his father before him. So the voices said.

Deborah, too, was trying not to hear what was still sounding from inside her head after her fall in the last big horse show:

The doctor: You barely escaped concussion, young lady.

Clyde: I just never saw your timing go off like that. I can't get over it.

Emma: You'd better let it go for a while, honey. There're other things, so many other things.

Back home, she later said to Emma: "Oh, Mama, I know you're right sometimes, and sometimes I'm sick of it all, but Clyde depends on me, he always has, and now look—"

"Yes, and 'Now look' is right, he has to be out with it to keep it all running. You got your wish, is all I can say."

Emma was frequently over at her sister-in-law Marian's farm these days. The ladies were aging, Marian especially down in the back, and those twilights in the house alone were more and more all that Deedee had to keep herself company with. Sometimes the phone rang and there'd be Clyde on it, to say he'd be late again. Or there'd be no call at all. And once she (of all people) pressed some curtains and hung them, and once hunted for old photographs, and once, standing in the middle of the little-used parlor among the walnut Victorian furniture upholstered in gold and blue and rose, she had said "Daddy?" right out loud, like he might have been there to answer, really been there. It had surprised her, the word falling out like that as though a thought took reality all by itself and made a word on its own.

And once there came a knock at the door.

All she thought, though she hadn't heard the car, was that it was Clyde and that he'd forgotten his key, or seeing her there, his arms loaded maybe, was asking her to let him in. It was past dark. Though times were a little more chancy now, LaGrange was a safe place. People nearer to town used to brag that if they went off for any length of time less than a weekend and locked the doors, the neighbors would get their feelings hurt; and if the Tylers lived further out and "locked up," the feeling for it was ritual mainly, a precaution.

She glanced through the sidelight, saw what she took for Clyde, and opened the door. There were cedars in the front yard, not too near the house, but dense enough to block out whatever gathering of light there might have been from the long slope of property beyond the front gate. There was no moon.

The man she took for Clyde, instead of stepping through the door or up to the threshold to greet her, withdrew a step and leaned down and to one side, turning outward as though to pick up something. It was she who stepped forward, to greet, help, inquire; for deep within was the idea her mother had seen to it was firmly and forever planted: that one day one of them was going to get too badly hurt by "those things" ever to be patched up.

So it was in outer dark, three paces from the safe threshold and to the left of the area where the light was falling outward, a dim single sidelight

234

near the mantelpiece having been all she had switched on, too faint to pene-
trate the sheer gathered curtains of the sidelight, that the man at the door
rose up, that he tried to take her. The first she knew of it, his face was in
hers, not Clyde's but something like it and at Clyde's exact height, so that
for the moment she thought that some joke was on, and then the strange
hand caught the parting of her blouse, a new mouth fell hard on her own,
one knee thrust her legs apart, the free hand diving in to clutch and press
against the thin nylon between her thighs. She recoiled at the same time that
she felt, touched in the quick, the painful glory of desire brought on too
fast—looking back on that instant's two-edged meaning, she would never
hear about rape without the lightning quiver of ambivalence within the
word. However, at the time no meditation stopped her knee from coming
up into the nameless groin and nothing stopped her from tearing back her
mouth slathered with spit so suddenly smeared into it as to drag it into the
shape of a scream she was unable yet to find voice for. Her good right arm
struck like a hard backhand against a line-smoking tennis serve. Then from
the driveway came the stream of twin headlights thrusting through the
cedars.

"Bitch!" The word, distorted and low, was like a groan; she had hurt
him, freed herself for a moment, but the struggle would have just begun
except for the lights, and the screams that were just trying to get out of her.
"You fucking bitch." He saw the car lights, wavered, then turned. His leap
into the shrubbery was bent, like a hunchback's. She stopped screaming
suddenly. Hurt where he lived, she thought. The animal motion, wounded,
drew her curiosity for a second. Saved, she saw the car sweep round the
drive, but watched the bushes shake, put up her hand to touch but not to
close the torn halves of the blouse, which was ripped open to her waist.

Inside, she stood looking down at herself in the dim light. There was a
nail scratch near the left nipple, two teeth marks between elbow and wrist
where she'd smashed into his mouth. She wiped her own mouth on the back
of her hand, gagging at the taste of cigarette smoke, bitterly staled. Animals!
She'd always had a special feeling for them, a helpless tenderness. In her
memory the bushes, shaking to a crippled flight, shook forever.

She went upstairs, stood trembling in her mother's room (Emma was away), combed her hair with her mother's comb. Then, hearing Clyde's voice calling her below, she stripped off her ravaged blouse and hastened across to their own rooms to hide it in a drawer, change into a fresh one, come downstairs. She had made her decision already. Who was this man? A nothing . . . an unknown. She hated women who shouted Rape! Rape! It was an incident, but once she told it everyone would know, along with the police, and would add to it: they'd say she'd been violated. It was an incident, but Clyde, once he knew, would trace him down. Clyde would kill him.

"Did you know the door was wide open?" He was standing in the living room.

"I know. I must have opened it when I heard the car. I thought you were stopping in the front."

"Well, I hardly ever do."

"Sometimes you do."

"Deedee, have you been drinking?"

"Drinking . . . ? Me?" She squinted at him, joking in her own way; it was a standing quarrel now that alone she sometimes poured one or two.

He would check her breath but not her marked body. Lust with him was mole-dark now, not desire in the soft increase of morning light, or on slowly westering afternoons, or by the nightlight's glow. He would kill for her because she was his wife. . . .

"Who was that man?"

Uptown one winter afternoon late, she had seen him again. He had been coming out of the hamburger place and looking back, seeing her through the streetlights, he had turned quickly into an alley. She had hurried to catch up, to see. But only a form was hastening there, deeper into the unlit slit between brick walls, down toward a street and a section nobody went into without good reason.

"That man," she repeated to the owner (also the proprietor and cook) in the hamburger place. "He was in here just now."

"I don't know him. He hangs around. Wondered myself. You know him?"

"I think he used to work for us once, two or three years ago. I just wondered."

"I thought I seen him somewhere myself."

"He looks a little bit like Clyde."

"Maybe so. Now you mention it." He wiped the counter with a wet rag. "Get you anything, Miss Deborah?"

"I got to get home."

"Y'all got yourselves some prizes, huh?"

"Aw, just some good luck." She was gone.

Prizes, yes. Two trophies at the Shelby County Fair, one in Brownsville where she'd almost lost control again, and Clyde not worrying about her so much as scolding her. His recent theory was that she was out to spite him. He would think it if he was guilty about the women, and she didn't doubt anymore that he was. But worse than spite was what had got to her, hating as she did to admit it.

It was fear.

She'd never known it before. When it first started she hadn't even known what the name of it was.

Over two years ago, Clyde had started buying colts not broken yet from a stud farm south of Nashville, bringing them home for him and Deborah to get in shape together. It saved a pile of money to do it that way. She'd been thrown in consequence three times, trampled once, a terrifying moment as the double reins had caught up her outstretched arm so she couldn't fall free. Now when she closed her eyes at night, steel hooves sometimes hung through the dark above them, and she felt hard ground beneath her head, smelt smeared grass on cheek and elbow. To Clyde she murmured in the dark: "I'm not good at it anymore." "Why, Deeds, you were always good. It's temporary, honey. That was a bad luck day."

A great couple. That's what Clyde thought of them. But more than half their name had been made by her, by the sight of her, Deborah Mecklin, out in full dress, black broadcloth and white satin stock with hair drawn trimly back beneath the smooth rise of the hat, entering the show ring. She looked damned good back of the glossy neck's steep arch, the pointed ears and lacquered hooves which hardly touched earth before springing upward, as though in the instant before actual flight. There was always the stillness, then the murmur, the rustle of the crowd. At top form she could even get applause. A fame for a time spread round them. The Mecklins. Great riders. "Ridgewood Stables. Blood horses trained. Saddle and Show." He'd had it put up in wrought iron, with a sign as well, old English style, of a horseman spurring.

("Well, you got to make money," said Miss Emma to her son-in-law. "And don't I know it," she said. "But I just hate to think how many times I kept those historical people from putting up a marker on this place. And now all I do is worry one of y'all's going to break your neck. If it wasn't for Marian needing me and all . . . I just can't sleep a wink over here."

("You like to be over there anyway, Mama," Deborah said. "You know we want you here."

("Sure, we want you here," said Clyde. "As for the property, we talked it all out beforehand. I don't think I've damaged it any way."

("I just never saw it as a horse farm. But it's you all I worry about. It's the danger.")

Deborah drove home.

When the working man her mother had hired three years before had stolen things and left, he had left too, on the garage wall inside, a long pair of crossing diagonal lines, brown, in mud, she thought, until she smelled what it was, and there were the blood-stained menstrual pads she later came across in the driveway, dug up out of the garbage, strewed out into the yard.

She told Clyde about the first but not the second discovery. "Some critters are mean," he'd shrugged it off. "Some critters are just mean."

They'd been dancing, out at the club. And so in love back then, he'd turned and turned her, far apart, then close, talking into her ear, making her laugh and answer, but finally he said: "Are you a mean critter, Deedee? Some critters are mean." And she'd remembered what she didn't tell.

But in those days Clyde was passionate and fun, both marvelously together, and the devil appearing at midnight in the bend of a country road would not have scared her. Nothing would have. It was the day of her life when they bought the first two horses.

"I thought I seen him somewhere myself."

"He looks a little bit like Clyde."

And dusk again, a third and final time.

The parking lot where she'd come after a movie was empty except for a few cars. The small office was unlighted, but a man she took for the attendant was bending to the door on the far side of a long cream-colored sedan near the back fence. "Want my ticket?" she called. The man straightened, head rising above the body frame, and she knew him. Had he been about to steal a car, or was he breaking in for whatever he could find, or was it her coming all alone that he was waiting for? However it was, he knew her as instantly as she knew him. Each other was what they had, by whatever design or absence of it, found. Deborah did not cry out or stir.

Who knew how many lines life had cut away from him down through the years till the moment when an arrogant woman on a horse had ridden him down with lust and laughter? He wasn't bad looking; his eyes were beautiful; he was the kind to whom nothing good could happen. From that bright day to this chilly dusk, it had probably just been the same old story.

Deborah waited. Someway or other, what was coming, threading through the scars like an animal lost for years catching the scent of a former owner, was her own.

("You're losing nerve, Deedee," Clyde had told her recently. "That's what's really bothering me. You're scared, aren't you?")

The bitter-stale smell of cigarette breath, though not so near as before, not forced against her mouth, was still unmistakably familiar. But the prod of a gun's nuzzle just under the rise of her breast was not. It had never happened to her before. She shuddered at the touch with a chill springlike start of something like life, which was also something like death.

"Get inside," he said.

"Are you the same one?" she asked. "Just tell me that. Three years ago, Mama hired somebody. Was that you?"

"Get in the car."

She opened the door, slid over to the driver's seat, found him beside her. The gun, thrust under his crossed arm, resumed its place against her.

"Drive."

"Was it you the other night at the door?" Her voice trembled as the motor started, the gear caught.

"He left me with the lot; ain't nobody coming."

The car eased into an empty street.

"Go out of town. The Memphis road."

She was driving past familiar, cared-for lawns and houses, trees and intersections. Someone waved from a car at a stoplight, taking them for her and Clyde. She was frightened and accepting fear which come to think of it was all she'd been doing for months, working with those horses. ("Don't let him bluff you, Deedee. It's you or him. He'll do it if he can.")

"What do you want with me? What is it you want?"

He spoke straight outward, only his mouth moving, watching the road, never turning his head to her. "You're going out on that Memphis road and you're going up a side road with me. There's some woods I know. When I'm through with you you ain't never going to have nothing to ask nobody about me because you're going to know it all and it ain't going to make you laugh none, I guarantee."

Deborah cleared the town and swinging into the highway wondered at herself. Did she want him? She had waited when she might have run. Did she want, trembling, pleading, degraded, finally to let him have every single thing his own way?

(Do you see steel hooves above you over and over because you want them one day to smash into your brain?

("Daddy, Daddy," she had murmured long ago when the old unshaven tramp had come up into the lawn, bleary-eyed, face blood-burst with years of drink and weather, frightening as the boogeyman, "raw head and bloody bones," like the Negro women scared her with. That day the sky streamed with end-of-the-world fire. But she hadn't called so loudly as she might have, she'd let him come closer, to look at him better, until the threatening voice of her father behind her, just on the door's slamming, had cried: "What do you want in this yard? What you think you want here? Deborah! You come in this house this minute!" But the mystery still lay dark within her, forgotten for years, then stirring to life again: When I said "Daddy, Daddy?" was I calling to the tramp or to the house? Did I think the tramp was him in some sort of joke or dream or trick? If not, why did I say it? Why?

("Why do you ride a horse so fast, Deedee? Why do you like to do that?" *I'm going where the sky breaks open.* "I just like to." "Why do you like to drive so fast?" "I don't know.")

Suppose he kills me, too, thought Deborah, striking the straight stretch on the Memphis road, the beginning of the long rolling run through farms and woods. She stole a glance to her right. He looked like Clyde, all right. What right did he have to look like Clyde?

("It's you or him, Deedee." All her life they'd said that to her from the time her first pony, scared at something, didn't want to cross a bridge. "Don't let him get away with it. It's you or him.")

Righting the big car into the road ahead, she understood what was demanded of her. She pressed the accelerator gradually downward toward the floor.

"And by the time he realized," she said, sitting straight in her chair at supper between Clyde and Emma, who by chance were there that night together; "—by the time he knew, we were hitting above seventy-five, and he said, 'What you speeding for?' and I said, 'I want to get it over with.' And he said, 'Okay, but that's too fast.' By that time we were touching eighty and he said, 'What the fucking hell—' Excuse me, Mama, '—you think you're doing? You slow this thing down.' So I said, 'I tell you what I'm doing. This is a rolling road with high banks and trees and lots of curves. If you try to take the wheel away from me, I'm going to wreck us both. If you try to sit there with that gun in my side I'm going to go faster and faster and sooner or later something will happen, like a curve too sharp to take or a car too many to pass with a big truck coming and we're both going to get smashed up at the very least. It won't do any good to shoot me when it's more than likely both of us will die. You want that?'

"He grabbed at the wheel but I put on another spurt of speed and when he pulled at the wheel we side-rolled, skidded back, and another car coming almost didn't get out of the way. I said, 'You see what you're doing, I guess.' And he said, 'Jesus God.' Then I knew I had him, had whipped him down.

"But it was another two or three miles like that before he said, 'Okay, okay, so I quit. Just slow down and let's forget it.' And I said, 'You give me that gun. The mood I'm in, I can drive with one hand or no hands at all, and don't think I won't do it.' But he wanted his gun at least, I could tell. He didn't give in till a truck was ahead and we passed but barely missed a car that was coming (it had to run off the concrete), and he put it down, in my lap."

(Like a dog, she could have said, but didn't. And I felt sorry for him, she could have added, because it was his glory's end.)

"So I said, 'Get over, way over,' and he did, and I coasted from fast to slow. I turned the gun around on him and let him out on an empty stretch of road, by a rise with a wood and a country side road rambling off, real pretty, and I thought, maybe that's where he was talking about, where he meant to screw hell—Excuse me, Mama—out of me. I held the gun till he closed the door and went down in the ditch a little way, then I put the safety catch on and threw it at him. It hit his shoulder then fell in the weeds. I saw it fall, driving off."

"Oh, my poor baby," said Emma. "Oh, my precious child."

It was Clyde who rose, came round the table to her, drew her to her feet, held her close. "That's nerve," he said. "That's class." He let her go and she sat down again. "Why didn't you shoot him?"

"I don't know."

"He was that one we hired that time," Emma said. "I'd be willing to bet you anything."

"No, it wasn't," said Deborah quickly. "This one was blond and short,

242

red-nosed from too much drinking, I guess. Awful like Mickey Rooney, gone and gotten old. Like the boogeyman, I guess.''

"The poor woman's Mickey Rooney. You women find yourselves the damnedest men.''

"She's not right about that,'' said Emma. "What do you want to tell that for? I know it was him. I feel like it was.''

"Why'd you throw the gun away?'' Clyde asked. "We could trace that.''

"It's what I felt like doing,'' she said. She had seen it strike, how his shoulder, struck, went back a little.

Clyde Mecklin sat watching his wife. She had scarcely touched her food and now, pale, distracted, she had risen to wander toward the windows, look out at the empty lawn, the shrubs and flowers, the stretch of white painted fence, ghostly by moonlight.

"It's the last horse I'll ever break,'' she said, more to herself than not, but Clyde heard and stood up and was coming to her.

"Now, Deedee—''

"When you know you know,'' she said, and turned, her face set against him: her anger, her victory, held up like a blade against his stubborn willfulness. "I want my children now,'' she said.

At the mention of children, Emma's presence with them became multiple and vague; it trembled with thanksgiving, it spiraled on wings of joy.

Deborah turned again, back to the window. Whenever she looked away, the eyes by the road were there below her: they were worthless, nothing, but infinite, never finishing—the surface there was no touching bottom of—taking to them, into themselves, the self that was hers no longer.

ELIZABETH COOK-LYNN

The Power of Horses

The mother and daughter steadied themselves, feet planted squarely, foreheads glistening with perspiration, and each grasped a handle of the large, steaming kettle.

"Ready?"

"Un-huh."

"Take it, then," the mother said. "Careful." Together they lifted the tub of boiled beets from the flame of the burners on the gas stove and set it heavily on the table across the room. The girl let the towel which had served as a makeshift pot holder drop to the floor as the heat penetrated to the skin, and she slapped her hand against the coolness of the smooth, painted wall and then against her thigh, feeling the roughness of the heavy jeans with tingling fingers. To stop the tingling, she cupped her fingers to her mouth and blew on them, then raised her apologetic eyes and looked at her mother. Without speaking, as if that was the end of it, she sank into the chrome chair and picked up the towel and began wiping the sweat from her face. The sun came relentlessly through the thin gauze curtains, and the hot wind blew gently across the stove, almost extinguishing the gas flames of the burners, making the blue edges turn yellow and then orange and then white. The towel was damp now and stained purple from the beets, and the girl leaned back in the chair and laid the towel across her face, feeling her own hot breath around her nose and mouth.

"Your hands get used to it, Marleen," the mother said, not even glancing at the girl, nor at her own rough, brown hands, "just have to keep at it," saying this not so much from believing it as from the need to stop this feeling of futility in the girl and the silence between them. The mother gingerly grasped the bleached stems of several beets and dropped them into a pan of cold water, rolling one and then another of the beets like balls in her hands, pushing the purple-black skins this way and that, quickly, deftly removing the peel and stem and tossing the shiny vegetable into another container. Finishing one, she hurriedly picked up another, as if by hurrying she could forestall the girl's rebellion.

The woman's arms, like her hands, were large, powerful. But, despite the years of heavy work, her sloping shoulders and smooth, long neck were part of a tender femininity only recently showing small signs of decline and age. The dark stains on her dark face might have seemed like age spots or a disfigurement on someone else, but on the woman they spread delicately across her cheeks, forehead, and neck like a sweep of darkened cloud, making her somehow vulnerable and defenseless.

"Your hands'll get used to it, Marleen," she repeated, again attempting to keep the girl's unwillingness in check, and an avenue to reasonable tolerance and cooperation open.

The brief rest with the towel on her face seemed to diminish the girl's weariness, and for an instant more she sat silently, breathing peacefully into the damp towel. As the girl drew the towel across her face and away from her eyes, something like fear began to rise in her, and she peered out the window, where she saw her father standing with a white man she had never seen before. Her father was looking straight ahead down the draw where the horses stood near the corral. They always want something from him, she thought, and as she watched the white man put a cigarette in his mouth and turn sideways out of the wind, the flame of his lighter licking toward his bony profile, she wondered what it was this time. She watched the man's quick mannerisms, and she saw that he began to talk earnestly and gesture toward his green pickup truck, which was parked close to the barbed-wire fence encircling the house and yard.

The girl was startled out of her musings at the sound of her mother's "*yu-u-u-u*," the softly uttered indication of disapproval, insistent, always compelling a change in the girl's behavior. And she turned quickly to get started with her share of the hot beets, handling them inexpertly, but peeling their hot skins away as best she could. After a few minutes, during which the women worked in silence, only the monotonous hiss of the burning gas flame between them, the girl, surprised, thought: her sounds of disapproval aren't because I'm wasting time; instead, they are made because she is afraid my father and the white man will see me watching them. Spontaneously, defensively, she said, "They didn't see me." She looked into the brown-stained face but saw only her mother's careful pretense of being preoccupied with the beets, as she picked up a small knife to begin slicing them. All last winter, every time I came home, I spied on him for you, thought the girl, even riding my horse over to Chekpa's through the snow to see if he was there. And when I came back and told you that he was, you acted as if you hadn't heard anything, like now. So this is not the beginning of the story, nor is it the part of the story that matters, probably, thought the girl, and she started to recognize a long, long history of acrimony between her parents, thinking, in hindsight, that it would have been better if she had stayed at Stephen Mission. But then, she remembered her last talk with Brother Otto at the Mission as he sat before her, one leg languidly draped over the other, his collar open, showing his sparse red chest hairs, his watery, pale eyes looking at her searchingly, and she knew that it wasn't better to have stayed there.

He had sat quivering with sympathy as she had tried to tell him that to go home was to be used by her mother against her father. I rode over to Chekpa's, she told him, hating herself that she was letting out the symptoms of her childish grief, despising him for his delicate white skin, his rapt gaze, the vicariousness of his measly existence, and *Até* was there, cutting wood for the eldest of the Tatiopa women, Rosalie, the one he was supposed to marry, you know, but, instead, he married my mother. My mother sent me there, and when I rode into the yard and saw him, he stood in uncertainty, humiliated in the eyes of Chekpa, his old friend, as well as all of those in the Tatiopa family. Worse yet, she knew, humiliated in the eyes of his nine-year-old daughter.

In her memory of that awful moment, she didn't speak, nor did her father, and so she had ridden out of the yard as abruptly as she had come and home at a dead gallop, standing easily in the stirrups, her face turned toward her right shoulder out of the wind, watching the slush fly behind the horse's hooves. She didn't cut across Archie's field as she usually did, but took the long way, riding as hard as she could alongside the road. When she got to the gate she reined in, dismounted, and led her horse through the gate and then, slowly, down the sloping hill to the tack shed. She stood for a long time with her head against the wide, smooth leather of the stirrup shaft, her eyes closed tightly and the smell of wet horse hair in her nostrils. Much later she had recited the event as fully as she could bear to the mission school priest, much as she had been taught to recite the events of her sinful life: I have taken the Lord's name in vain, I have taken the Lord's name in vain, I have tak . . .

Damn beets, damn all these damn beets, the girl thought, and she turned away from the table back to the stove, where she stirred the second, smaller, pot of sliced beets, and she looked out through the gauze curtains to see if her father and the white man were still there. They had just run the horses into the corral from the small fenced pasture where they usually grazed when they were brought down to the place.

"He must be getting ready to sell them, is he?" she asked her mother.

Her mother said nothing.

"How come? I didn't know he was going to sell," the girl said slowly, noticing that her horse, two quarter-horse broodmares, and a half-Shetland black-and-white gelding she had always called *Shōta* had been cut out of the herd and were standing at the far corner of the pasture, grazing. The heat shimmered above the long buffalo grass, and the girl's thoughts drifted, and, vaguely, she heard her mother say, "You'd better spoon those sliced ones into these hot jars, Marleen," and then, almost to herself, her mother started talking as if in recognition of what the girl did not know about the factual and philosophical sources from which present life emerges. "I used to have land, myself, daughter," she began, "and on it my grandfather had many horses. What happened to it was that some white men from Washington came and took it away from me when my grandfather died because, they said, they were going to breed game birds there; geese, I think.

"There was no one to do anything about it," she continued, "there was only this old woman who was a mother to me, and she really didn't know what to do, who to see, or how to prevent this from happening.

"Among the horses there on my land was a pair of broodmares just like those two out there." She pointed with her chin to the two bays at the end of the pasture. And, looking at the black-and-white horse called *Shōta*, she said, "And there was also another strange, mysterious horse, *su'ka wak a'*," *i-e-e-e*, she had used the word for "mysterious dog" in the Dakota language. And the mother and daughter stood looking out the window at the *shōta* horse beside the bays, watching them pick their way through the shimmering heat and through the tall grass, slowly, unhurried. The beets were forgotten, momentarily, and the aging woman remembered the magic of those horses and especially the one that resembled the *shōta* horse, thinking about that time, that primordial time when an old couple of the tribe received a gift horse from a little bird, and the horse produced many offspring for the old man and woman, and the people were never poor after that. Her grandfather, old Bowed Head, the man with many horses, had told her that story often during her childhood when he wished to speak of those days when all creatures knew one another . . . and it was a reassuring thing. "I wish this tribe to be strong and good," the mysterious horse had told the old man, "and so I keep giving my offspring every year and the tribe will have many horses and this good thing will be among you always."

"They were really fast horses," said the mother, musing still, filling in the texture of her imagination and memory, "they were known throughout our country for their speed, and the old man allowed worthy men in the tribe to use them in war or to go on a hunt with them. It is an old story," the woman concluded, as though the story were finished, as though commenting upon its history made everything comprehensible.

As the girl watched her mother's extraordinary vitality, which rose during the telling of these events, she also noted the abruptness with which the story seemed to end and the kind of formidable reserve and closure which fell upon the dark, stained features as the older woman turned again to the stove.

"What happened to the horses?" the girl wanted to know. "Did someone steal them? Did they die?"

After a long silence her mother said, "Yes, I suppose so," and the silence again deepened between them as they fell to filling hot jars with sliced beets and sealing hot lids upon them, wiping and stroking them meticulously and setting them one by one on a dim pantry shelf.

The girl's frustration was gone now, and she seemed mindless of the heat, her own physical discomfort, and the miserableness of the small, squalid kitchen where she and her mother moved quietly about, informed now with the wonder of the past, the awesomeness of the imagination.

The sun moved west and the kitchen fell into shadow, the wind died down, and the mother and daughter finished their tedious task and carried the large tub of hot water out through the entryway a few feet from the door and emptied its contents upon the ground. The girl watched the red beet juice stain the dry, parched earth in which there was no resistance, and she stepped away from the redness of the water, which gushed like strokes of a painter's brush, suddenly black and ominous, as it sank into the ground. She looked up to see the white man's green pickup truck disappear over the rise, the dust billowing behind the heavy wheels, settling gently in the heat.

The nameless fear struck at her again and she felt a knot being drawn tightly inside her and she looked anxiously toward the corral. Nothing around her seemed to be moving, the air suddenly still, the sweat standing out in beads on her face and her hands, oddly, moist and cold. As she ran toward the corral, she saw her mother out of the corner of her eye, still grasping one handle of the boiler tub, strangely composed, her head and shoulders radiant in the sun.

At the corral, moments later, she saw her father's nearly lifeless form lying facedown in the dirt, his long gray hair spread out like a fan above him, pitifully untidy for a man who ordinarily took meticulous care with his appearance. He had his blue cotton scarf which he used as a handkerchief clutched tightly in his right hand, and he was moaning softly.

The odor of whiskey on his breath was strong as she helped him turn over and sit up, and in that instant the silent presence of the past lay monumentally between them, so that he did not look at her nor did he speak. In that instant she dimly perceived her own innocence and was filled with regret that she would never know those times to which *Até* would return, if he could, again and again. She watched as he walked unsteadily toward the house, rumpled and drunk, a man of grave dignity made comic and sad and helpless by circumstances which his daughter could only regard with wonderment.

Keyapi: Late one night, when the old man had tied the horses near his lodge, someone crept through the draw and made ready to steal them; it was even said that they wanted to kill the wonderful horses. The mysterious gift horse called to the sleeping old man and told him that an evil lurked nearby. And he told the old man that since such a threat as this had come upon them and all the people of the tribe, the power of the horses would be diminished, and no more colts would be born and the people would have to go back to their miserable ways.

As her father made his way to the house, walking stiffly past her mother, who pretended to be scrubbing the black residue from the boiler, the girl turned and walked quickly away from the corral in the opposite direction.

I must look: she thought, into the distance, and as she lifted her eyes and squinted into the evening light, she saw the Fort George road across the river, beyond the bend in the river, so far away that it would take most of the day for anyone to get there from where she walked. I must look: at the ground in front of me where my grandmothers made paths to the ti(n)psina beds and carried home with them long braided strands over their shoulders. I must look: she thought, into the past for the horse that speaks to humans.

She took long strides and walked into the deepening dusk. She walked for a long time before returning to the darkened house, where she crept into her bed and lay listening to the summer's night insect sounds, thinking apocalyptic thoughts in regard to what her mother's horse story might have to do with the day's events.

She awoke with a start, her father shaking her shoulder. "You must ride with me today, daughter, before the horse buyer comes back," he said. "I wish to take the horses way out to the far side of the north pasture. I am ready to go, so please hurry."

The girl dressed quickly, and just as dawn was breaking, she and her father, each leading two horses, with the others following, set out over the prairie hills. These were the hills, she knew, to which the people had come when the Uprising was finished and the U.S. Cavalry fell to arguing with missionaries and settlers about the "Indian problem." These were the hills, dark blue in this morning light, which she knew as repositories of sacred worlds unknown to all but its most ancient tenants.

When they reached the ridge above Dry Creek, the girl and her father stopped and let the horses go their way, wildly. The *shōta* horse led them down the steep prairie hills and into the dry creek bed and, one by one, the horses of the herd disappeared into the stand of heavy cottonwood trees which lined the ravine.

She stood beside her father and watched them go. "Why were you going to sell them?" she asked abruptly.

"There are too many," he replied, "and the grass is short this summer. It's been too hot," he said, wiping his face with the blue handkerchief, and he repeated, "The grass is short this summer."

With that, they mounted their horses and rode home together.

HORSES AND LOVE

PAM HOUSTON

What Shock Heard

It was late spring, but the dry winds had started already, and we were trying to load Shock into the horse trailer for a trip to the vet and the third set of X rays on her fetlock. She's just barely green-broke, and after months of being lame she was hot as a pistol and not willing to come within twenty yards of the trailer. Katie and Irwin, who own the barn, and know a lot more than me, had lip chains out, and lunge ropes and tranquilizer guns, but for all their contraptions they couldn't even get close enough to her to give her the shot. Crazy Billy was there too, screaming about two-by-fours and electric prods, and women being too damned ignorant to train a horse right. His horses would stand while he somersaulted in and out of the saddle. They'd stand where he ground-tied them, two feet from the train tracks, one foot off the highway. He lost a horse under a semi once, and almost killed the driver. All the women were afraid of him, and the cowboys said he trained with Quaaludes. I was watching him close, trying to be patient with Katie and Irwin and my brat of a horse, but I didn't want Billy within ten feet of Shock, no matter how long it took to get her in the trailer.

That's when the new cowboy walked up, like out of nowhere with a carrot in his hands, whispered something in Shock's ear, and she walked right behind him into the trailer. He winked at me and I smiled back and poor Irwin and Katie were just standing there all tied up in their own whips and chains.

The cowboy walked on into the barn then, and I got into the truck with

255

Katie and Irwin and didn't see him again for two months when Shock finally got sound and I was starting to ride her in short sessions and trying to teach her some of the things any five-year-old horse should know.

It was the middle of prairie summer by then and it was brutal just thinking about putting on long pants to ride, but I went off Shock so often I had to. The cowboy told me his name was Zeke, short for Ezekiel, and I asked him if he was religious and he said only about certain things.

I said my name was Raye, and he said that was his mother's name and her twin sister's name was Faye, and I said I could never understand why people did things like that to their children. I said that I was developing a theory that what people called you had everything to do with the person you turned out to become, and he said he doubted it 'cause that was just words, and was I going to stand there all day or was I going to come riding with him. He winked at Billy then and Billy grinned and I pretended not to see and hoped to myself that they weren't the same kind of asshole.

I knew Shock wasn't really up to the kind of riding I'd have to do to impress this cowboy, but it had been so long since I'd been out on the meadows I couldn't say no. There was something about the prairie for me—it wasn't where I had come from, but when I moved there it just took me in and I knew I couldn't ever stop living under that big sky. When I was a little girl driving with my family from our cabin in Montana across Nebraska to all the grandparents in Illinois, I used to be scared of the flatness because I didn't know what was holding all the air in.

Some people have such a fear of the prairie it makes them crazy, my ex-husband was one, and they even have a word for it: "agoraphobia." But when I looked it up in Greek it said "fear of the marketplace," and that seems like the opposite kind of fear to me. He was afraid of the high wind and the big storms that never even came while he was alive. When he shot himself, people said it was my fault for making him move here and making him stay, but his chart only said *acute agoraphobia* and I think he did it because his life wasn't as much like a book as he wanted it to be. He taught me about literature and language, and even though he used language in a bad way—to make up worlds that hurt us—I learned about its power and it got me a job, if nothing else, writing for enough money to pay off his debts.

But I wasn't thinking about any of that when I set off across the meadow at an easy hand gallop behind Zeke and his gelding Jesse. The sun was low in the sky, but it wasn't too long after solstice and in the summer the sun never seemed to fall, it seeped toward the horizon and then melted into it. The fields were losing heat, though, and at that pace we could feel the bands of warmth and cool coming out of the earth like it was some perfectly regulated machine. I could tell Zeke wasn't a talker, so I didn't bother riding up with him; I didn't want Shock to try and race on her leg. I hung back and watched the way his body moved with the big quarter horse: brown skin stretched across muscle and horseflesh, black mane and sandy hair, breath and sweat and one dust cloud rose around them till there was no way to separate the rider from the ride.

Zeke was a hunter. He made his living as a hunter's guide, in Alaska, in places so remote, he said, that the presence of one man with a gun was insignificant. He invited me home for moose steaks, and partly because I loved the way the two words sounded together, I accepted.

It was my first date in almost six years and once I got that into my head it wouldn't leave me alone. It had been almost two years since I'd been with a man, two years almost to the day that Charlie sat on our front-porch swing and blew his brains out with a gun so big the stains splattered three sets of windows and even wrapped around the corner of the house. I thought I had enough reason to swear off men for a while, and Charlie wasn't in the ground three months when I got another one.

It was in October of that same year, already cold and getting dark too early, and Shock and I got back to the barn about an hour after sunset. Katie and Irwin were either in town or in bed and the barn was as dark as the house. I walked Shock into her stall and was starting to take off her saddle when Billy stepped out of the shadows with a shoeing tool in his hand. Women always say they know when it's going to happen, and I did, as soon as he slid the stall door open. I went down when the metal hit my shoulder and I couldn't see anything but I could feel his body shuddering already and little flecks of spit coming out of his mouth. The straw wasn't clean and Shock was nervous and I concentrated on the sound her hooves made as they snapped the air searchingly behind her. I imagined them connecting with Billy's skull and how the blood on the white wall would look like Charlie's, but Shock was much too honest a horse to aim for impact. Billy had the arm that wasn't numb pinned down with one knee through the whole thing, but I bit him once right on the jawline and he's still got that scar; a half-moon of my teeth in his face.

He said he'd kill me if I told, and the way my life was going it seemed reasonable to take him at his word. I had a hard time getting excited about meeting men after that. I'd learned to live without it, but not very well.

Shock had pitched me over her head twice the day that Zeke asked me to dinner, and by the time I got to his house my neck was so stiff I had to turn my whole body to look at him.

"Why don't you just jump in the hot tub before dinner," he said, and I swung my head and shoulders around from him to the wood-heated hot tub in the middle of the living room and I must have gone real white then because he said, "But you know, the heater's messing up and it's just not getting as hot as it should."

While he went outside to light the charcoals I sat on a hard wooden bench covered with skins facing what he called the trophy wall. A brown-and-white speckled owl stared down its pointed beak at me from above the doorway, its wings and talons poised as if ready for attack, a violence in its huge yellow eyes that is never so complete in humans.

He came back in and caught me staring into the face of the grizzly bear that covered most of the wall. "It's an eight-foot-square bear," he said, and then explained, by rubbing his hand across the fur, that it was eight feet long from the tip of its nose to the tip of its tail, and from the razor edge of one outstretched front claw to the other. He smoothed the fur back down with strong even strokes. He picked something off one of its teeth.

258

"It's a decent-sized bear," he said, "but they get much bigger."

I told him about the time I was walking with my dogs along the Salmon River and I saw a deer carcass lying in the middle of an active spawning ground. The salmon were deeper than the water and their tails slapped the surface as they clustered around the deer. One dog ran in to chase them, and they didn't even notice, they swam around her ankles till she got scared and came out.

He laughed and reached towards me and I thought *for* me, but then his hand came down on the neck of a six-point mule deer mounted on the wall behind me. "Isn't he beautiful?" he asked. His hands rubbed the short hair around the deer's ears. It was hanging closer to me than I realized, and when I touched its nose it was warmer than my hands.

He went back outside then and I tried to think of more stories to tell him but I got nervous all over and started fidgeting with something that I realized too late was the foot of a small furry animal. The thing I was sitting on reminded me a little too much of my dog to allow me to relax.

The moose steaks were lean and tender and it was easy to eat them until he started telling me about their history, about the bull that had come to the clearing for water, and had seen Zeke there, had seen the gun even, and trusted him not to fire. I couldn't look right at him then, and he waited awhile and he said, "Do you have any idea what they do to cows?"

We talked about other things after that, horses and the prairie and the mountains we had both left for it. At two I said I should go home, and he said he was too tired to take me. I wanted him to touch me the way he touched the mule deer but he threw a blanket over me and told me to lift up for the pillow. Then he climbed up and into a loft I hadn't even noticed, and left me down there in the dark under all those frightened eyes.

The most remarkable thing about him, I guess, was his calm: his hands were quieter on Jesse's mane even than mine were on Shock's. I never heard him raise his voice, even in laughter. There wasn't an animal in the barn he couldn't turn to putty, and I knew it must be the same with the ones he shot.

On our second ride he talked more, even about himself some, horses he'd sold, and ex-lovers; there was a darkness in him I couldn't locate.

It was the hottest day of that summer and it wouldn't have been right to run the horses, so we let them walk along the creek bank all afternoon, clear into the next county, I think.

He asked me why I didn't move to the city, why I hadn't, at least, while Charlie was sick, and I wondered what version of my life he had heard. I told him I needed the emptiness and the grasses and the storm threats. I told him about my job and the articles I was working on and how I knew if I moved to the city, or the ocean, or even back to the mountains, I'd be paralyzed. I told him that it seemed as if the right words could only come to me out of the perfect semicircular space of the prairie.

He rubbed his hands together fist to palm and smiled, and asked if I wanted to rest. He said he might nap, if it was quiet, and I said I knew I always talked too much, and he said it was okay because I didn't mind if he didn't always listen.

I told him words were all we had, something that Charlie had told me, and something I had believed because it let me fall into a vacuum where I didn't have to justify my life.

Zeke was stretching his neck in a funny way, so without asking I went over and gave him a back rub and when I was finished he said, "For a writer lady you do some pretty good communicating without words," but he didn't touch me even then, and I sat very still while the sun melted, embarrassed and afraid to even look at him.

Finally, he stood up and stretched.

"Billy says you two go out sometimes."

"Billy lies," I said.

"He knows a lot about you," he said.

"No more than everyone else in town," I said. "People talk. It's just what they do. I'll tell you all about it if you want to know."

"We're a long way from the barn," he said, in a way that I couldn't tell if it was good or bad. He was rubbing one palm against the other so slowly it was making my skin crawl.

"Shock's got good night vision," I said, as evenly as I could.

He reached for a strand of Shock's mane and she rubbed her whole neck against him. I pulled her forelock out from under the brow band. She nosed his back pockets, where the carrots were. She knocked his cap off his head and scratched her nose between his shoulder blades. He put both hands up on her withers and rubbed little circles. She stretched her neck out long and low.

"Your horse is a whore, Raye," he said.

"I want to know what you said to her to make her follow you into the trailer," I said.

"What I said to her?" he said. "Christ, Raye, there aren't any words for that."

Then he was up and in the saddle and waiting for me to get back on Shock. He took off when I had only one foot in the stirrup, and I just hung around Shock's neck for the first quarter mile till he slowed up.

The creek trail was narrow and Shock wanted to race, so I got my stirrup and let her fly past him on the outside, the wheat so high it whipped across Shock's shoulder and my thigh. Once we were in the lead, Shock really turned it on and I could feel her strength and the give of her muscles and the solidity of the healed fetlock every time it hit the ground. Then I heard Jesse coming on the creek side, right at Shock's flank, and I knew we were coming to the big ditch, and I knew Shock would take it if Jesse did, but neither of us wanted to give up the lead. Shock hit the edge first and sailed over it and I came way up on her neck and held my breath when her front legs hit, but then we were down on the other side and she was just as strong and as sound as ever. Jesse edged up again and I knew we couldn't hold the lead for much longer. I felt Zeke's boots on my calf and our stirrups locked once for an instant and then he pulled away. I let Shock slow then, and when Jesse's dust cleared, the darkening sky opened around me like an invitation.

It wasn't light enough to run anymore and we were still ten miles from the barn. Jupiter was up, and Mars. There wasn't any moon.

Zeke said, "Watching you ride made me almost forget to beat you." I couldn't see his face in the shadows.

He wanted silence but it was too dark not to talk, so I showed him the constellations. I told him the stories I knew about them: Cassiopeia weeping on the King's shoulder while the great winged Pegasus carries her daughter off across the eastern sky. Cygnus, the swan, flying south along the milky way, the Great Bear spinning slowly head over tail in the north. I showed him Andromeda, the galaxy closest to our own. I said, "It's two hundred million light-years away. Do you know what that means?" And when he didn't answer I said, "It means the light we see left that galaxy two hundred million years ago." And then I said, "Doesn't that make you feel insignificant?"

And he said, "No."

"How does it make you feel?" I said.

"Like I've gotten something I might not deserve," he said.

Then he went away hunting in Montana for six weeks. I kept thinking about him up there in the mountains I had come from and wondering if he saw them the way I did, if he saw how they held the air. He didn't write or call once, and I didn't either, because I thought I was being tested and I wanted to pass. He left me a key so I could water his plants and keep chemicals in his hot tub. I got friendly with the animals on the wall, and even talked to them sometimes, like I did to the plants. The only one I avoided was the Dall sheep. Perfect in its whiteness, and with a face as gentle and wise as Buddha. I didn't want to imagine Zeke's hands pulling the trigger that stained the white neck with blood the taxidermist must have struggled to remove.

He asked me to keep Jesse in shape for him too, and I did. I'd work Shock in the ring for an hour and then take Jesse out on the trails. He was a little nervous around me, being used to Zeke's uncanny calm, I guess, so I sang the songs to him that I remembered from Zeke's records: "Angel from Montgomery," "City of New Orleans," "L.A. Freeway," places I'd never been or cared to go. I didn't know any songs about Montana.

When we'd get back to the barn I'd brush Jesse till he shone, rubbing around his face and ears with a chamois cloth till he finally let down his guard a little and leaned into my hands. I fed him boxes full of carrots while Shock looked a question at me out of the corner of her eye.

One night Jesse and I got back late from a ride and the only car left at the barn was Billy's. I walked Jesse up and down the road twice before I thought to look in Zeke's saddlebags for the hunting knife I should have known would be there all along. I put it in the inside pocket of my jean jacket and felt powerful, even though I hadn't thought ahead as far as using it. When I walked through the barn door I hit the breaker switch that turned on every light and there was Billy leaning against the door to Jesse's stall.

"So now she's riding his horse," he said.

"You want to open that door?" I said. I stood as tall as I could between him and Jesse.

"Does that mean you're going steady?"

"Let me by," I said.

"It'd be a shame if he came back and there wasn't any horse to ride," he said, and I grabbed for Jesse's reins but he moved forward faster, spooking Jesse, who reared and spun and clattered out the open barn door. I listened to his hooves on the stone and then outside on the hard dirt till he got so far away I only imagined it.

Billy shoved me backwards into a wheelbarrow and when my head hit the manure I reached for the knife and got it between us and he took a step backwards and wiped the spit off his mouth.

"You weren't that much fun the first time," he said, and ran for the door. I heard him get into his car and screech out the driveway, and I lay there in the manure, breathing horse piss and praying he wouldn't hit Jesse out on the hard road. I got up slow and went into the tack room for a towel and I tried to clean my hair with it but it was Zeke's and it smelled like him and I couldn't understand why my timing had been so bad all my life. I wrapped my face in it so tight I could barely breathe and sat on his tack box and leaned into the wall, but then I remembered Jesse and put some grain in a bucket and went out into the darkness and whistled.

It was late September and almost midnight and all the stars I'd shown Zeke had shifted a half turn to the west. Orion was on the horizon, his bow drawn back, aimed across the Milky Way at the Great Bear, I guess, if space curves the way Earth does. Jesse wasn't anywhere, and I walked half the night looking for him. I went to sleep in my truck and at dawn Irwin and Jesse showed up at the barn door together.

"He got spooked," I told Irwin. "I was too worried to go home."

Irwin looked hard at me. "Hear anything from Zeke?" he said.

I spent a lot of time imagining his homecoming. I'd make up the kind of scenes in my head I knew would never happen, the kind that never happen to anyone, where the man gets out of the car so fast he tears his jacket, and when he lifts the woman up against the sky she is so light that she thinks she may be absorbed into the atmosphere.

I had just come back from a four-hour ride when his truck did pull up to the barn, six weeks to the day from when he left. He got out slow as ever, and then went around back to where he kept his carrots. From the tack-room window I watched him rub Jesse and feed him, pick up one of his front hooves, run his fingers through his tail.

I wanted to look busy but I'd just got done putting everything away so I sat on the floor and started oiling my tack and then wished I hadn't because of what I'd smell like when he saw me. It was fifteen minutes before he even came looking, and I had the bridle apart, giving it the oil job of its life. He put his hands on the doorjamb and smiled big.

"Put that thing back together and come riding with me," he said.

"I just got back," I said. "Jesse and I've been all over."

"That'll make it easier for you to beat me on your horse," he said. "Come on, it's getting dark earlier every night."

He stepped over me and pulled his saddle off the rack, and I put the bridle back together as fast as I could. He was still ready before I was and he stood real close while I tried to make Shock behave and get tacked up and tried not to let my hands shake when I fastened the buckles.

Then we were out in the late sunshine and it was like he'd never left, except this time he was galloping before he hit the end of the driveway.

"Let's see that horse run," he called to me, and Jesse shot across the

264

road and the creek trail and plunged right through the middle of the wheat field. The wheat was so tall I could barely see Zeke's head, but the footing was good and Shock was gaining on him. I thought about the farmer who'd shoot us if he saw us, and I thought about all the hours I'd spent on Jesse keeping him in shape so that Zeke could come home and win another race. The sky was black to the west and coming in fast, and I tried to remember if I'd heard a forecast and to feel if there was any direction to the wind. Then we were out in a hay field that had just been cut and rolled, and it smelled so strong and sweet it made me light-headed and I thought maybe we weren't touching ground at all but flying along above it, buoyed up by the fragrance and the swirl of the wind. I drove Shock straight at a couple of bales that were tied together and made her take them, and she did, but by the time we hit the irrigation ditch we'd lost another couple of seconds on Zeke.

I felt the first drops of rain and tried to yell up to Zeke, but the wind came up suddenly and blasted my voice back into my mouth. I knew there was no chance of catching him then, but I dug my heels in and yipped a little and Shock dug in even harder, but then I felt her front hoof hit a gopher hole and the bottom dropped out and she went down and I went forward over her neck and then she came down over me. My face hit first and I tasted blood and a hoof came down on the back of my head and I heard reins snap and waited for another hoof to hit, but then it was quiet and I knew she had cleared me. At least I'm not dead, I thought, but my head hurt too bad to even move.

I felt the grit inside my mouth and thought of Zeke galloping on across the prairie, enclosed in the motion, oblivious to my fall. It would be a mile, maybe two, before he slowed down and looked behind him, another before he'd stop, aware of my absence, and come back for me.

I opened one eye and saw Shock grazing nearby, broken reins hanging uneven below her belly. If she'd re-pulled the tendon in her fetlock it would be weeks, maybe months, before I could ride with him again. My mouth was full of blood and my lips were swelling so much it was running out the sides, though I kept my jaw clamped and my head down. The wind was coming in little gusts now, interrupted by longer and longer periods of calm, but the sky was getting darker and I lifted my head to look for Zeke. I got dizzy, and I closed my eyes and tried to breathe regularly. In what seemed like a long time I started to hear a rhythm in my head and I pressed my ear into the dust and knew it was Zeke coming back across the field at a gallop, balanced and steady, around the holes and over them. Then I heard his boots hit ground. He tied Jesse first, and then caught Shock, which was smart, I guess, and then he knelt next to my head and I opened the eye that wasn't in the dirt and he smiled and put his hands on his knees.

"Your mouth," he said, without laughing, but I knew what I must've looked like, so I raised up on one elbow and started to tell him I was okay and he said,

"Don't talk. It'll hurt."

And he was right, it did, but I kept on talking and soon I was telling him about the pain in my mouth and the back of my head and what Billy had done that day in the barn, and the ghosts I carry with me. Blood was coming out with the words and pieces of tooth, and I kept talking till I told him everything, but when I looked at his face I knew all I'd done was make the gap wider with the words I'd picked so carefully that he didn't want to hear. The wind started up again and the rain was getting steady.

I was crying then, but not hard, and you couldn't tell through all the dirt and blood, and the rain and the noise the wind was making. I was crying, I think, but I wanted to laugh because he would have said there weren't any words for what I didn't tell him, and that was that I loved him and even more I loved the prairie that wouldn't let you hide anything, even if you wanted to.

Then he reached across the space my words had made around me and put his long brown finger against my swollen lips. I closed my eyes tight as his hand wrapped up my jaw and I fell into his chest and whatever it was that drove him to me, and I held myself there unbreathing, like waiting for the sound of hooves on the sand, like waiting for a tornado.

TESS SLESINGER

Relax Is All

She rode Comanche badly, sitting him with no sense of ease or mastership, she let him jog her this way or that as he wanted, and when he turned his captious neck homeward, because if he couldn't keep up with the others he would rather get back and brood by himself in the corral, she let him have his head for several yards before she could succeed in guiding him back to the narrow, sandy path that edged the lake. He despised her anyway because of the way her citified old-maid bottom bounced up and down on his back, sliding her weight first to this side, then to that, of the saddle. But chiefly he despised her because she rode him so far behind the others; he wanted to be up in front with his kind, he wanted to spatter them with sand when he bounded suddenly ahead, he even wanted sand and water splashed in his own rheumy eyes when he fell behind; he wanted to nose his big head between Piute's slim, mustang rear and the great, powerful hind quarters of Coyote, he wanted to dash playfully beyond Chiquita who was ridden by Bud, and then when Chiquit', who was an old lead horse and could bear no more than her cowboy rider to be anywhere but in the lead, spurted leaping and panting past him he wanted to flick her good-naturedly with his tail, side-step in a cute way he had, and elbow Chiquita and Bud gently into the water. But not with bony, downeast, old-maid gal on his back, who held him in (through fear, God knows: she would have given up her position in New York to follow them once, be one of them on their mad gallops down the beach) while the others dashed off the minute their hooves met the hard sand.

Ethel Blake knew that she enjoyed no respect from her horse, although she had learned to saddle him herself and did so tenderly, being careful not to fasten the cinch too tight round his great belly, and although God knew she more than obeyed Bud's injunction never to run a horse till he dropped. But when she entered the corral she imagined Comanche's face fell, that he eyed her gloomily and shied away as though hoping against hope that she would change her mind about catching him. In the beginning, before his spirit was broken and before he had grown ashamed to look his fellows in the face, he had fought her; once he had set the bit and run with her clinging to the pommel, her feet clasping his belly, the stirrups flying wild, while he dashed over rocks and leaped sage until she was frightened nearly to death. A better rider, Bud had said afterward, would probably have fallen. But Miss Blake—you ride so stiff, can't you relax more, he kept saying (his blue eyes wandering to Mrs. Montague who sat her horse like the upper part of a centaur) can't you just take it easy; relax is all, he said.

Relax! Back east in New York Miss Blake had a desk, she had an office; there was Winter, and Spring, Summer, then Fall; and in all those seasons except just for two months of the Summer Miss Blake could be found behind her desk and in her office—and what would happen if she relaxed? Relax, the cowboy said (who despised her as much as her horse did). Imagine Ethel Blake "relaxing." Why, her name would waltz off the printed letterheads, her files would tip over and spill out their carefully catalogued contents, mixing the cases which needed immediate attention with the cases she had marked with her own red pencil "Closed—E. B." Imagine Dr. Stratton coming for the Monday afternoon seminar held in her office and finding *Miss Blake* relaxing!

But the very thought of Dr. Stratton (after a decade of sitting side by side and nodding intellectually behind their glasses at lectures on neuroses, on conditioned reflexes, on sublimation, she was sure they had come to look alike)—the very thought of Stratton, and the Decade Report she was supposed to be working on while curing her asthma, filled her with disgust. She had shoved it all back in her trunk the second night on the ranch and she would have blushed with shame if any of the others had stumbled upon it.

She wished she could have laid away her glasses on top of the pile of folders. But she couldn't see to the lake without them.

The others of course were riding a quarter mile's run ahead of her, along the curve of the beach. It was a short distance, especially when viewed with blinking eyes across the blazing Nevada sand, which danced a little with heat waves in the air. But it was an insurmountable distance to Miss Blake, who had shut away her real life in a trunk, who could read Proust in French and had been wishing all Summer that she couldn't, who would now gladly have sold her diplomas and her printed articles and her scholastic reputation to catch up just once with the others, to hear Bud say once, Hot diggity, gal! how you can ride! to have Comanche turn round and nip her affectionately on the toe of her boot.

The thing was, she thought, she had made of her horse a symbol, a something to conquer. If she could not control a horse then how on earth was she to control that more shapeless thing, her life? Yes, she had published her modest articles on pedagogy, she had seen her name in print (and Stratton told her her articles were more than meaty, they were brilliant, he said), but none of it mattered any more, and it had stopped mattering the very first day when Bud had helped her to mount Comanche for the first time and she sat there getting the feel of him in her unaccustomed limbs while Bud stood on the ground beside her, grinning: Now all you got to do is just sit back and relax, let yourself go; relax is all.

It seemed a sort of madness when she thought of how she talked all day with the little boy Jimmie (her only friend on the ranch; she *did* have a "way" with other people's children, and the fat little boy and herself were always together being left out of things) about sitting a horse and grooming a horse and how Bud had said Jimmie held his feet well in the stirrups and that Miss Blake was beginning to put her shoulders back and how a horse caught cold in the corral if you didn't walk him home to cool him off. And then she would fall asleep and wake in the night screaming or trying to, because there would be Comanche in her dream, looming twice his height with his head (rather human, and his lower lip stretched out like Bud's) carried toward her on a neck that stretched longer and longer as though to attack. So it's come to this, she thought, sighing and putting her hand forward timidly to touch Comanche's neck; I came out with work to do and books to read, and I have thrown them all away and my past life too because I have fallen in love with a horse who does not reciprocate. . . .

But the others, a quarter mile ahead, were deserting the shore path and cutting across the broad sandy beach toward a rocky formation a hundred jagged meters high, topped by the accidental perfection of an Indian's profile which gave it its name: Indian Head it was called, and it was said to contain a mysterious cave if only one were lucky enough to find the entrance. She could see them going slowly at last, because Bud at this point always reminded them that the soft sand was bad to canter over, the horses' legs might double under them. She had heard him say it in his drawling voice a hundred times, and he always added, "Now old Chiquit' here, she got stuck one time with one of her forelegs and where any other horse would have gone haywire and thrown her rider and busted her own leg, Chiquit' here just pulled herself up by the bootstrap and laughed; laughed is all."

She tried to prod Comanche into moving faster. But she had developed a sullen horse, and each time she prodded him he broke into a small, deceitful trot which he abandoned the second her heel left his flank. And so they approached the group, walking stiltedly until they reached the point where the hooves of Comanche's friends turned up, leaving their little hollowed prints in the soft sand. And then because he was so glad to see his fellows again, Comanche without any warning and totally disregarding the danger to his own legs, sprinted forward, exposing her to his difficult, jouncy trot before the eyes of his kind and her kind.

Already the horses were standing in their patient, restful line, each one with the rein of his colleague behind him slung over his own pommel, and his own rein slung over the pommel of the friend who stood before him. Ethel Blake dismounted in her awkward way, and watched while little Jimmie threw her rein over the pommel of Chiquita's saddle.

They were sprawled leaning and lying against the great rock, handing

the canteen that had been carried round Chiquita's neck from one to another. Now Mrs. Montague passed it with a kindly gesture, handing it to
Bud and nodding upward toward Miss Blake. But Bud with his insolent grin
lifted it as though he would drink a toast and tilted it to his own lips. She
watched him as he sat drinking with his eyes closed and the long sun-
bleached lashes coming down on his cheeks like a baby's, his ridiculous
cowboy hat pushed far back off his sweating forehead. She took in the boots
that were the pride of his life with the green butterflies stitched on the sides;
the HOT BABY tattooed in color on his chest, left bare under the theatrical
knotted handkerchief round his neck; the ring with the big Nevada tur-
quoise, bluer and greener than a stone of any value, on his brown finger; the
gaudy snakeskin band on his hat. She discovered that he was cheap as well
as stupid; a Nevada edition of a Broadway go-getter. Then he passed the
canteen on to her, and the thing felt warm on the outside, and it smelled
horsey a little, from the sweat on Chiquita's neck. She thought she detected
a salty taste of Bud's healthy spittle around the canteen's mouth, and although it disgusted her sharply for an instant, she put her lips around it
nevertheless and felt comforted by its warmth which was the warmth of another person.

"Let us be up and doing!" cried Mrs. Montague. "Let's explore! now
that we've rested and drunk."

Bud had come prepared with a flashlight for the inside of the cave, and
now they all caught sight of a sheath knife hanging from his belt as well.

"Good heavens, what's the knife for?"

"Rattlers is all," said Bud, shooting his blue gaze at them all and
smiling because he was too stupid to understand fear: he thought it a
dude affectation.

"Rattlers!" Mrs. Montague's eyes brightened. "But not for my little
boy. Jimmie, you are staying here with the horses."

The little boy with his fat, freckled, brooding face looked as though he
would have wept then and there if he hadn't been ashamed before Bud. Miss
Blake thought: what is it to me if I see the inside of an Indian cave? what is it
to any of them if I go in with them or stay outside, on the outside, with my

271

damn brains and eyeglasses and thin legs and my admirable way with other people's children? So she said, "I'll stay with you, Jimmie, we can tan our legs and keep old Midnight from rolling in the sand."

"What a gal," said Bud. "See you don't do anything I wouldn't do, Jimmie."

Mrs. Montague, relieved, flashed her dazzling smile: "Oh Miss Blake, you're a darling! I wouldn't dream of letting you, only I know how you and Jimmie simply adore being together!" Down over one eye she pulled her scarlet beret, and then she was up and over the rocks following after Bud and the others.

They could hear their voices as they skirted the rocky base, seeking entrance. Somebody shouted, and they were alone in the world, an old maid, a little boy, and half a dozen horses.

All the horses stood together, now and then rubbing a nose against the backside of a friend, now whisking a tail, now sleepily rolling a great stupid eye toward Jimmie and Ethel Blake. Then there was commotion among them; all of them were realizing that it was a longish rest and they settled down to it, turning round as far as their bridles would permit, until at last they stood, broken into pairs, almost static, Midnight and Piute standing flank touching flank, and Chiquita's long neck stretched in peace over Comanche's thick and sturdy one.

"Don't you think Buddy's just great?" said Jimmie with a little tremor in his voice.

"Yes," said Ethel Blake absently.

"I wish I could ride with a silver dollar between me and the saddle, like Bud. I wish I had a nickname. Do you think I'll be anything like Bud when I grow up, Miss Blake?"

She had never before gone back on Jimmie or on any child. But suddenly it seemed that she must assert herself in some way, if only by being rude to a youngster.

"How foolish you are, Jimmie," she said sharply; "why Bud is nothing but an ignorant cowboy." She tore her eyes from the boy's hurt gaze to look out and out over a lake that filled her chest with pain. The bitterest sense of frustration came over her. It was as though she had never believed before that this was she, this pinched old-maid lady, who spent her evenings wearing herself out at seminars and meetings to keep herself from ever having a moment in which to feel something. The trouble with this desert climate and this western life was that they made one dizzy with a sense of potentiality and weak with the knowledge of it squandered. She felt it in her lungs, in her breast, in her brain, in the very muscles of her legs, the knowledge that she might have power for the first time in her life, and that it was bottled up tight in her because no one came to draw it out.

"I think you're a fine little boy, and you'll be a fine man, Jimmie darling," she said sadly. But he was hurt beyond repair.

"I wish they'd hurry, don't you, Miss Blake?"

They waited sadly beside the rock. Miss Blake felt that she would never recover from the failure that she had learned herself to be this summer. Chiquita stamped a foot in her sleep, and Comanche, stirring and shifting his weight, whinnied softly; Miss Blake wished for a good friend who would whinny to her.

"I hear them!" said Jimmie at last.

"Oh, the scariest place! Spiders . . . Bones . . . not white because they've been in the dark for dear knows how long . . . an arrowhead for Jimmie . . . perfectly fascinating, Miss Blake . . ."

"My hatband!" said Bud in a squeaky voice. And took off his large and idiotic cowboy hat, and sure enough his snakeskin band, brand new, was gone. He kept twirling the hat round and round on his finger but it wasn't there.

"Someone will find it next century," said Mrs. Montague.

"I'm going back to find it *now*," said Bud.

"My God, get another, silly," they all cried.

"Someone's got to come in and hold the flashlight," said Bud obstinately.

And "Nobody's going to go back with you," they all cried. "What a fuss to make."

"I'm going to find it is all," said Bud. "I'm not going back till I've found it."

"Well, nobody's going to wait," they cried, moving toward the horses.

All but Ethel Blake. They didn't *get* him, she saw that. She was used to children; she understood them; she had a way with them. Here was a twenty-nine-year-old child who had lost his snake hatband; he would never be happy again if he didn't find it; if he found it he would forget it tomorrow, he would be dreaming about the green butterflies on his boots or a dirty scene he wanted tattooed on his thigh. But if he didn't find it he would have a lost place, a hurt place, inside of his chest forever, he would be thinking all of his life (and even if he didn't know it himself, Miss Blake couldn't bear knowing it for him) of the hatband lying abandoned, lying rotting in a dark cave, maybe waiting, maybe feeling hurt, for him to come back and save it. He would be thinking how all his luck had changed for the worse since the day that he had lost it; how for the two days he had had it he was the luckiest cowboy in Nevada. He frowned now, he was sulky, sullen, angry. But she knew he frowned because if he didn't look that way he would weep before them all.

"Well, I'm not tired," she said calmly. "I'll go back in with you and hold the flashlight."

His blue eyes rested on her in astonishment. "Will you? Say, that's mighty nice."

She thought as she turned to follow him that Mrs. Montague gave her an amused look; but she stared right back, grave and a little stubborn, and then she thought Mrs. Montague's look became definitely kind and not in the least malicious. She followed Bud around the rocky base and when she saw him at last put his great boot on a ledge and start to climb swiftly without a thought or a backward glance for her she wondered if she dared to follow him further. But something seemed to be driving her so that she could have stopped no more than a ball rolling downhill. Her foot with surprising ease found the ledge, her second foot came after, and there was Miss Blake (oh terribly afraid of high places; who had almost taken Dr. Stratton by the arm once in Carnegie Hall because her breath faded away when she

274

looked down), there was Miss Blake stepping calmly over crevices that revealed long slits of distance between herself and the ground, and running to catch up over narrow plateaus that held their breath on the edge of steep walls which dropped sheer a hundred feet. But she wasn't in the least afraid now. There was real danger, so she wasn't in the least afraid now, besides, she *couldn't* have stopped.

She saw him stoop; his legs went down; he was lowering himself, and coming after, she saw that here was the way in. She followed him down and they were in sudden darkness until she clicked the flashlight. Crouching all the time they climbed round and in, deeper into the heart of the rock; all the time the passage grew damper and darker, and looking back she could see the hole of daylight above them growing smaller and farther away. Round and round the path wound, every minute farther from reality, from day, from air, till the hole of light was a speck and then nothing. Round and round, like a path into the heart of a magnified seashell.

"Flash it lower," he called brutally. She flashed the light round and round, expertly, while she watched him stoop and snoop and cover every inch of the ground with his nose down like a hound following out a scent. "It wouldn't have been here," he said. "Flash it over on the left. Not here, damn it."

It was not there and it was not there. Miss Blake shared his sorrow. But they climbed farther in. She was frightened of the place. But she was very happy. Wherever her light flashed it illuminated spider webs with spiders as large and coarse and fierce as crabs. A bat whirred past her ears. There might be snakes. But she hoped their sojourn in the cave would never end.

"God damn it," he whined, near to crying, although surely he didn't know it himself. "God damn it, we're nearly through, we'll be coming out soon, and I haven't found the God damn thing."

Ethel Blake knew suddenly that they must find it. If they didn't, then her Summer was surely the total loss she had been thinking it was and her life an irretrievable failure. She would crawl back home to New York and let her body droop and let herself go quietly to pieces until she died. She must find it and she must give it to him.

She saw it. It looked pathetic, lost, unwanted. For the thousandth time in her life she thought how an inanimate thing had a quality, borrowed a something of its possessor, like a woman or a child. The band lay curled with sweat, partly on its side, very lonely and brave and scared.

It was directly ahead of Bud, caught on the side of the wall. She flashed her light quickly on the opposite side. He was crawling ahead faster now, he was miserable, bitter, he had just about given it up.

She held her breath.

He was safely past it!

She waited a moment because her heart was beating terribly. "I've found it, Bud," she said.

"What? you've *got* it? Are you *sure?*"

She held it swaggeringly above her head and with her other hand flashed the light directly on it.

He looked at it and reached out for it. Suddenly, and perhaps for the first time in her life, Ethel Blake grew coy, she dangled something and she withheld something, she felt her power come true and she let a man's eye rest on a thing she held in her hand and then deliberately she stuck her hand behind her back. The cowboy started laughing; it was a game he knew, a game he played, as easily and naturally as he swooped down from the back of a running horse and picked up a fallen bandana. He could afford to stand there laughing, because he knew Miss Blake could not withhold for long. And as for Ethel Blake, she became female and powerful, she felt as she stood there putting her head on one side and smiling that she must even, for the only time in her life, look *cute.*

"Give it here, gal." His voice was taunting. His blue eyes gazed laughing into hers.

She had no practice in this sort of thing.

"Wouldn't you really like it, though?" she said shyly, and loved herself for being so hard and so soft all at once.

"Will you lissen at the gal?" said Bud.

"Try and get it," said Ethel Blake faintly.

"Can't hit a gal with glasses," said Bud.

She almost brushed them off.

"Now put down the flashlight."

Trembling she put it down.

"Bet you can't," she whispered.

And then he was holding both of her wrists in his hands. But she hid her right hand behind her back, clutching the snake-band in a fist which would open only when the right time came.

He twisted her wrist. He bent over her and his laughing became panting as they struggled. His breath came in her face, went down her neck. She never stopped laughing, not for a minute, but it was serious laughter as laughter should be; laughter at something real and something really gay.

Her wrists burned, and when the cowboy reached around her back and found the hand that clasped his band nestled tight against the small of her back, her fist relaxed because it knew it was time. He unfolded every finger of her hand slowly, with a tortuous and tactical strength, a strength that held itself in check only because it was biding its time. One by one her fingers died pleasantly in his grasp, and then he wheedled the snake-band out of her palm and at the same moment kicked the flashlight so that it rolled over and went out and left them in the dark.

He was stuffing his snake-band into the back pocket of his jeans with one hand but with the other he held her firmly. Their laughter stopped. His right hand came back and traveled rapidly to her heart, while he took his lips away from her mouth to whisper slyly: "You'll never guess what I've found." She smelled horse on him, she smelled Chiquita, his other love. She smelled sweat and she smelled the clean desert dust on his jeans that had grown there through a whole Summer, because he said to wash blue jeans was to shrink them so they would never span a saddle again. She felt his legs wrapping strongly about hers with those muscles that were used to hugging the flanks of a horse, and she felt with her bold fingers the strength in his neck which was stout and hard, stubborn, like the neck of Comanche when Comanche was going to have his way with her. Then his lips came down hard over hers and with her last conscious, verbalized thought she imagined him drawling, Relax, gal; just let yourself go; relax is all.

* * *

They came out into the world again, and Chiquita and Comanche were standing there together, Chiquit' with her head across Comanche's neck, and both of them fast asleep with their eyes wide open and each with one foot curled delicately at rest. Chiquita lifted her head and saw Bud, rolled her nostrils bitterly, and waggled her ears like a wife who had had a perfectly good time but was going to give her man hell nevertheless.

Bud went straight to the fastening of his snake-band onto his hat. But Miss Blake, who might have helped him, who might have leaned over and reminded him of her presence under Chiquita's jealous eye, was filled with strength and pride and a desire to show Comanche. So she tossed his bridle free of Chiquita's pommel and tightened the cinch which had come loose around his belly, tucking in the end so it would not dangle and brush against his legs. Bud meanwhile sat by, intent upon his hatband, murmuring conciliatingly, "Chiquit', old Chiquit', hello Chiquit' old gal," as Chiquita angrily stamped her foot. He scarcely saw Miss Blake until she had slipped her foot into the stirrup and leaped up over Comanche's back. Then he looked up in surprise, remembering, and cried out: "Hey, wait a minute there, gal! wait for Bud!"

She laughed and dug her heels into Comanche's flank. Comanche didn't believe it. Comanche was for waiting for Chiquita and he couldn't see Ethel Blake not waiting for Bud. So he stood still stubbornly. She pressed her heels again, hard and sudden as though she meant business, and Comanche started in surprise across the soft sand. When they reached the path that ran along the lake he took the little leap over the bank and then stopped dead as much as to say a joke's a joke but this one has gone far enough; but Ethel Blake, hearing Bud's taunting laugh from across the beach, would have none of it, and she kept kicking and kicking her horse until she had kicked him into spirit again, kicked him out of surprise and into a nice even canter on the hard sand.

Rocked in the valley between his great hillock of a behind and the up-twist of his thick, sturdy neck, she sat with her legs strongly outspread embracing his sides, her body following his rhythm as easily as though they had

278

been a pair of expert tango partners. Beside the large forward movement there was a smaller motion of rolling, backward and forward, too gentle to be sliding, backward and forward and very gently up and down, almost circular, a lilting motion, powerful and very gay.

Ethel Blake and Comanche heard them coming up behind. Ethel Blake seized the end of her bridle and stung Comanche as far back as she could reach and at the same moment she dug both of her heels into his flanks, and when Comanche shook his head to show her that she was still like a city gal holding him in with the reins, she caught on suddenly to the art of riding and gave him his head with a thorough confidence that she had mastered him at last. He broke into a full run, leaping over the little bays on the shore's edge or splashing through the water because he had not time to slacken his speed or to waste going around the little scallops. Chiquita came dancing in their rear, her breath coming angry and joyful behind them, until she was so close that her nose snuggled against Comanche's backside, and "Faster! Faster!" cried Ethel Blake, and slapped Comanche on both sides with the end of the rein and kicked him with all her strength.

Now for Miss Blake there was no motion, nothing at all but sitting tight and flying through space with the ecstatic assurance that she would be caught and beaten; so paralyzed with joy and with terror and with a kind of unbearable excited suspense that she thought she would die when the horses came parallel.

The path was too narrow for two great horses. Chiquita nudged Comanche out of her way, sprinted forward; there was a wild whoop from Bud who reached out suddenly and touched her shoulder, and then the two horses were exactly parallel and Bud and Ethel Blake were riding side by side like lovers, and Ethel Blake knew that this was the finest moment in her thirty-five years of life.

For a few seconds the horses ran abreast, and then Bud dashed ahead on Chiquita. When Comanche saw his friend beating him he sprinted desperately, but Chiquita was an old lead horse as against his having been brought up to round cattle, so he decided to be game, and side-stepping in that cute way he had almost forgotten, he elbowed Chiquita gently into the water. Chiquit' stumbled and splashed, righted herself under Bud's expert guiding hand, and when she had regained the path she was already ahead of Comanche. So there was nothing for Comanche to do but to stretch his neck and ever so lightly nip Chiquita's hind parts and then fall behind, which is where a cattle horse belongs.

Miss Blake pulled him out of his gallop and helped him to subside back into his jouncy trot. And then they walked slowly together like friends. In Ethel Blake's heart (which was still pounding furiously from the run and the terror) there was a peace which she had never guessed existed, almost as though she had died, but died such a brilliant death that it didn't matter if she never came alive again. But Comanche's sides were running with sweat, and his whole big frame was collapsing and swelling with his quick and happy breathing; every few steps his legs shot out from under him as though he would be off again on a run, although there was no strength left in him. Ethel Blake put out a hand on his hot neck and spoke to him softly, to calm him. "There, Comanche; take it easy, darling. Simple and natural, relax—relax is all." He quivered. Then her touch and her voice succeeded in soothing him. Turning his long head with a kind of solemn humor he nipped gently at the toe of her boot. And then he threw up his head and laughed; laughed is all.

RICK BASS

Wild Horses

Karen was twenty-six. She had been engaged twice, married once. Her husband had run away with another woman after only six months. It still made her angry when she thought about it, which was not often.

The second man she had loved more, the most. He was the one she had been engaged to, but had not married. His name was Henry. He had drowned in the Mississippi the day before they were to be married. They never even found the body. He had a marker in the cemetery, but it was a sham. All her life, Karen had heard those stories about fiancés dying the day before the wedding; and then it had happened to her.

Henry and some of his friends, including his best friend, Sydney Bean, had been sitting up on the old railroad trestle, the old highway that ran so far and across that river, above the wide muddiness. Louisiana and trees on one side; Mississippi and trees, and some farms, on the other side—the place from which they had come. There had been a full moon and no wind, and they had been sitting above the water, maybe a hundred feet above it, laughing, and drinking Psychos from the Daiquiri World over in Delta, Louisiana. The Psychos contained rum and Coca-Cola and various fruit juices and blue food coloring. They came in styrofoam cups the size of small trash cans, so large they had to be held with both hands. They had had too many of them: two, maybe three apiece.

Henry had stood up, beaten his chest like Tarzan, shouted, and then dived in. It had taken him forever, just to hit the water; the light from the moon was good, and they had been able to watch him, all the way down.

Sometimes Sydney Bean still came by to visit Karen. Sydney was gentle and sad, her own age, and he worked somewhere on a farm, out past Utica, back to the east, where he broke and sometimes trained horses.

Once a month—at the end of each month—Sydney would stay over on Karen's farm, and they would go into her big empty closet, and he would let her hit him: striking him with her fists, kicking him, kneeing him, slapping his face until his ears rang and his nose bled; slapping and swinging at him until she was crying and her hair was wild and in her eyes, and the palms of her hands hurt too much to hit him any more.

It built up, the ache and the anger in Karen; and then, hitting Sydney, it went away for a while. He was a good friend. But the trouble was that it always came back.

Sometimes Sydney would try to help her in other ways. He would tell her that some day she was going to have to realize that Henry would not be coming back. Not ever—not in any form—but to remember what she had had, to keep *that* from going away.

Sydney would stand there, in the closet, and let her strike him. But the rules were strict: she had to keep her mouth closed. He would not let her call him names while she was hitting him.

Though she wanted to.

After it was over, and she was crying, more drained than she had felt since the last time, sobbing, her feelings laid bare, Sydney would help her up. He would take her into the bedroom and towel her forehead with a cool washcloth. Karen would be crying in a child's gulping sobs, and he would brush her hair, hold her hand, even hold her against him, and pat her back while she moaned.

Farm sounds would come from the field, and when she looked out the window, she might see her neighbor, old Dr. Lynly, the vet, driving along in his ancient blue truck, moving along the bayou, down along the trees, with his dog, Buster, running alongside, barking; herding the cows together for vaccinations.

* * *

"I can still feel the hurt," Karen would tell Sydney sometimes, when Sydney came over, not to be beaten up, but to cook supper for her, or to just sit on the back porch with her, and to watch the fields.

Sydney would nod whenever Karen said that she still hurt, and he would study his hands.

"I could have grabbed him," he'd say, and then look up and out at the field some more. "I keep thinking that one of these years, I'm going to get a second chance." Sydney would shake his head again. "I think I could have grabbed him," he'd say.

"Or you could have dived in after him," Karen would say, hopefully, wistfully. "Maybe you could have dived in after him."

Her voice would trail off, and her face would be flat and weary.

On these occasions, Sydney Bean wanted the beatings to come once a week, or even daily. But they hurt, too, almost as much as the loss of his friend, and he said nothing. He still felt as if he owed Henry something. He didn't know what.

Sometimes, when he was down on his knees, and Karen was kicking him or elbowing him, he felt close to it—and he almost felt angry at Karen—but he could never catch the shape of it, only the feeling.

He wanted to know what was owed, so he could go on.

On his own farm, there were cattle down in the fields, and they would get lost, separated from one another, and would low all through the night. It was a sound like soft thunder in the night, before the rain comes, and he liked it.

He raised the cattle, and trained horses too: he saddle-broke the young ones that had never been ridden before, the one- and two-year olds, the stallions, the wild mares. That pounding, and the evil, four-footed stamp-and-spin they went into when they could not shake him; when they began to do that, he knew he had them beaten. He charged $250 a horse, and sometimes it took him a month.

Old Dr. Lynly needed a helper, but couldn't pay much, and Sydney, who had done some business with the vet, helped Karen get the job. She needed something to do besides sitting around on her back porch, waiting for the end of each month.

Dr. Lynly was older than Karen had thought he would be, when she met him up close. He had that look to him that told her it might be the last year of his life. It wasn't so much any illness or feebleness or disability. It was just a finished look.

He and Buster—an Airedale, six years old—lived within the city limits of Vicksburg, down below the battlefield, hidden in one of the ravines—his house was up on blocks, the yard flooded with almost every rain—and in his yard, in various corrals and pens, were chickens, ducks, goats, sheep, ponies, horses, cows, and an ostrich. It was illegal to keep them as pets, and the city newspaper editor was after him to get rid of them, but Dr. Lynly claimed they were all being treated by his tiny clinic.

"You're keeping these animals too long, Doc," the editor told him. Dr. Lynly would pretend to be senile, and would pretend to think the editor was asking for a prescription, and would begin quoting various and random chemical names.

The Airedale minded Dr. Lynly exquisitely. He brought the paper, the slippers, he left the room on command, and he brought the chickens' eggs, daily, into the kitchen, making several trips for his and Dr. Lynly's breakfast. Dr. Lynly would have six eggs, fried for himself, and Buster would get a dozen or so, broken into his bowl raw. Any extras went into the refrigerator for Dr. Lynly to take on his rounds, though he no longer had many; only the very oldest people, who remembered him, and the very poorest, who knew he worked for free. They knew he would charge them only for the medicine.

Buster's coat was glossy from the eggs, and burnished, black and tan. His eyes, deep in the curls, were bright, sometimes like the brightest things in the world. He watched Dr. Lynly all the time.

Sometimes Karen watched Dr. Lynly play with Buster, bending down and swatting him in the chest, slapping his shoulders. She had thought it would be mostly kittens and lambs. Mostly, though, he told her, it would be the horses.

The strongest creatures were the ones that got the sickest, and their pain was unspeakable when they finally did yield to it. On the rounds with Dr. Lynly, Karen forgot to think about Henry at all. Though she was horrified by the pain, and almost wished it were hers, bearing it rather than watching it, when the horses suffered.

Once, when Sydney was with her, he had reached out and taken her hand in his. When she looked down and saw it, she had at first been puzzled, not recognizing what it was, and then repulsed, as if it were a giant slug: and she threw Sydney's hand off hers quickly, and ran into her room.

Sydney stayed out on the porch. It was heavy blue twilight and all the cattle down in the fields were feeding.

"I'm sorry," he called out. "But I can't bring him back!" He waited for her to answer, but could only hear her sobs. It had been three years, he thought.

He knew he was wrong to have caught her off-balance like that: but he was tired of her unhappiness, and frustrated that he could do nothing to end it. The sounds of her crying carried, and the cows down in the fields began to move closer, with interest. The light had dimmed, there were only dark shadows and pale lights, and a low gold thumbnail of a moon—a wet moon—came up over the ragged tear of trees by the bayou.

The beauty of the evening, being on Karen's back porch and in her life, when it should have been Henry, flooded Sydney with a sudden guilt. He had been fighting it, and holding it back, constantly: and then, suddenly, the quietness of the evening, and the stillness, released it.

He heard himself saying a crazy thing.

"I pushed him off, you know," he said, loudly enough so she could hear. "I finished my drink, and put both hands on his skinny-ass little shoulders, and said, 'Take a deep breath, Henry.' I just pushed him off," said Sydney.

It felt good, making up the lie. He was surprised at the relief he felt: it was as if he had control of the situation. It was like when he was on the horses, breaking them, trying to stay on.

Presently, Karen came back out with a small blue pistol, a .38, and she went down the steps and out to where he was standing, and she put it next to his head.

"Let's get in the truck," she said.

He knew where they were going.

The river was about ten miles away, and they drove slowly. There was fog flowing across the low parts of the road and through the fields and meadows like smoke, coming from the woods, and he was thinking about how cold and hard the water would be when he finally hit.

He felt as if he were already falling towards it, the way it had taken Henry forever to fall. But he didn't say anything, and though it didn't feel right, he wondered if perhaps it was this simple, as if this was what was owed after all.

They drove on, past the blue fields and the great spills of fog. The roofs of the hay barns were bright silver polished tin, under the little moon and stars. There were small lakes, cattle stock tanks, and steam rose from them.

They drove with the windows down; it was a hot night, full of flying bugs, and about two miles from the river, Karen told him to stop.

He pulled off to the side of the road, and wondered what she was going to do with his body. A cattle egret flew by, ghostly white and large, flying slowly, and Sydney was amazed that he had never recognized their beauty before, though he had seen millions. It flew right across their windshield, from across the road, and it startled both of them.

The radiator ticked.

"You didn't really push him off, did you?" Karen asked. She still had the pistol against his head, and had switched hands.

Like frost burning off the grass in a bright morning sun, there was in his mind a sudden, sugary, watery feeling—like something dissolving. She was not going to kill him after all.

"No," he said.

"But you could have saved him," she said, for the thousandth time.

"I could have reached out and grabbed him," Sydney agreed. He was going to live. He was going to get to keep feeling things, was going to get to keep seeing things.

He kept his hands in his lap, not wanting to alarm Karen, but his eyes moved all around as he looked for more egrets. He was eager to see another one.

Karen watched him for a while, still holding the pistol against him, and then turned it around and looked at the open barrel of it, cross-eyed, and held it there, right in her face, for several seconds. Then she reached out and put it in the glove box.

Sydney Bean was shuddering.

"Thank you," he said. "Thank you for not shooting yourself."

He put his head down on the steering wheel, in the moonlight, and shuddered again. There were crickets calling all around them. They sat like that for a long time, Sydney leaning against the wheel, and Karen sitting up straight, just looking out at the fields.

Then the cattle began to move up the hill towards them, thinking that Karen's old truck was the one that had come to feed them, and slowly, drifting up the hill from all over the fields, coming from out of the woods, and from their nearby resting spots on the sandbars along the little dry creek that ran down into the bayou—eventually, they all assembled around the truck, like schoolchildren.

They stood there in the moonlight, some with white faces like skulls, all about the same size, and chewed grass and watched the truck. One, bolder than the rest—a yearling black Angus—moved in close, bumped the grill of the truck with his nose, playing, and then leapt back again, scattering some of the others.

"How much would you say that one weighs?" Karen asked. "How much, Sydney?"

They drove the last two miles to the river slowly. It was about four A.M. The yearling cow was bleating and trying to break free; Sydney had tied him up with his belt, and with jumper cables and shoelaces, and an old shirt. His lip was bloody from where the calf had butted him.

But he had wrestled larger steers than that before.

They parked at the old bridge, the one across which the trains still ran. Farther downriver, they could see an occasional car, two round spots of headlight moving slowly and steadily across the new bridge, so far above the river, going very slowly. Sydney put his shoulders under the calf's belly and lifted it with his back and legs, and like a prisoner in the stock, he carried it out to the center of the bridge. Karen followed. It took about fifteen minutes to get there, and Sydney was trembling, dripping with sweat, when finally they gauged they had reached the middle. The deepest part.

They sat there, soothing the frightened calf, stroking its ears, patting its flanks, and waited for the sun to come up. When it did, pale orange behind the great steaminess of the trees and river below—the fog from the river and trees a gunmetal gray, the whole world washed in gray flatness, except for the fruit of the sun—they untied the calf, and pushed him over.

They watched him forever and forever, a black object and then a black spot against the great background of no-colored river, and then there was a tiny white splash, lost almost immediately in the river's current. Logs, which looked like twigs from up on the bridge, swept across the spot. Everything headed south, moving south, and there were no eddies, no pauses.

"I am halfway over him," Karen said.

And then, walking back, she said: "So that was really what it was like?"

She had a good appetite, and they stopped at the Waffle House and ate eggs and pancakes, and had sausage and biscuits and bacon and orange juice. She excused herself to go to the restroom, and when she came back out, her face was washed, her hair brushed and clean-looking. Sydney paid for the meal, and when they stepped outside, the morning was growing hot.

"I have to work today," Karen said, when they got back to her house. "We have to go see about a mule."

"Me, too," said Sydney. "I've got a stallion who thinks he's a bad-ass."

She studied him for a second, and felt like telling him to be careful, but didn't. Something was in her, a thing like hope stirring, and she felt guilty for it.

Sydney whistled, driving home, and tapped his hands on the steering wheel, though the radio did not work.

* * *

Dr. Lynly and Karen drove until the truck wouldn't go any farther, bogged down in the clay, and then they got out and walked. It was cool beneath all the big trees, and the forest seemed to be trying to press in on them. Dr. Lynly carried his heavy bag, stopping and switching arms frequently. Buster trotted slightly ahead, between the two of them, looking left and right, and up the road, and even up into the tops of the trees.

There was a sawmill, deep in the woods, where the delta's farmland in the northern part of the county settled at the river and then went into dark mystery; hardwoods, and muddy roads, then no roads. The men at the sawmill used mules to drag their trees to the cutting. There had never been money for bulldozers, or even tractors. The woods were quiet, and foreboding; it seemed to be a place without sound or light.

When they got near the sawmill, they could hear the sound of axes. Four men, shirtless, in muddy boots with the laces undone, were working on the biggest tree Karen had ever seen. It was a tree too big for chain saws. Had any of the men owned one, the tree would have ruined the saw.

One of the men kept swinging at the tree: putting his back into it, with rhythmic, stroking cuts. The other three stepped back, hitched their pants, and wiped their faces with their forearms.

The fourth man stopped cutting finally. There was no fat on him and he was pale, even standing in the beam of sunlight that was coming down through an opening in the trees—and he looked old; fifty, maybe, or sixty. Some of his fingers were missing.

"The mule'll be back in a minute," he said. He wasn't even breathing hard. "He's gone to bring a load up out of the bottom." He pointed with his ax, down into the swamp.

"We'll just wait," said Dr. Lynly. He bent back and tried to look up at the top of the trees. "Y'all just go right ahead with your cutting."

But the pale muscled man was already swinging again, and the other three, with another tug at their beltless pants, joined in: an odd, pausing drumbeat, as four successive whacks hit the tree; then four more again; and then, almost immediately, the cadence stretching out, growing irregular, as the older man chopped faster.

All around them were the soft pittings, like hail, of tree chips, raining into the bushes. One of the chips hit Buster in the nose, and he rubbed it with his paw, and turned and looked up at Dr. Lynly.

They heard the mule before they saw him: he was groaning, like a person. He was coming up the hill that led out of the swamp; he was coming towards them.

They could see the tops of small trees and saplings shaking as he dragged his load through them. Then they could see the tops of his ears; then his huge head, and after that they saw his chest. Veins raced against the chestnut thickness of it.

Then the tops of his legs.

Then his knee. Karen stared at it and then she started to tremble. She sat down in the mud, and hugged herself—the men stopped swinging, for just a moment—and Dr. Lynly had to help her up.

It was the mule's right knee that was injured, and it had swollen to the size of a basketball. It buckled, with every step he took, pulling the sled up the slick and muddy hill, but he kept his footing and he did not stop. Flies buzzed around the knee, around the infections, where the loggers had pierced the skin with nails and the ends of their knives, trying to drain the pus. Dried blood ran down in streaks to the mule's hoof, to the mud.

The sawlogs on the back of the sled smelled good, fresh. They smelled like they were still alive.

Dr. Lynly walked over to the mule and touched the knee. The mule closed his eyes and trembled slightly, as Karen had done, or even as if in ecstasy, at the chance to rest. The three younger men, plus the sledder, gathered around.

"We can't stop workin' him," the sledder said. "We can't shoot him, either. We've got to keep him alive. He's all we've got. If he dies, it's us that'll have to pull them logs up here."

A cedar moth, from the woods, passed over the mule's ears, fluttering blindly. It rested on the mule's forehead briefly, and then flew off. The mule did not open his eyes. Dr. Lynly frowned and rubbed his chin. Karen felt faint again, and leaned against the mule's sweaty back to keep from falling.

"You sure you've got to keep working him?" Dr. Lynly asked.

"Yes, sir."

The pale logger was still swinging: tiny chips flying in batches.

Dr. Lynly opened his bag. He took out a needle and rag, and a bottle of alcohol. He cleaned the mule's infections. The mule drooled a little when the needle went in, but did not open his eyes. The needle was slender, and it bent and flexed, and slowly Dr. Lynly drained the fluid.

Karen held on to the mule's wet back and vomited into the mud: both her hands on the mule as if she were being arrested against the hood of a car, and her feet spread out wide. The men gripped their axes awkwardly.

Dr. Lynly gave one of them a large plastic jug of pills.

"These will kill his pain," he said. "The knee will get big again, though. I'll be back out, to drain it again." He handed Karen a clean rag from his satchel, and led her away from the mule, away from the mess.

One of the ax men carried their satchel all the way back to the truck. Dr. Lynly let Karen get up into the truck first, and then Buster; then the ax man rocked and shoved, pushing on the hood of the truck as the tires spun, and helped them back it out of the mud: their payment for healing the mule. A smell of burning rubber and smoke hung in the trees after they left.

They didn't talk much. Dr. Lynly was thinking about the pain killers: how, for a moment, he had almost given the death pills instead.

Karen was thinking how she would not let him pay her for that day's work. Also she was thinking about Sydney Bean: she would sit on the porch with him again, and maybe drink a beer and watch the fields.

He was sitting on the back porch, when she got in; he was on the wooden bench next to the hammock, and he had a tray set up for her with a pitcher of cold orange juice. There was froth in the pitcher, a light creamy foaminess from where he had been stirring it, and the ice cubes were circling around. Beads of condensation slid down the pitcher, rolling slowly, then quickly, like tears. She could feel her heart giving. The field was rich summer green, and then, past the field, the dark line of trees. A long string of cattle egrets flew past, headed down to their rookery in the swamp.

Sydney poured her a small glass of orange juice. He had a metal pail of cold water and a clean washcloth. It was hot on the back porch, even for evening. He helped her get into the hammock; then he wrung the washcloth out and put it across her forehead, her eyes. Sydney smelled as if he had just gotten out of the shower, and he was wearing clean white duckcloth pants and a bright blue shirt.

She felt dizzy, and leaned back in the hammock. The washcloth over her eyes felt so good. She sipped the orange juice, not looking at it, and licked the light foam of it from her lips. Owls were beginning to call, down in the swamp.

She felt as if she were younger, going back to a place, some place she had not been in a long time but could remember fondly. It felt like she was in love. She knew that she could not be, but that was what it felt like.

Sydney sat behind her and rubbed her temples.

It grew dark, and the moon came up.

"It was a rough day," she said, around ten o'clock.

But he just kept rubbing.

Around eleven o'clock, she dozed off, and he woke her, helped her from the hammock, and led her inside, not turning on any lights, and helped her get in bed.

Then he went back outside, locking the door behind him. He sat on the porch a little longer, watching the moon, so high above him, and then he drove home, slowly, cautiously, as ever. Accidents were everywhere; they could happen at any time, from any direction.

Sydney moved carefully, and tried to look ahead and be ready for the next one.

He really wanted her. He wanted her in his life. Sydney didn't know if the guilt was there for that—the wanting—or because he was alive, still seeing things, still feeling. He wanted someone in his life, and it didn't seem right to feel guilty about it. But he did.

* * *

Sometimes, at night, he would hear the horses running, thundering across the hard summer-baked flatness of his pasture, running wild—and he would imagine they were laughing at him for wasting his time feeling guilty, but it was a feeling he could not shake, could not ride down, and his sleep was often poor and restless.

Sydney often wondered if horses were even meant to be ridden at all.

It was always such a struggle.

The thing about the broncs, he realized—and he never realized it until they were rolling on top of him in the dust, or rubbing him off against a tree, or against the side of a barn, trying to break his leg—was that if the horses didn't get broken, tamed, they'd get wilder. There was nothing as wild as a horse that had never been broken. It just got meaner, each day.

So he held on. He bucked and spun and arched and twisted, shooting up and down with the mad horses' leaps; and when the horse tried to hurt itself, by running straight into something—a fence, a barn, the lake—he stayed on.

If there was, once in a blue moon, a horse not only stronger, but more stubborn than he, then he would have to destroy it.

The cattle were easy to work with, they would do anything for food, and once one did it, they would all follow; but working with the horses made him think ahead, and sometimes he wondered, in streaks and bits of paranoia, if perhaps all the horses in the world did not have some battle against him, and were destined, all of them, to pass through his corrals, each one testing him before he was allowed to stop.

Because like all bronc-busters, that was what Sydney someday allowed himself to consider and savor, in moments of rest: the day when he could stop. A run of successes. A string of wins so satisfying and continuous that it would seem—even though he would be sore, and tired—that a horse would never beat him again, and he would be convinced of it, and then he could quit.

Mornings in summers past, Henry used to come over, and sit on the railing and watch. He had been an elementary school teacher, and frail, almost anemic: but he had loved to watch Sydney Bean ride the horses. He taught only a few classes in the summers, and he would sip coffee and grade a few papers while Sydney and the horse fought out in the center.

Sometimes Henry had set a broken bone for Sydney—Sydney had shown him how—and other times Sydney, if he was alone, would set his own bones, if he even bothered with them. Then he would wrap them up and keep riding. Dr. Lynly had set some of his bones, on the bad breaks.

Sydney was feeling old, since Henry had drowned. Not so much in the mornings, when everything was new and cool, and had promise; but in the evenings, he could feel the crooked shapes of his bones, within him. He would drink beers, and watch his horses, and other people's horses in his pasture, as they ran. The horses never seemed to feel old, not even in the evenings, and he was jealous of them, of their strength.

He called Karen one weekend. "Come out and watch me break horses," he said.

He was feeling particularly sore and tired. For some reason he wanted her to see that he could always do it; that the horses were always broken. He wanted her to see what it looked like, and how it always turned out.

"Oh, I don't know," she said, after she had considered it. "I'm just so *tired.*" It was a bad and crooked road, bumpy, from her house to his, and it took nearly an hour to drive it.

"I'll come get you . . . ?" he said. He wanted to shake her. But he said nothing; he nodded, and then remembered he was on the phone and said, "I understand."

She did let him sit on the porch with her, whenever he drove over to her farm. She had to have someone.

"Do you want to hit me?" he asked one evening, almost hopefully.

But she just shook her head sadly.

He saw that she was getting comfortable with her sorrow, was settling down into it, like an old way of life, and he wanted to shock her out of it, but felt paralyzed and mute, like the dumbest of animals.

Sydney stared at his crooked hands, with the scars from the cuts, made over the years by the fencing tools. Silently, he cursed all the many things he did not know. He could lift bales of hay. He could string barbed-wire fences. He could lift things. That was all he knew. He wished he were a chemist, an electrician, a poet, or a preacher. The things he had—what little of them there were—wouldn't help her.

She had never thought to ask how drunk Henry had been. Sydney thought that made a difference: whether you jumped off the bridge with one beer in you, or two, or a six-pack; or with a sea of purple Psychos rolling around in your stomach—but she never asked.

He admired her confidence, and doubted his ability to be as strong, as stubborn. She never considered that it might have been her fault, or Henry's; that some little spat might have prompted it, or general disillusionment.

It was his fault, Sydney's, square and simple, and she seemed comfortable, if not happy, with the fact.

Dr. Lynly treated horses, but he did not seem to love them, thought Karen.

"Stupid creatures," he would grumble, when they would not do as he wanted, when he was trying to doctor them. "Utter idiots." He and Buster and Karen would try to herd the horse into the trailer, or the corral, pulling on the reins and swatting the horse with green branches.

"Brickheads," Dr. Lynly would growl, pulling the reins and then walking around and slapping, feebly, the horse's flank. "Brickheads and fatheads." He had been loading horses for fifty years, and Karen would giggle, because the horses' stupidity always seemed to surprise, and then anger Dr. Lynly, and she thought it was sweet.

It was as if he had not yet really learned that that was how they always were.

But Karen had seen that right away. She knew that a lot of girls, and women, were infatuated with horses, in love with them even, for their great size and strength, and for their wildness—but Karen, as she saw more and more of the sick horses, the ailing ones, the ones most people did not see

295

regularly, knew that all horses were dumb, simple, and trusting, and that even the smartest ones could be made to do as they were told.

And they could be so dumb, so loyal, and so oblivious to pain. It was as if—even if they could feel it—they could never, ever acknowledge it.

It was sweet, she thought, and dumb.

Karen let Sydney rub her temples and brush her hair. She would go into the bathroom, and wash it while he sat on the porch. He had taken up whittling; one of the stallions had broken Sydney's leg by throwing him into a fence and then trampling him, and the leg was in a heavy cast. So Sydney had decided to take a break for a few days.

He had bought a whittling kit at the hardware store, and was going to try hard to learn how to do it. There were instructions. The kit had a square, light piece of balsa wood, almost the weight of nothing, and a plain curved whittling knife. There was a dotted outline in the shape of a duck's head on the balsa wood that showed what the shape of his finished work would be.

After he learned to whittle, Sydney wanted to learn to play the harmonica. That was next, after whittling.

He would hear the water running, and hear Karen splashing, as she put her head under the faucet and rinsed.

She would come out in her robe, drying her hair, and then would let him sit in the hammock with her and brush her hair. It was September, and the cottonwoods were tinging, were making the skies hazy, soft, and frozen. Nothing seemed to move.

Her hair came down to the middle of her back. She had stopped cutting it. The robe was old and worn, the color of an old blue dish. Something about the shampoo she used reminded him of apples. She wore moccasins that had a shearling lining in them, and Sydney and Karen would rock in the hammock, slightly. Sometimes Karen would get up and bring out two Cokes from the refrigerator, and they would drink those.

"Be sure to clean up those shavings when you go," she told him. There were little balsa wood curls all over the porch. Her hair, almost dry, would be light and soft. "Be sure not to leave a mess when you go," she would say.

It would be dark then, Venus out beyond them.

"Yes," he said.

Before he left, she reached out from the hammock, and caught his hand. She squeezed it, and then let go.

He drove home slowly, thinking of Henry, and of how he had once taken Henry fishing for the first time. They had caught a catfish so large that it had scared Henry. They drank beers, and sat in the boat, and talked.

One of Sydney Bean's headlights faltered, on the drive home, then went out, and it took him an hour and a half to get home.

The days got cold and brittle. It was hard, working with the horses: Sydney's leg hurt all the time. Sometimes the horse would leap, and come down with all four hooves bunched in close together, and the pain and shock of it would travel all the way up Sydney's leg and into his shoulder, and down into his wrists: the break was in his ankle.

He was sleeping past sun-up, some days, and was being thrown, now, nearly every day; sometimes several times in the same day.

There was always a strong wind. Rains began to blow in. It was cool, getting cold, crisp as apples, and it was the weather that in the summer everyone said they would be looking forward to. One night there was a frost, and a full moon.

On her back porch, sitting in the hammock by herself with a heavy blanket around her, Karen saw a stray blasa shaving caught between the cracks of her porch floor. It was white, in the moonlight—the whole porch was—and the field was blue—the cattle stood out in the moonlight like blue statues—and she almost called Sydney.

She even went as far as to get up and call information, to find out his number; it was that close.

But then the silence and absence of a thing—she presumed it was Henry, but did not know for sure what it was—closed in around her, and the field beyond her porch, like the inside of her heart, seemed to be deathly still—and she did not call.

She thought angrily, I can love who I want to love. But she was angry at

Sydney Bean, for having tried to pull her so far out, into a place where she did not want to go.

She fell asleep in the hammock, and dreamed that Dr. Lynly was trying to wake her up, and was taking her blood pressure, feeling her forehead, and, craziest of all, swatting at her with green branches.

She awoke from the dream, and decided to call him after all. Sydney answered the phone as if he, too, had been awake.

"Hello?" he said. She could tell by the true questioning in his voice that he did not get many phone calls.

"Hello," said Karen. "I just—wanted to call, and tell you hello." She paused; almost a falter. "And that I feel better. That I feel good, I mean. That's all."

"Well," said Sydney Bean. "well, good. I mean, great."

"That's all," said Karen. "Bye," she said.

"Good-bye," said Sydney.

On Thanksgiving Day, Karen and Dr. Lynly headed back out to the swamp, to check up on the loggers' mule. It was the hardest cold of the year, and there was bright ice on the bridges, and it was not thawing, even in the sun. The inside of Dr. Lynly's old truck was no warmer than the air outside. Buster, in his wooliness, lay across Karen to keep her warm.

They turned onto a gravel road, and started down into the swamp. Smoke, low and spreading, was all in the woods, like a fog. The men had little fires going all throughout the woods; they were each working on a different tree, and had small warming fires where they stood and shivered when resting.

Karen found herself looking for the pale ugly logger.

He was swinging the ax, but he only had one arm, he was swinging at the tree with one arm. The left arm was gone, and there was a sort of a sleeve over it, like a sock. The man was sweating, and a small boy stepped up and quickly toweled him dry each time the pale man stepped back to take a rest.

They stopped the truck and got out and walked up to him, and he stepped back—wet, already, again, the boy toweled him off, standing on a low stool and starting with the man's neck and shoulders, and then going down the great back—and the man told them that the mule was better but that if they wanted to see him, he was lower in the swamp.

They followed the little path towards the river. All around them were downed trees, and stumps, and stacks of logs, but the woods looked no different. The haze from the fires made it seem colder. Acorns popped under their feet.

About halfway down the road, they met the mule. He was coming back up towards them, and he was pulling a good load. A small boy was in front of him, holding out a carrot, only partially eaten. The mule's knee looked much better, though it was still a little swollen, and probably always would be.

The boy stopped, and let the mule take another bite of carrot, making him lean far forward in the trace. His great rubbery lips stretched and quavered, and then flapped, as he tried to get it, and then there was the crunch when he did.

They could smell the carrot as the mule ground it with his old teeth. It was a wild carrot, dug from the woods, and not very big: but it smelled good.

Karen had brought an apple and some sugar cubes, and she started forward to give them to the mule, but instead, handed them to the little boy, who ate the sugar cubes himself, and put the apple in his pocket.

The mule was wearing an old straw hat, and looked casual, out-of-place. The boy switched him, and he shut his eyes and started up: his chest swelled, tight and sweaty, to fit the dark soft stained leather harness, and the big load behind him started in motion, too.

Buster whined, as the mule went by.

It was spring again then, the month in which Henry had left them, and they were on the back porch. Karen had purchased a Clydesdale yearling, a great and huge animal, whose mane and fur she had shaved to keep it cool in the warming weather, and she had asked a little boy from a nearby farm with time on his hands to train it, in the afternoons. The horse was already gentled, but needed to be stronger. She was having the boy walk him around in the fields, pulling a makeshift sled of stones and tree stumps and old rotten bales of hay.

In the fall, when the Clydesdale was strong enough, she and Dr. Lynly were going to trailer it out to the swamp, and trade it for the mule.

Sydney Bean's leg had healed, been broken again, and was now healing once more. The stallion he was trying to break was showing signs of weakening. There was something in the whites of his eyes, Sydney thought, when he reared up, and he was not slamming himself into the barn—so it seemed to Sydney, anyway—with quite as much anger. Sydney thought that perhaps this coming summer would be the one in which he broke all of his horses, day after day, week after week.

They sat in the hammock and drank Cokes and nibbled radishes, celery, which Karen had washed and put on a little tray. They watched the boy, or one of his friends, his blue shirt a tiny spot against the treeline, as he followed the big dark form of the Clydesdale. The sky was a wide spread of crimson, all along the western trees, towards the river. They couldn't tell which of the local children it was, behind the big horse; it could have been any of them.

"I really miss him," said Sydney Bean. "I really hurt."

"I know," Karen said. She put her hand on Sydney's, and rested it there. "I will help you," she said.

Out in the field, a few cattle egrets fluttered and hopped behind the horse and the boy. The great young draft horse lifted his thick legs high and free of the mud with each step, free from the mud made soft by the rains of spring, and slowly—they could tell—he was skidding the sled forward.

The egrets hopped and danced, following at a slight distance, but neither the boy nor the horse seemed to notice. They kept their heads down, and moved forward.

Acknowledgments

"Wild Horses" reprinted from *The Watch: Stories* by Rick Bass with the permission of W. W. Norton & Company, Inc. Copyright © 1989 by Rick Bass. Originally appeared in *The Paris Review*.

"Episode in the Life of an Ancestor" from *Fifty Stories* by Kay Boyle. Reprinted by permission of the author and the Watkins / Loomis Agency.

"The Horse of the Sword" by Manuel Buaken, copyright © 1943, is now in the public domain.

"Bush River" by Joyce Cary, reprinted from *Spring Song and Other Stories*. Copyright © 1960 by Joyce Cary, by permission of JLA Cary Estate.

"The Power of Horses" from *The Power of Horses and Other Stories* by Elizabeth Cook-Lynn. Copyright © 1990 by Elizabeth Cook-Lynn. Reprinted by permission of the author.

"Champ's Roan Colt" from *Drinking Dry Clouds: Wyoming Stories* by Gretel Ehrlich. Copyright © 1991 by Gretel Ehrlich. Reprinted by permission of Capra Press.

"Engine Horse" by Patricia Highsmith, copyright © 1975 by Patricia Highsmith, is from her story collection *The Animal-Lover's Book of Beastly Murder*, published by William Heinemann Ltd., London, and Penzler Books, New York. Reprinted by permission of Diogenes Verlag AG, Switzerland.

"What Shock Heard" from *Cowboys Are My Weakness: Stories* by Pam Houston. Copyright © 1992 by Pam Houston. Reprinted by permission of W. W. Norton & Company, Inc.

"The Maltese Cat" by Rudyard Kipling is in the public domain.

"Dry Point of Horses" from *Soulstorm: Stories* by Clarice Lispector. Copyright © 1974 by Clarice Lispector. Reprinted by permission of New Directions Publishing Corporation.

"The Splendid Outcast" by Beryl Markham from *The Splendid Outcast: Beryl Markham's African Stories.* Copyright © 1944 by the Estate of Beryl Markham. Reprinted by permission of the Estate of Beryl Markham.

"The Old Hunter" from *Short Stories of Liam O'Flaherty.* Reprinted by permission of the Estate of Liam O'Flaherty.

"We'll Have Fun" from *The Collected Short Stories of John O'Hara.* Copyright © 1963 by John O'Hara. Reprinted by permission of Random House, Inc.

"Beautiful My Mane in the Wind" by Catherine Petroski from *Gravity* (Fiction International, 1981). Copyright © 1975 by Catherine Petroski. Originally appeared in *The North American Review* and *Ms.* Reprinted by permission of San Diego State University Press / *Fiction International.*

"The Brogue" by Saki (H. H. Munro), published by Viking Press, is in the public domain.

"Twenty Minutes" from *Dusk and Other Stories* by James Salter. Copyright © 1988 by James Salter. Reprinted by permission of North Point Press, a division of Farrar Straus & Giroux, Inc.

"The Summer of the Beautiful White Horse" reprinted from *My Name Is Aram,* by William Saroyan, by permission of Harcourt, Brace & Co., Inc. Copyright © 1938 by William Saroyan.

"Relax Is All" from *On Being Told That Her Second Husband Has Taken His First Lover* by Tess Slesinger. Copyright © 1971 by Quadrangle / The New York Times Book Company. Reprinted by permission of Times Books, a division of Random House, Inc.

"A Horse in Bed" is excerpted from *The Stray Lamb* by Thorne Smith. Copyright © renewed 1956 by the Estate of Thorne Smith. Reprinted by permission of Harold Matson Company, Inc.